What others are saying

The Brands from the Burning series

"What a splendid story! From the palaces of 1500 Japan to the war-ravaged lands of the 1940s, Linda Thompson's *The Mulberry Leaf Whispers* rivals *Shogun* with its sweeping story of passion and faith, of survival and hope. I love this story, the rich language and fresh imagery that brings the reader into the bone-aching choices of these characters. You'll want to read every word of every page. I did. Be prepared to be enriched, moved and deeply satisfied."
--Jane Kirkpatrick, Award-winning author of *Something Worth Doing*

"In lovely prose, *The Mulberry Leaf Whispers* describes the beauty and the danger of feudal Japan as well as the difficulties for Japanese prisoners of war during World War II. Full of fascinating detail, the story highlights two family members, hundreds of years apart, who face difficult choices. Linda Thompson does an excellent job with this gorgeous, not-to-be missed novel."
--Sarah Sundin, bestselling and Carol Award-winning author of *When Twilight Breaks* and the Sunrise at Normandy series

"In her remarkable novel, *The Mulberry Leaf Whispers*, Linda Thompson immerses readers in two periods of Japanese history. She brilliantly captures the strict social structures that ruled every life, rich or poor, in the sixteenth century under lord regents and shoguns and then in the years after World War II, when those social structures had been shattered. For those like me who know very little about Japanese history, Thompson has given us two compelling, parallel stories. I was captured from page one and couldn't stop reading!"
--Louise M. Gouge, award-winning author of *Winning Amber*

"Linda Thompson attacks the publishing world like a Mitsubishi Zero swooping from the Japanese sky. Her first novel, *The Plum Blooms in Winter,* proves a taut, crisp, debut achievement that colorfully evokes the Pacific theater of World War II. Start this one forewarned: it's a stay-up-all-night read."

--Jerry B. Jenkins, 21-time *New York Times* bestselling author *(Left Behind, et al)*

"*The Plum Blooms in Winter* is a poignant story about bitter defeat and the power of forgiveness. With her lovely prose, Linda Thompson sweeps readers away on a journey to Japan and China during and after World War II, crafting a novel about the remarkable beauty and strength that bloomed in the midst of adversity. A brilliant debut!"

--Melanie Dobson, Carol Award-winning author of *The Curator's Daughter* and *Memories of Glass*

The Mulberry Leaf Whispers

Brands from the Burning Series

Book One: The Plum Blooms in Winter
Book Two: The Mulberry Leaf Whispers

The Mulberry Leaf Whispers

Brands from the Burning Series: Book Two

By
Linda Thompson

The Mulberry Leaf Whispers
Published by Mountain Brook Ink
White Salmon, WA U.S.A.

Scripture quotations are taken from the King James Version of the Bible. Public domain.
ISBN 978-1-943959-94-5
© 2020 Linda Thompson

The Team: Miralee Ferrell, Jenny Mertes, Robin Patchen, Alyssa Roat, Nikki Wright, Kristen Johnson and Cindy Jackson

Cover Design: Indie Cover Design, Lynnette Bonner Designer

The Author is represented by and this book is published in association with the literary agency of WordServe Literary Group., Ltd, www.wordserveliterary.com.

Mountain Brook Ink is an inspirational publisher offering fiction you can believe in.
Printed in the United States of America

Dedication

"To appoint unto them that mourn in Zion... beauty for ashes, the oil of joy for mourning, the garment of praise for the spirit of heaviness...." (Is 61:3)

This novel is dedicated to the men and women who lived out the history that inspired it:

Rev. Jacob and Florence DeShazer

Capt. Mitsuo Fuchida and Sub-Lieutenant Kanegasaki Kazuo

The "Hopevale Martyrs" and Professor James H. and Charma Covell, along with their children Peggy, David and Alice

...And to all the men and women who return from wars forever changed by experiences they will never talk about.

Author Note

My author journey started a little differently than many others I've heard about. Most authors seem to experience a calling to be a writer, then search for the story they will tell. For me it happened the other way around. The story spoke to me out of a history book and demanded that I retell it.

The history, of course, was bigger than a single novel could convey. It involved five interconnected lives. My first novel, *The Plum Blooms in Winter*, reflected two of those lives. I guess that made it inevitable that *The Mulberry Leaf Whispers* would also clamor to be written to provide some echo of the missing voices.

This novel, like *The Plum Blooms in Winter*, begins on April 18, 1942. The day of the Doolittle Raid, the first U.S. air raid on Japan.

I'd like to issue an important disclaimer around some of the verbiage used in the story. Denigrating slang terms, such as "Jap" and others, are included to authentically represent the perspective of the characters toward their military opponents at that point in history. In no way do they represent my perspective, nor do I personally agree with the use of such unkind language. But presenting readers with an authentic journey demands certain liberties.

Finally, if you feel mystified by the use of Japanese honorifics such as -san and -chan, please know you are not alone! Here's a brief introduction. The use of -san after a name is a respectful title, somewhat equivalent to Mr., Mrs., or Ms. in English. The Japanese use -san for both genders, and since Japanese society at that time was structured and formal, -san would be employed in most interactions. In a more intimate friendship with someone who would be considered your equal or perhaps lower on the social scale, less formal honorifics (-chan for women or -kun for men) come into play.

With that, let the story roll!

Reader Bonuses

I have a free eBook featuring more short fiction of World War Two's Pacific War, *A Matter of Mind and Heart*, exclusive to subscribers of my newsletter. Plus, other bonuses that will deepen your experience with this *Brands from the Burning* series. Please come check them out at: www. lthompsonbooks.com/reader-bonuses

I'd Love to Hear from You

As an author, I place tremendous value on your feedback! Reviews weigh heavily with readers when shopping for books, so if you enjoy this novel, please consider leaving one! You could help another reader experience the power of this story. If you're willing, you can leave a review on Amazon Kindle version by simply swiping left from the last page of an Amazon Kindle book. The bonus page I mentioned above (www.lthompsonbooks.com/reader-bonuses) provides easy links to leave reviews in other venues.

Acknowledgments

I'm so grateful to my husband, Michael, who introduced me to the moving, true story that inspired both my novels. He has always supported and encouraged my writing journey, even when it has required him to put up with a lot of divided attention.

I'm deeply thankful to my parents for teaching me to love books, and to appreciate the magic and the beauty in well-chosen words. And for loving my books enough to read multiple early versions.

It turns out it takes a whole village to write a novel. I'd never have gotten anywhere with this writing adventure if not for my teacher and mentor, Les Edgerton. Les is leaving a tremendous legacy in the writing community. I'm grateful to my ever upbeat and highly effective agent, Sarah Joy Freese of WordServe Literary. I'm deeply thankful to Miralee Ferrell and the stellar team at Mountain Brook Ink for taking a chance on me.

Many others had a big hand in shaping this story. Jenny Mertes and Robin Patchen, who worked with me as professional editors. Also, Mary Edelson and Holly Love, my longsuffering critique partners. I'm confident I'll see you both at your own book signings soon.

Love and thanks go to Carla, Johanna, Kimberly, Liz, Mary Rose, Suzie, Terry, and my team of prayer warriors for much-needed "air cover"—you know who you are. And to early readers Becca, Jan, Jeanne, Jeremy Neely, and Pam, who gave me honest feedback and some much-needed prayer support as well. Wouldn't be here without all of you!

With Love and Gratitude,
Linda

Chapter One

Saturday 18 April 1942
Pacific Ocean, 650 Nautical Miles off the Coast of Japan

SUB-LIEUTENANT MATSUURA AKIRA PACED THE open bridge of *Nitto Maru*. He had the dawn watch, as usual. Capt. Yoshiwara wasn't much good before noon. Like his vessel, the captain had seen better days.

Rough seas that morning. It was raining, but not hard. All the same, the swells towered twenty feet above his head.

A stiff breeze drove icy spray into Akira's face. He filled his lungs, and the bracing tang of sea air assailed his senses. It smacked of everything he loved about life in the Imperial Navy. Rigor. Discipline. And with his nation triumphing against the U.S. and British fleets, a golden opportunity to follow Papa-san in glorious deeds. To prove himself worthy of his long line of ancestors, the ancient lords of Hirado domain.

He'd been born for this—the emperor's navy. If destiny favored him with a long career, he might even surpass his father's prestige.

And why shouldn't it favor him? Why shouldn't he spend his life winning glory on the seas, as his father and grandfather had done? He, Matsuura Akira, would mark a path his little brother, Hiroshi, would be proud to follow. And his own sons, when he had them. And give the Matsuura women, Mama-san and his sister Miyako, full right to stand tall.

Although this first assignment was a bit...limiting. There wasn't much chance of glory on this former fishing trawler doing patrol duty a few hundred miles off Japan's coast.

Ensign Nagai ambled onto the narrow deck ten feet below him, making his rounds, reliable as rain on the China Sea. Even his square face and solid frame conveyed a sense of something immovable.

The ensign paced halfway across the deck, then turned and lifted his face to Akira. The wind whipped the end of his thick muffler. He grabbed it and mouthed something. With an exaggerated gesture, he pointed at the sky, then cocked his head and brought one hand to his ear.

Listen.

Akira cupped his hands behind his ears. Wind. Waves. Spars thrashing. And above it all...

The whine of a propeller in the clouds.

He let out a soft whistle. *Odd...*especially considering the transmission they'd received a couple days earlier. Command had raised the alert level. They'd have to radio this in.

The thirty-meter boat crested a swell. He scanned the pewter-gray clouds. About half a nautical mile to the east, above the spot where an inch-wide strip of oily light shone on the horizon, the cloud cover thinned.

There. A cross-shaped fleck against the sky, exposed for just seconds. She banked immediately and vanished, bearing east-southeast. *Almost as if she turned when she spotted us.* He made a little snort at himself. His imagination was working overtime.

But Tokyo had received some piece of intelligence that made them wary. He mused over the question for the twentieth time. With the Americans still nursing the wounds Japan's navy had inflicted at Pearl Harbor, and with the trouncing the emperor's fleet had recently given the British at Ceylon, what could the threat be?

Nagai loped across the deck toward him, bounded up the ladder, and saluted. Akira returned his salute.

"Did you identify the aircraft, ensign?"

"Maybe a Zero out of Yokosuka, sir. But I didn't have a good view."

Akira heaved a sigh. "Nor did I. And I didn't see the insignia. We'll follow protocol and call this in to *Kiso*. Alert Onishi. I'll join you in the radio room." *After I do the dirty work of waking the captain.*

Nagai descended the ladder and disappeared into the room beneath the open bridge where they'd been standing. Akira followed his ensign to the deck, then took a second ladder below. He walked through the hold, past three seamen snoring in their hammocks, and along a narrow passageway to the captain's cabin.

He pounded on the door and braced himself for Yoshiwara's displeasure.

Nothing.

He knocked harder. "Pardon the interruption, sir. We sighted a plane. Shall we report it to *Kiso*?"

The captain coughed. He said something Akira couldn't make out.

"Permission granted, sir?"

This time the harrumph from the other side of the door was more distinct.

"*Hai.*" Akira bowed at the closed door.

He mounted the ladder to the deck. The brisk sea air struck his face again—a vast improvement over the reek of fish offal in the hold. The old fishing trawler would never lose that stench, no matter how the Imperial Navy overhauled her.

He went to the radio room. A gust rattled the door he'd just closed and buffeted the windows.

Midshipman Onishi, at twenty-six the oldest among them save the captain, had his pencil and notepad out and his cipher book open. He stood. "I'm working on the transmission, sir."

Akira gave him a brisk nod. "Very good. Get it done." This simple surveillance mission, this foul-smelling vessel— they were Akira's duty. And he would not see it carried out in a manner that was one whit short of stellar. Even if it was routine.

He dispatched Nagai back to the bridge and helped himself to a cup of lukewarm tea from the flask on the table. He perched on a stool and observed Onishi working out his ciphers. The man seemed to be doing all he could.

Nagai burst back in, his cheeks flushed from the wind. "You might be interested to step outside, sir. Two of our beautiful carriers are on the horizon."

What's this? Command should have informed him of any operation in their area. He planted his cup on the table so firmly that tea sloshed out. "Where?" He strode past Nagai onto the deck.

In the distance, gray water met gray sky. He spotted them there—two darker flecks near the horizon, almost due east. He raised his binoculars and dialed them in. The flecks resolved into enormous vessels with elongated decks. Aircraft clustered in neat rows at their sterns. Commanding islands towered amidships.

Two carriers, indeed. *Enormous* carriers. Along with two—no, *three* smaller vessels. Cruisers. A sizable task force, bearing toward Japan.

He focused on one of the carriers and took a slow, deliberate breath. This ship looked like nothing he'd seen. He'd toured the emperor's newest carrier, *Shokaku*, in the shipyard at Kobe. Its island sat like a stack of blocks. It had a standard curved prow.

The vessel in front of him boasted a dramatic, squared-off prow. And its island stretched above its deck, graceful as a *geisha*'s neck. She was not the emperor's.

Nitto Maru's situation swirled into focus in his mind like his binoculars had focused the scene before him. Only three nations in the world boasted aircraft carriers. His own. And two nations Japan was at war with.

He was witnessing something that hadn't happened in seven centuries. No enemy since the Mongols had dared venture an invasion of Nippon, the Land of the Gods. And Hachiman himself, the great god of war, had destroyed that fleet with a *kamikaze*, a divine wind.

Generations of ancestral spirits, fabled warriors all, murmured the truth into his soul. All his life, he'd prepared for the moment he would face an enemy. That moment had come, and he was unlikely to survive it. *Nitto Maru* was on patrol for one purpose—to radio an alarm to the cruiser *Kiso* to relay to Tokyo. When his crew accomplished that, the enemy would hear them and almost certainly hunt them.

Barring Hachiman providing another divine wind, this was a battle they would not win. All that was left for him was to make his death a worthy one. Prove it meant something to carry the blood of the Matsuura, the ancient naval power of Hirado Island. And do his best to ensure the crew did the same.

His pulse took up a drumbeat in his ears.

Calm your own mind. The foremost act of war. Ancient wisdom Papa-san had taught him.

He wrestled back a tendril of fear. Tore his focus from the enemy warships and turned to Nagai. "Those carriers are beautiful. But they are not ours."

The ensign's eyes went wide. "Sir?"

"Call the men to battle stations. I'll alert the captain. And ensign—make sure every man puts on his life preserver."

Eighteenth Day of the Fifth Month, Anno Domini 1587
Sakaguchi, Omura Domain, Kyushu Island

Omura Sono plucked the last arrow from the bucket at her feet and nocked it. She raised the bow and arrow above her head. She brought her left arm down in a strong arc as she drew the bowstring past her ear. Then farther back, in time with her slow exhale. The polished bamboo shaft glided across her knuckle until everything from her right fingers to her left forearm burned.

She squinted along the shaft at the wooden target set on an easel between two rows of tea bushes, a third of the way down the field. Cicada song throbbed from the stand of mulberry trees behind her.

"Steady." Capt. Fujita's voice flowed from behind her in a guiding whisper, nothing like the thunder of command he used with her older brother's men. "Calm your own mind. *That* may be called the foremost act of war."

Sono focused on the center of the target. The hum of cicadas and the wheeze of the captain's breath disappeared as the target transformed into a fearsome Shimazu warrior charging her on horseback in full armor, his *naginata* pike aimed at her heart.

She parted her fingers. The bowstring thrummed. The arrow hissed past her ear and whooshed above the brilliant green rows of tea bushes, and...buried itself in the earth behind the target. The bow vibrated in her left hand.

"*Che!*" She couldn't help a little stomp of her foot. Only

four of her fifteen arrows had pierced the target. The first three had fallen into the bushes well short of it.

"Patience, Sono-chan," Capt. Fujita said. "Your muscles need time to grow accustomed to the longer bow."

She huffed out a sigh. "It seems so, *sensei*." She had recently graduated to this bow, which stood nearly her own height. Not as long as the bows the *samurai* used in mounted archery, but powerful enough to make her a worthy defender, shooting around a corner or through a port in a castle wall.

Footsteps crunched the gravel path behind them. She glanced over her shoulder to see her younger brother, Suminobu. This was his fourteenth year but, annoyingly, he had come back from the Jesuit school in Arima standing taller than she did at seventeen. Between his two years at Jesuit school and his eight years as a hostage of their former enemies, the Ryuzoji, she'd had too little time to get to know him.

A familiar twinge of envy jabbed her belly. At least boys went on journeys. As a woman, she would spend her life anchored to a man's castle. Her father's. Her brother's. And soon enough, her husband's.

She moved her right arm in a slow circle to ease the knot in her shoulder. If she was to be tied to a castle, she would know how to defend it.

Suminobu made a deep bow to the captain. "Greetings, *sensei*." And a shallower bow to her. "Honored sister, I thought I would see how you are coming along. You will need a bigger quiver with an aim like that. And a page tagging after you to carry it." He said it with a superior smirk.

It took real effort to banish the irritation from her voice and show him the deference owed a brother—even an irritating younger one. "Papa-san says I must keep applying myself." The thought of her father brought a catch to her throat. Trapped by disease inside the elegantly paneled walls of the country mansion to which he had retired when he yielded his domain to her older brother. That was only eighteen months earlier. Now he withered away, barely able to speak, that horrible cough pulling blood from his lungs.

Exactly the thing she was trying not to think about.

The captain grunted. "I do not recall your sister Luzia being so interested in the warrior's way, Lady Sono."

And your father saw Luzia well married. No doubt that was the captain's thought, although he did not say it. Luzia had gone in a good marriage to further an important alliance with a neighboring *Kirishitan* clan. And she'd already borne a boy.

The question of how well Sono would marry had hung over her for as many of her seventeen years as she could recall. Anxiety squeezed her chest. The problem would soon be her older brother's.

She pushed that thought away—hard. Her fingers went to her cross pendant. "I want to be ready in case—"

"In case you have to take on the whole Shimazu clan alone?" Suminobu folded his arms across his chest.

"*Hai.*" She lifted her chin and squared her shoulders. "Or the Matsuura—cursed pirates—while you are out on campaign." The skepticism on her brother's face pushed her further. "You know as well as I that such a thing took place mere months ago, in Bungo. Myorin-ni fought off sixteen enemy advances against her son's castle. She was clever and bold. Everyone says it."

And why should I not be clever and bold as well?

"Everyone does say it. The old widow made an admirable general." Fujita scowled at Suminobu. "Do not mock your sister. You may not be old enough to remember how hard we fought to repulse the Ryuzoji, but your sister does. And before that? It was the Goto and the Saito with the Matsuura. And before that?" The captain took a ponderous step or two across the platform. "The Matsuura, when they had the gall to sail out from Hirado Island and board the Portuguese Black Ship itself. In *our* harbor."

"I remember well, *sensei.*" Sono watched him lurch on his bad leg. "I remember Mama-san tending to your thigh in the castle courtyard."

And she would never rub out those memories. How they carried the captain in from the battle raging outside their gates, blood from an angry gash in his leg dripping through the cotton stretcher. The cries of the wounded still haunted her nights, their groans rising above the distant cannon fire. The smell of their blood. And the fear that ran through it all. If the enemies who had done that to Fujita breached the castle walls, what would they do to her? To her mother?

In the end Papa-san had bought peace by submitting to the Ryuzoji and their demands. She had little memory of the much-older half-sister Papa-san had bartered away to their enemy clan as a bride. But when a grinning *samurai* in Ryuzoji livery had scooped the infant Suminobu, her own baby brother, up onto his big horse and borne him away as a hostage, that loss was keen.

The captain shifted his weight, bringing her back to the present. He puffed out his chest and peered at Suminobu, back home with them at last. "Alliances can be fluid. Your father knows this as well as anyone. His stance as a *Kirishitan* has won him few friends. And bigger and bigger *koi* seem to find their way into our pond." His eyes rested on Sono. The furrows around his mouth softened. "You never know when one heart full of courage can make all the difference."

Suminobu's smirk faded. "Of course, *sensei*." He directed a bow at her. "Forgive me, honored sister. It is noble to discipline your mind by developing your skills. And wise to be prepared for the worst."

Even if you are but a girl. He didn't have to say it.

"It is nothing." Forgiving him came as easily now as the ripple of annoyance had earlier.

He went on. "And to desire greatness is admirable. But we can be honest, ah? Your most likely path there will be—"

"Bearing a lord's heir." She said it with him, then stifled her deep sigh.

Fujita shot a glare at Suminobu. He inclined his head toward Sono. "Do not let your brother discourage you. That was nice work this morning, lady. You will do better with time."

"*Hai, sensei.*" His words were kind, but there'd been an odd hesitancy in the way he said *do better with time.* And something strange about the way he focused off into the fields. As if he knew something she was not meant to know.

Her father had spent his life playing a giant game of *Go* versus his many enemies. As his last remaining marriageable daughter, she represented a critical piece to place. But unlike *Go* stones, daughters aged. Lost their marriageable luster. Had her father decided it was time to put her on the board? At seventeen years, her value was at its peak.

If so, she'd have no more say in where he placed her than a stone had.

She thrust her anxious speculations away. "I had best go back up to Papa-san."

Before the captain answered, one of their father's servants hurried from the trees, calling out as he came. "Excuse me, Master Suminobu. Excuse me."

She took in the boy's panting breaths and wide eyes, and everything around her froze. A sound like ocean breakers swelled in her ears.

"Papa-san?" Suminobu's voice, barely audible through the roaring.

"*Hai.*" The boy bowed to her brother, then to her. "Lady Omura summons you both to your father's mansion. At once."

Chapter Two

Saturday 18 April 1942

AKIRA SPRINTED DOWN THE PASSAGEWAY TO Capt. Yoshiwara's cabin and hammered on the door. "Please excuse me, captain."

Deep coughs, then muffled curses. "What? What is it?"

He hesitated. The magnitude of the news he had to deliver made his throat feel thick. "You're needed on the bridge, sir. At once."

More curses. "Give me a minute, Matsuura-kun."

Akira shifted his feet with impatience. *Time. Something they had very little of.* His thoughts flicked from *Nitto Maru*'s captain to his own father, Matsuura Saburo, captain of the heavy cruiser *Aoba*. Six hundred fifty men serving under his command.

What Yoshiwara had been five years earlier.

Akira was not the only one who had dreamed of progressing to a better assignment. But where Akira's career showed every promise of stretching for long years ahead of him, Capt. Yoshiwara's was adrift in a backwater. No wonder the man pounded down whiskey every night to dull his frustration.

The door cracked open, and the captain's thickset face and tousled head appeared. The odor of sweat and stale liquor permeated the passageway.

Akira took a half step back and saluted. "I beg to inform you we've sighted a task force, sir. I believe it's the enemy."

"The enemy? Impossible!" The door flew open. Yoshiwara threw his heavy raincoat over his pajamas and grabbed his binoculars. He pushed past Akira and vaulted up the ladder.

Akira followed in the captain's wake. It was the fastest he'd seen the man move.

The captain called down to Akira. "Bearing?"

"One twelve, sir."

The captain brought his binoculars to his eyes and

scanned the horizon while *Nitto Maru* slid into a trough as deep as its radio tower was tall, then rode up another swell. The distant flecks wove in and out of view.

Nagai came up beside them, waiting for orders.

The captain let the binoculars drop against his chest and turned to Akira. He spoke in a ponderous voice. "I concur, Matsuura-kun. Those are not our carriers." Without another word he walked back to the hatch, legs stiff and head bowed as if he'd aged twenty years.

Akira trailed him. "Orders, sir?"

"You have the con, Akira-kun." Without a glance in Akira's direction, the captain stepped onto the ladder and disappeared below.

Akira glared after him, the outrage of it a punch to the gut. Like himself, the captain had been born into an ancient family and had been bred for command. But when it came to the crisis point—when the need for leadership was desperate—the man was a child's wooden sword with no edge.

Ensign Nagai stood slack jawed.

Akira swore beneath his breath. No time to concern himself with Yoshiwara. No time for anything but the mission.

Nagai. The men. They need me to lead.

His *nation* needed him to lead.

"Ensign, bring us around to two twenty. Order the engine to full speed. And tell the helm to steer for troughs."

Nagai jerked to attention and rushed up the ladder toward the bank of voicepipes on the bridge.

Akira hustled through the door to the radio room. "Onishi. Status?"

Onishi stood. "Transmission complete, sir."

"Very good. Alert the *Kiso*. We've sighted..." He trailed off, the enormity of it hitting again.

"The plane, sir? If you have a description, I'll send it to *Kiso*."

"No." He gave Onishi a level gaze. "Seaman, we've encountered an enemy task force."

Onishi froze. "I, ah...I don't understand, sir."

"I don't either. But they're out there. Two carriers with support vessels. The captain agrees they're not ours."

Nagai stepped in, bringing a wild gust of ocean wind, and slammed the door behind him.

Onishi spoke up in a choking voice. "If we transmit, they'll hear us, sir."

He steeled himself. He'd been born for sacrifice—and by definition, sacrifice came at a cost. "If they do?" He held Onishi's eyes for a moment, then Nagai's. "This is our moment, men. The day we rise up to defend Nippon in the spirit of our *samurai* forebears. We'll evade the enemy if possible. But should this end in our glorious deaths, we'll fall selflessly as cherry blossoms. Proud we were given the opportunity to spend ourselves in defense of our nation and assured our spirits will join the boldest of our ancestors."

Eighteenth Day of the Fifth Month, Anno Domini 1587

Sono slung her bow over her shoulder and rushed up the path to Papa-san's mansion, silently cursing her long skirt and courtly sandals. Suminobu, in his wide silk trousers and sturdy laced shoes, was well ahead of her.

The morning had started out breezy and beautiful, but the summer heat was rising. Pine fragrance floated on the breeze. She took no joy in it—it brought only an image of Papa-san, so content repeating Latin prayers in his pine-ringed garden. But that was before the disease came that made his throat swell and sent heat to devastate his lungs.

Suminobu barely slowed his pace at the ornamented entrance gate, bobbing a bow to the guards in passing. She trailed him along the fine gravel path that led through the garden to Papa-san's place of retirement.

Papa-san had one of his coughing fits. The sound filtered through the paper *shoji* even before she reached the slate steps. He was so much feebler now, each cough tearing out more of his lungs—and ripping at her heart.

She rushed along the broad planked patio—the warrior's run—that circled the mansion. She handed her bow to one of the guards outside her father's chamber. The other slid the *shoji* aside. A glance confirmed her worst fears. She stifled a little gasp, stepped inside, and dropped into a deep bow.

Her father had not moved from where she'd seen him last. He lay on a thick *futon* swathed in heavy silk embroidered with their family crest. His eyes seemed more sunken, above unnaturally sharp cheekbones. Labored breathing alternated with the heartbreaking coughs.

A small table set with his medicinal tea stood in its usual spot near his head. But the servants had placed two additional tables beside it, draped with white cloth.

For the last rites. To see him peacefully to paradise.

Mama-san knelt to his left. Tears glistened on her cheeks. She gently swabbed his mouth with a silk handkerchief. Two cushions awaited Sono and her brother. He fell to his knees on one. She took the other.

Papa-san's eyes rested on Suminobu and he parted his lips as if to say something. A shadow crossed his face before he convulsed in another fit of coughing. He crumpled his sheet up in a hand like a gnarled claw.

Mama-san caressed it. "Pray, my lord. Do not exert yourself."

Those hands. So strong, wrapped around a horse's reins. Brandishing a *katana*. So patient, clasped in fervent prayer. But now his skin stretched over bones that appeared as fragile as porcelain. The veins running up the back of his wrists were distinct as pale-blue lines painted on rice paper.

His coughing ran its course and tailed off into a wheeze. Then silence.

How close is the old warrior to giving up the fight? She held her own breath for what seemed like an endless moment. At last he parted his lips and breathed again.

The *shoji* partition at the back of the room stood open to the interior courtyard. Shifting light from the *koi* pond played on the ceiling and across one end of the wall, where a large crucifix hung. Bands of pale gold light danced across the bright gold of *Iesu*'s figure on the cross.

Sono fixed her eyes on His image and silently repeated

a memorized prayer. *By His passion and His cross, be brought to the glory of His Resurrection.* She blinked away tears that burned behind her eyelids.

Papa-san took a gasping little pant and opened his eyes. His focus drifted somewhere above the ceiling before settling on his wife. Mama-san gave him a soft smile.

Male voices rose in the garden outside. A guard called in from the warrior's run. "Pardon, madam. Your son has returned from battle."

Gratitude flooded Sono's heart. Her weeks of worry for her older brother lifted like a heavy blanket.

"What? How..." Mama-san's face softened with relieved surprise. "*Graças a Deusu!*" She glanced at Papa-san and her voice broke. "Please usher him in."

Yoshiaki's voice boomed as he greeted the sentries. He strode into the room, showing every sign of a hard ride—shoulders drooping with exhaustion, *samurai* top-knot askew. Perspiration glistened on his forehead. Mud splattered his shin guards to his knees.

He made it in time. He exuded a new confidence, sun-bronzed and hardened from his time on campaign. It seemed leading their column to battle agreed with him.

Sono rose with her mother and younger brother and they bowed in unison.

Yoshiaki's face folded with grief. He fell to his knees next to Papa-san. "Father, how are you?"

"Tired. So..." He took a labored breath. "Tired."

Sono choked back a sob.

Papa-san's eyes didn't stray from his oldest son. He opened his mouth as if to speak, but only a soft moan came. Mama-san patted his hand and spoke for him. "We were not expecting you so soon, son. How did you manage it?"

"The Shimazu have surrendered." Triumph rang through his voice.

Mama-san's features lit with surprise. "Surrendered? How marvelous!"

"It is true. The Lord Regent's great army has ensured their house will trouble our island no longer. I will tell you the whole tale another time."

Mama-san stroked her husband's arm. "Such wonderful tidings! Now, I believe your father has something important to say."

Papa-san gave a small nod. "Ah, my son." His focus moved to Yoshiaki's face. "You have made me...so proud. One charge...I leave you. Both of you. Live as I have raised you—as *Kirishitan*. Protect...protect the padres. No matter the cost."

"*Hai*, Papa-san." Yoshiaki and Suminobu said it in virtual unison.

"You must not"—his eyes drifted closed—"must *not* go back to the cult of spirits and ancestors." The expression ebbed from his face.

Sono sat motionless, battling her disappointment. Would he have no word for her, then?

Her mother touched his shoulder. "Lord Omura. Sono-chan..."

Papa-san flinched and started. "Sono? Daughter?"

"I am here, Papa-san." She leaned over to rest her hand against his temple. She did her best not to notice the smell of his dying—an odd note like pitch on his breath mixed with hints of stale sake and licorice from his medicine.

He fixed bleary eyes on her. "I have a request of you too. It is..." He labored to draw in air. "A very difficult thing."

Her mother, her brother, the shifting light...all gone. There was only his face—and it looked weary to death. "Anything, Papa-san." Her mouth felt dry as an autumn field.

"This will be...hard for you." His gaze drifted to Yoshiaki.

Her older brother's jaw tensed. "Shall I tell her, Papa-san?"

He made no objection. Yoshiaki went on. "We have been forced to strike a peace deal, Sono-chan."

A peace deal. All those couriers back and forth. Had they agreed to bargain her off as a pledge?

Otomo. Arima. Those were the other *Kirishitan* houses on Kyushu. Luzia, her sister, had gone to the Arima. Masamuro, her sister-in-law, had come from the same house. She had never dreamed she would marry outside that circle.

But there were other *Kirishitan* clans, farther away. So much farther, on the big island of Honshu.

Papa-san studied her, eyes glistening. "I am fortunate to have many daughters. I must do...very hard thing with you."

She managed to swallow. "*Hai*, Papa-san."

His eyes drifted closed and stayed that way. "I am sorry...dear daughter. It's hard to go..."

He lay very still for a moment. Fear he would not continue drove the air from her lungs.

But he did. "I find I must...part now from everything I love." The corners of his lips rose in a faint suggestion of a smile. "Except...*Iesu Kirisuto*."

The *shoji* cracked open. "Your pardon, Lady Omura. Padre Lucena is here."

Relief washed over her mother's face again. "Ah, good. Let him enter."

Papa-san heaved a sigh. "We can no longer afford...enemy right down the coast. Yoshiaki made...contract with...Matsuura. You marry...Matsuura Hisanobu."

Matsuura. She gaped at him. Had that name really dropped from his lips?

Matsuura, their sworn enemy for decades?

And not just *their* enemy. An enemy of the cross. Had she not heard the stories all her life? How Hisanobu's father, Shigenobu, desecrated a holy painting intended for a new *Kirishitan* church in his domain. Of course, the Portuguese *Kirishitan* captain reacted and sailed the enormous Black Ship down the coast to her father's port. How Lord Matsuura had the gall to pursue and attack the Portuguese ship itself, at anchor in an Omura port.

Married off to a hater of *Deusu*. She'd known for years that the number one son of that house was near to her age, but this she had never expected. Not from her father. Or from her older brother.

Or from her mother. Disbelief numbing her, she turned her eyes to Lady Omura.

Concern creased her mother's forehead, but she gave Sono a tiny nod.

Yoshiaki shifted his weight. "The Lord Regent commanded it, Sono-chan. We dared not refuse. Master Hisanobu and his father will come to meet you on their way back to Hirado."

It was true then. Sono fought to maintain her composure even as the shifting light from the *koi* pond seemed to spread through the room, dissolving the walls around her.

How? How could Papa-san leave her *and* give her away to the enemy, all in the same day? She swallowed to moisten her dry mouth. "But...honored brother, what does that mean? As a *Kirishitan*, I will be scorned in a clan that is not of the faith."

Padre Lucena, the mission superior from Nagasaki, swept in, followed by a pair of younger padres burdened with a large ceremonial crucifix and a wooden chest. Their unadorned capes and somber dark cassocks fit the occasion much better than the embroidered silks and brightly painted panels that filled the room.

Everyone around Papa-san's futon stood and bowed. Sono was the last to find her feet.

"*Pax huic dómui*," Padre Lucena said. *Peace be in this house.*

They recited the response in unison. "*Et ómnibus habitántibus in ea.*" *And in all who live here.*

Sono mouthed the words, but nothing inside her connected with them. Peace? In *all* who lived there? How could they speak of peace when a cannonball had reduced her life to splinters?

Padre Lucena sank to his knees beside Papa-san. "How are you, my lord?"

The pain that pinched his features relaxed a bit at seeing his old friend and confidante. "Very...glad...you have come, Padre."

They all settled back into their places around Papa-san.

Mama-san echoed her husband's gratitude. "It is good you have come now, Padre. Lord Omura was talking to our daughter about our arrangement with the Matsuura."

Padre Lucena regarded Sono with solemn eyes. "*Deusu*'s will is at times mysterious."

Heat rose to her face. So he knew all about it. Everyone knew, it seemed. Except her.

The Portuguese father went on. "This marriage may not be what we would have chosen. But we cannot deny it presents opportunity."

Opportunity? She stared at him. "Padre, I thought marriage to an unbeliever is a grievous sin."

He exchanged glances with her mother. "In this case, it seems it cannot be helped. The Lord Regent has directed it. Your brother was able to secure Lord Matsuura's assurance that his son, the Matsuura heir, will accept a *Kirishitan* marriage. And you will be allowed the sacrament of baptism for your children. Under these considerations, we will grant a special dispensation."

Special dispensation. Her thoughts spun into a whirl of astonishment. Had he said those words? The padres were *Deusu*'s mouthpiece to man, and as the superior to the grand mission in Nagasaki, Padre Lucena was the saintliest person among them. Hearing him speak might not be quite the same as hearing from *Deusu* Himself, but it was the closest she would get to it.

If Padre said this was *Deusu*'s will, it had to be so. But it was more than a mystery. It was a dreadful disaster.

Padre was still speaking. "It may not be an easy road for you. But think of it, Lady Sono. You can place a *Kirishitan* lord in Hirado Castle. You can shift the path of an entire domain. An important one." Something flashed behind his eyes. Something with almost the appearance of greed.

She pushed that thought away. Padre Lucena was a holy man. His desires could only reflect *Deusu*'s. If he had greed, it was a godly greed for souls. And if her future was to be sacrificed in a bid to bring the *Kirishitan* faith into the ruling house of Hirado, that had to be *Deusu*'s mysterious will.

A fresh question pressed on her so hard she was compelled to voice it. "By *Kirishitan* marriage, this means my future husband will not keep a concubine, yes? It will be just the two of us?"

"They have agreed to a *Kirishitan* marriage." It was not a direct answer.

"Your father knows well what a sacrifice he asks of you, Sono-chan." Mama-san's voice was soft but firm. "You must trust him in this. He would never ask if he were not convinced it is best for all concerned."

She gaped at her mother. All concerned? Shouldn't she be included in the "all"? Was she so insignificant?

The question wasn't worth asking. The answer was clear.

Her mother's slender white index finger traced the embroidered pattern down her silk kimono sleeve, lingering on a delicate cherry blossom. "You know that a *samurai* must give himself—"

Sono sighed. "As heedlessly as a cherry blossom. *Hai,* Mama-san."

"The same is true of a *samurai*'s daughter, yes?"

Everyone seemed to be staring at her. Suminobu made a noise in his throat.

Papa-san. Mama-san. Her number one brother, Yoshiaki, who was now also her lord. Even dear Padre Lucena, and by extension, *Deusu* Himself. They were all ready to bundle her off to Hirado, to live as the lone embattled *Kirishitan* in a Buddhist house. One thin little voice whispering for *Deusu*, amidst a din of temple drums and bells sending up a clamor to eight million deities.

She turned a pleading gaze into her father's red-rimmed eyes. His trembling hand lifted in a vague gesture. "It must be, Sono-chan."

Yoshiaki weighed in again, his voice firm. "The Lord Regent brokered the peace agreement, sister. We had little choice."

So, this was a battle she could not win. Could not even fight.

She placed her hands on the mat in front of her knees and bowed her head to the floor. "*Hai,* Papa-san." Again the right words, connecting to nothing in her hollow heart.

An inexpressible sadness crossed Padre Lucena's face.

"We must begin the extreme unction, Lady Omura. Do you wish to summon anyone else?"

Sono's eyes settled on the figure of *Iesu*, writhing in dying agony on the big crucifix the Jesuits had brought in.

Agnus Dei—Lamb of God. *Iesu*, the Lord of Lords, led like a lamb to slaughter. For the sake of her own soul.

Love your enemies. Could she love the Matsuura, the ancient enemies of her house?

Could she at least not hate them?

She dabbed away a tear. The marriage *Deusu* had apparently ordained for her. The dynasty they all expected her to build. She would have long years to concern herself with the consequences of those maneuvers. On this day, she could concern herself with only one thing—the fact that her father was leaving her.

Saturday 18 April 1942

Onishi gaped at Akira across the radio room. He set his jaw and flipped to a fresh page in his notepad. "*Hai.* What's the message, sir?"

"Inform *Kiso* we've sighted enemy carriers six hundred fifty nautical miles east of Inubo Saki."

"*Hai.*"

"Keep transmitting until they respond. If you need anything, we're on the bridge."

"*Hai.*" The radio operator bent over his cipher book.

"Ensign. With me." He exited the radio room, Nagai following. Started down the ladder to the deck below.

Bang.

A pistol shot. Even muffled by wind and rain, the report was unmistakable. He froze.

Nagai all but skidded to a halt. His eyes met Akira's, whites showing all around the irises. "What was that?"

Akira cursed. "It came from below."

The ensign sucked his breath in through his teeth. "The captain?"

Akira gave him a curt nod. He and Yoshiwara were the only men with sidearms. "Get the medic and send him to the captain's cabin."

Chapter Three

PADRE LUCENA SAT LONG WITH SONO'S father after he concluded the rite, reading passages from *The Imitation of Christ* and from the Bible. "Purify me with hyssop, Lord..." Papa-san's lips moved in time with the padre's lovely words.

Sono lingered until her father's face slackened into sleep. It gratified her heart to see him so peaceful. But then a fierce desire to escape took over. She'd had more than her fill of kneeling in that chamber watching him, or what was left of him.

She excused herself. then slung the bow over her shoulder and followed the rugged path that led to the archery range. The mid-afternoon sun glared without mercy into her eyes.

She paused at an outcropping where the path flirted with a steep drop, catching her breath at the sweeping view of the glistening bay below. The white-washed walls and peaked roofs of Sanjo Castle, her clan's ancestral fortress, were just visible in the distance, crowning the promontory at the far end of Omura Bay.

Their castle. Their land. Their bay. Even if her future father-in-law had once thought he could sail up and take it by storm.

A wave of sadness nearly made her knees buckle. She loved it here. But she had known all her life she was destined to leave.

A dragonfly hovered over a little pool next to the path. Sunlight caught its wings before it darted down the hillside. Even that tiny creature was free to flit where it pleased, no one commanding it here or there.

She blinked back hot tears and walked on. She mounted the archery platform and shot off three or four arrows before her eyes misted. When she could no longer aim, she sank down on the platform's edge, her bow across her lap.

She could not have said how long she sat alone with

her grief before her handmaid appeared. The daughter of one of Papa-san's senior advisers, Iya had been Sono's companion so long she felt like a sister. Iya settled next to her, wordless. Sono rested her head on her dear friend's shoulder and dissolved into tears.

Her handmaid slipped a comforting arm around her. "I know. It is a hard thing."

"You know?" She sniffed. "About the Mat—?" The name stuck at her lips.

"*Hai.*" Iya gave her waist an encouraging squeeze. "My father says he would be honored if you would choose me to come with you."

"He does?" She would not be alone on their horrid island after all. "Ah, Iya! Of course I want you to come with me. Those are the only good tidings I've had today."

Iya dropped her eyes and bit her lip. "Your mother summons you."

"Is it...?" Sono stood and brushed off her skirt.

"I fear so."

Sono rushed up the path and into her father's chamber. Mama-san knelt across from Yoshiaki and Padre Lucena, gazing at her husband. When Sono crossed the threshold, her mother spoke quietly, her voice flat. "He slipped away in his sleep." Tears streaked her face powder, usually so immaculate.

"Ah! Papa-san." Sono dropped to her knees beside him. His face was already taking on an ashen hue. Death had overtaken the warrior.

Tears blurred her view of him. She lay her hands on the floor in front of her and prostrated herself. Pressed her forehead into the mat until she could feel the fine weave in the straw and smell the faint odor of autumn fields. The first sob forced its way through, breaching her dam of restraint. The next came faster, and then sobs wracked her.

Others entered. Mama-san greeted them. Padre Lucena spoke words no doubt intended to encourage them all. There was comfort in the deep bass of his voice, but it flowed around Sono like water glides past the hull of a ship. The truth was cold and hard as stone, and nothing anyone said could budge it.

Papa-san was gone. And she was leaving—a peace offering to their bitter enemies.

Saturday 18 April 1942

Akira rushed down the ladder and pounded on Yoshiwara's door. "Captain?"

No response.

He tried to twist the knob. Locked.

He let out a stream of curses. *No time for finesse.* Thank the deities the door to the captain's cabin was polished wood rather than steel. That and the cabin's wood paneling were the vessel's sole touch of luxury.

Akira sprinted to the main hold and grabbed the hatchet from the fire equipment cabinet. He launched himself back down the passageway and slammed the blade into a seam in the door. The hardwood splintered.

The emergency medic, Ichiro, rushed up. His face shone pale in the light from the bare bulb in the ceiling. "What happened, sir?"

"We'll know soon." Akira smashed the hatchet into the door again, rending a rift large enough to put his arm through. He felt inside for the handle, popped the lock open, and pushed into the room.

Yoshiwara's body sprawled across his berth, blood streaming from his gaping mouth. Dead eyes fixed on the ceiling.

"*Che.*" Ichiro's voice quavered.

A growing circle of angry crimson pooled beneath the captain's head, glaring in stark contrast to the white sheets and the crisp dress uniform he'd changed into. His right arm lay flung over the sheets, fingers open toward his Nampu Fourteen pistol. Blood marked the weapon's muzzle.

Ichiro gasped and sank to his knees beside the berth. He listened at Yoshiwara's chest. Probed his wrist for a pulse.

The medic's efforts were wasted. The captain was dead.

Ichiro let the captain's wrist drop and stared up at Akira.

Akira looked away, swallowing hard against the bile that mounted his throat. *Think about this later. Think about it...later.*

A square of elegant mulberry paper lay in the precise center of the captain's writing desk. Elaborate *kanji* characters moved in purposeful columns down the page.

The captain's death poem.

Later.

There might be a day for remembering the captain. A day for delivering his death poem to the people who loved him. For making up tales of his glorious end and telling them to his wife and children. To the captain's son, Matsuo, with whom Akira had shared a few classes at the naval academy on Eta Jima.

A day for burning incense and watching cherry blossoms fall, showing the same heedless disregard for their own mortality the captain had. For appreciating the man's lifetime of service to the emperor—and for forgetting the way a single mishap four years ago had destroyed his career.

But only if Akira and the men—*his* men now—survived *this* day.

He turned to the medic. "Get back to the engine room. We'll do everything that's proper for Captain Yoshiwara later."

If there was a later.

He pressed the blotting paper onto the blood and fresh ink on the captain's death poem. He tucked the poem inside his raincoat with as much care as he could, then rushed into the cabin he shared with Nagai. He grabbed his life jacket from its peg and pulled a folded, cream-colored sash from his top dresser drawer.

His *senninbari*. Its embroidered pattern consisting of a thousand stitches from a thousand different hands, each stitch worked with a prayer. If legend was to be believed, it would provide supernatural protection in battle. His little sister Miyako had probably invested a hundred hours standing on street corners, begging each passing woman to contribute a stitch.

Something in his chest went liquid at the thought of

not seeing them again—his sister, and Mama-san. A deep regret that he'd failed to show them the appreciation they deserved.

He slammed that thought into a hollow place he could access later. *Time to defend them. Do your duty and leave them proud.*

He paused long enough to honor his grandfather's photo, in a silver frame on his desk. Two deep bows, two strong claps for Grandfather's spirit, and by extension, all the long line of noteworthy Matsuura ancestors. Then another deep bow.

Grandfather, whatever happens, allow me to honor you today. And all our noble lineage.

He wasn't convinced Grandfather could hear him, much less help him. But having thirty-seven generations of *daimyo*—high-born warlords—in your lineage conferred a certain weight of obligation.

He jogged up to the radio room, the *senninbari's* silk smooth in his hand and the life preserver looped over his arm. He and *Nitto Maru* were going to need all the help they could get.

Nagai and Onishi came to attention when he entered. Onishi reported. "I've completed several transmissions, sir. No response."

Nagai's eyes searched his face. "The captain, sir?"

Akira gave him a grim shake of the head. He wound the *senninbari* around his waist beneath his shirt and slipped the life preserver over his jacket. Protection in both the physical and the spiritual planes.

Beyond the plate-glass windshield, the clouds above the eastern horizon flared with reflected fire. Shells whistled from a cruiser's fearsome gun turrets, hurtling across miles of ocean.

At them.

His heart hammered in his chest. *So it begins.* "I'll be on the bridge. Nagai, with me."

Before he could reach the door, the ship jumped and took a violent pitch to starboard. He slammed shoulder-first into the wall. Nagai's weight smashed into his ribs. The light from the bulb on the ceiling flickered.

They'll aim better with the next one. Fear crouched like a *sumo* wrestler ready to take him on.

Akira took a controlled breath. There was work to do. He pushed himself out from behind Nagai.

Nothing but static on the radio. Onishi sat rubbing his elbow.

"Are you all right, seaman?" Akira said.

"Yes, sir."

"Good man. Keep up the transmission." Akira walked out onto the deck.

Nagai followed on his heels. "*Kiso* didn't hear us," the ensign said. "But it seems the enemy did."

A second salvo boomed in the distance. More shells screeched their way.

"Grab on!" Akira took hold of one leg of the ladder to the bridge and laced his arms through the rungs. Nagai grabbed the other leg.

Projectiles splashed in the waves just meters off *Nitto Maru*'s gunwales. Monstrous geysers erupted in every direction. Multiple concussions rang against the iron hull. The ship lurched, cabin windows rattling and joists crying like they would wrench open.

Water slammed into Akira's back. He clung to that ladder with every ounce of strength. Fear lunged and gripped him. Got him in a chokehold.

Calm. The foremost act of war. He took a deep breath and threw it off.

For a moment that felt like forever, there was nothing but the sea punching and thrusting at him. And the primal battle to hold on—to the ship, to life. He clutched the ladder, adrenaline lending strength to his grip. In the mad rush of water, he could feel Nagai's mass next to him. Feel Nagai's muscles strain in the same battle to hang on.

Feel Nagai start to slip.

It was a reflex and not a decision. He let go of the ladder with one arm and circled it around Nagai, bracing him. They fought a mighty battle together against the buffeting waves. It took endless seconds, but Nagai forced his arm forward and got his hand back on the ladder.

The torrent ebbed. Akira filled his lungs. His feet were

invisible beneath six inches of churning foam. Nagai stood next to him, panting, water streaming from his hood.

The others. Sakamoto. Konishi. Relief swelled through his chest to see both men at the forward cannon, clinging to the gun mount.

He scrambled up the swaying ladder to the open bridge, Nagai on his heels. *Nitto Maru* crested a wave and the enemy cruiser's big guns lit up once more. Its artillery took up a steady roar—very audible, even over the smashing waves and even from at least six kilometers away.

Huge billows of smoke obscured the enemy gunship. Enough firepower to obliterate a city, focused on a single speck in the water—his own *Nitto Maru.*

A sense of awe pressed a crushing weight into his chest. *How long can we stay afloat in this?* It wasn't a matter of *if* they would go under. It was a matter of when.

His head throbbed.

Focus. "The troughs, ensign. Tell Takeshi to steer into the troughs." If *Nitto Maru* couldn't see the enemy, the enemy couldn't see them. Staying in the troughs might give them a chance—or at least, precious extra minutes to get their message through.

Nagai barked the order into a voicepipe. He turned to Akira, grimacing. "Hear that, sir? Planes."

Akira stood still. Above the booming guns and the frenzied water smashing into the hull and the ship's joints complaining, he heard it—a steady whine.

Prop noise. And more than one plane.

Air cover from the second carrier. He swore and glanced around at the men.

Che! We're all so exposed. The *sumo* wrestler crouched again, an ugly leer on his face.

No sound from the aft gun. He hadn't checked on Omeda. He pushed away the sick feeling that churned his gut as he pictured the seaman's strong-boned face. Had he washed overboard?

"Ensign. See what's going on with the aft gun. Send the gunners from the fore cannon back if Onishi—"

"*Hai.*" Nagai put his mouth to another voicepipe.

That was it. Every tactic Akira could think of that might

improve the odds for his men—and himself. All that remained was to make sure *Nitto Maru* discharged her mission. Then if they all went to join their ancestors, they did it with honor.

A fresh barrage of shells hurtled toward them. A new wall of water shot into the air. Akira wrapped both arms around the handrail and held on. Nagai did the same.

The prop-whine swelled to a roar. Beyond a thick curtain of spray, a pair of sleek fighters glinted as they broke from the clouds.

The ensign was only three feet away, but Akira screamed to make himself heard. "Nagai! Take cover!" He threw himself into the corner of the bridge where the half-height wall would at least give him some protection. Nagai landed beside him.

The lead plane opened up its fifty-caliber guns. Bullets sprinted up the radio-room wall, puncturing the metal with an ear-piercing din.

Calm your own mind...

But with bullets punching jagged holes as wide as his thumb in the iron deck a meter from his knees, that wasn't so easy. Bullets went through the iron like cardboard—right into the radio room. A hoarse yell sounded from beneath his feet.

The lead plane roared overhead. Akira could make out the whine of more aircraft in the distance, carrying above the deep-throated boom of artillery.

The second plane dove at them. Two guns blazed from its fuselage and two from either wing. Their bullets converged to a single line that sliced across the foredeck.

A tremendous noise splintered the air. *Nitto Maru* rocked like a bathtub toy. The line of bullets came at the bridge.

Akira crammed into the corner beside Nagai and huddled with his head down. He nurtured a crazy idea that his *senninbari* would give the two of them a charmed circle of invulnerability. Or that the war god Hachiman would send a raging divine wind to drive off the attackers, like in the old story.

The sound of shattering glass came from the radio-room window a few feet below his knees. A bullet whizzed through the deck in front of him. His heart lurched in his chest. Beside him, Nagai let loose a wild shriek.

The fighters whooshed overhead and away.

Nagai lay crumpled like a rag doll on the deck where a bit of shrapnel had flung him, mouth stretched wide in a scream. He clutched a bloody four-inch stump that had been his right arm.

Akira's stomach heaved. He managed not to retch.

Calm... "Shh, shh. Here." He stripped off his leather belt, lashed it around what was left of Nagai's arm, and pulled it as tight as he could.

Fresh prop-noise swelled from the east.

A plane broke from the clouds, then another. Something smashed into the waves in front of him. Something much bigger than a six-inch shell.

There was a split second when everything was roaring and ripping and crashing water and twisting iron and crushing force.

Then there was—

Chapter Four

SENTRIES' FEET TRAMPED OUTSIDE SONO'S CHAMBER, as they had day and night since Papa-san left her for *Deusu's* paradise and she had returned to what was now her brother's castle.

The bustle here felt overwhelming. Stealing away from Papa-san's haven of retirement had been as simple as a walk across the garden and a shallow bow to the sentries at a single gate. But to exit Sanjo castle entailed passing through a network of courtyards and two-story gatehouses, where gun barrels angled through rows of firing ports. And down long flights of exposed steps where untold numbers of eyes tracked her every movement.

It all added to a surreal sensation her body no longer belonged to her. And given how they had bartered her away, that was no mere fancy. It was true.

The evening before, Yoshiaki had summoned her to his chamber. "Lord Matsuura and his son plan to visit us at mid-day tomorrow, Sono-chan. Tomorrow will decide whether you become Hisanobu's bride."

Now Mama-san hovered, making small adjustments to Sono's hair bows and the arrangement of her best *obi*. "You're stunning. Remember, you are simply there to serve a platter of sweets to the men. You need not speak unless they address you."

"*Hai*, Mama-san."

Mama-san stepped back and studied her. "Could you manage a happier expression?"

A tang like sour plum filled her mouth. She swallowed. The taste did not go away. "Mama-san, how did *you* feel?"

Her mother stood very tall. "My situation was...different. You could be less fortunate than you are."

A small shock of surprise jolted her, as it always did when something jarred her into acknowledging her mother's past. Mama-san made such an elegant figure in her beautiful lavender kimono. But she had not come to Papa-san from a noble house. And she had not come as a bride. She grew up a swordsmith's daughter in the castle village. Papa-san had bought her for his concubine when his first wife failed to produce a son. She bore him Luzia and Yoshiaki before Papa-san's first wife passed away. A baptism and a church wedding had made the concubine over into Lady Omura.

The tang of sour plum grew stronger. If a lord was not *Kirishitan*, pretty girls were quite affordable.

Still—resentment needled her—Mama-san's father had not shipped her off to some far domain, or to her family's ancient enemies.

Mama-san took Sono's hand between hers. "If you can't manage *happy*, try for *content*, ah?"

Sono glowered. "I have a question, Mama-san. Papa-san said he was compelled to accept this. So am I a bride? Or a hostage?"

"You shall have the honor to serve as a token of a new alliance."

A token. A symbolic item to be exchanged. She sighed.

"Are you not tired of it, Sono-chan? All the battles, all the losses, all the hardship? This will mean one less enemy to storm our gates. At least our corner of Kyushu will be at peace, thanks to you."

Peace. The word breathed a sort of perfume into her soul. How many times had she watched their castle gate swing open, sending their brave column out to glorious battle? How many times had a smaller column straggled back, ragged and bandaged, weeks or months later?

Mama-san applied a red-tinged brush to Sono's lips. "And you will have the honor of seeing your son rule their domain. *Hai*, our house has had a long history with the Matsuura. But your marriage will mark the dawn of a new era of alliance." She lifted the brush away and examined her work.

"You speak of alliances, Mama-san? We all know the alliance that did the most for our house was not with any house on this island. It was the outsiders—the padres and the Portuguese."

"*Hai.* And you heard Padre Lucena's pronouncement on this." Her mother tried the same coaxing voice she'd employed when Sono was a small girl. "None of us would have chosen it"—she patted Sono's hand as if she could transfer some confidence—"but *Deusu* has decreed it. *Deusu* willing, the sons you bear will change the destiny of Hirado and lift up the cause of *Kirisitu* in all of Kyushu."

Mama-san's handmaid appeared at the *shoji.* "It is time, Lady Sono."

Mama-san offered a parting thought. "It is a sacrifice, my dear. We all know that to be so. But this is the path *Deusu* has decreed for you."

Tuesday 21 April 1942

Akira woke slowly to a world of searing pain. Why did it hurt so much to be dead?

He wrenched his eyes open to find himself on his back in a gray-walled room that was much too bright. A contraption hung above him, with a heavy steel bar suspending a line of ropes and pulleys. A traction harness.

I'm not dead. I'm in a sick bay.

Relief washed over him, followed an instant later by a sharp twinge of shame that overwhelmed it. Where was he? What had become of his crew?

His eyes landed on the profile of a pale, freckled face. *Gaijin demon. What's he doing here?* He started and grabbed for his pistol.

He couldn't reach his hip. He couldn't reach anything. The harness pulleys jangled above him. Scorching tongues of fire licked up every nerve. He clenched his teeth to keep from crying out.

The room swayed. His weight shifted with the ship's movement, pressing his left ribs into the bed. Fresh pain jolted him, and he let out a sharp cry.

Oh! I'm still at sea.

The freckled medic turned and took a step to his bedside. "Hey! Slow down, buddy." The man studied him for a moment. "Speakee any English?"

English. Akira had a little knowledge tucked in some long-neglected corner of his mind. Classes at high school and at the naval academy made for ill-formed memories. "My...ship. My...men. Where?"

The medic's wide mouth went slack in a mocking grin. "Your ship? Gone—blasted to hell, I hope. Your crew? Gone too. You're it, fellow."

Images assaulted his mind in confused splinters. Enemy ships, flecks on the horizon. Yoshiwara in a pool of blood. Nagai, his cabin-mate, lying mangled in a corner of the bridge. The *senninbari* his sister had made for him, his own fingers knotting it around his waist.

Despite all Miyako's efforts, his *senninbari* had failed to protect anyone.

And Onishi. Sakamoto. Konishi. Brave men he'd spent months with. In Nagai's case, years. *His* brave men, persisting in their duty in the teeth of the enemy barrage.

"Me? Only?" He managed to choke out the words.

"Yep."

He closed his eyes while the *gaijin's* statement sank in. His men. His friends. Every single man on *Nitto Maru*. Dead.

But I'm a prisoner? Why was there still light in the world?

The medic's grotesque freckled face grated on his nerves. How was this man alive when his worthy crew was dead? Worse, how was *he* alive?

Captured. Shame engulfed him. Never in his worst moments had he imagined this could be his end.

"I was thinking you might want to know where you are." The man's voice had a drawl that jarred Akira's ears and made him hard to understand.

"I am *horyo.*" A prisoner. The most ignoble fate that could befall a warrior of Japan. *Where* he was hardly mattered.

"I don't understand that. But you're on *U.S.S. Nashville*—and lucky to be alive."

"What...how am I bad?"

"How are you *in*-jured? Crushed ribcage." He ran a hand along his own side to illustrate. "Broken leg. Crushed hand. Burns over thirty percent of your body." He formed a three and a circle with his fingers.

Akira screwed his eyes shut and thrust his head back into the pillow.

Lucky. Didn't that mean something like *fortunate?* The foreigner understood nothing. The men who'd gone down—they were the fortunate ones. He'd give anything to be where they were. To join them in glorious death in the emperor's service.

All those generations of his ancestors. The long line of noble heroes, their spirits entombed at half a dozen temples dotting the verdant hills of Hirado. He'd always known he'd share their glory one day. What chance did he have of that now?

The medic's voice intruded into his misery. "Like I said, welcome to *U.S.S. Nashville.* Eight hundred"—some language he couldn't follow—"men on board. And you." His eyes narrowed into an expression of tangible scorn. "The only Jap."

The man picked up a syringe from the steel table next to Akira's berth. He said something that included "hospital."

"So sorry. I don't understand."

"You go hos-pi-tal." He drew the words out, then gave Akira a pointed look up and down. "Why we're so nice to *you,* I don't know."

An excellent question. What use was he? Right hand and right leg immobilized in plaster casts. From what he could tell, bandages covered half the rest of his dysfunctional body—his torso, arm, hips, and leg.

What kind of life was left for such a husk of a man? He could never return to Japan. A prisoner who failed the Land of the Gods deserved no better than a quick execution. Or a long life of infamous shame.

The medic twirled the syringe slowly in front of Akira's face, his eyes lit with a strange glow. "This is morphine. For pain. I don't s'pose you want any of this?"

Moruhine. Akira understood that much. He squared his jaw. "No. Thank you." He deserved nothing but pain.

"Suit yourself. It's all one to me." The orderly put the

syringe on a table at the far end of the room. He turned for his parting shot. "You know we did it, don't you?"

Akira focused past the pain with an effort. Peered into the man's strange sky-colored eyes. "What?"

"Jimmy Doolittle bombed your God-forsaken Tokyo, genius. That's what."

Tokyo. He jerked with alarm. "Excuse me." His voice rasped through vocal chords he hadn't used for...how long? A day? Two?

"What is it?"

"The emperor..." He could barely bring the words to his lips.

The medic's jaw hardened. "Your Hirohito's fine. Our boys stayed clear of the Imperial Palace." He narrowed his eyes. "Shame, if you ask me." He turned and left the room.

Akira lay studying the gray paint globs on the ceiling rivets. A picture rose in his mind—a massive gray ship against a gray horizon. Gray planes clustered on its deck.

Those planes had lived to rain fire on Tokyo.

Rage sent his pulse pounding against his skull. His men had sacrificed their lives to report the *gaijin* incursion up the chain. How had those bombers made it in range to threaten the emperor himself?

He and *Nitto Maru* had done their best. Even so, they'd failed Japan. He should have died with his ship. He could never recover from the anguish of this shame.

Something woke Akira, if you could call it waking. It was more of a slow fade into a less hazy state of being.

Two facts towered like granite mountaintops above the fog in his brain.

His nightmare hadn't gone away. Immobile in a traction harness. Pain sharp enough to steal his breath when he wasn't flooded with morphine to hold it at bay. Steel walls and a port-hole window. He was still *horyo* on an enemy warship.

And there was only one honorable path for him. The one Yoshiwara had taken.

A man-shape loomed over his berth. A *gaijin*'s pale skin, with chiseled features and a cleft chin. Gray-flecked dark hair. The bearing of an officer.

"Welcome to *U.S.S. Nashville.* I'm Lieutenant Commander Prescott." The intruder perched on the empty bed next to Akira's. "Cigarette?" He pulled a pack from his breast pocket along with a lighter.

"*Hai*—Yes. Thank you." Akira reached for it with a trembling left hand and brought it to his lips. It was the first cigarette he'd held since the *Nitto Maru.*

"What's your name, sailor?" And then something else Akira didn't follow.

"I'm sorry, sir. I don't understand."

The commander sighed with an exasperated shake of his head. "Your name, sailor." He followed this with a few more words in something between a grumble and a growl. Akira couldn't track it, but he made out *tell family* and *alive.*

Those words were a boom slamming into his chest. Did the man think he was being kind? The last thing he wanted was for anyone at home to know of his enduring shame. Much better for them to hold their heads high, thinking him dead defending Japan. Any end would be better than smearing their ancient family name with the insult of a *horyo* who'd failed them all.

"My, ah... name? It is..." He grasped at the first name he thought of—the Yamiuri Giants' famous star pitcher. "Sawamura. Sawamura Akira, sir."

Comdr. Prescott gave him a slight nod. "Slow down. I want to make sure I get that right."

Akira spelled out his new name in English letters. The officer uttered more words. They echoed somewhere at the fringe of Akira's thoughts as he drifted back to forgetfulness.

One honorable path. But it was hard for a wounded prisoner to dispatch himself. Harder than Akira had ever imagined.

His mind swam most of the time, either with merciful morphine or merciless pain. He had no weapon. Not a *tanto* knife, which would have been the proper thing. Nor a pistol—a Nampu Fourteen had been good enough for the captain. Nor even a weapon as crass but effective as a grenade.

He would have to improvise.

A baby-faced medic was peeling back the bandage on his chest, exposing the cracked and blistered flesh that covered him from the right side of his neck down to his groin.

Just keep your eyes on the ceiling. But a sick fascination always drew them to the skin beneath the bandage. He snapped his gaze away and forced back the bile that rose in his mouth. Was that mangled torso really him? He *couldn't* be stuck in this hideous body for the rest of his life.

The pasty-faced medic, who had to be a demon in disguise, wrenched up a few more inches of bandage. Darts of pain shot up every nerve.

"That hurts. I know. But..." The *gaijin* said a few words Akira didn't track, in a voice that rang with contrived cheer. "You could be dead, you know. You have to think about that."

Akira did. Constantly. He sent pleas to his ancestors for it.

The *gaijin* continued his insipid patter. "The doc says"—more words—"could have killed you." More babble, then: "...a hole in your lung."

He sponged at the flesh that covered Akira's broken ribs. "Doc says... extra careful here. Don't wanna move these ribs around..."

Akira tensed at the pain, clenching his good fist. He begged the deities with every ounce of fervor in him to join his men in death. Dying had to be easier.

Chapter Five

SONO GLIDED INTO THE RECEPTION HALL where her brother hosted the Matsuura men. Her pulse pounded in her ears so hard she felt lightheaded. An odd floating feeling filled her, as if her feet never grazed the ground.

Keep the tray level. Keep an even pace.

The morning sun filtered from behind her as she walked, bathing the space in a warm glow. Four men knelt formally on brocade cushions. Grief stabbed her—hard. It felt odd seeing her older brother in Papa-san's place, but he had to mature into the warlord he was born to be.

Suminobu knelt to his right. Sono's sister-in-law, Masamaro, was positioned behind them where she could easily pour their *sake,* just as Sono's mother had always done for Papa-san. Pain wrenched her chest again.

The two men to Yoshiaki's left sported the misshapen mulberry-leaf crest of the Matsuura. Lord Matsuura Shigenobu and his son. They had the same hard, vibrant air as Yoshiaki.

Mama-san hovered discretely behind them all to oversee the service.

Curiosity consumed Sono, but it would be inconceivably impolite to stare. One brief glimpse of her future father-in-law, stolen before she dropped into a bow, sent a tremor of surprise through her. This enemy who had attacked their harbor, the man she'd heard so many stories about, had a prominent nose and chin that gave him the air of a hawk prepared to dive and a powerful build that belied his nearly forty years. But his dark eyebrows were poised at a quizzical angle, and his lips bore a pleasant curve that made him appear intelligent and not ill-humored.

She knelt and placed the tray with care on a low table before her brother.

"*Arigato,* sister. It is a delight to see you." Yoshiaki's face bore a flush of pride. Her mother's efforts to make her beautiful must have paid off.

With her gaze anchored on the mats at her knees, she moved back a few inches and settled into a kneel while Yoshiaki introduced her. She bowed her head to the floor and counted slowly to three. At last, at *last* she could move her focus up to Lord Matsuura's face, and then to his son. The man *Deusu* had slated to be her husband.

Apparently, no one had told *him* it was impolite to stare. Hisanobu devoured her with brazen eyes as if she were a persimmon he was about to bite into.

He is handsome. A younger version of his father, which translated into striking good looks. About her own age. Lively eyes, strong features, his father's intelligent mouth. White teeth shone in bright contrast to swarthy skin.

An uncomfortable warmth crept up her cheeks. She dropped her eyes again.

Lord Matsuura plucked a bean-curd delicacy off the tray. "Lady Sono, your brother tells me you are quite a student of the way of the bow."

"I assure you my skills are lacking. But my father encouraged me to pursue it."

Hisanobu's eyes flashed. "Your father was wise in this." His lip curled in a derisive arc. "Omura Sumitada had many enemies." His eyes moved to the crucifix displayed in the alcove, and open scorn crossed his features.

The expression on his face sent a blast of chill air into her chest. It was gone in an instant, but she knew what she had seen. Worse than mocking her—he had the gall to mock her father's faith.

He has no more choice in this than I do. He must have been raised on stories about *her* Papa-san, the great *Kirishitan* enemy of the Matsuura. Just as she'd grown up hearing about the pirates of Hirado. He could hardly welcome being bound to her in a monogamous *Kirishitan* marriage.

All Mama-san's flowery words about peace. About destiny. They were soft rain breaking over the cold steel reality of this battle-hardened young man in front of her, who scorned her and her faith.

Lord Matsuura regarded her with a slight smile. "Your house has acquired more than its share of enemies. But those days are behind us, yes? We all serve the Lord Regent now." He selected a fig.

Hisanobu downed his tea and said nothing.

Mama-san refilled Lord Matsuura's cup. "Congratulations to you all on your tremendous victory. We hope for years of peace."

Yoshiaki made a grand gesture that encompassed both the Matsuura men. "Our honorable guests distinguished themselves in the seaborne assault. And the Lord Regent took note."

Lord Matsuura grunted. "You lopped off quite a number of heads yourself, Lord Omura."

Sono gaped as if Yoshiaki had taken a cobra's guise. It seemed he'd missed the barb buried in Hisanobu's comment about Papa-san's many enemies. Somehow. But to sit here trading compliments with Papa-san's old enemy as if they were best friends?

Perhaps they had saved each other's lives in battle. Or perhaps, in her brother's mind, the new prestige the House of Matsuura had gained made up for their open scorn for the *Kirishitan* faith. That thought pushed a sour taste into her mouth.

Lord Matsuura eyed her. "What of the gentler arts, Lady Sono? Are you proficient in poetry?"

"I do favor reading poems, Lord Matsuura."

"Very good. Perhaps you could recite something for us, ah?" He bit into another delicacy.

I said read, not recite! But she inclined her head to their guest, cringing inside. "'Twould be an honor." She worked to compose herself. She glanced at Yoshiaki, and an impish impulse quickened her pulse. Did she dare?

She dressed her features in her mildest guise. "Here is one of my favorites.

"The mountain hamlet
buries me in wintry gloom.
People gone. And grass
and green things withered, lifeless.
Wistful memories."

Lord Matsuura's eyebrows lifted in surprise. "Ah, the

LINDA THOMPSON | 41

poignant beauty that dwells in transient things. A dour theme for a lovely maiden, ah?"

She gave Yoshiaki a direct stare. "*The grass withers, and the flowers.* A verse from our *Kirishitan* scripture. Does it not make you think of Papa-san, and how fleeting the glory men spend their lives seeking proves?" She drove in her own barb. "Even glory in battle."

Yoshiaki winced. Hisanobu set his *sake* cup down. "Lord Omura failed to mention his sister is a philosopher." Her future husband ran a finger around the rim of his cup and eyed her, amusement tugging at his lips.

"My condolences on your father's death," Lord Matsuura said. "He and I did not agree on some matters, but he was a great warlord. Ever a worthy opponent."

Did not agree on some matters. Was that what he called sailing into someone else's harbor and blasting away at ships under their protection? The man had quite a way of wording things.

Mama-san arched her eyebrows and inclined her head. "*Arigato* for bringing the sweets, Sono-chan." It was a dismissal.

"Of course." Sono rose smoothly and bowed to Lord Matsuura and his son. "What a pleasure to meet you."

"The pleasure is ours." Lord Matsuura raised his cup to her. He turned to Yoshiaki. "Your sister's beauty exceeds all reports, Lord Omura."

She bowed her way out of the hall, the smooth silk of her kimono swishing around her thighs as she moved. She managed a sidelong glance at Hisanobu. His eyes followed her, the same vexing half-smile playing at his lips.

Once she was safely past the guard and out of view, she stopped and braced herself against a pillar.

He could have uttered one *word to me that wasn't sarcastic.* Of course, the two lords were expected to carry the conversation, but some slight acknowledgment of his future wife would have been a nice gesture.

And the way he had glared at the crucifix. They thought she was going to build a *Kirishitan* dynasty with this young man? He appeared quite set against it.

Iya hurried toward her. "Well? How did it go? Is he as handsome as the servant girls say?"

"Oh, he's handsome. But..."

"But what?"

"I think he despises me. And our faith. And I can't imagine my honored brother is too happy with me either." A sigh wrenched itself from some deep place in her core. "Padre says this is *Deusu*'s will, and they all envision a *Kirishitan* heir for Hirado. But perhaps I am too weak in faith."

Wednesday 22 April 1942

Akira woke to find the infirmary dark and silent. The medic's words jumped into his mind with bell-like clarity.

A hole in your lung. Don't wanna move these ribs.

Could a broken rib still kill him? Poke a hole in his lung? His fractured ribcage wasn't protected by any kind of cast or splint. Just yards of bandages.

He draped his good arm over the railing at the side of his berth, levered his torso up, and pulled. He jammed himself against the railing hard enough to make it grind into his ribs. Pain shot through him and he let go, biting back a howl.

Like every officer, he'd memorized the words of the *Instructions for the Battlefield*.

Never live to experience shame as a prisoner. Better to die and avoid leaving the outrage of a dishonorable name.

If he did that again, with all his strength, could he puncture a lung and end his tortured life?

The thing was worth trying. He screwed his eyes shut and dwelt on an imagined scene. Made it as real as he could in his mind. He knelt on a white cloth, robed in white. A *tanto* knife shone in his hand. He wrapped his fist around its solid steel hilt wrapped in silk cord.

Grandfather awaited him already at Yasukuni Shrine, the most sacred spot in Japan. In the broad hall on Kudan Hill, where Japan's heroes rested in immortal glory. Papa-san's spirit would surely arrive there soon. And in that inevitable someday, he would be there to meet his father— assuming he went through with this. Profound pride would light his father's face when he learned his eldest son had done what was needed to ensure an honorable death. In spite of everything. In spite of failure and capture.

He steeled himself with the determination that was his birthright, looped his arm around the steel railing again, and slammed his torso against it with all the strength he could muster.

The bed let out a creak. The pain was excruciating, but he could still pull breath into his lungs. He tried again. Then again, pushing past the agony to get into a rhythm. The bed jumped. The creaking echoed through the room, together with rhythmic thuds as rubber-coated feet struck linoleum flooring.

The fourth time he slammed himself against the steel, something cracked, triggering an explosion of pain. It took every ounce of determination he possessed not to scream.

He inhaled. Pain flared across his torso from his waist up to his shoulder. He sensed at once he hadn't pulled in enough air.

His mind soared with glee. He'd done it. He'd killed himself.

But dying was hard. His flesh rebelled. His lungs worked, gasping for breath, each movement bringing fresh torment. He thrashed in the traction harness, every muscle in his body joining the involuntary fight for oxygen.

His left side burned. Sweat streamed down his face. Gray invaded the edges of his vision.

His mind drifted on a rising tide of animal panic. But somewhere above it, a last thin glimmer of conscious thought remained.

This was how it felt to die.

The freckled medic ran in. "What the..." A stream of forceful language followed. He grabbed a blanket, wedged a muscular arm between Akira and the railing, and wadded the blanket around the metal. He glowered at Akira. "If you're so determined to die, Jap, I should let you."

Hai. Let me die. If only he had some way to

communicate that—to beg for it. But he was beyond speaking, and vision and hearing were fading.

The medic shouted something into the hall. Footsteps pounded to his bedside. More expletives in a different voice. A doctor loomed over him. "What's going on?"

The medic pressed him into the mattress with both forearms, sending a fresh wave of pain crashing through his torso. The doctor probed up and down his ribs, then stabbed something into his chest. Air whooshed through the puncture with an audible hiss. The burning pressure in his side was relieved in an instant.

He gasped, and oxygen flooded in. He howled inside. *Why?* Why couldn't these cursed Americans let a warrior die with his last shred of dignity intact?

The medic jabbed another needle into his arm. Medication stung its way into his veins.

Voices clamored above him, but he made no effort to follow. Consciousness slipped away leaving one final thought.

He'd failed. Again.

Twenty-fifth Day of the Fifth Month, Anno Domini 1587

Sono and Iya made their way back to Sono's chamber. Iya tuned her *shamisen*, laid the instrument's long neck across her lap, and plucked every melody she knew on its strings— some of their favorites twice—while Sono awaited her summons to bid the Matsuura farewell. At last, Mama-san's handmaid came to fetch her.

Sono rustled along, still in her best kimono, hastening to join the rest of her family outside the arched portal that led to the main entrance courtyard. The din of preparation carried through from the courtyard. Horses whinnied. Hooves scuffed fine gravel. The Matsuura men stood stroking and murmuring to their nickering steeds. The sun shone on sleek pelts and meticulously groomed manes.

Yoshiaki shot her a frown. "That was a pretty performance," he said in a low voice.

She dropped into a deep bow. "Pray pardon me, my

lord." She straightened and faced him. "But the pirate wanted a poem."

"Sono-chan!" Mama-san said with an exasperated huff. She looked her over, then tweaked her hair bow.

"You are incorrigible, as always." But Yoshiaki's eyes glinted. "Much as you may have hoped to scuttle the arrangement, it's settled."

"Settled!" Her voice bounced back at her off the plaster wall, louder than she intended. She lowered it. "Did you not see how he scowled at the crucifix? How am I to raise *Kirishitan* sons with—"

Yoshiaki broke in on her, jaw jutting. "It was our father's great regret"—he rested his fist on the hilt of his sword, an heirloom Papa-san had carried, and three generations of Omura lords before him—"that we wasted so much blood warring with the Matsuura. And his cherished wish and prayer that we attain an enduring peace with them. He told you this himself, yes?"

Sono dropped her eyes and heaved a sigh. "He did, my lord."

Mama-san added her voice. "And think how many men's lives you will save by keeping us from warring with the Matsuura. Is that a small thing?"

Fifteen paces away, Hisanobu stood stroking his horse's acorn-colored coat. Sunlight shone on the young man's thick hair in its sleek topknot and gleamed from the black silk that rippled across his well-muscled chest. He turned and saw Sono. His gaze lingered, traveling up and down the length of her. He caught her eyes and gave her a slight bow before he sprang into his saddle.

"Padre Lucena has affirmed the match as *Deusu*'s will," Yoshiaki said. "Need anything else be said?"

She found sudden interest in the stones beneath her toes. "No, my lord."

He placed a hand on her shoulder. "Very good. We will join them in the courtyard, and you will give them your most courteous goodbye—for now."

Chapter Six

A MONTH PASSED, WITH MAMA-SAN WORKING through long days commissioning the trousseau that would journey with Sono to her new home. Hundreds of items were needed, and even the narrowest cosmetic brush had to fully reflect the Omura family's stature.

Sono peered into an open trunk in her mother's chamber. Lacquered boxes. Tea implements. Hand mirror. Every ornate object finely crafted and richly gilded, tokens of her family's prestige.

And as for herself, she would serve as a token too, a symbol of their houses' new alliance. They might as well ship her off in a trunk, like the other decorative objects.

A morning came when the mansion buzzed with a fresh undercurrent of commotion. Sentries carried on low-voiced conversations on the warriors' run. Servants pattered rapidly back and forth. A rumor flew through the castle that an emissary had come from the Lord Regent himself.

When Iya told Sono, she started up a frenetic rhythm with her fan. "Are we mustered to war? I wonder where Yoshiaki will be off to this time. And if he'll take Suminobu along."

"Your little brother must begin to prove himself in the way of the warrior, yes?" A bit of moisture gleamed at the corner of Iya's eye. Her brother had ridden off to prove himself when the Ryuzoji stormed their gates—and had not survived the day.

Sono circled her arm around her handmaid.

"The Lord Regent will call out the Matsuura too, ah?" Iya said.

Sono nodded. If the Lord Regent called out her clan, why not their neighbors? Hisanobu would ride out to battle. The wedding would be postponed. Perhaps her fate wasn't so fixed. A maelstrom of confused emotions buffeted her. A glimmer of guilty hope shot through with a thread of anxiety. "I may not be eager to marry Hisanobu, but..."

"You do not want him to perish."

"No."

It was mid-afternoon before her sister-in-law's handmaid summoned them to the reception hall. Dread wrapped cold fingers around Sono's heart and squeezed. She took her place on a cushion while the other women of her house assembled.

Yoshiaki sat on the raised dais at the head of the hall, appearing every bit a proper warlord. But he seemed painfully preoccupied. He kept repositioning two oversized sheets of paper on the low writing desk in front of him.

The Lord Regent's message.

Their younger brother knelt to his left and Yoshiaki's wife, Masamuro, to his right. None of them would meet Sono's eyes.

When all the noble ladies and their handmaids had settled into place, Yoshiaki shuffled the papers once more and began. "I will come straight to it. The Lord Regent has issued new edicts. You are all welcome to read them, but I will list the key directives."

Those directives struck dangerously close to home. Yoshiaki covered several points, each of them a sweeping condemnation of the padres—and of *Kirishitan* houses like their own. Every sentence he read spurred a bigger wave of shock than the last. But the centerpiece was the final point, which had the most direct bearing on their house.

"'When a vassal receives a fief, he must consider it as property entrusted to him on a temporary basis. However, some vassals—'" Yoshiaki broke off and pressed a clenched fist against the table next to the scroll. "'Some vassals illegally commend part of their fiefs to the *Kirishitan* church. This is a culpable offense.'"

Mama-san's voice trembled with emotion. "So my husband acted illegally when he ceded his port of Nagasaki to the padres."

"*Hai*, according to the Lord Regent. Needless to say, the shame this casts on our house is immeasurable."

Everything in Sono recoiled at the implications of the Lord Regent's words. "If Papa-san were here—"

"If Papa-san were here, this edict would mean the end

for him," Yoshiaki said. "Everyone would expect him to ask the Lord Regent for permission to commit *seppuku*. Of course, as a *Kirishitan*, he could not do so."

Sono's throat felt so tight she could barely breathe. "What happens now?"

"That, Sono-chan, is the worst part." He paused, his jaw working. "The Lord Regent is taking our port of Nagasaki. It will be his own possession. And the padres..." He gazed steadily into his mother's eyes. "The padres are expelled."

"No!" The exclamation was out of Sono's lips before she knew she'd said it.

Mama-san's features could have been carved in stone. She repeated Yoshiaki's words, slowly and deliberately. "Expelled. From the Lord Regent's entire realm."

Yoshiaki nodded, his expression equally grim. "They have twenty days. Eighteen days now, since the edict is dated the day before yesterday. After that, they remain on pain of death."

Mama-san's hand flew to her mouth. "Where are they supposed to go? The great Portuguese ship is not even here."

Sono's voice rang with a fervor that surprised her. "We cannot let that come to pass. So many have found the true faith. How are they to serve *Deusu* without the padres?"

Yoshiaki replied in an even voice. "Sister. You have to realize this places our house in a vulnerable position. *Very* vulnerable. You should have seen the magnificent army the Lord Regent brought to besiege the Shimazu."

She lapsed into silence, an old memory playing through her mind—standing on tiptoe to peek through one of the gun ports in their castle wall. Bold enemy banners arrayed as far as she could see, conveying a fear that had threatened to choke her.

Yoshiaki stepped down from the dais and paced the center of the hall. "Of course we will do what we can to protect the padres. But we cannot defy the Lord Regent. Not openly. Even if all the *Kirishitan* houses banded together, he is much too strong. Think how such a move would end! Disaster—not just for our house, but possibly for all the

Kirishitan in Japan."

Mama-san made a delicate grimace and nodded.

He paced on. "Many of the padres will have to leave. But a few..." He stopped in front of Mama-san. "A few can stay, if they are willing, and carry out their work in secret."

"At risk of their lives." Mama-san shifted on her cushion. "And how are they supposed to disappear, ah? The Portuguese ship will not arrive for six months. There is no means by which so many can leave Japan at once."

"If they appeal to the Lord Regent, surely he will see that fulfilling his edict is impossible. *Deusu* willing, he will grant them more time."

"*Deusu* willing." Mama-san glanced at Sono. "And Sono-chan's position also needs to be considered."

"*Arigato*, Mama-san." Sono said it in a muffled voice. She'd been sure they had all forgotten her.

"*Hai*." Yoshiaki returned to his seat on the dais. "In view of this new edict, the Matsuura may no longer be willing to accept a *Kirishitan* marriage. In that case, we are free to seek a new match for Sono."

"And, ah..." Sono was careful to keep her voice steady. "If the Matsuura *are* still willing?"

"Then the match must move forward. I am sorry, sister, but to break the engagement would be a terrible affront."

Sono's voice sounded small in her own ears. She *felt* small, but something had been whispering in the back of her mind. "It still seems very, very hard. What is a mere wife compared to a lord? And in such a strong Buddhist house. Surely my weak efforts to persuade anyone in Hirado Castle to embrace the true faith will be as futile as painting calligraphy on water. Still, Padre says *Deusu* wants me in Hirado. He must have good reason. If the Matsuura will take me in a *Kirishitan* marriage, I will go willingly."

Suminobu glared at her as if she were an imbecile. "A wife may not be anything compared to a lord, sister. But she can bear one."

A fresh thought made Mama-san's eyes widen. "You will have to be married before the padres leave. Or how can you have a *Kirishitan* marriage?" She stood. "Eighteen days, Sono-chan!"

Eighteen days. So much sooner than she had expected—not another month at home. The thought of leaving them all ripped her to bits. But since it seemed the thing was decided, perhaps it was best to get it done.

Sunday 26 April 1942
Oahu, Hawaii

Birdsong. The sound tugged Akira back into consciousness, but he resisted, squeezing his eyes tightly closed.

He wasn't a captive on a *gaijin* warship. He was at his grandparents' vacation cottage in Shimoda. In a moment, he'd roll over and open his eyes to see his little brother Hiroshi asleep on the futon next to his.

In a moment he would rise, pad down the narrow hallway in stockinged feet and his grandmother would greet him. But there was no hurry now to break the magic of the birdsong. He lingered with his eyes closed, ruthlessly pushing all other thoughts away.

A rasping metallic creak shattered the spell. He opened his eyes and the pain and despair flooded in.

The creak had come from a door hinge. A nurse breezed toward him. Young, pretty, with soft almond eyes and smooth dark hair pinned up beneath her cap. Japanese.

He tried to get his bearings. Another hospital room. Another steel traction harness brooded over his white bedding. Everything was either glistening stainless steel or white. And outside the big, open window, a lush garden burst with tropical color.

The nurse greeted him in his language. "You're awake now, ah?"

Where on earth was he? And would it ever stop hurting?

"I know you're disoriented." He hadn't heard an accent like hers before. "You're on the island of Oahu, Hawaii. At Tripler Army Medical Center. Today is April 26. You were taken on April 18, after the Doolittle Raid."

"Hawaii?" He struggled to sit up. A stab of pain shot through his ribcage while a bigger one shot through his soul.

Three thousand nautical miles. They'd carried him three thousand nautical miles from the waters where he'd lost *Nitto Maru,* to deposit him in American territory. And he remembered none of it after he'd punctured his lung.

He slumped onto the mattress. He'd dared to hope when he saw her that he wasn't a prisoner, that his life wasn't over. But he was, and it was.

"Shh." She let the hiss taper off in an un-Japanese way. "Please calm yourself, Sub-Lieutenant Matsuura. I know it's a lot to take in."

He drew his breath in sharply. "My name is Sawamura." Summoning the air to speak sent acute jabs of pain through his chest.

Her eyes flashed. "I can read your dog tags, sub-lieutenant."

"You read Japanese?" Nothing made any sense. Except his sore ribs.

"*Hai.*" She bristled. "I speak it too, as you see." She relented and gave him a soft smile. "Although I'm sure I sound funny to you." She leaned toward him and lowered her voice. "But if you prefer to be Sawamura, it's all right. I don't have to tell."

"*Arigato.*" He hadn't seen a woman in weeks, and his pulse picked up at the nearness of this one. But maybe she wasn't full Japanese. Her skin seemed a shade too fair, her cheeks a hint too pink, her eyes a bit too round. She could be a mixed-blood girl. It didn't make her less pretty. But it did make her harder to trust.

Anyway, what woman would desire him now? Even a mixed-blood woman. If she did, all he had to do was take off his shirt. His mangled skin would smash any interest.

"You're American?" Disdain put an edge on his voice.

"*Hai.* I'm *nisei.* Second-generation Japanese. My parents came here from Hokkaido."

He studied her, suspicious he wasn't getting the whole story. How could a Japanese stoop to mingle pure blood with that of another race?

She sighed, all business again. "But back to you. They had you on a very high dosage of morphine. We're gradually bringing you to a more standard program of treatment. I'm sorry, but you'll probably experience withdrawal symptoms. We'll watch that closely."

Why? "They won't execute me?"

Her eyes snapped to his. "No! Is that what you expect?"

"Enemy. Prisoner." He put it simply, to save spending precious air.

"I assure you, you'll be treated according to the Geneva Convention. America is a civilized nation." A shadow flicked over her face. "For the most part. I would hope Japan would do likewise for an American."

He sat as straight as he could in his bed, giving himself as much dignity as a flimsy hospital gown would afford. "If you won't kill me, I must kill myself."

She responded with a steady gaze. "I know you've tried." She pressed her lips into a line. "My brothers went to school in Japan. They told me how they cram all that death and glory nonsense into you. Don't believe it. You still have a whole life ahead of you. You may not see this now, but you can be useful and productive. And happy, even, if you let yourself."

She brandished a thermometer. "Rest assured we'll do everything in our power to prevent you from taking your life. Open, please." She slid it under his tongue and took a half step back. "I understand they do what they feel they must out at sea. But what's coming will not be fun for you."

She pulled out the thermometer and read it. She fitted a cuff around his arm and squeezed the rubber bulb several times to inflate it.

He opened his mouth to say something.

She turned on that melting smile again, with a vigorous shake of her head. "Don't talk. I know it hurts." She walked to the window and pushed the curtains wider. "See what a beautiful spot this is, ah? Rest here and let us help you get well. Okay?"

She waited until he nodded, then gave him a brisk nod in response. "Good. I'll consider that your commitment. I'll let Doctor Hansen know everything's within normal range."

He observed the curve of her hips as she went out the

door. His mind's eye followed that swaying skirt as the clack of her heels faded down the corridor and birdsong took over the room again.

A spring breeze carried in a delicious floral scent from the garden. A small tree stood outside the window, its glossy spear-shaped leaves studded with flowers like white-and-yellow stars. A gust ruffled the curtain and stirred the foliage. A lone blossom relinquished its grip on a branch and drifted toward the lawn. He pictured it joining a company of blooms that had gone before it.

As he should have joined Nagai and the others. Papa-san's voice whispered through his head. "You remember the lesson of the cherry blossom, don't you?"

Years earlier, Papa-san had led Akira and his little brother, Hiro-chan up the tropical slopes of Hirado. They'd climbed all the way to Saikyo-ji, the venerable temple that crowned the high ridge behind the ancient town. They'd wandered the overgrown paths through the temple grounds and mounted the broken granite steps that led to a moss-covered altar of piled stone. It stood as high as Hiro-chan was tall.

The rough-hewn memorial stone of Shigenobu, the twenty-sixth hereditary warlord of the noble Matsuura clan, balanced in the center of the altar. A shallow offering bowl stood before it for those who wished to honor the *daimyo*.

He and his little brother had answered Papa-san's question almost in unison. "*Hai*, Papa-san."

Papa-san's eyes crinkled as he peered down at his youngest son. "Tell me then."

Hiro-chan panted and blew his fringe of bangs off his forehead. He piped his response. "In Hirado town, we saw cherry trees. A blossom fell, and you said a warrior must always be prepared to throw his life away. As recklessly as that blossom."

"Exactly. That is how our great ancestors lived, and how you must live as well. To fear death is to die."

An island breeze played at the hospital curtains, tugging Akira back to his wretched present. He studied the view out the window, where Oahu's verdant hills rose above the roofs of the *gaijin* fort.

He knew what Papa-san would make of this. If there was a man under heaven who had no reason to cling to life, Akira was that man. What use could he be? As long as he lived, he would bear the disfigurement of his burns. And he would spend eternity disfigured by his failure and shame.

He had thought he understood the lesson of the cherry blossom. Thought he was more than ready to hurl himself into the next world like a spent bloom. Yet here he was in a *gaijin* hospital, clinging to his useless life like a withered old branch. Unworthy creature that he was, the truth was he wanted to live. He didn't have the will to try to take his own life again.

A pathetic weakling like him could never return to Japan. And he could never insult his family by using his real name.

To fear death is to die. Matsuura Akira was already dead. Only wretched Sawamura Akira would live on.

He closed his eyes, pictured Papa-san's face, and let his wrenching shame consume him.

Chapter Seven

FOUR DAYS LATER, A MISSIVE ARRIVED from Sono's new clan confirming they were willing to go forward with the marriage. A week and a half rushed past, and the dreaded morning came. She clung to the railing of their junk as it slipped away from their private dock, bound for Hirado.

She had done her best to deny her sorrow a foothold—although it had confronted her with every turn of thought. This marriage was *Deusu's* will, as well as her father's and brother's. A warrior had to stare even death in the eye, unflinching.

She would face her destiny like a warrior. She would lock her feelings away.

Iya leaned on the vessel's railing beside her. Mama-san and her older brother stood a little farther aft. Their tiny flotilla—one junk sailed ahead and another behind theirs—bore a detail of seventy *samurai* to guard them. And to guard the treasure they carried—pile after pile of trunks with her bridal trousseau.

A half-dozen gulls wheeled above their vessel, sending desolate cries back and forth. The locked-up place in Sono's heart yearned to cry out with them.

She shaded her eyes to take in the great stone retaining walls and the peaked tile roofs of Sanjo Castle's towering keep. Every angle of those walls, every balcony on those buildings held a memory.

Iya spoke in a voice so soft it barely carried above the breeze and the sloshing of the waves against the bow. "The main gate seems so small from here."

The memories rushed in. "And the keep too. Remember how Yoshiaki used to chase us up all those stairs?"

Her handmaid broke into a light laugh. "*Hai.* Remember painting the moon from the balconies?"

"Remember when Suminobu came home in triumph through that gate, after all those years as a hostage?"

Other memories were not so cheerful. The light on the

waves dimmed. "Iya-chan, you remember the day we met, ah?"

Iya nodded, her smile fading. "I will remember it all my life, my lady."

It was the afternoon the Ryuzoji had carried the hot breath of battle within earshot of that gate. Sono had lugged bucket after heavy bucket along rows of wounded men, bringing water in a ladle to one moaning mouth after another.

A young *samurai* had been next. Blood soaked the gold-embroidered cross on his white-liveried chest. A girl even littler than Sono clung to his arm, sobbing.

Iya. Sono poured a trickle of water into the boy's gaping mouth. Whispered a memorized prayer. *By His passion and His cross, be brought to the glory of His Resurrection.*

Tears had left furrows through the dirt and blood that stained Iya's cheeks. "Today was his first battle."

Sono pushed back that memory and peered up the dazzling blue waters of Omura Bay. The waves swarmed with the ghosts of dozens of enemy ships. How many times had an armada sailed up these waters to raid Sanjo Castle? To burn their ports? How many times had the Matsuura been responsible?

Yoshiaki crossed the deck to confer with the *samurai* captain. His sweet wife had caught Sono's arm that morning. She'd leaned to her ear to whisper. "I'll tell you my secret now, since you're leaving. I think I'm pregnant."

Her face had glowed like the light rippling across the water. Sono watched the shifting patterns, her heart ripping in two. With Omura fading into the distance, would she ever get to see the baby?

But with this union, Yoshiaki should never have to defend his baby, at least from Matsuura raiders. No *samurai* on big horses, snatching his children up to bear them away. Like her own little brother.

She squeezed Iya's hand. "That's why we are making this journey, Iya-chan. For my brother's peace. For your brother's memory. I will marry a Matsuura pirate and stem the bloodshed. And"—she pulled her spine straight, resolute—"I will see my son reign over their domain. If *Deusu* wills that, this alliance will last."

"And," Iya said, "if we can unite our banners under the cause of *Kirisuto*, this alliance will bind us as staunchly as our alliance with the Arima. It is a great work you are doing, Sono-chan."

If. She nodded, resisting a pang of anxiety. "That is something to hope for. *Deusu* willing."

Mama-san walked up, examined her, and clucked. "You need to sit under the awning. You want flawless skin on your wedding day."

Wedding day. Hisanobu strutted into her thoughts as she'd seen him last, all those weeks before—glossy topknot, powerful shoulders, strong jawline, fiery dark eyes.

A few days earlier, he had sent her a gift by courier. It came in a beautiful sandalwood box. She had brushed her fingers along the polished wood that felt like silk. The cover boasted an inlaid design—a sailing vessel with oars. The sails were abalone, lustrous in the sun. A pattern of roiling waves, cresting and throwing off gold-leaf spray, trailed down the box.

It was intricate, magnificent, and a little wild. *A perfect gift for a pirate to send.*

Pirate or not, she was charmed. The scroll in the box wasn't large. A little longer than her forearm. The paper was of the best quality, the smoothest mulberry fiber edged with gold leaf. Well-formed characters marched down the scroll, bold strokes laid out in even rows.

It read:

This mulberry leaf
Whispers a simple oxherd's
Words of deep longing,
Pining for his noblest love.
When will our eyes and arms meet?

A pair of green-and-gold painted mulberry leaves accented the bottom right corner.

Mama-san had beamed a smile at her. "Ah! How sweet! He has made himself the oxherd in the legend of the star lovers. And you are the celestial princess, the daughter of the Sky King. He awaits your crossing the River of Heaven to him." She let out a girlish giggle. "Of course we do not believe in starry lovers in the sky. But just the same, your voyage up the water—so funny how that fits!"

Iya shook her head in wonder. "He is clever. Tonight is the eve of the star couple's festival day."

Hisanobu had even gotten his mulberry, her new house's crest, into the verse—another clever play. And he'd signed the bottom. He had done the calligraphy himself.

Intriguing. Her pirate had a thoughtful side. That was a nice surprise. Maybe she had judged him too harshly.

She had stroked the box, the chill she'd placed on her heart beginning to thaw. Could she love this man—her pirate prince?

But now the box was packed away in one of the dozens of trunks in the hold. And the beloved promontory where their castle perched shrank behind her while the northern mouth of the bay grew ahead. A hard knot of apprehension formed at the base of her stomach.

Her groom on faraway Hirado had seen her twice, weeks ago. Would he still like her now? The suspense sent twists through her core—another surprise. She very much wanted him to like her. Very much wanted to feel those muscular arms circle her. To see his striking eyes gaze down at her, soft with love.

The same eyes that had blazed with disdain when they landed on Papa-san's crucifix? The knot in her stomach hardened. If a man hated *Deusu,* how could she render him the respect due a husband?

It would be her duty to ensure harmony between them, no matter how unreasonable he might prove. She followed Mama-san's advice and ducked under the awning. Love was not required of her, but obedience was.

It was afternoon before Sono saw the bay give way to open sea along an undulating coast. Small islands littered the water like lumps of uncut jade scattered by a careless hand. Fishing villages dotted their shores.

Hirado formed a growing gray-green mass before her. A mysterious land haunted by pirates and *Deusu*-haters. Her heart sank under such a weight of apprehension she wondered how the vessel stayed afloat.

The sun beat down from the top of the sky the next day before she got her first glimpse of her new home. Strong white walls enclosed the top of a peninsula that pushed into the channel like a fist. The tall keep thrust a sharply pointed roof upward from the peninsula's crown.

The pirate clan had secured itself well. Hirado Castle was the picture of a coastal stronghold. Should Hisanobu become Lord Matsuura, she could be responsible for defending his fortress when he rode out on campaign. Studying Hirado Castle through the eyes of a future general, she approved. But through the eyes of a soon-to-be bride, every massive stone fed her dark weight of dread.

Special dispensation. Deusu's inscrutable will. She had a great work to do in that forbidding place—so everyone said.

An angel's words to another virgin whispered through her mind. *Fear not. Deusu is with thee. Mariya,* too, had been destined to bear a crucial child. A Prince of Peace. She, too, had left her home—and never returned.

Sono was no saint. She wore no halo. Still, for some reason *Deusu* had chosen her for this. Padre had said so.

No more pirate armadas sailing for Omura. I will give them a prince of peace. She closed her eyes and breathed strength into her resolve.

Wednesday 15 August 1945
Camp Carson, El Paso County, Colorado

Akira slid his tray along the buffet counter in the prisoners' officers' mess. For three years and four months they'd kept him from war and glory, locked up in camps like this one. Camp Carson, in the vast open prairie of the American West, was the fourth.

How much longer could this war drag on? Anxiety made a hard knot congeal inside him every time he asked that question.

A big P.O.W. with a florid face stood behind the

counter. He used his sleeve to blot a streak of sweat from the spot where his curly hair disappeared beneath his white chef's hat. He shoveled a pair of sausages onto a plate and thrust it at Akira, saying something in his own lilting language. Whatever he said, it made the second Italian serving the fried eggs snigger.

The Italians seemed elated their war was over and that they would soon go home. Their crushing dishonor as prisoners didn't appear to weigh on them. Akira couldn't understand it. He knew what would confront him when he returned to Japan. The family and friends who wouldn't acknowledge him. The derisive glares on the streets. The death threats.

Execution, even. It would be no more than he deserved. If there was any way to avoid going back to face all that, he would lunge for it.

There wasn't.

He turned and walked the length of the officers' mess. Past the three tables where the German contingent was assembling and the two that would accommodate raucous Italians. He and his four fellow Japanese officers kept their own company at the table in the back corner. If you could call it company.

He saluted Capt. Yoshigumi, the ranking Japanese officer. The captain acknowledged him with his habitual grunt. Akira exchanged bows with the others. Arrogant army men, all four of them, who consoled themselves for the disastrous turn the war had taken by blaming the Imperial Navy for bungling it. A war the army militarists had forced on the country—over the admiralty's objections, if the whispers he'd heard around the camps were true.

As the sole Japanese naval officer at Camp Carson, Akira inhabited a lonely place. But his isolation had driven one positive outcome—a dramatic improvement to his command of written English. The camp library offered the best hiding place he'd found from his fellow officers.

He stopped in daily to digest the American newspapers—and lately, the news for Japan had been more horrific by the day. Hard fighting across the Pacific islands. Cities bombed. Ships, whole fleets destroyed.

His fellow officers dismissed it all as propaganda, and he no longer bothered to tell them what he read. He kept the despair that darkened even the bright blue above the Rocky Mountain skyline to himself. But every time he read of heavy damage to a Japanese cruiser, concern for Papa-san swelled. And the headlines about air raids on Tokyo and Osaka made him agonize, having no news of Mama-san or his brother and sister.

He took his seat at the end of the table and stabbed at one of the sausages. The European prisoners ate this food with gusto, but he couldn't learn to like it. At least at breakfast, they didn't try to make him choke down that strange German dish called sauerkraut.

An American orderly rushed in from outside and took brisk strides to their table. "Colonel Simmons would like you to report to his office in twenty. All you Jap officers."

Yoshigumi gave him a curt dismissal. The officers exchanged glances across their breakfast trays. This would make the third time they'd been summoned to the camp commander's office in two weeks.

Both the previous meetings had started the same way. "I have very bad news for you, gentlemen," Simmons had said. Then he'd handed Yoshigumi the morning paper. The captain had grunted and passed it on to Akira to translate the dour headlines.

Atomic Bomb Dropped on Japan

2000 Times More Explosive Power Than Any Bomb Ever Used

Fukuyama Hit by 100 Superforts; City Scorched

Japan Not Expected to Resist Long

This morning had brought another summons. What did it mean? What city had the Americans targeted with their big new atomic bomb this time? Tokyo? Kyoto?

Osaka? As far as he knew, that's where his mother, brother, and sister lived now. Paralyzing fear narrowed his throat.

The bits of burnt crust on the flanks of his sausages soured his stomach. He pushed his plate away. The other men's forks weren't moving, either.

Akira followed Yoshigumi and his fellow officers up the wooden steps and through the double doors into the admin building. An orderly ushered them into Col. Simmons's office.

Once again, the colonel had a newspaper on his broad steel desk, face down so the headline didn't show. But a boxed subhead stood out in the middle of the far-right column.

Super-Forts Hit Home Isles in 800 Plane Attack

Akira's insides hollowed as he lined up with his fellow officers. Eight hundred flying fortresses. Enough to level whole districts in multiple cities.

He should have paid with his life to prevent this. Instead, he stood here. Alive, while his nation incinerated to death.

Yoshigumi led them in saluting the colonel, as if they were all men of arms in good standing with no lifelong shame to bear. The American returned their salute, his expression grave. "Please take a seat, gentlemen." He observed their faces as they settled in their chairs, perhaps mustering his strength for the revelation that was coming.

"Coffee?" he said.

They all shook their heads.

"Tea perhaps?"

"No, thank you." Yoshigumi's refusal was emphatic.

Olive-colored cotton rippled across the colonel's broad shoulders. He gave the captain a brisk nod. "I'll get to the point, then. It's over. Japan has done the intelligent thing and"—a slight pause—"surrendered."

An invisible mallet slammed into Akira's diaphragm, driving the air from his lungs. He sagged against the back of his chair, the edges of items in the room going liquid and bleeding together.

Yoshigumi leapt to his feet. "Liar! All Japanese die before this happen."

Col. Simmons shrugged and handed him the paper. "You don't have to believe me. Believe the *Denver Post*."

The captain glared at the headline. The bold English

words seemed clear.

Japan Surrenders, End of War!

Yoshigumi sank into his chair, clutching the paper, eyes wide with disbelief.

Akira's gut coiled. Generations of his forebears had devoted their lives to the military glory of the empire of Japan. All of that had ended now, in mushroom clouds and miles of decimated cityscape. If there was any truth to the ancient idea that ancestral spirits concerned themselves with the affairs of this world, the heavens were howling with anguish.

Simmons's uniform hat and jacket dangled from a coatrack behind him. Their gold braid and insignia caught the light the way Papa-san's always had. Where was Akira's father now? Would he survive the day this news hit him?

Simmons leaned back with a profound sigh. "You don't believe it? You can hear it from Hirohito himself. He's doing a radio broadcast at noon Tokyo."

Any sense of reality Akira still possessed vaporized. That Japan would surrender? Unimaginable. But this was past unimaginable. For the Son of Heaven to speak directly to anyone outside his closest circle flew in the face of centuries—no, a millenia—of practice.

Yoshigumi was on his feet again, jaw jutting. "The emperor? On radio? Now I know you lie." A vein on his temple throbbed, blue against his skin.

The colonel's lips quirked with something that could have been veiled amusement. "That's in the paper too."

Yoshigumi thrust it in Lt. Toyoshima's direction instead of in Akira's. "What does this say?" he cried out in Japanese, his voice vibrating with outrage.

The lieutenant squinted at the subheads. A moment passed before he began a halting translation. "Emperor Accepts Allied Rule. Surrender"—he broke off, brow furrowed in puzzlement, and held the paper out toward Akira. He'd tripped over the word *unconditional*.

Yoshigumi roared. "I don't want to hear it from Sawamura. I want to hear it from a man I can trust."

The colonel glowered at him and thundered. "Enough. If

you can't calm down, captain, I'll dismiss you so I can carry on a civil conversation with your subordinates."

The captain sputtered to silence.

The colonel rubbed one temple along the line where his sandy-gray hair thinned out. "Sub-lieutenant, please help me here."

Akira translated the concept that the surrender was absolute into Japanese. His voice fell on his own ears with a distant sound, as if someone else were delivering this horrific news.

The captain shook his head violently. "Impossible. His august majesty the emperor would never agree to this thing." He stood and addressed the colonel in English. "Nippon no surrender."

Simmons grimaced. "We're not here to debate whether facts are facts, but I'd like your help figuring out how best to convey those facts to your men. I would think there would be at least a little relief that you can go back to your families while there's still something left of those islands of yours." He squared his jaw. "Noon Tokyo will be twenty-one hundred here. I plan to put Hirohito's broadcast over the P.A. for the entire camp. I'd prefer to prevent filling my hospital with suicide casualties, if at all possible. Can you help me with that, captain?"

Yoshigumi gave him a glare soaked with scorn. "This is useless. Nippon Imperial Army not surrender."

Simmons huffed out an exasperated breath. "Fine. Dismissed. Everyone except Sawamura."

The captain stood and stalked from the room. The others followed. As he trooped out, Lt. Toyoshima shot a dark glare over his shoulder at Akira.

The camp commander watched them leave. "Well, that was pleasant." He turned his attention to Akira. "I could use another cup of coffee. You?"

Akira stared past him in numb silence, unable to connect the concept of coffee with anything that mattered.

"Maybe I should give you a minute. I'll be back."

Akira managed a nod.

Chapter Eight

SONO STOOD IN HIRADO CASTLE'S ENTRANCE courtyard. Her enemies' ancient stronghold—and her new home.

Yoshiaki swung down from the stallion the Matsuura had loaned him for the occasion. Horses stamped and snorted. *Samurai* wearing the mulberry-leaf crest of the Matsuura dismounted around her.

Anxiety made her knees want to buckle. She'd strained her eyes searching for her groom even before they had made landfall. No sign of him, or of his father, yet.

She made a small adjustment to the lay of her kimono and reached for the parasol Iya held open for her. Why had she not stayed under that awning, as Mama-san had bid her? Two days of sun off the water had almost certainly darkened her cheeks.

Her groom had seen her twice. When he saw her again, would he be pleased with his choice?

And for her part, she only knew what he looked like. What would he *be* like?

Her eyes stopped on an immense statue of the Shinto deity, Hachiman, frowning down at her from a pedestal. She caught her breath. His stone eyes seemed to drill into her, gold paint giving them fire.

This was no Buddhist monk in lotus position, Hachiman's usual guise. Here at Hirado, he was every bit the god of war. He stood taller than she did, bore a scowl as fierce as any Buddhist demon, and carried a long bow of bronze.

She pulled her eyes away from the cursed idol with a determined effort. *Deusu* had sent her, had He not?

A conch-shell horn wailed. Two men in rich versions of the Matsuura livery emerged through the main gatehouse. Shigenobu, her soon-to-be father-in-law, with a boy of about her younger brother's years—Hisanobu's brother, no doubt. Disappointment pricked the pit of her stomach. She hadn't seen Hisanobu in weeks. Had he not cared to come to greet her?

A woman of roughly Mama-san's years followed a discrete distance behind the Matsuura men. Lady Matsuura cut a slender figure in her striking green kimono, but in an angular way, not in a graceful dancer's way like willowy Iya. Sono knew exactly two things about this woman she would call "honored mother." She went by the name Chiyo, and she came from a long line of Buddhist priests.

What was her new honored mother's opinion of the agreement that would someday put a *Kirishitan* grandson over her husband's domain? It was not the first time Sono had pondered the question. But as her new family members stood with the Hachiman's fearsome image towering behind them, the forces arrayed against her seemed to radiate a thick cloud of hostility.

And not just against her. They stood arrayed against the mustard seed of *Kirishitan* faith she carried. Yet the men she loved and trusted—Papa-san, Padre Lucena, her older brother—had sent her here, expecting her to nurture that puny seed into a sturdy tree destined to cast far-reaching shade over this forbidding soil.

She shivered at the crushing weight of expectation.

Lord Matsuura made the proper introductions, then led the men toward the gatehouse. "We can relax over tea until all is prepared. My wife will direct the ladies."

Lady Matsuura regarded Sono and her mother and handmaid with a fixed smile. "So you have come. Welcome." The lady turned with a stark no-nonsense air and started through the gatehouse, trailing the men.

Sono flinched like she'd been stung. It was a cold welcome. Was she so unimportant to the woman she must honor as her mother?

She moved past Hachiman's fiery golden eyes, feeling very small. The air around the icon seemed to pulse with malevolent energy. She could not walk fast enough to get the monstrous thing out of view.

Lady Matsuura tackled the hill with an energetic gait, leading them through a bewildering maze of defensive structures. Flights of stairs set at rakish angles, a succession of gatehouses, then yet another set of broad steps brought them to the Matsuura mansion. They passed several large rooms with magnificent gold-painted screens before they reached a forbidding wooden door guarded by a pair of *samurai*.

Lady Matsuura inclined her head to Sono. "The women's wing. Men may not enter here, except our husbands." A guard slid the heavy bolt aside.

The door led to an inner courtyard, with a patio that circled a garden graced by a *koi* pond. Several chambers opened onto it. Their *shoji* stood open, revealing glimpses of rich furnishings. The air echoed with birdsong.

Everything was lovely, but the only entrance was through that forbidding guarded door.

Sono already felt like a bird flying at the bars of its cage. And the waist-high figurine of Marishiten that glowered out from a niche behind a small Zen garden was no help. The six-armed war goddess glared at her from the back of a fearsome three-headed boar.

Lady Matsuura followed her gaze to the figurine. "She is splendid, ah? A priceless antique. But you've always been a *Kirishitan*, of course. Perhaps you are not aware that when Kukai brought True Word Buddhism here from China, he observed his first fire ritual right here on Hirado."

Sono averted her eyes from the statue. "I did not know it."

"I suspect there is a great deal you don't know." Her tone was withering.

Deities and fire rituals and a frosty welcome from the woman she must now call mother. Her chest felt heavy. Her new life was going to be even harder than she'd feared. And she would pine for her old life and family more than she'd imagined.

Lady Matsuura showed her to her chamber. Even empty, it was grand. Larger than the one she had left at Sanjo Castle, as befit her new status. The furnishings would come from the trunks Mama-san had fretted over.

But nothing in those elegant trunks would make this a home. And that very evening, she would marry a stranger.

For better or for worse. Thus far, worse was winning. It was no contest.

Mama-san asked after Padre Lucena. Lady Matsuura drew herself up and gave a barely audible sniff. "Ah, yes. The Portuguese is here. I will have you taken to him." She shot a wilting glance at Sono's rumpled clothing. "We were hoping to have the ceremony at sunset. But I see we have work to do."

Lady Matsuura clapped imperiously. Her handmaid hurried in. The lady made a brusque introduction, then bid her show Sono and Iya to the bathhouse. The handmaid—her name was Rin—led them around the garden and through a wisteria-covered patio in its back corner, twittering about the wedding all the way. "We are setting up the room at the top of the keep for the occasion. The views at dusk should be stunning. Do you think you can be ready by then?"

"*Hai*, I believe so. Iya can work miracles."

"Excellent. The ladies here seldom get to see the rooms in the keep. They stay in the women's wing unless they are summoned. Or Lady Matsuura approves it."

Unless Lady Matsuura approves it. "Are you telling me the Matsuura women cannot leave the mansion without Lady Matsuura's blessing? *This wing* of the mansion?"

Rin's eyebrows rose. "It is for your protection, you know. But you will want to speak with Lord Hisanobu about what he expects of you."

An invisible band squeezed the air from Sono's chest. *Protection?* What kind of people would expect a woman to spend her days trapped in a single wing of a house?

Rin bustled off and Iya helped Sono out of her sticky kimono. Iya uttered a hasty apology, then excused herself to hunt for Sono's wedding clothes among her trunks.

Sono slipped into the warm water, stifled a groan, and rolled her eyes up to the ceiling. She would smother in all the luxury here if they held her to that rule. It was a conversation she would have with Hisanobu—soon. Before she went mad as a hungry ghost.

Rin ushered Sono's mother in. Mama-san dismissed her, then took a sharp glance around for listening ears before settling beside the tub and pulling a fan from her sleeve. She spoke in a whisper. "I am so sorry, my dear child. You do have your hands full with that woman. I hope your husband will make it worthwhile."

"I think I am going to see a lot more of dear Lady Matsuura than her son." A dull pain throbbed in Sono's temples. She massaged them with her knuckles and told her mother with a sinking heart what Rin had revealed about the shape of her new life.

"Ah, Sono-chan! *Hai,* that is the custom of some lords with their women. Well, try not to despair. Your husband's wishes may be different." She clicked her tongue. "A matter for prayer."

"From this day forward, I am going to have an impressive prayer life. But what did you learn from Padre Lucena?"

Mama-san leaned in so Sono could feel her breath against her ear. "Padre tells me they do not plan to leave Kyushu yet."

Sono jolted straight with surprise. "Not leave? What of the edict?"

"The Lord Regent has seen reason. He will give them until the Black Ship can take them." She put her fan to work. "So we had no need to rush the wedding. But here we are. And you will never guess the Lord Regent's condition for letting them stay."

Sono shook her head, wordless.

"All the padres must come here, to Hirado, to await the ship."

Sono couldn't help the little cry that escaped her. "Here! You will lose Padre Lucena?"

Her mother nodded. "Strictly between you and me, I wonder whether they all plan to sail." She snapped her fan closed with a grin. "But it is your wedding day! Shall we dwell on more cheerful subjects? I am so glad Padre was here to work out the details. Of course they tried to insist on a spirit dancer, but Padre told them we will not be inviting the Shinto spirits in." She arched her eyebrows. "Apparently it was quite a battle."

The first of many. The irony of it drove a tart taste into her mouth. From his deathbed, Papa-san had cautioned her brothers against the cult of spirits and ancestors. Yet he had sent her into its very lair.

But with all the padres clustered in Hirado, the town should overflow with so much grace the Divine Presence would be felt all the way up in the Matsuura mansion.

She sighed. It was something to hope for, anyway.

By the time the late afternoon bells sounded, Sono stood with her hair waxed and artfully draped down her back, secured in a long column by elegant bows. Mama-san had finished her face powder and had the brush ready to rouge her lips.

Shadows now owned the garden. Lady Matsuura strode in and gave Sono an appraising stare. "You look splendid, my dear. Quite a transformation. You are ready, then? Except for your wedding cloak and veil." She turned to her handmaid. "Rin-chan, let everyone know it's time."

Lady Matsuura's handmaid hurried out. Mama-san draped the heavy wedding veil over Sono's head, then painted Sono's lips with practiced strokes. "You are stunning." Her voice carried a subtle quaver.

Lady Matsuura actually produced a smile from her arsenal of facial expressions. "You do make a nice picture, my dear. Let us not keep them waiting to see it. Come along."

Wednesday 15 August 1945

Akira had recovered enough to come to attention when Col. Simmons returned.

"At ease," the colonel said. "I'll renew my offer. Tea, maybe?"

"*Hai.* Thank you, sir." He'd also regained the ability to form simple thoughts into words.

Simmons hailed the orderly and made the arrangement. He settled in the leather chair behind his desk. "What about you, sub-lieutenant? You believe it, don't you?"

The window above the colonel's shoulder gave Akira a

clear view out to open fields beyond the camp's perimeter, where an enormous tractor crawled along geometric rows of glossy, broad-leafed sugar beets. It was agriculture on a scale that could never exist in Japan.

Other images pressed on his mind. Train engines pulling hundreds of cars across broad grasslands. Laden ships crowding Pearl Harbor the day he left Hawaii, mere months after the harbor's complete decimation.

What had his nation's generals been thinking? How had they concluded they had any chance of winning a war against such an enormous and well-equipped foe? Had they failed, in their arrogance, to even consider Sun Tzu's five factors of strategy?

He'd never voiced such questions, and it had taken him years to admit it, but for the past weeks the knowledge had pressed on him like a roller dragging across soft earth. Defeat was a matter of time. How many more Japanese cities would be leveled first? How many more people would die?

And how long until they sent him home to face his shattered life?

He met the colonel's gaze and choked out the words he didn't want to think, much less speak. "I believe the papers, sir."

"Good man. I thought you'd be reasonable." The colonel downed a hearty swig of coffee. "Since your captain can't seem to provide any advice worth hearing, maybe you can help me. The reaction Yoshigumi just gave me is exactly the one I'd like to avoid getting from your rank and file."

"This thing is very difficult, colonel. Surrender. Defeat. These are hard words. Maybe you can say things in"—he groped for a good word—"nicer way. Easier for hearing."

"Avoid the plain facts, in other words."

The orderly set Akira's tea in front of him. He studied the steam coming off the liquid. "You Americans are very...straight in how you say things. Japanese are not this way." He pulled out the tea bag and sipped at the tea, suddenly aware of his dry mouth. "The broadcast. Emperor Hirohito. We will hear him?"

"The paper says the major networks will carry it."

"Then maybe let them hear the emperor say it himself. In Japanese way. This they must accept."

Simmons gave him a grave nod. "Which is precisely why there's a broadcast."

"*Hai*. This is a very big thing, sir. You don't understand how big, I think. The emperor isn't like your president. The emperor never talk to ordinary people this way."

He stopped, tense with frustration. The English he could muster wasn't adequate. This radio broadcast would be a once-in-a-lifetime event. No, not even that. You could live endless lives and never hope to hear the emperor's voice. "The voice of the crane," as they said—the sacred bird that passes above the clouds, unseen.

Simmons's lips quirked. "Yes. Descended from the sun goddess, or something like that. That broadcast is going to be interesting. I've barred them from distributing the papers this morning, but I'm sure the men will hear about this well before twenty-one hundred rolls around. I have to give some message to them now. And I'd like to do it in a way that won't result in suicides."

Akira discovered new interest in the line of bubbles at the edge of his tea. Hirohito, the human expression of the deities. The glory of the heavens represented in a man. Defeated, what did that make him?

This was a thing to ponder another time. "I think just tell them what the newspapers say. And they will hear more on the radio."

"Sounds like good advice. I'll have them call the men to assemble at eighty thirty. Could you do me a favor? Could you please circulate among the men today and keep an eye out for trouble?"

"Yes, sir." It would be helpful to have a sense of purpose.

Chapter Nine

AKIRA WALKED OUT THE BUILDING'S main entrance. Three army trucks stood in the parking lot in front of him. A rich stew of English, German, and Italian phrases mingled in the air as clumps of prisoners loaded onto them, headed out for daily work details on surrounding beet farms.

But no Japanese. They weren't assigned off-camp work. On another day, a twinge of envy would have writhed through him. It seemed American farmers were prepared to accept that not all Germans were Nazis, but the same logic did not apply to Japanese and "the yellow menace."

Still, having the forty-three Japanese enlisted men contained on base would be useful today. It might help ensure no one did anything rash, like plunging a knife into his own belly or into one of these smug Americans.

Did he feel like doing something rash himself? No. He felt numb. The grief of this catastrophe was far too big to be fixed with a knife or a rifle or a fist. It was a *tsunami* wave bearing down on his entire nation, and he was helpless before it.

Would another man—a Yoshigumi—react differently? Rail at fate and strike out? Perhaps. And suicides could take the form of a desperate mass charge. Was Yoshigumi capable of working the men up to charging the fence, or worse?

Japan had suffered enough at the hands of Yoshigumi and his ilk. If Akira could do something to keep the men from getting embroiled in some stupid plot, he was willing.

But was he able? At that moment, his despair was too crippling for words. He had no desire to talk to anyone.

By the time he reached the assembly area at the front of his barracks complex, forty-three Japanese prisoners stood there in clusters, speaking in muted voices. Hurt and bewildered and questioning glances came his way. He had no comfort for them.

Yoshigumi stalked into the assembly area, along with

the other officers. The men fell silent and formed up in rows. All were present.

Akira lined up with Yoshigumi and his lackeys. At eight thirty precisely, Col. Simmons marched up the sidewalk, flanked by Majors Hillson and Fredericks. Lt. Toyoshima called the prisoners to attention.

Simmons stopped before Yoshigumi. "At ease, men. Sub-Lieutenant Sawamura, step forward."

Akira stepped out two paces.

"Could you please translate what I'm about to say? I want to make sure every man here understands."

"*Hai*, sir."

"Thank you." Col. Simmons wore a grim expression. "I have news, soldiers, which many of you may have already heard. There have been rumors in the papers for days that the end of this brutal war is near." He paused while Akira translated. "Today the paper says the Japanese government has taken a concrete step to effect this. While some may say this information is unconfirmed,"—he shot a glance at Yoshigumi, who jerked up straighter and scowled—"a remarkable thing has happened. It has been announced that Emperor Hirohito himself will make a radio broadcast later today."

A stir coursed through the prisoners like a breeze through cedars. Someone made a little gasp of surprise, then a choking sound.

Simmons gave the details. Noon Tokyo. Twenty-one hundred hours there. Every man expected to turn out.

He took a half step toward the men. "Men, I realize how sad you find this turn of events. But if the rumor is true, it will mean the chance to return to your homes and families and help rebuild your nation." His voice rose with conviction. "Japan will need you. This is where your focus must rest, not in some dead vision of battlefield glory."

Akira translated. Yoshigumi looked as sour as if someone had stuffed a lemon in his mouth.

The colonel announced that he'd canceled their work details and cleared his schedule for any who might wish to speak with him. "And I'd like to point you to one further resource. No one here is an expert on what's going on in Tokyo or Washington or Bern. But Sub-Lieutenant Sawamura has a good grasp of the events reported in the English-language papers and can communicate them to you as clearly as anyone. If you have any questions, you may prefer to address them to Sawamura."

Akira swallowed his astonishment. Lt. Toyoshima shot him a poisoned glare.

Dozens of eyes fixed on Akira, anchoring expressions that ranged from careful ambivalence to open hostility. Yoshigumi regarded him with malevolence.

Akira kept his gaze riveted forward, emotions waging a pitched battle inside him. He did believe in peace. More than that, he longed for it. Not for anything it would do for him, but because it was the right path for Japan. The bombs would stop when the Americans took over. Yes, *gaijin* boots would tramp across the sacred Land of the Gods. At least there would still be a land for them to tramp. But Simmons's notion of a Japan that would welcome *horyo* like them back was an ignorant delusion.

The colonel took two more paces. "I'd suggest you spend your down time today considering the role you might play in a peaceful Japan." He gave Akira a brisk nod. "Thank you, sub-lieutenant."

Akira returned to his position beside Lt. Toyoshima.

"Captain Yoshigumi, do you have anything to add?"

"*Hai.*" Yoshigumi walked forward and pivoted to face the men. He addressed them in a ringing voice, in Japanese. "As good Japanese soldiers, I urge you to remember who you are. I assure you the lies you've heard this morning will be exposed as filthy propaganda. Take heart. If you believe our nation can be defeated, you are unworthy of the uniform." He shot a pointed glance at Akira. "If Sub-Lieutenant Sawamura, or anyone else, advises you otherwise, you will hold that man in highest contempt."

Col. Simmons had no way to know what Yoshigumi had

said. He gave him a nod. "Very good. We'll reassemble here at twenty-one hundred hours."

A dejected silence reigned. The prisoners filed out, shoulders limp and eyes anchored on the pavement.

The colonel turned to Yoshigumi and the other officers. "I'll be in my office if any of you need me."

Yoshigumi greeted this with cold formality. "*Arigato,* sir." He watched with narrowed eyes while the colonel disappeared between the buildings, then spun on Akira. "Conducting private meetings with the camp commander, ah?"

The hairs at the base of Akira's scalp prickled. It wasn't the first time they'd hinted he was some kind of collaborator.

A prisoner *and* a collaborator. As if he didn't have enough trouble already. A suspicion like that could follow him all the way back to Japan. "I've never met with him before. And I didn't ask for this meeting."

Yoshigumi was working himself up to full rant. "But you'll entertain the idea that Japan would surrender."

Akira chose his words with care. "You can't deny that Okinawa fell, and Iwo Jima. And that the Americans are close enough now to bomb our cities to ash."

Yoshigumi snorted. "If you're the kind of fool who believes their newspapers. Spread these lies among the men, and you will answer for it." The captain's hand twitched to the place at his hip where the hilt of a *katana* would once have rested. "My conscience will never fault me for honoring my emperor to my last breath. Like a true Japanese."

You didn't. Any more than I did. We're both here.

Akira wandered through the barracks as Simmons had requested. But Yoshigumi's little speech had eliminated any chance of an honest conversation with anyone. The men pointedly avoided his eyes or turned away as they saw him coming. Worse, he spotted the captain several times in hushed conversation with men he knew as ringleaders.

Yoshigumi was taking full advantage of these idle

hours. For what purpose?

Akira settled on a concrete stoop at the edge of camp, facing the perimeter fence—two lengths of electrified barbed-wire with a broad no-man's land stretching between them. He lit his last cigarette. A Marine guard ambled past, the muzzle of his M1 carbine glinting behind his shoulder. A monstrous dog that was all taut muscle trotted at his side, its tongue lolling over jagged teeth.

The gleam of gunmetal brought a photo he'd seen in the *Denver Post* to mind. A jagged five-foot breach in a chain-link fence like the one in front of him. When was that? The summer before?

In far-away Australia, Japanese prisoners had set their barracks on fire during the night. With the camp in an uproar, they'd charged a perimeter like this one. They somehow broken through the fences, overwhelmed a guard tower, and hundreds escaped into the Australian bush.

What a futile exercise. All prisoners recaptured. Nothing accomplished, except that those who wished to die got a chance to do so. More than two hundred of them did. And some men who never left the barracks burned to death anyway.

Akira's chest swelled with rage. If a *horyo* chose to end his life, that was understandable. But no one should force that decision on another man.

Dark clouds brooded on the horizon, mirroring the apprehension that had carved a hole in his chest. He stood. Yoshigumi might call what he was about to do disloyal to Japan, but he had no concern for the opinions of men like him.

Maybe he was wrong about Yoshigumi's intentions, but it was time to share his doubts with the colonel. It could avert a deadly disaster.

He strode to the admin building. The orderly ushered him straight into the colonel's office.

Col. Simmons stood to greet him. "Nice to see you. What's up?"

"Nothing, maybe, sir. But I'm worried." He described

what he'd seen.

"Hmm." Simmons leaned back in his chair and pursed his lips. "But you don't have anything definite?"

He shook his head. "No, sir. None of them talk to me. I think this also is fear of the captain."

"I don't like to put a man in the brig without clear cause."

"Maybe more guards tonight?"

Simmons gave him a slow nod. "I can put the guards on alert. And I'll impose a curfew after dinner."

"I think that's good, sir."

"If you get anything more specific, by all means let me know."

"Yes, sir." Akira left the colonel's office burning with irritation at himself. What did he think he would accomplish, bringing up a bunch of vague suspicions? All he'd done was play the fool in front of the colonel—and invite more trouble for himself.

Ninth Day of the Seventh Month, Anno Domini 1587

Sono's heart clattered with anxiety as she joined the other ladies trailing Lady Matsuura from the women's wing. Every step past the magnificent reception rooms carried her closer to her groom. The pirate who had chilled her soul by scoffing at her faith. The prince whose lovely gift had softened the freeze on her heart.

They mounted a steep path that led toward the keep at the crown of the hill. Walked past a contingent of guards at yet another gatehouse and through the arch into a courtyard—

And after weeks of suspense, she gazed into his eyes. Her groom awaited her at the base of the broad steps that led to the entrance of the five-story keep. His father and grandfather stood to his right, Yoshiaki with Padre Lucena to his left.

His face was enough to make her heart stop—more

handsome than she remembered. He held himself straight as a bamboo rod, his broad chest and strong shoulders filling out his formal black silk jacket.

She dropped into a bow, but not before she'd seen his eyes glow and his expressive lips form a smile. A torrent of relief overwhelmed her, so strong she thought her knees might buckle. *Graças a Deusu*, he seemed to like her well enough.

Lord Matsuura's voice filled the courtyard. "Our new daughter is a vision. Shall we conclude the matter?"

Something like thirty people had assembled in the courtyard, most of them strangers to Sono. Strangers she would have named among her house's many enemies a few weeks earlier. In an hour, they would be her family.

Hisanobu mounted the first step and turned toward her. His long *katana* swung at his side, and the hilt of his short sword showed at his sash. With his flashing eyes, determined brows, and sun-darkened skin, he embodied the pirate prince.

But what portion prince? What portion pirate? After weeks of wondering, she would soon know.

Another man-sized statue of the war-god Hachiman cast a shadow across him from the top of the steps. This one was in his god-of-culture guise, seated on a lotus blossom with eyes closed and an enraptured expression.

Everything here felt so foreign. Especially her new honored mother, and that insane idea she would pass all her days confined to their women's wing. No escape from the woman's sharp eyes. The thought squeezed like a band around her ribcage, and a wild desire to run pulsed through her.

Ah, Papa-san. What were you thinking? When he committed her to this, did he know the kind of life he had chosen for his daughter?

He was once an unbelieving prince. Then an unbelieving lord. He must have known.

Sono's eyes sought her groom. *Prince or pirate?* Meditative lotus-seated icon, or the war-god's demon-faced guise?

If Papa-san could undergo such a transformation, so could this man—her husband. With *Deusu* all things were possible.

Hisanobu gave her a smile. He seemed nervous too.

And he is so handsome.

Padre said a few words of greeting, then the whole party ascended four flights of stairs to the keep's top level. The balcony yielded breathtaking views—forested hills and glittering stretches of water. The sun had dropped behind the peaks, staining the clouds with pearlescent pinks.

Padre led Sono and her bridegroom into the wedding chamber and onto a dais. The soft light from paper lanterns glowed on her groom's cheeks and glistened from his hair. His eyes, framed with those dark lashes, drew her in. And his strong arms—the thought of them twined around her sent a new sensation chasing up her spine. Eagerness shot through with anxiety. A ball like clay formed at the base of her stomach.

She glanced up at him with a jittery smile. *For better or for worse.*

Padre delivered a brief message about *Kirishitan* marriage, with a Japanese brother translating. He fixed Hisanobu with a direct stare and led him in the *Kiristitan* vows.

Esteem, honor, hold, protect. Forsake all other women, as long as both their lives endured.

Forsake all other women. Sono might have imagined that Padre give those words a bit of extra emphasis. Perhaps Hisanobu gave a slight flinch, or perhaps a breeze made the lamplight flicker. But he reached for her hands and clasped them both between his larger ones. He looked at her with fervent eyes. "*Hai.*"

He'd done it. He had agreed to a monogamous, as-long-as-we-live *Kirishitan* marriage. Warmth like the summer sun flooded from his strong hands into hers and up her arms.

Padre paused, and she was pretty sure he let a tiny

sigh of relief escape before he started her portion.

Last chance to say no. Last chance to pick up my skirts and flee this gilded birdcage. After this moment, it would be forever.

Her mother and brother knelt directly behind her. A subtle tingle ran up her back—Mama-san's loving eyes, resting on her. Her brother's too. Trusting her to do what was needful.

She drew herself up straight. Of course she would not rebel against her father's will. Or *Deusu*'s, no matter how foreign the path it would lead her down. And no Matsuura boats would bear her nephews away, hostages like her brother.

Time to purchase peace for Omura. With this word. With my life.

She gazed into Hisanobu's eyes. "*Hai.*" It was like stepping off the balcony outside and hoping a cloud would catch her.

Chapter Ten

WITH THE VOWS EXCHANGED AND THE union cemented, Sono sat beside her handsome new husband at a splendid dinner. There was toasting, and moonlight, and music. But the inevitable moment came to leave their guests. Hisanobu's hand found her thigh beneath the table and rested there. Heat ran up her leg like he'd placed a glowing coal beside her. She set her chopsticks down.

He gazed directly into her eyes. "Perhaps we should retire, ah?"

She managed a tiny nod. "*Hai*, my lord."

He stood and took his leave of their guests. She stood, bowed, and took a heartbreaking last glance at Mama-san and her brother. This marked the end of her life with them.

She turned and followed her new husband back down all those stairs. Moonlight bathed their way with an ethereal glow. Every few paces, he glanced at her over his shoulder. The second time he did so, she met his eyes and he gave her a tentative smile.

Mama-san had explained what would come next. Had told her about his eel and her cave. "You'll learn to enjoy it," she'd said. "You can remind him to be gentle if you need to."

Her eyes lingered on the powerful angles of his shoulders and the way his loose jacket fell across his hips. She wasn't sure how she felt about any of it. Would she need to caution a pirate? Or would she melt into the arms of her prince?

They passed through the gatehouse onto the more secluded path to the mansion. He stopped and turned to her. "You're not cold, are you? Surely you don't need that big coat you're wearing."

She dropped her gaze, heat searing her cheeks. "No, my lord."

Crickets filled the air with pulsing song, and jasmine flowers exhaled a sultry fragrance. He walked back toward her with a sharp, almost hungry expression on his face. He slipped the heavy wedding coat off her shoulders and draped it over his arm. "Better." His eyes caressed her form. "Sono-chan, you are exquisite. A prize well worth winning."

A prize? That was better than a hostage, but too much like a token.

He ran his fingers down her neck. His fingertips grazed the skin just beneath the collar of her kimono.

That glowing heat surged up her spine. Her lips parted on their own. He had to duck under her headdress, but he found her mouth. His lips brushed hers, then pressed against them. A thrill of surprise ran through her at the velvet feel of them.

He pulled her firmly against him for a moment, then stepped back. She gazed at him, winded. It was all she could do to stay steady on her feet. His eyes lingered on hers, and he grinned.

Hostage? Prize? Or bride? She felt like a bride now, and gossamer wings could just as well have been wafting her to *Deusu's* paradise.

His hand moved to her hip. "Walk beside me, Sono-chan."

"*Hai*, my lord."

"And you can say something besides '*Hai*, my lord.'"

She laughed and dipped her head in a bow. "Pray excuse me, Lord Hisanobu." She glanced around at the unfamiliar shapes of trees and bushes and retaining walls. "I guess I am a little overwhelmed."

His eyes glowed as he studied her. "Me too."

Sono woke with a start and a throb of panic. *Where am I?*

A solid arm weighed on her ribs. Soft breathing buzzed in her ears. Hisanobu stirred beside her, the smell of sake floating on his breath.

Hai. Of course. It was really true. She was a married woman now, sharing her pirate prince's silk bed. She ran her fingertips along his muscular upper arm with a soft smile.

"Mmph." He pulled her closer, then resumed his rhythmic breathing.

She studied him, and quiet satisfaction filled her.

Filtered moonlight highlighted the strong lines of his face and neck. The gloss of his hair, its precise topknot skewed. Dark lashes formed twin crescent moons against his smooth cheeks.

So this was her life now. This young man's castle. This young man's bed. And in time, by *Deusu's* grace, his children, and Hirado's *Kirishitan* heir.

She rolled over and snuggled against him with a contented sigh. *Hai*, he'd shown himself as young and unschooled in the bedchamber as she. Still, married life seemed pleasing enough thus far.

At least the marriage part of it. A small jade statue of Hachiman glowered at her from the alcove at the back of her new husband's chamber.

A sense of oppression settled over her like a thick blanket. There was something knowing in that statue's expression. As if the fearful demon-god was aware of why she'd come to Hirado, and brooded over her, determined to stop her.

She slipped her fingers around her cross. *Deusu* was there too. And no idol was His equal.

The next morning brought the heartbreaking moment when Sono stood in the courtyard and watched an attendant swing open the enormous castle gate. A *samurai* escort waited outside it to conduct her mother and brother to the dock.

It wrenched her heart to watch Mama-san gather her skirts to leave. Yoshiaki gazed down on Sono from his mount. His eyes lingered in a way that made her think he might even miss her.

Would she see them again? Omura was so far away. She blinked hard against the tears and the burning hollow in her heart. She could not trust herself to utter a word.

Later, tears. Later. With Iya. Graças a Deusu for Iya. She longed for a chance to sob on her handmaid's shoulder, but Hisanobu offered her a tour of the grounds instead.

He was thoughtful, to want to distract her. And her heart did an extra skip at the opportunity to diffuse the idea they could imprison her in the women's wing. "*Arigato.* I would love a tour of the defenses. I have been eager to view the archery range."

His eyebrows arched. "Defenses and archery range. I expected you to be interested in the rooms and gardens. But I forget your reputation with the way of the bow."

He led her up the maze of defenses that protected the keep. Would she ever learn her way around this impossible labyrinth?

It will certainly take some time if I can't leave the women's wing.

She was dabbing sweat from her brow by the time they mounted the final set of stairs to the balcony at the top of the keep. A pair of *samurai* paced by them on patrol, long swords glinting at their thighs.

The view made her gasp with wonder. It swept across the castle grounds and over the walls, out to the island's rugged terrain. He talked her through the intricate network of barriers that made up the castle's defensive system. It was truly impressive.

And clenched inside all those layers of defenses, a pearl tightly guarded by an oyster's shell? The keep where she stood, and the mansion where they proposed to hold her captive.

Brooding storm clouds hung in the distance above a silvery line of sea she could just make out between two hills. A pagoda stood in proud silhouette against the sky like a nail piercing the horizon.

The ocean breeze did not produce the sudden chill that moved across her shoulders. The whole landscape felt hostile.

His chest swelled as he surveyed the forbidding view. "This fortress has been our work for generations. I want you to be happy here, as the lady of my castle. I want you to be happy and healthy and bear big, healthy boys."

As if she could control whether she bore boys. Still... *I want you to be happy.* He'd said it twice. This was her opportunity to plead for liberty.

Blessed Deusu, *have mercy.* "What if I require my freedom to be happy?"

"What do you mean?"

"What if I want to practice archery when my lord is occupied? Or linger in the teahouse? Or take in the views from this balcony?"

His fingers locked around the strand of hair he'd been playing with. "Do you intend to wander the castle by yourself?"

"Not by myself. I would go with my handmaid."

"Your father permitted this in his castle?"

"Of course."

He pressed his lips into a line. "And in town?"

"When there was occasion. Properly veiled, of course."

"You would be on display before dozens of men. That strikes me as very unseemly."

Hot rage at the injustice exploded through her. "But my handmaid may travel where she pleases, ah? I do not understand."

"Your handmaid is not a noble's wife." He studied her, his jaw resolute. "This would not please me, Sono-chan."

She bit her lip and dropped her eyes. A tense silence floated between them.

"Do you realize how beautiful you are? Am I wrong to keep you to myself?" He slipped the errant strand of hair behind her ear. "No, Sono-chan. Being a noble's wife on Hirado comes with certain restrictions. You will need to accustom yourself to them."

He slid his hand up her arm, under her sleeve. His eyes had that gleam again. "And of course, when I am free, we will go all those places. Nothing would please me more."

This would please me, Sono-chan. That would not please me, Sono-chan. She gave him a fixed smile meant to hide her despair.

Calm your own mind, as Capt. Fujita used to say. The thought of her former teacher carried a fresh pang of homesickness with it.

She replied in what she hoped was an even tone. "*Hai,* my lord. Then I will live for my hours at your side."

He had the gall to give her a self-satisfied nod. "I will be glad of that."

She took a deep breath. *Deusu, help me.* "There is one other thing, my lord. Every seventh day, *Kirishitan* go to church to hear mass."

"I am aware of this."

"Would my lord care to escort me there? Nothing would please *my* heart more."

His jaw hardened. "You know we follow Hachiman. We have agreed to permit you your choice of religion, but make no mistake. The House of Matsuura will not compromise ours."

So the pleasing did not work both ways. Not that this surprised her. "How can I practice my religion, then?" No mass. No confession. No access to the Lord's grace through communion. No padres to lead her in prayer.

A stifling fear of impending loss pushed her heart into her throat. If her husband was going to stick to this, she would lose every lifeline. Every channel to *Deusu.*

Her mind whirred with barely controlled panic. "If I cannot go to mass, perhaps you could allow one of the padres to come to me?"

He let out a disdainful snort. "There are enough of them around. Hirado town is full of them, thanks to the Lord Regent's edict. It might be good to give them some employment." He studied her in the waning light and his expression softened. "It is that important to you, ah?"

"It is desperately important, my lord."

"I will discuss your request with Father and Grandfather. But for now"—he pulled her against him—"that twenty-eighth lord awaits conceiving."

Wednesday 15 August 1945

There was no need to call the prisoners to assemble that evening. With the last ragged shards of dusk fading behind the mountain peaks and twenty-one hundred hours approaching, all forty-three enlisted men gathered in clusters on the assembly ground.

At seven minutes before the hour, Col. Simmons took

his place in front of them and asked Akira to translate again. The colonel said a few words of introduction, then static hummed as the radio came across the P.A. loudspeakers.

A male voice echoed off wooden buildings and concrete pavement, emphasizing the import of the occasion—the first time an occupant of the ancient Chrysanthemum Throne had spoken to his people in his own voice. But Western listeners would hear Emperor Hirohito's message in translation.

"Now"—joyful excitement throbbed through the announcer's voice—"let me welcome our distinguished translator, Mr. Hirakawa of the Japan Broadcasting Company."

The new voice, equally smooth, carried a distinct Japanese accent. "Hello, listening friends. Hirakawa Tadaichi here. Let me assure you of the authenticity of this message. I translated it myself from the recording the emperor made last night. Without further preliminaries, here is Emperor Hirohito's message.

"To our good and loyal subjects: After..."

Akira closed his eyes and listened hard. The English was elaborate, and he missed quite a bit of it.

"We have ordered our government..."—more words he couldn't follow—"Our empire accepts the provisions of their Joint Declaration."

The Joint Declaration. The document in which the Allied nations had insisted on unconditional surrender. The emperor—the Son of Heaven—was telling the entire world that he'd accepted it.

Akira's mind numbed. A roaring like the ocean pounded in his head. But the prisoners in front of him stood in uncomprehending silence.

Eloquent phrases followed about "the well-being of our subjects" and obligations handed down by imperial ancestors. The prisoners' eyes focused fixedly ahead or dropped to the pavement in increasing desolation and bewilderment.

The statement came to the point. "We have ordered the

acceptance of the provisions of the Joint Declaration of the Powers."

Screams and cheers like a *sumo* match echoed from the sections of the camp that housed American personnel.

Akira had expected this surrender, but expecting it and hearing it pronounced were different things. What he felt now was too overwhelming for tears. The prisoners lined up before him could not have understood the broadcast, but they'd clearly gotten the idea. Shoulders slumped and heads hung. One prisoner in the front row and another in the middle wept openly.

The announcer-voice went on with words no doubt meant to console. And perhaps they would later, when letters would stare from a page. But at that moment, Akira had no capacity to absorb them.

Then, finally, "We have resolved to pave the way for grand peace for all the generations to come by enduring the unendurable and suffering what is insufferable."

The broadcaster fell silent. The men shifted from foot to foot. Several anchored their eyes on Akira, their faces full of questions.

Yoshigumi grumbled in Japanese, loudly enough for everyone around him to hear. "Did anyone understand any of that?"

The voice over the loudspeaker wrapped up his address. "The full text of the message will run in the papers." The loudspeaker went quiet.

"I am sorry, men. I was under the impression you'd get to hear the emperor's original statement." Simmons turned to Akira. "Sub-lieutenant, perhaps you could relay what you heard?"

Akira tried to swallow away the swelling that was closing his throat as the magnitude of what he'd heard sank in. He had no desire to meet Yoshigumi's eyes, but the captain's puffed-out chest and huffed-out breaths were impossible to miss.

He focused beyond Yoshigumi on the rows of faces behind him and spoke in a wooden voice. "The emperor has told his government to accept our enemies' terms. Which means complete and total surrender. No conditions."

Yoshigumi emitted a growl. Lt. Toyoshima appeared frozen in place. The men who had just had any last desperate hope squashed stared straight forward in disbelieving shock.

Akira summarized the rest as well as he could. He ended with, "His Majesty has elected to cut short the suffering by ending the war."

He dropped his eyes to the pavement and let his grief consume him.

The voice of the crane. To hear it even once would be a privilege beyond imagining. An awed envy swelled through him, imagining the tens of millions in Japan who'd just had that experience.

But his gut roiled at what they'd heard that voice utter.

Endure the unendurable.

Suffer what is insufferable.

The impact of those phrases sent a tremor running from his core through his fingertips. This was it. This was forever. A nation that had never known defeat or occupation would now suffer both.

The colonel said a few more words intended to bolster morale. They were received in dejected silence. He dismissed them, and the enlisted men filed into their barracks. Akira followed. He sank onto his bottom bunk and rested unfocused eyes on the gray cement floor.

Yoshigumi walked in, with Toyoshima and the other junior officers on his heels.

The captain stalked toward him with a malevolent glare. "Look who beat us here." He cocked his arm back and slapped Akira across the face with force enough to rock his head back.

The five of them formed a threatening circle in front of him.

Che! Akira groaned as he found his feet. He worked his jaw. It didn't seem to be broken. "What is this?"

Yoshigumi snorted. "Why do you help advance this farce? We were told we would hear from the emperor."

His mouth felt dry as the prairie grasses. "We heard His Majesty's words."

"We heard some words. We heard a voice. The voice wasn't the emperor's. How do we know the words were, ah?" The captain made a disgruntled *harumph*. "How do we even know this so-called journalist is who he says he is?"

Akira gaped at the man like some new species of lizard. Then the truth flashed through his mind. He'd chosen to believe the broadcast because he wanted it to be true. The war had to end for Japan to survive. And it seemed the emperor had come to believe that too.

Yoshigumi loomed over him. "Thanks to you, these *gaijin* have succeeded in duping some of the simple-minded here."

Akira's chest swelled with a blinding rage. "Really? I'll tell you who has duped the simple-minded. The militarists that told us our nation was invulnerable. That bombs would never fall on the Land of the Gods." He was done trying to hide his outrage. His voice shook with it. "See what's become of Tokyo. Of Osaka. Of all our great cities."

All five of them lunged, and Akira crumpled against the wall beneath a hail of blows.

Chapter Eleven

Ninth Day of the Seventh Month, Anno Domini 1587

IT WAS MID-AFTERNOON BEFORE SONO RETURNED to the women's wing. Lady Matsuura's handmaid, Rin, saw her first. "See who is here! Our new princess has returned."

Sono groaned inside. With her lips sore from kissing and her hair disheveled, she had hoped to slip in unnoticed. But the wing's other occupants—two concubines and their handmaids—hurried from rooms and terraces to greet her.

Several of the *shoji* stood open, making the chambers clustered around the garden one common space. *Graças a Deusu*, Lady Matsuura made no appearance. Even so, the small confines of that space were as cloyingly heavy around her as her wedding coat.

She had made the two concubines' acquaintance the afternoon before. Tatsuko was the older one. She'd passed perhaps forty summers and had belonged to Hisanobu's aged grandfather since her fifteenth year. She had an elegant figure and creamy skin. Still handsome, despite crows' feet and a few thin streaks of gray—and a wistful droop to her eyes. She spoke little.

The younger concubine, perky Akiko, belonged to Lord Matsuura. She had brought her two adorable boys by Sono's chamber shortly after she arrived. Both sported wooden swords thrust through their sashes. The older one was a merry little soul, and he stood very tall in his miniature *samurai* garb. His little brother simply stared at Sono with big dark eyes.

Meeting Akiko's boys drove an unexpected twinge of sympathy for Lady Matsuura through her chest. To be expected to stand by while your husband fathered children with a woman ten years younger. Or your father, with a woman of your own years.

Forsake all other women. Hisanobu had vowed it. He meant to keep that vow, yes? She pressed her lips together and thrust the question away, a knot congealing in her stomach.

The ladies tagged along behind her in an informal procession. It seemed they all wished to see how she would like her chamber. Iya slid the *shoji* aside with a flourish. "A place to make new memories, my lady."

A thrill of amazement ran through Sono. Her handmaid had indeed worked a dazzling transformation. The crowning touch was the magnificent painted screen that stretched along one wall.

Papa-san's pines. They had once graced his chamber. This was a surprise—she did not know Mama-san had bundled it into their cargo.

How delightful. She would always have a hint of Papa-san with her.

She took everything in with a wistful ache in her chest. "It's perfect, Iya-chan. *Arigato.*" She turned from the screen with its knobby pine trunk and larger-than-life crane strutting across a gilded background. The knot inside her thickened.

If only she could bolt from the building into an actual pine forest. When Papa-san bargained her off to Hirado, did he know he was locking her away from the pines they'd enjoyed so much together?

The ladies cooed over everything like doves. The embroidered bed linens. The gilded lacquer shelves, with their artful arrangement of inlaid boxes and cosmetic brushes. Finally, there was nothing left to admire, and they trooped out, leaving her alone with Iya.

"At last!" She lifted up another sincere *graças a Deusu* and sank onto her futon. She laid her fingers against her lips and listened. A little too much water music from the pond filtered in through the *shoji*. The sound of her voice would flow out just as readily.

"You do not know how I long to talk, Iya-chan." She arched an eyebrow and tipped her chin at the *shoji* that led to the garden. "But could you play something for me?"

Iya's eyes followed hers and she nodded. "Of course." She disappeared for a moment, then returned and unwrapped her *shamisen*.

Sono slipped onto the mat beside Iya, as close as she could get to her handmaid's ear. Rin's face hovered in her mind. "You know someone is listening. We will need to take care."

Iya transitioned seamlessly into a piece that required vigorous strumming. "*Hai.* It will be hard to keep any secrets here."

Sono listened. *Better.* She murmured all her news into Iya's ear. When she got to the conversation at the keep, frustration wrenched out bitter words. "I swear he has two guises, like that Hachiman idol of theirs. One minute he says he wants to see me happy, and he seems to mean it. But the next, he agrees with his mother and says I am not to leave this wing. I have to sit here unless he shows up to collect me or gives express permission to someone else.

"And it gets worse." Her gaze settled on her crucifix, now on display in her alcove. "He denies me permission to hear mass."

Iya's mouth fell open with outrage. "Did they not pledge you could keep your religion?"

"*Hai,* but they seem to think I can somehow be a *Kirishitan* without crossing the threshold of a church. Without mass, without confession, without communion? What kind of *Kirishitan* will I be? But it seems these rules don't apply to you."

Iya's face glowed with relief. "*Arigato,* my lady. Although I feel guilty to get good tidings when you—"

"Don't be sorry. I am glad of it. You can be my eyes and ears."

Twilight stained the sky when Sono's husband came to collect her, fulfilling his pledge to show her the archery range. He led her on a path that plunged down the slope behind the keep. Her bow jostled against her shoulder, filling her with a delicious sense of exhilaration.

He ushered her onto the platform at the near end of the range, then stepped back to observe her form.

She swung her arms to loosen her shoulders, dragonflies darting through her belly at the thought of him evaluating her skills. "It has been at least a week since I touched this bow, my lord. I am out of practice."

He folded his arms, still wearing his amused smile. "That is why we came out."

Cicadas and bullfrogs had already struck up their night chorus. The smell of new-mown hay filled her nostrils. Two targets hung on stands in the field, one at a quarter *cho*—the distance she was used to—and another half again as far beyond it.

She plucked an arrow from her quiver and nocked it. She inhaled, filling her lungs with the delicious scent of the thick stand of pines behind her, and raised the bow above her head. She drew the arrow back and took aim, doing her best to lose every thought but the target's painted center.

He's eyeing my bare arm....

Her skin tingled. She let the arrow fly, and it hissed past her ear. The instant it left the string, she knew she'd shot wild. She bit her lip and watched it loft past the target, well to its right. The bowstring thrummed.

"Do not be discouraged," he said from behind her. "You have the distance. The way of the bow requires consistent devotion, as you know. Try again."

She did, twice. The third time, he stepped up behind her and shifted her elbow a little. "I think this will steady your aim." The nearness of his strong chest sent a thrill along her spine.

"Steady," he said. "Focus."

Easy for him to say. She squinted down the shaft. This time the arrow shot true, burying itself in the target's outer circle with a satisfying thunk.

"There it is! See? We just need to get you out more often."

They shot until her muscles burned. "I am afraid I am done for tonight, my lord. I could not draw another arrow if an entire army charged me."

A shadow crossed his face. "You might be surprised what you could do if an entire army charged you. But that is not a subject for a pleasant evening."

The bullfrogs swelled their chorus. He rested a hand on her arm. "I spoke with my father about your request."

She stared at him. "About mass?" Why did he not tell her right away? A shred of hope rose in her heart like morning mist. "What did he say?"

"He did not welcome the idea of a padre coming here."

"I see." She focused on the woodgrain at her feet, deflated.

"I am sorry, Sono-chan. I know you are disappointed."

Disappointed? How would you feel if someone tried to cage you like a bird? She bit back the words. "I am, my lord."

"One of Papa-san's *Kirishitan* retainers made a suggestion." He seemed as pleased with himself as a cat who'd brought her a fresh mouse. "Koteda-san thought his wife and a few other *Kirishitan* ladies could visit you. You could discuss the teachings of the padres with them."

It was something. *Deusu* was granting her a bit of grace. She bowed and thanked him with all the contentment she could muster.

But it took several days to get the meetings set up, over Lady Matsuura's vehement objections. The woman swore she could not accept that *Kirishitan* would soil her women's wing with their foreign religion.

In the end, Lord Matsuura was compelled to offer his prized teahouse for Sono's meetings. Which delighted her— she adored the teahouse. Soon enough Koteda Yasuki, with her ample form and ready laugh, became part of Sono's intimate circle, along with her lively daughter Kai and their neighbor Satoko. The three ladies would walk up from Hirado town, bringing *Kirishitan* literature and key discussion points from the Sunday teachings. For Sono, the time always sped past on hawks' wings until they closed each meeting in prayer.

But Sono and Iya always found a whiff of frankincense when they entered the room. Sono's honored mother had been there before them, burning incense and invoking her deities' protection against the wicked influence of the *Kirishitan*.

Wednesday 15 August 1945

Akira passed agonizing hours in silence on his bunk, phasing in and out of consciousness. Every inhale set off a flaming ball of pain on the left side of his back.

Something was wrong with him.

When he came to himself for the third or fourth time, snores and deep breathing were all he heard. He could creep out at last and get help. He managed to pull himself to his feet and stumble to the door. Thankfully, the hinges moved without waking any of them.

He closed the door behind him, let out a sigh of relief at his escape, then doubled up and retched loudly.

A sentry jogged toward him. "Hey! You Japs are under curfew."

Akira straightened as best he could. "I need a doctor."

"What's wrong? You drink too much?" The sentry frisked him.

Akira groaned and just managed not to jump as the American patted down his lower back.

The guard shot him a surprised stare. "Did that hurt?"

Akira nodded. A sharp pang creased his stomach, but he had nothing left to throw up.

"You know where the clinic is?"

"*Hai.*" Akira took two steps. The ground lurched.

"Wait," the sentry said. He came up beside him and steadied him. "You sit over here. I'll get you some help." He supported him to a stoop a few feet away. "What happened to you anyway?"

Akira tried to see the man, but he couldn't bring his face into focus. "I'm... not... sure." It was almost the truth.

Light throbbed through Akira's eyelids, but it was too much trouble to open his eyes.

He was on his back, a mattress beneath him. Voices

hummed above. The hum resolved into a babble of conversation.

He didn't care to follow it. His head was pounding. He tried to twist away from the light, but the glare was everywhere. Pain shot through his lower back when he moved.

"He's waking up." A female voice. American. Musical.

"About time." Another woman. This one's voice fell harder on his ears. "Sub-Lieutenant Sawamura?"

Who— *Hai.* He was Sawamura. He forced his eyes open. A hospital, again. Where? How long?

The face attached to the musical voice was a red-haired nurse around forty. "Oh, good." She smiled down at him. "Do you know where you are?"

His thoughts floated like wisps of incense smoke. He closed his eyes and did his best to gather them.

Towering blue mountains. Acres of glossy-leafed sugar beets.

I am horyo. He let out a deep sigh as the light in the room seemed to fade. "Camp Carson."

She gave him a dazzling grin. "Good."

A doctor walked in and joined her. "How is our patient?"

"Back with us, Doctor Hessel."

The doctor peered into Akira's eyes. "Nice to meet you, sub-lieutenant. I don't think you've been our guest before. Watch this, please." He moved a finger slowly across Akira's field of view. "Good. Do you know what happened to you?"

He pushed his thoughts back in time. Something niggled back there. Something horrible.

Men in the assembly area. Voices over loudspeakers. Words about—

"The emperor." Despair settled on him in a dark cloud.

The doctor nodded. "Yes. You heard the emperor's broadcast last night. Do you remember it?"

Akira squeezed his eyes closed, tears burning against his eyelids.

"Yes, you remember. And after that? Do you recall anything?"

Yoshigumi's contorted face swam into Akira's mind,

insults streaming from his lips. He stiffened. He opened his mouth to speak, but he thought better of it. Satisfying as seeing that arrogant mongrel jailed for assault would be, all those army men snapped to obey his commands like slavish puppies. He should think the thing through before he accused the man.

He pressed his lips closed and shook his head.

"Hmm." Dr. Hessel's eyebrows rose. He asked a few more questions, testing Akira's memory, then assessed his injuries. He stepped back and shook his head. "Someone roughed you up pretty good. Your urine test showed blood, which makes me suspect kidney damage. I think you should heal on your own. But we'll need to keep you on bed rest and observe you closely. You still might need surgery—to go under the knife. Do you understand?"

"Yes, sir."

The nurse nodded. "I'll let Colonel Simmons know right away. He's very concerned about you."

Dr. Hessel settled on the chair next to Akira's bed and made a few notes on his chart. He peered at Akira. "You don't remember what happened?"

Akira grimaced and shook his head.

"I hope something will come back to you. The M.P.s have all your roommates in the guardhouse, but oddly, none of them seems to know what happened either. If we can establish who was responsible, they won't go back to Japan for some time."

The words "back to Japan" gave Akira's unformed despair a name, and it cut through his chest like a sword.

"You are going to need rest. Nurse Carr will dispense aspirin and do whatever she can to make you more comfortable. And, sub-lieutenant"—he rested a reassuring hand on Akira's shoulder—"it seems some of your countrymen aren't happy with you. But Colonel Simmons is grateful. We will keep you safe here."

Chapter Twelve

Thirteenth Day of the Eighth Month, Anno Domini 1587

IT WAS A RAINY SUNDAY AFTERNOON, AND Iya had just returned from town. She shook water off her wet coat. "Koteda-san and Brother Bartholomeu send you their regards."

"*Arigato.*" Sono forced a smile through a pang of envy.

Iya padded across the floor to Sono and spoke in a whisper. "And Brother Bartholomeu sends you this." She slipped a small scroll from her sleeve.

"Intriguing!" The scroll bore Padre Lucena's signature. The handwriting was unadorned but clear. Bartholomeu or one of the other Japanese brothers must have written it out for him.

Sono's pulse picked up as she read.

Dearest Lady Sono,

I send you my warmest greetings in the name of Deusu, and salutations from your brothers and your sisters here. I write to convey a request that must remain our secret. Doubtless you know that the Black Ship has docked in Nagasaki and will sail again with favorable winds. You also know it is not our desire that Japan should be left without the witness of the Gospel.

The plight of your family in Omura weighs on my heart most gravely. This unfortunate edict has left them without access to the grace of Deusu which the church provides through the blessed sacraments.

That weighed on her as well. She had spent a month cut off from the blessed Church herself. Padre Lucena passed his days in Hirado town, in full view of her castle walls, but he might as well be in Osaka.

A wave of pity for her family shook her. *Graças a Deusu*, she had Koteda-san to bring her the padres' teachings. In Omura, they lacked even that.

She read on.

I have a man who would risk going to them in secret with a glad heart. But traveling, even privily, requires means. I know your willing heart, my child. I pray that Deusu might lead you to contribute to this effort with your devoted prayers, but also in some material way.

In His surpassing love,

Padre Lucena

She stuffed the scroll in a box, feeling light-headed. Every thought of the padre now triggered an unsettling memory. The strange glint in his eyes when he'd first spoken of *Deusu*'s will embarking her to Hirado.

Still, one of the foreign padres was willing to risk his life to make the journey to serve Omura domain.

The strings on Iya's instrument let out strident wails of protest as she tuned them. Sono settled next to her. "Did you read it?" she whispered.

Iya shook her head.

"It's from Padre Lucena himself. He asks me to contribute"—she glanced at the wall between her chamber and Lady Matsuura's and lowered her voice further—"to defying the Lord Regent's edict. *In some material way*, as he puts it. He will use the money to send a padre in secret to Omura." She let out a caustic laugh. "How am I to do that? He of all people knows the constraints I live under. I am not free to speak my thoughts in the privacy of my own chamber without taking great pains." *And he was quick enough to send me into this.*

She glanced at Papa-san's pine trees on her painted screen. *Along with Papa-san. And the rest of them.*

Iya studied her, then bit her lower lip and gave her head a slow shake. "Does Padre believe you have money, my lady? You do not."

"No." She took an appraising look around the chamber. "But it sickens me to think of them in the same condition as myself. With no access to the grace *Deusu* gives through the padres."

She walked to the magnificent lacquer shelves that had come with her to Hirado and eyed her lacquered writing box. "There are more beautiful things in this chamber than I could use in three lifetimes. If only they were mine to give away." She ran her fingertips across the gilded pattern on the box's lid. "This, for example. I've used it since I was a small girl. Even so, since it came with my dowry, it's the property of the House of Matsuura now."

They both studied the luxurious items around them. Beautiful lacquer boxes. Cosmetics, gilded brushes, her hand mirror. Her teapot and utensils. It was surely worth enough to send a padre all the way to China. But none of it belonged to her.

Iya narrowed her eyes in thought. "There are things in this chamber that no one would miss. Kimonos in your trunks you have not yet worn. Or your fans, for example. 'Twould be easy enough to tuck a couple in my sleeve."

"Your sleeve!" Sono hissed the air in past her teeth. "We know what the penalty for theft could be, if you are found leaving the castle with something that belongs to the House of Matsuura."

Iya made a grim face and drew a finger across her neck.

"You told me they cut a boy's head off last week for stealing a dinghy, did you not?" Sono shuddered. "And the fact that I gave you the fan might not help—since it's not mine to give."

Iya fairly attacked her instrument's strings. "*Hai.* But think of the risk that padre is ready to take. To serve your family. And mine."

"And this may be the last thing Padre Lucena ever asks of me—of us. Since they are under orders to sail with the Black Ship." She sank to her futon and hugged her knees to her chest in a miserable ball. She couldn't remember a time when Padre Lucena wasn't a beloved presence when he came to her father's home. "How will we get along without them to guide us? To intercede for us? To draw us to *Deusu*'s throne?"

Iya's fingers rested for an instant. "Omura can still have that. *If* we risk this."

Iya played on, and Sono let the strains from the *shamisen* flow over her. Longed-for faces passed in front of her—mother, brothers, pregnant sister-in-law. Brave Fujita, who had taken a bullet in his leg defending her. As for the padres, more than once the Portuguese gunships they had summoned had driven back her house's enemies. She owed the padres more than she could ever repay.

She thrust her new nagging questions aside. "We have to do it, ah?"

Iya nodded.

But what could Iya carry? Used fans would be easy to conceal, but even the most artfully decorated might not fetch enough to be worth the risk. Sono's cosmetic brushes were exquisite, but they were a set, and even one could be missed.

"A kimono would be too bulky to carry. But you could wear it, ah? Under your traveling coat. We could hitch it up so the hem would not show." She tossed her head. "Surely no one would have the effrontery to search my handmaid."

Iya bit her lip. "But if I am discovered, somehow—"

"Ah, Iya. I will not let them think you stole it. No matter what price I pay. But that might not stay them from punishing you." She put a hand on Iya's arm. "The choice has to be yours."

Iya gazed at the floor for a moment, then lifted determined eyes to hers and gave her a grim nod. "This is for my family too. And for all the *Kirishitan* in Omura domain."

Sono nodded back as her heart sank like a boulder. "For Omura." Her voice trembled. To protect her family from the Lord Regent's edict, she was forced to put her only friend in Hirado at risk.

Sono picked out a lovely kimono with Iya's help. Brown brocade with an all-over pattern of embroidered peacocks. Much too expensive for a handmaid. A new winter kimono, so no one had seen her don it yet.

When Sunday morning came, she helped Iya slip it on under her other garments. She cinched a silk tie around her handmaid's waist. Her fingers shook so that she had trouble working the knot. She adjusted the garment so the hem fell below Iya's knees, three hands' breadths above where her outer garments would end. She arranged Iya's other clothes to cover it all, then stepped back.

"Spin around."

Iya did. She stopped, facing Sono. Her cheeks showed nearly as pallid as the collar of her white under-kimono.

"Oh, Iya. You can't look so unnerved." Sono dabbed a bit of perspiration off her handmaid's forehead. Her own felt moist too. "You need not take this kind of risk for me. We can find another way."

Iya's eyes flashed. "I do not take it for you, my lady. I take it for my father and for the *Kirishitan* of Omura." She gave her chin a resolute lift. "And my veil will hide my face, ah? But I need to leave now."

Sono's heart swelled with admiration for her friend while anxiety churned through her. "I hate the thought of you taking such a risk. I wish I could do this myself."

She helped Iya position her broad-brimmed traveling hat with its sweeping white veil. *Do this myself.* Face obscured behind the veil. Form concealed beneath a loose coat. They were about the same size.

Why can't I? "No. I am not going to ask you to go through with this. I will put on your traveling outfit, and I will take the kimono to the padre."

Iya backed away from her, shaking her head violently.

"Why not, ah? We're the same size. In your coat and that veil, no one will know it's me." She reached for Iya's hat. "I can serve as the carp on the cutting board."

Iya clutched her hat's brim with both hands. "No, my lady. It would only work until you speak. And someone would notice your absence here. I would answer for that. No. You have to let me do this."

"Iya—"

"It is my honor, my lady." Iya squared her shoulders. "So...here I go."

"*Deusu* guard you." Sono sank to her knees and clasped her hands in prayer. She listened for the dour thud of the heavy door to the women's wing closing behind her handmaid.

The morning hours stretched long as she repeated prayer after anxious prayer. Her mind produced an expanding litany of ways Iya could be discovered. Letting her dear friend agree to this had been the most thin-livered thing she had ever done.

From this day forward, I am going to have an impressive prayer life. Her words to her mother mocked her. She had never imagined how true they would be.

Her knees were sore, and the shadows in the garden spreading toward the east, by the time Iya returned. Without incident, and one kimono lighter.

As she did the next Sunday, after smuggling out another precious kimono and a pair of fans.

Thursday 16 August 1945

Akira spent much of that day asleep. Which was a mercy, since waking brought only torment. A vague aching premonition of disaster. A new effort to remember what it stemmed from. Then a fresh dose of cringing shame at the image of Americans tramping into his homeland with all the arrogance of an occupying power.

What would it look like, this end of everything he'd known? And what was a bruised kidney in the face of all this?

He was picking at his dinner when someone rapped on his door. A refreshingly girlish voice called in a polite greeting. "*Gomen kudasai.*" May I come in please?

He sat up, astonished, and invited her in. His surprise swelled when he saw her. A young woman. Tall and slender. Soft brown curls framed a fair-skinned face and large round eyes. Striking. And very American.

"*Konnichiwa, Sawamura-san. Watashi-wa* Covell *desu.*" Her accent wasn't flawless, but it was the best he'd heard from an American.

"Nice to meet you, Covell-san." He felt so mortified he stammered. What a pathetic figure he made in his hospital gown, the scars on his neck on full display. "Please." He gestured at the chair, more than a little perplexed.

She perched on it and settled her bag on the floor.

"Where did you learn to speak such good Japanese?"

"I grew up in Yokohama. And I work now with Japanese-Americans."

"Really? Where?"

Her smile dimmed. "Have you heard of Camp Amache?"

That piqued his interest. "*Hai.* It's not for war prisoners, is it?

"No. I do social work with Japanese-American civilians." Her infectious cheerfulness sprang back. "But I'm here to talk about you. You've been in the U.S. more than three years—the longest of anyone at Camp Carson. But you'll be going home soon. Are you happy?"

He formed a careful response. "I'm happy the war is over."

She peered into his eyes. "That wasn't quite an answer."

"No." He let his head fall back on his pillow, weariness flooding him.

"Sawamura-san, have you ever written a letter home? I can make sure it gets mailed for you."

He shook his head without lifting it from the pillow.

"You don't think your family wants to hear from you, ah? I heard that from one of your fellow prisoners." She leaned toward him with wide, ardent eyes. "If you'd drowned when your ship went down, how would that have helped Japan? But since you lived, you have a chance to help your nation enter a new era. Trust me. God still has a use for you, Sawamura-san."

The nurse on duty appeared at the door. "I'm so sorry, miss, but visiting hours are over."

"Of course." Covell-san rose. "You're a baseball fan, ah?"

He nodded, fresh perplexity hitting at the abrupt change in topic.

"I happen to know Sawamura Eiji's pitching record for the Yomiuri Giants. Incredible. He even struck out Babe Ruth in an exhibition game." Her eyes sparkled, and a conspiratorial smile tugged at her lips.

She was only the second American who'd caught on. He wasn't sure whether to feel annoyed or amused.

"Who did you leave at home?" she said. "Father? Mother?"

"*Hai.*"

"Siblings?"

"A brother and sister. I'm the oldest."

"I've spent my life among Japanese people." She tossed her head. "I don't believe you're so different in your hearts than we are. Your mother and father want to hear from you, I promise. And that brother and sister. They all long to know you're alive." She bowed. "I'll see you again tomorrow. And I'll have writing paper."

She left, and he went back to toying with his dinner. It was like the edge of a knife, this longing for people and places he would never know again.

Sleeping. Waking. Urine samples. And tortured thoughts about country, home, family.

A letter home? Never.

Nurse Carr had just left Akira's room with a jar of urine when Col. Simmons came in.

"Oh, good!" The colonel's voice boomed with sincere pleasure. "You're awake this time."

The camp commander considered him important enough to visit. A warm feeling rushed through him, but it carried along a twinge of anxiety. Simmons was sure to probe him regarding what he remembered of Yoshigumi's attack—a subject he was doing all he could to avoid.

He brushed off his anxiety.

"At ease, sub-lieutenant. May I?" The colonel settled in the chair beside him.

"You are very kind to worry for me, sir. You have so much important things."

"Perhaps." He took off his hat and balanced it across his thighs. "But the truth is I feel somewhat responsible for what happened to you." He shot a piercing glance at Akira. "You know we have your former roommates in the brig."

"Doctor Hessel said that, sir."

"I want to see the truth come out, and I want those men to bear the full consequences. The M.P.s are very interested in interviewing you as soon as you're ready."

He wasn't. "I'm sorry. I don't remember anything."

The thought that he'd derailed some plan of Yoshigumi's flooded him with grim satisfaction. If he told the whole truth, the man might stay locked up for a while. But what would Akira gain from that? And was it worth the price he might pay?

He'd made a decision not to decide for now, although keeping his mouth shut about what they'd done to him rankled him to the core.

"I think we all know what happened." The colonel cleared his throat. "And I suspect I had a hand in creating the hard feelings that landed you in this hospital bed."

"You didn't start the war, sir. The—how do you say it?—hard feelings. This is bigger than you or me."

"But maybe I helped you become a target for those feelings." He sighed. "I hear from Miss Covell that many of you Japanese are deeply concerned about what awaits you at home. Many of you seem to think your families don't want you back. Your *nation* doesn't want you back."

That's not a belief. It's a fact. "It's hard, I think, for Americans to understand the Japanese way."

He leaned toward Akira. "You've endured a great deal for your country. You should return home celebrated, not shattered and shamed. And I recognize that what's happened in the past days might make it more difficult for you to do so. That it might even"—the colonel stared directly into his eyes—"be dangerous for you now. I'd like to make amends."

"Make amends?"

"Make it right somehow. Do you understand?"

"I'm sorry. I do not."

The colonel gave him an apologetic smile. "Let me explain better. I received orders today concerning the repatriation process. Assuming Doctor Hessel feels you're well enough four days from now, I've got a berth for you on a hospital train." His smile became a self-satisfied smirk. "The rest of these men won't leave here for weeks, and when they do, I'll see to it they go a different direction."

"Thank you very much, colonel." He wanted to sound grateful, but the hard knot inside him tightened, and dread darkened the room. That train would put him that much closer to the boundless shame of returning home as a *horyo.*

"I'm not going to tell you, or anyone outside my office, where you're going. So no one will be able to track you down." The colonel knocked his hat twice against his thigh. "There's one more thing—and this is where I get really clever. As it happens, an old friend of mine runs Los Angeles operations for a shipping company, American President Lines. I took the liberty of talking to him. He said with normal operations resuming, they may have a position open. Your combination of maritime and language skills might make you a fit. If a position materializes, he'll try to give you some consideration. So if you hear from Robert Taylor, that's what it will be about."

"I might not have to go back to Japan?" From the day of the surrender, there'd been nothing in his future but black despair. Now the colonel was offering him a thin thread of bright hope. He seized at it with all the eagerness he had. "I don't know how to thank you, sir. Even if there's a small chance."

"Thank me when it's done. If Taylor's got something for you, I'll warn you that red tape is likely to be a problem. If there's anything I can do to help, I will." He stood with the jaunty air of a man who'd cleared his conscience. "These gray hairs ought to give me some clout."

Once the colonel left, Akira's mood deflated. May have a position...might be a fit...if it materializes...try to give consideration. What did that make the odds? Low. Still, it was some small glimmer of hope.

Chapter Thirteen

Autumn, Anno Domini 1587

WEEKS PASSED. THE TREES AROUND THE castle clothed themselves in magnificent robes of red and gold. Every time Sono saw her honored mother, her pulse thrummed in her ears, but nothing was said about the missing kimonos.

One breezy afternoon, Hisanobu invited her to take in a rare sight—the Portuguese Black Ship as it tacked into their harbor.

She hurried behind him, heart fluttering with excitement, as he passed through the maze of paths and gatehouses, then up the four narrow flights of stairs to the balcony on the keep's top level.

She'd heard about this ship all her life. But thrilled as she was to see it, its dark hull also served as a portent. The Black Ship in their harbor meant the padres would sail. And all Japan would be the poorer.

She rounded a corner and caught her breath as a magnificent view of the bay and harbor opened before her.

Hisanobu pointed. "There it is!"

She nodded, awe swelling through her breast. The Black Ship deserved its fame. She was several times the size of any vessel Sono had seen. Her six decks made her appear as tall as the hills on the channel's far side. The half-dozen men crawling up and down the rigging were little more than dots.

"What an enormous vessel! As tall as a temple pagoda." She watched it in unbridled admiration. "Your grandfather was very bold to attack such a ship."

He gave her hand a squeeze. "The Black Ship has not docked in Hirado since my grandfather's day. You know why it is here, ah?"

She worked to hold her voice steady. "I do, my lord. It will take on the padres in accordance with the edict."

And when the ship left without a full complement of them, the Lord Regent would rage. Blood would spill somewhere. She did not know Padre Lucena's plans, but for his sake she hoped he would sail with that ship.

An anxious evening stretched through to an anxious dawn, and Sono received no further tidings of the Black Ship or the padres. The sun had just begun to warm the garden when Rin announced that Hisanobu sought her again.

He never came so early. Her chest tightened as she hurried to greet him at the guarded door.

He shot her a glower that made her heart leap like a startled frog. "Walk with me."

She followed him onto the warrior's run and around the mansion, fear squeezing her chest. They reached a secluded stretch of path behind it. He halted in the shelter of a stand of golden mulberry trees, spun to face her, and pinned her with a glare. "Sono, a very strange thing came to pass this morning."

We are discovered. Deusu, *have mercy.* Had they executed anyone yet?

She quelled her panic as best she could. "What was that, my lord?"

Ice shards prickled through his tone. "The Black Ship pulled away from the dock at dawn—almost as if to leave by stealth. How many foreign padres do you think were on this island yesterday?"

She bristled. "How would I know, my lord? I have never left the castle."

"Your guess, then."

"Dozens, I suppose."

"How many of those padres did the Lord Regent expect to embark on the Portuguese ship?"

His questions came like blows, and she trembled inside to match the mulberry leaves above her head. "All of them. Why?"

He glared at her. "They took only five. What do you make of that, ah?"

Five. She drew in a gasp of genuine surprise.

"Five, Sono. And your Padre Lucena was not among

them." He grabbed her by the upper arm and squeezed so hard she had to stifle a yelp. "Do you know where Padre Lucena is?"

She went rigid with resentment. As her husband, he held the right of life and death over her. But it was the first time he had made her feel he might use it. "How should I, my lord? You know I have not laid eyes on him since our wedding."

He gave her a searching look. "I am not going to ask you, because if the answer is what I fear, I do not want to know. But if you have aided the padres to disobey the edict in any way, you will stop."

She kept her gaze as level as she could manage. "What could I have done for them?"

His eyes blazed. "This isn't a game, wife. If the Lord Regent concludes that the House of Matsuura has been derelict in our duty to ensure the padres boarded that ship, I do not have to tell you how severe the consequences could be. This could put our entire house at risk."

She quailed under his glare. "I understand, my lord."

He pushed her arm away, took a pace, then turned on her stiffly. "I have assured my father and my grandfather that my wife would not involve herself in any kind of disobedience to our Lord Regent. But if they find out differently, do not think your position will shield you. If you insist on these strange *Kirishitan* beliefs, we have agreed to accept that. But I cannot let you jeopardize our house."

So he suspected her, yet he'd been willing to lie for her—this time. But should it come up again, preserving his house would be more important than preserving his wife. A chill ran down her arms, and she pulled her jacket tighter. "I understand, my lord. *Arigato* for your faith in me."

Friday 17 August 1945

Covell-san appeared again at Akira's door that afternoon, as promised.

"Thanks for coming," he said. "I've been thinking about you."

She rewarded him with her charming smile. "Me? Why?"

He gestured toward his chair. "I've been thinking you must have good memories from growing up in my country, and I'd like to hear them."

She settled on it. "I do have many good memories."

"What brought your family there?"

Her face lit with a tinge of pride. "My father was a professor at Kanto Gakuin University." Did her voice catch a little? "We were missionaries. He taught Biblical studies."

He straightened with surprise. "The Christian Bible? There were students for that in Yokohama?"

She nodded.

"Please don't tell me your family is still in Japan." They'd forced all Americans who hadn't left into camps staffed with brutish guards, not gracious social workers like Covell-san. He'd heard nothing good about those places.

"I'll answer that, but only if you tell me what I can call you. Besides Sawamura-san." She fixed him with a clear gaze, and the goodness of her soul shone through it.

He could trust her, if he could trust anyone under heaven. He dropped his voice. "My name is Matsuura Akira."

"Thank you for your confidence in me. And if you can trust me..." Her brown eyes shifted to a spot above his shoulder. A deep sadness furrowed her face. "I would think you could trust the mother who raised you. No, my parents aren't in Japan. Their mission board moved them to the Philippines, and my father sent me back to the U.S. to college."

"They're in the Philippines, then? Will you see them again soon?"

She stared into her lap. When she raised her eyes to him, tears glittered on her lashes. "I will. But, Matsuura-san, it will only happen in paradise."

"Only in paradise? Why?"

She regarded him for a long moment and her chin took on a slight tremble. "The Japanese army killed my parents."

Akira froze inside. "What?"

She paused, her throat working. When she went on, her

words came in a flood. "My father was a vocal pacifist. Deeply opposed to the war in China. He felt Christians weren't doing enough to advocate for peace. His superiors in the mission felt he was endangering himself—and the mission."

"So they moved you to the Philippines, ah?"

The nod she gave him came with a sniffle. "My parents sent me home from Panay in 1940. And I will never see them again."

What could you say in the face of such a grievous loss? He fell back on the customary response. "I'm very sorry, Covell-san." It sounded hollow in his own ears.

She pulled a handkerchief from her purse. "It's still so hard to grasp that they're gone."

"But what happened to them?"

"When the Japanese took Panay, they ordered all Americans to report for internment, of course. But with my father's pre-war record, my parents were afraid to turn themselves in. They joined a group who went into hiding in the mountains. That much, my mother told me in her last letter."

She paused, dabbing at her eyes. She closed them briefly before going on. "I learned a few months ago that the Japanese army tracked them down, deep in the mountains. Beheaded them all as spies. My parents and fourteen others. Men, women, and children. Most of them were medical missionaries and teachers. I assure you none of them were spies."

He gaped at her, stunned. *Hai,* her parents had been fools to risk disobeying a direct order from the Japanese army. And fools to think they could hide. But such a devastating consequence!

Frank awe flooded his heart and put weight behind his words. "What are you doing here, Covell-san? Working for Japanese Americans. Trying to help me here. I don't understand. You should hate us."

"Let me tell you something, Matsuura-san." She balled her hands in her lap and bit her lip. "They say that, before they were executed, my parents asked for an hour to pray. I asked the Lord what they prayed, and He showed me."

"He showed you? Showed you what?"

"Do you know what *Iesu* said when they killed him on the cross? 'Father, forgive them, for they know not what they do.'"

"You think that's what they prayed?"

She nodded.

He blinked, still not sure he understood. "In Japan, we believe there is only one way to respond if someone murders your father. Revenge. It's a sacred duty."

She shook her head. "The Bible teaches that God is love, and He enables us to forgive. May I share something else the Bible teaches?"

The heartbreak behind those compassionate brown eyes. How could he say no? "Of course."

"There's a battle for the souls of men, Matsuura-san. A very old one. It goes back to the beginning. No matter how things may seem at any moment, there is a God in heaven who loves you. But—"

Nurse Carr poked her head in and caught Covell-san's eyes.

She responded with a little nod, then focused again on Akira. "There is also an enemy, and he will do anything to steal, kill, and destroy. He will tell you your life is worthless. That you have no future. That your family has no use for you. Those are all lies. You have to decide, Matsuura-san. You can follow God and trust Him to give your life worth, or you can believe the enemy's lies."

He shook his head. "Gods and demons." Hadn't he grown up in the Land of the Gods? Shrines and temples and priests and rituals and descendants of the Sun Goddess. What good had any of it done Japan?

He gave her a faint smile. "Frankly, Covell-san, you're the best evidence for any of this I've seen."

She dashed fresh tears from her cheeks. "Really?"

"*Hai.*"

"*Arigato.* That means a lot to me." She leaned toward him, her eyes wide and earnest. "Please let me leave you something. It's a little book in Japanese that talks more about what I just shared." She dug in her bag and held out a booklet to him. "Promise me you'll read it?"

The True Nature of God. It was blue with white lettering, a little larger than his hand. Cheaply produced with thin pages. Nothing about it appealed to him, but for her, he could try to digest it.

"I will." He set it carefully on the table beside his bed.

"And now you know why I want you to write that letter. There's nothing I can do to change my situation. But you can still change yours."

He studied a blank stretch of wall beyond the foot of his bed. Their faces rolled across it like a screen. Papa-san, laughing over a game of *Go* with his little brother Hiro-chan. Mama-san dressed for a wedding, striking in her formal black kimono. His sister Miyako-chan, blushing as she presented him with her parting gift, the *senninbari* she'd toiled over, thinking it would protect him.

Covell-san watched him, her eyes glinting with tears. He was fighting his own. "I appreciate your kindness. No, that's not enough to say. I'm overwhelmed by your goodness. But"—he straightened on his pillow and kept his voice firm—"my situation is different. As much as I yearn to see them, I must think of them first. I won't shame my parents with a letter. You said yesterday my brother and sister idolized me. They did. We will leave it that way."

Nineteenth Day of the Twelfth Month, Anno Domini 1587

On a winter day some weeks later, Hisanobu made a surprise appearance outside the women's wing. Iya gave Sono's face powder a quick touch-up, and she hurried out to him.

This was no pleasure outing. The glower on his face told her that.

Discovered? After all? Her mind flicked to a vignette of her handmaid, spinning in Sono's brown kimono, its hem hitched up so it would not show beneath Iya's own.

She dropped into a low bow, her pulse thundering so she could barely hear. "My lord." She rose and gave him her brightest smile, hoping to disguise the quaver in her voice. "What a pleasant surprise."

He eyed her, his expression anything but pleasant. "Walk with me."

Trouble. Her heart dropped in her chest.

He led her to the stand of mulberry trees where he had confronted her the day the Black Ship sailed. They were not alone this time. A *samurai* captain and one of his soldiers awaited them.

A third man knelt before them with his face to the ground. He wore the garb of a peasant—a rough-textured, simple jacket over narrow trousers of sturdy fabric. But he lacked the peasant's sun-darkened skin.

A merchant from Hirado town, probably. The poor man trembled with fear. Her own knees wobbled as well.

Hisanobu spun on her, his expression fierce. "Do you know this man?"

An anxious knot swelled in her belly. Would her kimono hide her quivering legs? "I do not know any men outside the castle, my lord." *I hardly know any within it.*

He jerked his chin at the captain, who gave the man a nudge with his foot. The merchant raised his eyes, wide with despair, and fixed them straight ahead of him.

Hisanobu glared down at the man, upper lip curving in disgust. "You are certain you do not recognize him?"

"No, my lord. Should I?"

Hisanobu nodded at the captain, who pulled a paper fan from his sleeve and handed it to his master.

"This merchant had this"—Hisanobu flicked the fan open with an imperious snap of his wrist—"on display in his shop. You may not know him, but you will not deny you know this."

The fan bore a pattern of wintry pine branches, beautifully painted and signed by a noted craftsman. The knot in her belly congealed to granite.

"*Hai,* my lord. It is one you graciously gave me."

"How did it come into this man's possession?"

A sense of unreality took hold. What explanation could she give that wouldn't get the poor man executed—along with the whole chain of men and women involved? And how could this have come to pass? The fans were not to be sold on Hirado. Everyone had agreed to that.

She rushed through an explanation, working hard to control the quaver in her voice. "Koteda-san's housemaid's young daughter has been sick with a fever to the point of death—such a tragic situation. Funds were needed for the girl's treatment. I gave the housemaid the fan as a gift." *Forgive me, Lord* Deusu, *for the half-truth.*

"You gave away a fan *I* commissioned for you? For a servant's daughter?" Did a glint of hurt hang behind the anger in his eyes? If so, it was gone in an instant, hidden behind a wall of suspicion. "In the future, if you want to make a gift to someone, you will seek my permission. I do not expect to learn of it when my mother's servant chances on it in a shop."

My mother's servant. Was this Lady Matsuura's doing?

She sank to her knees in humble supplication and lowered her face to the ground—the same posture as the townsman. "*Hai,* my lord." Gravel ground into her knees through the layers of silk. "Pray forgive me. The fault is mine. I adored the fan, but I wanted to do something to help. I will not transgress again."

Hisanobu's feet moved a few paces from her. Then pivoted back toward her. "Look at me, wife." It was a commanding snarl.

She lifted her gaze to his face. The cold expanse behind his eyes thrust icy spears into her chest.

He leaned toward her. "Remember this, Sono-chan." His voice reverberated with intensity. "I chose you. My father and I debated for hours concerning the wisdom of bringing a *Kirishitan* into our house. I knew 'twould not be easy, but you are here because"—he emphasized each individual syllable—"I chose you."

He straightened to his full height. "I expect to be rewarded for that choice. I expect gratitude. And obedience. And—it is not the first time I have said this, Sono—above all, I expect you to submit to the Lord Regent's edicts. Or you endanger our whole house."

He raised his voice in a ringing declaration. "Consider this your second warning." He swiveled to the *samurai.* "Execute him."

Sono gasped in horror. *For selling a fan?* "What? No—"

The captain slid his long sword from its scabbard, crouched into a fighting stance, and grasped the hilt firmly in both hands. He narrowed his eyes, focusing like a predator on the merchant's neck.

The man on the ground let out a low moan of despair. He hunched as if he hoped to fold up inside himself.

Outrage propelled her to her feet. "My lord! This poor man did nothing!"

"Silence!" Hisanobu thundered. His voice was a solid wall that drove her to her knees. It was all she could do not to press her hands to her ears and quail.

The sword arced up and back, then flashed through the air and cut a clean angle through the merchant's neck. The man's head spun from his torso and rolled onto the path, eyes frozen in his final expression of despair. His soulless stare seemed to fix on Sono's knees.

He was gone. Irreparably. As a result of a decision she had made.

Was she next?

The captain's facial expression did not change. He took a cloth from his sleeve, wiped his blade, and thrust it back into its scabbard.

She pushed to her feet and took a half step back, a surge of nausea making her weak. "Pardon me, my lord. But did he even know where the fan came from?"

Pray don't ask who else was involved. Horror filled her at the realization that she had already implicated Koteda-san.

Her husband's voice bore the same chill as his eyes. "This is not about a merchant, dear Sono. It is about you." He nudged the man's head so his vacant eyes met hers. "This man's life is forfeit as a lesson to you. And I will execute ten more like him, if I must, to make you understand. The House of Matsuura will not budge from compliance to the Lord Regent's edict."

Cold winter sunlight glistened off scarlet liquid seeping into the gravel at her feet. Vivid red streaks marred the silk of her skirt. The blood of a man who might not have understood the full import of what he perished for. He only knew it was something she did.

A chain twisted across the gravel where it had fallen from his neck. It attached to a simple iron cross that rested face-down on the blood-spattered gravel.

A magpie jeered knowingly at her from the branches above.

"Tell me you understand, wife," Hisanobu said.

For an instant, he wasn't her pirate prince, but a mask—a mocking mask disfigured with their war-deity Hachiman's beastly snarl. A violent chill ran through her.

She blinked and the mask faded. He was her husband again, but all she felt for him was raw disgust. A bitter taste took over her mouth.

Deusu's edicts before man's. She lifted her chin, defiance throbbing through her that she could not voice. "I understand, my lord. I understand perfectly."

He gave her a frigid smile. "Excellent. And always bear in mind—I could execute you just as easily."

She lifted her hands to her collar, slid her fingers under the silk, and pulled it away to expose her neck. "My life is in my lord's hands. But you can bear this in mind. If I disobey you, it is only to obey *Deusu.* Your quarrel is with Him."

Chapter Fourteen

THE INSTANT SONO REACHED THE HAVEN of her chamber, she tore off her sash and stripped off her kimono. She dropped the thing in a pile on the floor, bunching it so it landed with the worst of the bloody streaks inside. Violent tremors shook her. A sob tore from her throat as she sank to the mat in her under-kimono.

Iya came in on her heels. "What is it, my lady?" She knelt and reached for the kimono. "And what under heaven did you get on your skirt?"

"Don't touch that, Iya. Unless you mean to burn it."

Iya examined it. "It is blood, my lady. Are you well?" The kimono slipped from her hands. She swiveled on her knees to look at Sono, face full of questions.

His eyes. That head. "His stare, Iya-chan. He stared at me."

"Who, my lady? Hisanobu?"

"No. The poor, dead shopkeeper." She poured out the story in a bitter torrent of words. "I don't even know who the man was, yet his bones will come to an early grave because of me." She squeezed her hands into fists, then pressed her cheeks into them. "Because I helped the padres."

"I am so sorry, my lady. That is"—Iya paused, groping for a word—"monstrous."

"Of course my dear husband is no stranger to blood. All the warring—none of us has escaped the sight of a man dying, ah? I know he will lose no sleep over severing a head. But he admitted what it was about, Iya." Another sob welled up. "Controlling me. He executed that man to manage his wife. And"—she glared at the thin paper divider that separated her chamber from Lady Matsuura's and dropped her voice—"From the sound of it, his mother was the cause of it."

Iya spoke softly. "Is there anything I can do, my lady?"

"Please play something for me."

Iya lifted her *shamisen* to her lap and tuned it at full

volume. Sono took deep breaths, rocking a little on her knees, until Iya had transitioned into a soothing melody.

"My lady?" Iya whispered.

She shook off the image of the demon-like snarl on her husband's face and focused on her handmaid. "Nothing I can do will bring the poor man back. But I need to find out who he was. And if there may be some way I can help his family."

Iya gazed at her with enormous eyes. "Not another gift, my lady."

"Ah! Dear Lord, no. But pray see what you can find out. And we must make doubly sure none of my other things are lying around in shops here in my lord's domain. They need to be carried over to Kyushu for sale."

"I shall go today, my lady."

"And Iya-chan..." The horrible snarl was back to haunt her. "I hope Hisanobu does not ask for me any time soon. How can I act like nothing has changed?"

Lady Matsuura's grating voice pierced through the *shoji*. "May I come in, daughter?"

She exchanged a glance with Iya. If only there was a choice.

"Now, girls."

Iya slid the *shoji* open. Lady Matsuura stalked in. She scanned the room, eyes lingering on the bloodied kimono crumpled on the floor. A hint of a gloat flicked over her face.

Sono stood, outrage vibrating from every pore. She plucked the garment off the mat and thrust it at her honored mother. "Are you the cause of this?"

Lady Matsuura drew herself up and angled her chin. "No. *You* are the cause. A shopkeeper's life is of no consequence. If he was helping you violate the edict, he got what he deserved."

Sono's words came out pure vitriol. "I do not even know who he was. But now he is dead."

"But you don't deny giving the fan to raise alms for the padres." Sono's honored mother took a pace toward her and spoke in something akin to a growl. "My husband may have agreed to some ridiculous demands of your father's. But you will find they will not hold in my women's wing.

Continue to flout me with these vile foreign practices of yours, and I will see that you get what you deserve." She threw her parting words over the shoulder as she stalked from the chamber. "Like that wretched shopkeeper."

Sono had no will to see anyone. She huddled in a miserable ball on her futon. Iya put out word that she was ill—and she was sick, at heart. She couldn't sleep, had no desire to eat, and every time she closed her eyes a ghastly head rolled toward her feet.

Iya had trouble finding a believable reason to leave her side and make the trip to Hirado town. But she came up with an idea the next day. "I'll go after a concoction from the herbalist for you. He'll have something to aid your sleep."

Sono groaned. "Eyes. If I'm not seeing the shopkeeper's, I'm seeing hers. So triumphant we got caught. She couldn't have been happier if she devised it personally."

Devised it. The words rattled around her mind. "Iya, what if she did?"

"Her spy found it."

"But more than that. What if she actually made it happen?" Her thoughts spun until they formed a thick cord of certainty. "Did Koteda-san not assure you the fan would not go on sale in Hirado?"

"Absolutely, my lady."

"Then how could it have ended up in that shop? What if it never did, Iya-chan? Maybe someone who was supposed to take it off the island betrayed us. Maybe someone gave the fan to Lady Matsuura instead. We have only her word that it was ever in the poor man's shop."

Iya bit her lip. "So someone among the *Kirishitan* betrayed us."

"*Hai.* And perhaps Honored Mother was so determined to get at me that she sacrificed an innocent man to bring her point home. An innocent *Kirishitan*, of course."

She knelt on her *futon*, hugging her chest against a sudden chill. Lady Matsuura had been a vexation. Now she was a murderous threat.

And she was playing Sono's husband as glibly as Iya plucked her instrument's strings.

Sono spent that afternoon on her knees before her crucifix. By the time Iya returned, evening gloom had filled her chamber. Iya brought in a firebrand from the courtyard to light the paper lantern, then knelt without a word and tuned her *shamisen.*

Sono rose, stretched her stiff legs, and settled next to her handmaid. "What did you learn?"

Iya heaved a mournful sigh. "The merchant's name was Sato-san. He was well regarded, and everyone mourns him. He left three children and a pregnant wife. Koteda-san says they are doing all they can to console her. She has gone back to her father's house."

Iya played a few more melancholy measures, then spoke without glancing at Sono. "The father is antagonistic to our faith. Sato-san's oldest child is a daughter. I have seen her at mass. Very pretty, and nearing the age for marriage. She would fetch a good price with the Portuguese traders. Everyone is worried he might sell her off. He gambles."

Outrage sent blood throbbing through her veins. "No! I have to do something for them."

"Except"—Iya hit a sour note—"the captain of the guard at the gate stopped me and examined my sleeves. He said it was on Lady Matsuura's orders."

She gaped at her handmaid, stricken. "What? Everyone's sleeves? Or just yours?"

"Only mine, as far as I saw." She turned a harrowed face to Sono. "It seems we must abandon our smuggling venture, my lady."

Sono couldn't sleep. If she dozed for even a moment, she jerked awake horrified and sweaty. She would grope at her nightclothes in panic before relief swept over her at finding them dry after all. Not soaked in blood.

Her sick day turned into two and then three, while two questions circled endlessly through her mind. How did poor Sato-san get that fan? And what would become of his daughter?

Sunday morning came, and she insisted Iya leave her to go to mass. "Pray bring me back a good word from *Deusu*. I need one."

Iya returned in the early afternoon. She draped her cloak over the clothing rack at the back of the chamber and picked up her *shamisen*. She knelt next to Sono. "Everyone sends their warmest regards. Our dear friend Koteda-san says to tell you she knows well how upset you must be about what passed with Sato-san. You are not alone. It was a scandal. But it was not your fault."

Sono's stomach roiled. "I came to Hirado hoping to help people, not get them executed for no reason." She glared at the floor mat. "Except that it did not occur for no reason. My honored mother targeted that poor man, and my husband permitted her to do it. I cannot get that out of my mind. Or my dreams."

She pawed at her cotton kimono to banish the delusion that hot blood defiled it. "She may have circled poor Sato-san in a hoop like he was a barrel, but Hisanobu should have investigated things before..." She stopped, not wanting to put words to the travesty she had witnessed.

"Everyone suspects Lady Matsuura had it placed in his shop." Iya's fingers slowed. "And Koteda-san said something else."

"What?"

"This is all the more reason Hirado needs your son. You must ask *Deusu* for the grace to forgive Hisanobu and get on with married life."

Sono groaned in disgust. "I doubt he even realizes he needs forgiveness. The mighty Matsuura rule a dozen islands. Why should he not do exactly as he pleases?"

"*Iesu* commands us to forgive. Did He make the other person's attitude a condition?"

She huffed. "How can I feel anything other than disgust for people who would do something like this?"

"But it is hard to get pregnant by a man you do not see, ah?"

"Iya-chan, I cannot even bear the idea of bringing a child into this house. If I bear boys, they might grow up like their father, swaggering around and executing people for nothing. And if I bear girls, what life do they look forward to?" She arched an eyebrow and surveyed the chamber where they spent most of their days.

Fresh rage flared at the sight of the pine boughs on Papa-san's screen. The painted landscape mocked her now. How she would love to smell an actual pine forest! But Papa-san, the first man in the whole world she had thought she could trust, had committed her to this.

"But if you refuse Hisanobu," Iya said softly, "you give him every justification to take someone else to bed. He will produce a Matsuura heir, one way or the other. You know he will. If that heir comes from your womb, did they not agree you can raise him as a *Kirishitan*? You at least have that."

"Do I?" Desolation made her breath catch. Tears welled up, and it was all she could do to choke them back. "Papa-san sent me here thinking I could do something for the future of Hirado, but they stifle me at every turn. Why should I believe they will keep any promise they made him?" She walked up to the screen and fingered a fleck of gold-paint accent. "I no longer know why I'm here." She scrubbed her fingertip over the paint as if she could rub it out.

Iya put down her instrument, came up beside Sono and lifted her hand gently from the surface. She whispered in her ear. "Pray do not lose hope, my lady. You may not know why you are here, but *Deusu* does. Remember, when people betray us, that is all the more reason to look to the Lord. He never will."

Sono's sigh came from her core. "I know you're right." She sank onto her futon and buried her face in her hands. "I will have to make myself play wife again. I owe it to *Deusu*, no matter how I feel."

"I know this is not easy," Iya said. "But remember what you told Hisanobu about who his quarrel is with."

Sono trailed a fingertip down her neck. "I told him his quarrel is with *Deusu.*"

"*Hai.* And as for your part, why not let it rest there?"

That afternoon, Rin came by to tell her Hisanobu was outside the women's wing. She eyed the sturdy painted trunk on Papa-san's screen.

Had he known the lion's den he was sending her into? That question too, could rest with the Lord.

Her husband needed an heir. And her brother needed security in his castle. And while she had never laid eyes on more than a handful of them, Hirado's *Kirishitan* needed justice. For all those good ends, by *Deusu's* good grace, Hirado's heir had to be birthed from her womb. And for all those good ends, she could be resolute as the ancient tree on Papa-san's screen.

She slung her bow over her shoulder and went out to her husband, using a fixed smile to hide the dead wood inside her.

Tuesday 21 August 1945

Col. Simmons's "ticket" got Akira a berth on a hospital car bearing prisoner transfers from a medical center in Denver. Orderlies hoisted his stretcher onto a top berth. He felt every jolt, but at least they'd put him against a window. They gave him a pill, and he sank into a drugged sleep. Two days and a night passed while unearthly vistas of scrubby trees and rising heat waves and many-armed cacti taller than men rolled by his window.

An orderly handed him yet another pill cup. Some time later, a man jostled him awake. His window revealed a star-studded night sky. Ninety more minutes and he found himself lying at last on a firm bed between crisp white sheets, relieved to be done with all the bumping and lurching. His new home was Mitchell Convalescent Hospital. Almost against the California–Mexico border, they told him.

The next morning, an orderly brought in his breakfast tray and handed him a typewritten envelope. "You have a letter."

First mail he'd received in three and a half years. Akira opened it to find a typed letter featuring American President Lines' logo—a wide-winged eagle—on its top-right corner.

Sub-Lieutenant Sawamura,

Col. Simmons called me about you. His recommendation carries tremendous weight with me. However, I have researched it, and I can't make anything happen here in the U.S. The Army insists you will have to return to Japan. There's no allowance for P.O.W.s to remain here. But I hope you will come see us when you reach Yokohama. Ask for Harvey Glassman. He'll be expecting you.

Best of luck to you.

Sincerely,

Robert G. Taylor

Vice President, Los Angeles Operations

He slammed his head against the pillow with a grimace. He would board a repatriation ship after all.

Chapter Fifteen

WEEKS PASSED. SONO'S NIGHTMARES FADED AND her life resumed its previous rhythm. At least, outwardly. As the plum trees began their cycle of riotous bloom, something seemed to be blooming inside her. Her red day had never come so late.

The bright joy of a hundred sunrises wove through every moment of her days. But not a small tinge of anxiety colored the yarn. Some babies did not survive the birthing— and some women.

She spent her first hour each morning on her knees before the crucifix in her alcove, imploring *Deusu* to bring the heir Hirado needed. An heir who would uphold justice and cement a lasting peace.

And to bring the baby safely. Because whatever this baby was, its life was bound up with hers. Her heart swelled with love for it.

When she confessed to her husband that her red day was late, he laughed and covered her face with kisses. "What wonderful, fabulous, spectacular tidings! So we will have our little lord next autumn." He caught her against him, held her suspended in the air for a moment, then let her slip down his chest until her sandals met the ground.

A month earlier she would have stiffened at the feel of him. But now she could almost relax against him. She was learning to trust the Lord to deal with those who persecuted His children.

She did not join her husband's mirth. "I am delighted to make you so happy, my lord. My red day has never tarried so long. But pray let us keep this our secret. It is too soon to be sure." Wise words of caution, which she should remember to heed herself.

"You are pregnant. I know it. I made a special offering at the family shrine yesterday." He knelt and caressed her belly. "Are you listening in there? You are to be a big, strong, clever boy. You will have armies to lead and a domain to run."

She stroked the smooth, shaved skin in front of his topknot, cringing inside with anxiety. *So many expectations.*

The next morning, her prayers were all the more earnest.

There are few secrets in a castle and even fewer in a mansion with rice-paper walls. Although Sono had sworn Hisanobu to secrecy, within a week it seemed everyone was giving her good wishes for a healthy pregnancy. *Graças a Deusu*, her red day stayed absent.

Hisanobu was beside himself with excitement. He lavished her with attention. He gave her activities endless scrutiny—they were to be calming. And her diet—foods with cold *yin*, not warm *yang*.

She marveled over it to Iya. "He slices off a head in front of me and then has the delicacy to worry that my food might be spicy." But she dutifully ate her white gourd and lotus seeds, and mourned over her bow languishing unstrung in her alcove.

The weather warmed, and delicate buds formed on the cherry trees in the mansion's garden. The women's wing hummed with anticipation. The cherry-blossom festival would arrive soon.

Akiko could hardly contain her excitement. "The blossoms are so beautiful at Saikyo-ji temple! You know where that is, yes? It is the one on the ridge with the tall pagoda. Lady Matsuura's brother is the abbot there. He invites us every year. The priests put out hundreds of lanterns, so we can enjoy the blossoms into the night."

Sono gave a wistful sigh. "I would love to see that." *I would love to see anything outside these walls.*

When she returned to her chamber, she whispered the tidings to Iya. "I am looking forward to this so much. You remember our lovely cherry-blossom parties at Sanjo Castle. But the temple. I'm not so sure about going there. What do you think?"

"I think it will be very awkward if you do not join your honored father and mother when they invite you to a family outing."

"'Twould also be torment to miss it." She laughed, feeling more carefree than she had since the incident with Sato-san. "Or to miss any outing, for that matter."

"Koteda-san and my friends in town plan to walk up to the temple to view the blossoms after church this week."

"I guess it can't be so bad, then." She shook off a feeling of foreboding. "I am going to enjoy the cherry blossoms, not to make offerings, ah?"

Lady Matsuura scheduled the outing for the next fair afternoon, and it proved an elaborate enterprise. The ladies of the women's wing flitted about like so many jewel-toned dragonflies, putting on their brightest spring-themed kimonos, painting their lips, and powdering their faces.

At mid-afternoon's eight bells, Sono and the ladies joined a large entourage assembled inside the main gate. Many of the leading *samurai* were there. Horses snuffed and snorted. Porters bustled in and out, loading carts with sake casks and large lacquered trunks full of treats.

A line of palanquins—elaborate coffin-shaped boxes suspended on long, sturdy carrying poles—awaited the high-born ladies. This was the first time Sono had seen hers since the day she arrived in Hirado and it had borne her from the dock to the castle. One glance at the thing brought back the seasick feeling from that last experience.

She eyed it with a mixture of excitement and resentment. *Never thought I would be happy to see this stuffy little box again.* But she settled into its cushioned interior, Iya closed her in, and a pair of bearers lifted the conveyance to their shoulders. A delicious thrill ran through her as the gates swung open and she peered through a viewing lattice at a luscious slice of green hillside.

The view broadened as they crossed the drawbridge, which stretched over a precipitous gulch. "We are actually outside those cursed castle walls." She pronounced the words in joyful wonder.

Iya, walking alongside the palanquin to keep her company, broke into a carefree grin. "And it is the best day of the year, save Christmas and Easter."

Friday 17 September 1948
Habana de Cuba

The midday subtropical heat was passing into a sultry evening, and a welcome sea breeze rustled through palm fronds swaying high above Akira's head. Beside him, Stan Beaudoin's steps slowed. The third mate of American President Lines' *S.S. President Monroe* gestured toward the taxis queued across the street from the pier, and the line of well-heeled tourists—mostly American—lined up to board them. "What do you think, Sully? Head over to the Tropicana?"

Chief Mate Oscar Sullivan shot a sharp glance at Beaudoin and grimaced. "No thanks. I lost enough moolah last time. Besides, the girls are friendlier in Old Town."

Beaudoin snickered. "Friendly! They're all for sale. Remember that Negro girl who took such a shine to Matsuura here?"

"I'm sure he does." Sully gave Akira a leer. "But we'll keep to Old Havana tonight. Our Jap amigo would stick out at the Tropicana."

Akira stifled a jolt of resentment. "Thank you, sir." He usually got left behind on watch, and they made no secret as to why. Judging by the very white crowd queued for the taxis, he would stand out at the Tropicana.

But they'd left someone else on watch that night, and Akira was out to have a good time. Cuba was famous for hot music, cool rum drinks, and beautiful women. He aimed to drown himself in all three. For one night, he would find enough rum to still the ceaseless, scolding voice in his brain that told him he had no right to live.

A vision of that Cuban girl Beaudoin had mentioned played through his mind like a record skipping. Brazen grin. Swaying hips. Flawless skin the color of coffee with cream.

Beaudoin couldn't leave the topic, either. "Never understood why you didn't go upstairs with her. Guess you weren't man enough to handle her."

Akira sighed. "The truth is—it hit me she was about the same age as my little sister." As she'd gyrated in front of him, a vivid image had arisen in his mind. His own Japan flooded with Americans like Beaudoin, eager to take advantage of the desperation of the beautiful "native" girls.

Beaudoin made a mock gagging noise. "That would kill a moment."

Sully threw Akira a startled look. "You never told me you have a sister."

I don't think you ever asked. "I haven't seen her since she was fourteen."

Beaudoin put on an exaggerated leer. "I'll bet she's turning some heads now."

"Shut up, Beaudoin." Sully gaped at Akira. "You didn't see her when you went there after the war?"

Akira shook his head. "I wasn't there long." He'd seen Japan once since the war. Eighteen months earlier, a troop transport had deposited him on Japanese shores, along with three thousand other P.O.W.s. He spent hours in long lines of vacant-eyed men, waiting for processing at the repatriation center at Uraga. All of them drowning in their silent misery.

"You didn't see your family at all?" Sully said.

"I...wasn't able to find them." He hadn't tried. He had become Matsuura again by that time, hoping to frustrate any effort Yoshigumi might make to track him down. But as for his parents, his sister, his little brother—they all had burdens enough without weighing them down with their one-time number-one son and his all-consuming shame.

Thanks to Col. Simmons, unlike the thousands of men lined up with him, Akira was fortunate enough to hope he had options. As soon as the bureaucrats at the repatriation center released him, he'd boarded the first train to Yokohama and found the American President Lines office. And he soon had fresh reason to be grateful to the colonel. Simmons's recommendation bore weight even in Yokohoma, it turned out. Akira had a berth as junior third mate on an ocean liner within the week.

"Too bad." Sully said. "Bet that bothers you."

"It does. A lot." He longed for home and family. It was an ongoing battle to push his thoughts away from them, and everything he'd loved about his life before the war. But he'd made the decision to stay away, and he knew to the depths of his spirit he was doing the right thing. It was what they would want.

Tonight he'd made a pact with himself to forget all that.

Old Havana was the place to forget things. The city assailed him with a kaleidoscope of sound and color. Pulsing music poured onto the sidewalks from the doorways of countless bars and restaurants, along with the mouth-watering scents of frying oil, garlic, onion, and spices. Vendors hovered over carts piled to overflowing with fruits and vegetables and anything else a man could imagine. Men swaggered around like there was nothing to be anxious for in the whole world.

And the women! Oh, the women. A young one in a low-cut dress and the kind of strappy heels showgirls wore stepped in front of them. Her rouged lips curved in an inviting smile. "It's happy hour in the Club de los Bohemios. Half off drinks, *amigos*."

That turned out to be the first in a succession of bars. They forged a path deeper into Old Havana, as if they were infantry with one more hill to take. Two more bars, three more rum drinks, and a few colorful blocks later, they came to a broad, angled boulevard. A row of restaurants boasted signs in Chinese characters.

Beaudoin elbowed Akira. "Look there. A Chink joint."

"I hear there's a big Chinatown." Sully said. "I've never been."

They passed a Chinese restaurant with a colorful terrace. Red and gold paper lanterns dangled from a tiled roof overhead. Beaudoin grinned and tipped his head at the oriental-style gate to the patio. "Why not?"

Why not was the phrase of the evening. They walked in and seated themselves.

Before they'd even ordered, two young women came in

from the street. The taller one was striking. Shapely, with almond eyes and hair falling down her back in a long braid, like a Chinese girl. But the thick braid, the unruly tendrils escaping it, and her sensual full lips made her mixed blood.

Akira was quick to shift his eyes to the other girl. She was slender, her skin fairer than most of the Cuban faces he'd seen. Glossy black curls brushed her shoulders. This one appeared to be full Chinese. And pretty, in a less showy way. Much more to his liking.

Her almond eyes met his and she smiled. *"Hola,"* she said. And then, *"Nǐ hǎo."* His pulse drummed as she walked up to him, a seductive sway to her slim hips. She stood so close that he imagined he could feel her warmth. Citrus and jasmine from her perfume mixed with a faint odor of sweat from walking the sweltering sidewalks.

"Is it okay?" She slipped into the chair beside him. The other girl hovered between the Americans.

The Chinese girl fumbled in her purse, pulled out a pack of cigarettes, and lit one. There was a subtle tremble to her fingers. As her arm moved, Akira noticed something else. A pair of faint pinkish circles marred the soft flesh inside her elbow. They were exactly the size of her cigarette's glowing end.

He stared at her arm, and slow-burning heat surged through him. Someone had ground a lit cigarette into her tender skin. Was that how they kept her walking the streets?

His stomach soured. He'd thought he could put down enough rum to get as callous as Beaudoin. But this girl with the burn marks was someone's daughter. Probably someone's sister.

He hadn't had enough rum not to see those burns.

Beaudoin leaned back in his chair with a broad grin. "You ladies are in luck. Matsuura-san here"—he delivered this with exaggerated deference—"is going to buy your drinks."

Their waiter, a middle-aged Chinese man, walked up. He glared at Akira. "Matsuura-san. You Japanese?"

"Yes."

The girl sat with narrowed eyes fixed on him too.

The waiter's shoulders tensed. "We don't serve Japs. Not since Japs murdered my uncle in Nanjing. Your friends can stay, but you leave now."

Akira should have been insulted. But the marks on the girl's arm had filled his mouth with a bitter taste instead. He was glad for a reason to leave. He rose, his blood warming with indignation that he'd played any part in this scene.

He thought about telling the girl goodbye, but she kept her head turned the opposite direction. It seemed she didn't serve Japanese either.

He laid a five on the table in front of her. "Find a better boss." He bobbed his head at Sully. "I'll take a taxi back to *Monroe*. Enjoy your beer."

Sully gave him a resigned nod. "Fine. We'll catch up with you there."

He strode to the gate. Neither of the Americans rose from their seats. But the Chinese waiter followed him, herding him toward the street with the air of a menacing dog.

"Do you know who put cigarette burns on her arm?"

The man growled. "Stay out of our business, Jap. Go back to your island and leave ours alone."

It was tempting to let a fist fly in the waiter's smug face. But was a girl who'd given him the snub worth a "drunk and disorderly"? *Monroe* sailed the next day. It could cost him his job.

And it might do her more harm than good. He unclenched his fist, stalked out of the place, and found a taxi.

The driver whistled along with the Mambo music pouring from his radio. Pulsating rhythms spilled from brightly lit clubs on every block. The sidewalks thronged with people, all in couples or groups. In the entire city, only Akira was alone.

Go back to your island, Jap.

Those words bore the ring of bitter truth. It *was* time to go back to his island. In Japan, they'd called foreigners *gaijin*—outside persons. And they'd done it with a subtle sneer. Who was the outside person now?

He'd lived alone, a man without a country, for six and a half years. He couldn't keep going this way. A Japanese man without other Japanese was nothing.

And if the voices in his mind were right? If he was merely a burden to his family? Japan would be a fine place to end his life. Accomplish what he'd tried to do on *Nashville*.

Perhaps that was all that was left for him.

Fifth Day of the Third Month, Anno Domini 1588

After a dizzying climb in her palanquin through a magnificent green landscape, Sono waited with the other Matsuura ladies at the base of the stone steps that led to the temple gatehouse. Mounds of delicate pink blossoms massed above the white plaster of the temple wall. She filled her lungs with the bold scent of pine and gazed around, awestruck at the splendor. Her heart sang until she was sure everyone would hear its music. What a treat the evening was going to be!

The temple bells rang out the six strokes of dusk, and conch horns took up their strident blare. The majestic gates swung open, and Sono filed through with the crowd—the Matsuura household, their *samurai,* and their wives and children who had walked up from Hirado town. The plaster walls rang with merry laughter.

A world of soft pink exploded before her. Row upon row of lovely trees laden with mounds of delicate blossoms lined their path on either side. A light breeze stirred the treetops, making waves through a sea of color.

She gasped at the beauty. A pang speared her chest at all she'd been missing, locked away in her gilded cage.

The gravel path turned, opening onto a different vista. Beneath the brilliant pink boughs, two rows of gray granite figures faced each other across a mossy stone path. Eerie images of monk-men with elongated ears and simple robes—dozens and dozens of them. Each wore a bright red cap and a triangle of red fabric draped around its neck. Some stood, while others sat in lotus position. Fallen petals clung to their bald heads and nestled in the grooves between their crossed granite ankles. Petals stood in drifts against their bases like a thin layer of pink snow.

The line continued unbroken until their little caps were mere dots in the distance. The plaintive tones of distant flutes filtered through the trees. The skin on her arms prickled. She pulled her jacket tighter and shifted her steps to the precise center of the gravel, as far from the dozens of vacant stone stares as she could walk.

Tatsuko's gait slowed as she fixed worshipful eyes on a stony face. Sono caught up with the older concubine. "Tatsuko-san, what are they?" She kept her voice low, an irrational fear filling her that the monk-men's long ears were listening.

Tatsuko fixed wide, astonished eyes on her. "You do not know Jizo *Bosatsu?*"

"No. I'm sorry."

Tatsuko gently straightened the monk-man's red drape. "What, then, of *Kirishitan* children who perish? Who protects them in the spirit world?"

Sono hugged her jacket around her midsection. A child meeting an early death was not a vision she welcomed. "We believe there is only one protector of the faithful, young and old. *Iesu*, the Great Shepherd of all. And it is a great comfort to know that He said little children can always come to Him. Why do all the statues wear red?"

"For protection from demons. That's what Jizo does." The concubine brushed petals off the mossy pedestal at the statue's feet. "They say demons torment the souls of little children in the afterlife. Jizo keeps the dear ones safe in his long sleeves." She clamped her mouth shut and walked on, eyes moving between the granite faces.

Sono followed her, astounded. That was as many words as she had heard Tatsuko utter at one time.

They came to a wide grassy area facing the temple's main hall, with its tiled roofs and broad eaves. The priests had furnished the hall's raised front porch with luxurious cushions and low tables for Lord Matsuura's dining comfort. He mounted the stairs, elbow-to-elbow with his wife's brother, the temple abbot.

Facing the hall and the porch, a festive altar stood under a pavilion. The five-story pagoda Sono had seen all the way from Hirado Castle towered to her left. Her foreboding deepened. The House of Matsuura would dine on display, directly before the ritual altar to the rice god.

Hisanobu awaited her at the base of the steps. "Here you are. Excellent. We will sit in state with my father for the feast."

Panic surged through her. "For the prayer of invocation?"

"*Hai.*" He turned and walked toward his father.

She hesitated, but what could she do? She would have to go up with him. But she could enjoy the evening among them without participating in any prayers to their deities, couldn't she? She took her place on a cushion at his side with growing unease. She searched the faces on the lawn for Koteda-san's but didn't see her.

Bowing monks circulated, offering cups of sake. Sono waved hers away. "*Arigato*, but I prefer plum wine."

Hisanobu stared at her, startled. He took a cup of sake and held it out to her. "We have to start with the sake. We must thank the rice god for visiting the cherry trees."

The giant *taiko* drum struck up its soul-stirring rhythm, each resonant boom jarring something in her chest. She bit her lower lip and whispered in his ear. "My lord, I cannot drink. I came to view the blossoms, not to make offerings under them."

He glanced at Lady Matsuura. "My mother will be furious. Can you at least hold a cup? Maybe she will not notice that you do not sip."

She nodded, not trusting herself to speak, and took the cup from his hand. She raised her eyes to find Lady Matsuura's hawk-like gaze fixed on her.

The sun dipped into the treetops. The flute music swelled. Bright banners fluttered. A colorful procession of priests wended through the courtyard, coaxing haunting melodies from flutes and hand drums. The abbot paced majestically to the altar. He dropped into a low bow, then turned toward his guests of honor and began to chant.

Everyone rose and lifted their cups.

Hisanobu's voice sounded low in her ear. "Mama-san is watching. Is it so hard to take a sip?"

Mama-san is watching. Always watching. Like a cat with gleaming eyes and switching tail, ready to pounce at Sono's slightest motion out of conformance.

Perhaps it had been a mistake to come. Perhaps she had let her longing to leave the castle and experience the woods overcome the "still, small voice" of her Lord.

The little cup grew heavy in her fingers.

My dear Lord Deusu, *I pray You will pardon me. I never want to offend You, even in the smallest thing.*

While everyone around her sipped, she dropped her eyes and knelt to set her cup on the floorboards at her feet.

Hisanobu quaffed his, glaring at her over its lip. "You defied my mother. You defied me. You know there has to be a consequence."

She dropped into her deepest bow, heart dropping faster. "I am so sorry, my lord. But I would rather disappoint you than my Lord *Deusu.*"

He pivoted away from her. "Mama-san, Lady Sono has taken ill. Shall we have them bring up her palanquin?" The ice in his tone would have snuffed glowing embers.

Lady Matsuura stood as rigid as the ancient granite Buddha before the pagoda. "*Hai.* Rin will summon the bearers."

Hisanobu rounded on Sono, his lips pressed into a line. "It seems it was a mistake for you to leave the castle."

Tears burned in her eyes. "It seems it was."

Chapter Sixteen

SONO'S PALANQUIN AWAITED HER BEFORE THE temple gate, with a guard detail of ten *samurai* and three blazing torches to see her home. "You did the right thing, my lady," Iya murmured as she helped her in.

"*Hai.* But it still hurts."

"Obedience that hurts may be the best kind."

Her bearers shouldered her palanquin. Forest sounds took over as they started down the rough road. She determined to press every sight, sound, and smell into her memory, siphoning any drops of pleasure she could still glean from the evening. These impressions would have to last.

It was a mistake for you to leave the castle. Her husband's words rankled. She must make an effort to enjoy this journey home. When would they let her escape the castle again?

The air swelled with a chorus of cricket and bullfrog songs. An owl hooted in the distance. A three-quarter moon floated, entangled in the upper branches. Little of its light reached the ground, so they journeyed in an island of flickering torchlight.

Sono put her lips close to the lattice and spoke in a low voice to Iya. "Did you see Tatsuko-san when we spoke of Jizo *Bosatsu*? A bit strange, wasn't she?"

Iya smothered a giggle behind her fingers. "I think she had more to say about that Jizo than I have heard her say about anything."

"*Hai*, but it was more than that. Something about those statues affected her deeply." A chill prickled across her shoulders. "I found those rows and rows of stone eyes unnerving."

They had descended well into the forest when she first heard it—a hoarse howl that rose to a wild shriek, then suddenly broke off. She clutched the sides of her palanquin and stared through the lattice at Iya, her heart slamming against the cage of her chest. "What was that?"

Iya's wide eyes reflected her question back at her.

The *samurai* captain, Watanabe, turned and answered her in a reassuring tone. "It is a fox, my lady." He chuckled. "Their cries are unearthly."

"Ah! I have never heard one so close." She huddled into her jacket. "It is horrible. It sounds almost human."

Iya's voice quavered. "It sounds as if someone is being murdered."

Watanabe gave her a crisp nod. "It does, my lady. But do not be alarmed. The men and I are accustomed to the forest noises. If anything is amiss, we will know at once."

A second cry echoed from the other side of the path. Sono sat bolt upright and pressed a hand to her chest. This time, Watanabe's eyes reflected a glint of amusement. "That is its mate, my lady. This time of year, they travel in pairs."

From that point, the foxes' hideous cries kept them company until the road flattened out. A pinpoint of flickering light gleamed on the hillside ahead. The castle walls.

My prison. The sight of them brought a deep gloom into her heart. The first prick of light was soon joined by another. Dread pressed on her chest. She laid her head against the back wall of the palanquin, closed her eyes, and let the sounds of the forest fill her ears and the fragrance of the pines fill her lungs.

A deep yearning seized her to break free and run, elusive as those foxes. But an escape was hopeless— weighed down by all her silks, with ten armed men in pursuit. She gave her handmaid a rueful look. "Next time you come out here, pour the feeling in a cup and bring it back to me."

A new sound filtered into the palanquin. A faint wail that trailed off. Not as piercing as the foxes' cries. Had she imagined it? She held her breath and bent all her attention to her ears.

The cry came again. Weaker this time. Sono tapped on the palanquin door. "Iya-chan, did you hear that?"

"What, my lady?"

"Pray ask the men to stop."

Iya relayed the request.

Capt. Watanabe's voice boomed from in front of the

palanquin. "Halt!" His face appeared in her viewing lattice next to Iya's. "Is something amiss, my lady?"

"I heard something."

"The foxes—"

"No, captain. This was different."

He gave her a patronizing smile, but the party fell silent, and the bearers lowered the palanquin to the ground. Watanabe stood still, his face attentive, for a long moment.

He caught her eyes through the lattice and shook his head. "My lady, if you will permit us to go on—"

Iya put her fingers over her lips. The sound echoed again—a mere whimper this time. "There is something."

Sono pressed her face against the lattice. "It sounds like a baby. Why would someone have a baby out here at this time of night?"

Watanabe kept his eyes straight forward.

Iya shot Sono a pained stare. "You really do not know, my lady?"

"No."

She dropped her eyes and twined her fingers through the lattice. "This happens when a baby is unwanted, my lady. They leave it...out."

Sono recoiled. "What? Out here?" She wrapped both arms around her belly.

Watanabe turned to face her. "Many peasants struggle to feed the children they have, my lady. Or perhaps the child is not well. And Lord Jizo is so highly honored at Saikyo-ji. If a mother leaves a baby here, surely he will care for the child's spirit once it goes back."

"Goes back? Goes back where, ah?" Sono thrust the door to her palanquin open. "That baby's spirit is attached to a living body. I am charging you to keep it that way." She stepped onto the path and glared at him.

The captain took a stride back, letting out a subtle huff of exasperation. "My lady, pray return to your palanquin. If the parents chose to thin the child from their garden—"

A hideous howl echoed from the hillside behind them.

"A fox! Captain, you heard that. They travel in pairs—is

that not what you said? Its mate could be anywhere. Would you really leave that baby to them?"

Iya bowed to the captain. "Respectfully, captain, if the parents do not want the child, the *Kirishitan* will care for it. They are happy to accommodate foundlings at the Jesuit's House of Mercy."

Sono's sense of urgency choked her. Could he not see they lacked the time to exchange gracious words? She gave her foot a petulant stomp. "What are we standing here for? Those foxes! Start a search at once, captain."

He jutted his jaw and issued a resigned sigh. "As you wish, my lady. Men, get to it!"

Sono hitched up her skirts. She and Iya scouted the path along with the men, listening for any faint sounds.

Thin the child from their garden. A baby was a living, breathing miracle full of life only *Deusu* could give. How could anyone equate it to a weed?

One of the bearers cried out. "I think I hear something." Sono reached for Iya's wrist and squeezed it.

A torchbearer brandished his light. Two men pushed into the underbrush. Sono clutched at Iya's hand, and the women hovered at the torchbearer's elbow, taking care not to block the light.

I pray to thee, Lord Iesu—*spare this baby.*

"Here!" One of the men shouted from the thicket.

Sono's heart jumped. "Did you find a baby?"

"*Hai.*" The man emerged from the thicket carrying a baby-sized basket.

"Let us see." Sono and Iya pressed in on either side of him.

He pushed the crude basket at Iya. A bundle of coarse red fabric lay inside, with a tiny face at one end. The poor child let out a weak whimper as Iya lifted it out and cradled it to her chest. "Ah! *Graças a Deusu!*"

Sono whispered a fervent prayer of gratitude and brushed a clump of pine needles from the ragged blanket. Rough wool grated against her fingers. "The baby is so quiet. Is it well?" She gently stroked the tiny cheek. She fished a miniature hand from the sleeve of the baby's kimono and rubbed it with a tentative finger. "Poor thing! So small."

The infant didn't respond to the torchlight or to her caress.

"They have wet nurses at the House of Mercy." Iya's voice trembled.

Tears blurred Sono's vision. "This little one needs to go there without delay."

The infant let out another feeble whimper.

A *samurai* stepped forward and bowed to his captain. "Captain, I know the House of Mercy. May I have your permission to take the baby there?" Relief rushed through Sono's breast at the glint of torchlight off the corner of a silver cross dangling on the man's chest.

Watanabe-san gave him a curt nod. "Handle the matter and report back as soon as you can."

Iya gazed into the baby's face. "Shall I go with him, my lady?"

Sono started to say *hai*, but thought better of it. "He will move faster without you."

And Hisanobu wouldn't approve of your leaving me with these men. She had disappointed him enough for one night. That thought brought a pang of bitter anguish.

Iya gently handed the baby-bundle to the *samurai*. The man arranged his jacket over the baby while Iya closed Sono back in her box, like an elegant doll meant for display. One that might not be brought out for another year.

Something dropped from the *samurai*'s jacket onto the dirt path. Iya knelt to pick it up.

Sono leaned against the viewing lattice. "What is it?"

Iya closed her hand around it. "Nothing consequential."

Once they got underway, Iya opened her hand to show Sono what nestled in her palm. "The baby's mother must have left it."

A crudely carved wooden amulet. Flickering torchlight showed a rough depiction of a monk with oddly babyish features. A small piece of red cloth wrapped its neck, and it wore a red painted cap.

"Jizo," Sono whispered, and blinked back tears.

Iya peered at her through the lattice, thinly veiled rage

making her features sharp. "I suppose this bit of carved wood was meant to persuade the deity to care for the baby. Since—"

"Since father and mother chose not to." Sono's voice shook with indignation.

"I would like to go to town and check on the baby early tomorrow morning, if it pleases you, my lady."

"'Twould please me very much, Iya-chan." Angry tears stung her eyes again. She dashed them away and wrapped both arms around her midsection, giving her own unborn infant a hug. "How could a mother just abandon her little one? Carry it out here and..." *Leave it.* She could not bring the words to her lips.

Watanabe responded. "This world sometimes forces hard choices, my lady. It seems she believed the child would be happier in the spirit realm."

Tuesday 14 December 1948
Port of San Francisco

Three years and four months after the day Akira heard the emperor's broadcast—the *second* day tragedy had smashed a hole through his life—he stood on the forecastle of American President Lines' newly overhauled passenger liner, *S.S. General Meigs.* He drank in the tang of sea air.

In minutes, they'd sail for Honolulu. He tightened his fists around the steel handrail in front of him until the pressure burned through his forearms. He'd spent more than six years unable to conceive that he'd ever return home. Now he'd make Yokohama in two weeks.

Anxiety squeezed his chest, thinking about the green slopes of Japan, but he was done running. He'd wasted enough time sailing everywhere in the world except where the people he loved might need him. This time he intended to stay. At least long enough to find out whether anyone cared to know what had become of a former prisoner.

Off the ship's port side, the mighty steel span of the San Francisco Bay Bridge arched across the steel-gray sky. Excited passengers thronged the pier below him and filed up the gangplank. Some thirteen hundred paying passengers would sail with them. If only he shared their enthusiasm to reach Japan.

These weren't luxury travelers. The people who booked passage on *Meigs* were of the class chiefly interested in getting from point A to point B. And for that, *Meigs* was an excellent choice. She was fast. It would take her just two weeks to reach Yokohama, even with a two-night stopover in Honolulu.

One of the able-bodied seamen he was tasked with supervising leaned over the handrail. He chuckled. "There's something going on down there you don't see every day. Not on this proud vessel."

"What's that, Petersen?" A second sailor, Barclay, moved beside him.

Petersen pointed toward the pier. "Reporters braving the drizzle."

"Reporters? Someone famous booked passage on *Meigs*? This I've got to see."

Petersen clearly enjoyed his air of mystery. "We're playing host to a *bona fide* war hero."

"Who?"

"A Reverend Delham. A Doolittle Raider, no less."

A Doolittle Raider. The words were a truncheon in Akira's gut. It had been six-and-a-half years since the morning he'd watched that raid launch. He'd seen the first group of bombers lift from a carrier's deck, their bellies full of death.

That morning had blown his life forever off course. Good thing he was expert at hiding his feelings—what the men around him called a poker face.

Petersen was still talking. "One of Doolittle's lost crews. Captured after the raid. Barely survived his forty months of Jap hospitality, I hear."

Curiosity burned in Akira's chest. An interest he wouldn't betray to the seamen. The scorn in which this American crew held him was already apparent. He'd heard the men whisper their surprise that a Jap had been made an officer. He'd seen sudden, guilty silences as he rounded corners. Eyes that drifted to his scars.

He may not have made many friends on *Monroe*, but they'd stopped short of open scorn. This crew was different.

He huffed out air in a bitter little snort. Anything he faced on *Meigs* was nothing compared to what lay ahead in Japan. A man never outlived shame like his. Still, in his own way, he was doing his best to copy Covell-san's example of forgiveness.

A grinning crowd thronged the deck below him. The stream of passengers moving toward the gangplank eddied and broke around stationary clusters of spectators, standing like rocks in the current.

One group of two dozen men and women held up a long banner on poles. The banner read *Godspeed Reverend Delham*. That whole group had come out to see the Doolittle Raider depart. This was what it meant to be a war hero. Amazing to think that in America, a *horyo* could become one.

Petersen craned for a better view. "He piloted one of those birds, you know. He could make a decent living flying for an airline here. But I guess he got religion."

"And he spent the war as a P.O.W.? Why would he ever go back there?"

Akira stood rooted to the deck. Farther down the pier, several reporters clustered around a well-built man of medium height. Wavy dark hair receded from a broad forehead that disappeared into the brim of his hat. He had an arm draped around a striking woman with copper-colored hair in a tailored suit. They had two children with them—a small girl with bright red curls and a toddler boy.

Flashbulbs popped. So this was the Doolittle airman— the former *horyo*. In Japan, such a man would be worse than nothing.

Akira turned from the railing, shaking his head. He didn't count on any such reception in Japan. Nor did he deserve it. He'd failed twice that day, early in the war. He'd failed to stop Doolittle's bombers, and he'd failed to die trying.

Once *Meigs* got safely underway, he walked briskly aft and mounted several ladders to the bridge level. He paused for a moment, relishing the glint of water over the railings, before he pushed through the steel door into the wheelhouse where Chief Mate Healy presided.

Brass gleamed from fittings and instruments. From the helm. From the gyro compass's big metal helmet. From the corners of the chronometer's mahogany box. A dozen rubber cones topped voicepipes that stood ready to carry commands throughout the ship. All of it well engineered, efficient—and beautiful.

Healy gave him a sharp nod. "Everything shipshape, Jap-man?"

"Aye, sir." Akira winced inside. *Che! Wish he'd stop that.*

Healy was a continual, irritating reminder that forgiving your enemies was harder than Covell-san had made it sound. The chief mate had come up with his little nickname during the pre-voyage briefings. "Like Batman," he'd explained. "I don't mean nothing by it." But the malicious glint in his eyes made it clear those words were a lie.

Healy gave him a smug nod. "Good. You're dismissed until your watch."

"Thank you, sir." Akira left the wheelhouse and started down the ladder to his cabin.

It would be helpful to get some rest before his watch began. But that was going to be difficult. Forty-five hundred nautical miles of featureless ocean lay before them. *Meigs* would roughly retrace the route the carrier *Hornet* and her task force had taken before unleashing the raid that had captured him.

It wasn't the first time this had occurred to him, but as they steamed toward the vast gray waters beyond the Golden Gate, *Hornet*'s ghost emerged from the fog of his memory. And as he swung his cabin door open, Nagai's screams echoed for at least the thousandth time down the passageways of his mind.

Chapter Seventeen

Fifth Day of the Third Month, Anno Domini 1588

WATANABE SAW SONO AND IYA BACK to a silent women's wing, where they retreated to Sono's chamber.

Sono watched her handmaid put water on for tea, her insides twisting like a cord. "I keep thinking about that baby. Its poor cold little fingers! And"—she bit her lip— "something else we saw tonight, too."

As they'd left the castle, her palanquin had swayed past a corner of the mighty stone foundation wall. Several dozen men knelt in the shadow of a towering bamboo scaffold, their faces to the dust. A crew of peasant conscripts.

"You saw the workcrew, Iya-chan?"

Iya nodded as she loosened a knot on Sono's *obi.* "I saw them. It must be miserable work."

The peasants' burdens had rested beside them—heavy bundles of fist-sized stones for shoring up the wall. Ankles and elbows jutted from their rough clothing, dirt-streaked and bony. Many hands bore the spots and wrinkles of age.

Their *samurai* overseer had bowed as well, his twin swords swinging against his lustrous silk uniform. If any of the aged ones faltered in the heat, Sono knew how quickly that *katana* could bite.

She shuddered as it flashed through her mind again— the sword severing Sato's head from his body. The familiar sick feeling churned inside her. She slipped her scent packet from her kimono and breathed in its fragrance of sandalwood, jasmine, and citrus.

Her anguish of heart flowed out in her words. "*Hai.* Conscripts slave day after day on our strong walls, Iya-chan, while we sleep in silk and dine on delicacies within. Who feeds their babies while they labor for us, ah?" She pushed her gilded teabowl away. "If a fox had killed that baby, its death would have been on my head."

"That is not true, my lady." But Iya's retort lacked conviction. She busied herself with the teakettle.

Sono hadn't finished. "Does it not seem strange? I *must* bear, and when I do, my children will become lords like their father, or ladies like their mother. Why? Because we are the House of Matsuura. We inherited the right to rule twenty-seven generations ago from the sun goddess herself, so I'm told. Meanwhile that mother has to discard her baby like so much rubbish. If *Deusu* created them both, why is my baby worth more than hers?"

She turned the teabowl to study its golden mulberry-leaf design. "Look at our emblem. The mulberry. Such a useful thing. It lives to serve, furnishing leaves to the silkworm so it can spin. But what is the House of Matsuura? What are any of the great houses, ah? We are not mulberries. We are not even silkworms. We're leeches."

Iya took Sono's bowl and poured steaming water into it. "But someone must lead the people. And those castle walls protect them too."

"*Hai*, in time of war. But protect them from whom, ah? From other great houses that want to steal what we have." Sono stared into the pale green liquid in her bowl. "Iya-chan?"

"*Hai*."

"When you go to town tomorrow, perhaps you could go the long way. See if you hear any more abandoned babies. I can manage without you for an extra hour. Let us do what we can to prevent more babies going to the foxes."

It was late the next morning when Sono's handmaid's voice echoed in the courtyard. Sono dropped her chopsticks on her plate of lotus root and hurried to the *shoji* to greet her. "Ah! Iya-chan. What did you learn in town?"

Iya grinned with relief. "He made it through the night, my lady."

"He?" Sono nearly hopped up and down, she was so ecstatic. "A boy, ah? *Graças a Deusu*."

"*Hai*, my lady. The wet nurse had just fed him when I arrived. But he is very weak. His path will not be easy."

Outrage swelled through her again. "Do they ever find out who abandons these infants?"

"They do not inquire, my lady They assume only hunger would drive a mother to such an act."

There was a hint of hesitation to her words. She was holding something back. "What is it that you are not telling me, ah?"

Iya busied herself with folding her traveling cloak.

She rested her hand on Iya's upper arm. "What?"

Iya heaved a deep sigh. "The padres have learned nothing about the baby, but..."

"But?"

"I suppose you will find out in time, so perhaps it is best you hear it from me. As soon as I told her, Koteda-san knew. She said Sato-san's wife went into labor the day before yesterday."

The shopkeeper. His dead eyes stared accusingly at her again. She had to steady herself against a shelf. "What? I thought you said they were *Kirishitan.*"

"*Hai,* my lady. But once Sato-san's wife moved back in with her father, the *Kirishitan* in Hirado town saw less and less of her."

"No!" Horror wrapped dark tentacles around her brain. "So if not for me—"

"This is not your fault, my lady. She chose this. The House of Mercy was there for her. No matter what kind of pressure her father put on her, she did not have to sacrifice her baby boy."

"This is awful beyond saying." A wave of nausea roiled her belly. Anguish pushed her voice shrill. "I owe that child a huge debt, Iya-chan."

Saturday 25 December 1948

S.S. General Meigs cruised west-northwest toward Yokohama. Akira stood his twice-daily watches from eight to twelve, relieving Healy morning and evening. The air grew gradually cooler, the winds brisker, and each day a few minutes shorter than the last.

On the Americans' Christmas holiday, Akira went from a traditional turkey dinner straight to the monotony of his watch. It was his seventh Christmas, and he still didn't understand why Americans celebrated a son of God who never ruled a nation or founded a dynasty. Hirohito's claim to the title Son of Heaven would have seemed much stronger—until the day a few months after the war ended, when the god-like emperor Akira had sacrificed so much to defend announced he had never been divine.

So much for anyone's ability to be certain of anything in this supposed realm of gods and spirits.

Healy stood on the command wing outside the wheelhouse, his sextant to his eye. "Merry Christmas, sir," Akira said. "I'm reporting a little early to relieve you if you'd like."

Healy broke into a grin. "Well, thanks, Jap-man." His usual little joke was fresh sandpaper grating on Akira's nerves. "That's a mighty thoughtful gift. I'm off to my turkey, then." Healy walked into the wheelhouse, picked up a grease pencil, and marked a dot to record their position on the plastic sheet that protected the nav chart.

Seven hundred thirty nautical miles east-southeast of the coast of Japan.

Tension drained from Akira's shoulders the instant the door clanged shut behind the chief mate. Miller had relieved Jensen on the helm. Seaman Chalmers stood lookout. For the next four hours, it would be the three of them on the bridge.

Akira took his place at the navigation desk. Two nights earlier, he'd made a tiny tick mark on the chart. Easy to miss if you weren't looking for it, especially in the red night lighting. He rested his forefinger on the mark.

Healy's latest pencil dot was almost on top of it.

On the huge surface of that vast ocean, their course had brought him here. Would they cross the exact point where *Nitto Maru* rested? Who could know, ah? But that night *Meigs* would bring him the closest he was ever likely to get to the spot where *Nitto Maru* went down.

An eerie shiver ran through him. His old friend Nagai lay at rest somewhere in the quiet reaches beneath him. Away from striving and defeat and shame. All the weary business of the world.

And Akira was weary to the core.

He drifted from the wheelhouse with its little islands of lurid red light and stood on the wing. A fine drizzle dusted his face, but the western horizon was clear. He raised the sextant to his eye, then absently lowered it again. The dark surface of the water called to him. He leaned on the railing and watched the ocean, drawn in by the restless dance of the silver-tipped waves.

Somewhere over there, off the starboard bow. That would have been the spot where the smoldering corpse of *Nitto Maru* went down, dragging Nagai and Onishi and the rest to the bottom with her.

Good men. Brave men. They'd been honored to die gloriously in the emperor's service. An honor he'd spent every day of the six years and seven months since yearning to share.

Akira's watch ended at midnight, and he headed down the ladder to his cabin. The events of the past four years had fueled a healthy skepticism concerning the existence of any kind of spirit world, but there were moments when it felt right to honor the dead. This was one of them.

He kept incense and a bowl for such times. He set up the bowl and placed an incense stick in it. When he'd finished honoring his crew's sacrifice, he'd keep his usual ritual of lighting another stick for the peace of Covell-san's parents.

He brought out two drinking glasses and set one in front of the incense holder. He had no sake, so he cracked open a bottle of the strange Hawaiian liquor he'd picked up in port. He poured a finger into the glass for Nagai then three fingers into his own.

He lit a cigarette and left it to burn down in an ashtray. Its smoke would help mask the aroma of his incense. He put a match to the end of the stick, and a thin spiral of smoke bore the fragrance of burnt citrus into the air. Papa-san's words whispered through his head: *You remember the lesson of the cherry blossom, ah?*

Tears burned behind his eyes. Papa-san's voice was so clear—the clearest he'd heard it. And he remembered the lesson like it was emblazoned on his brain. His men—Nagai, Onishi, and the rest—had lived out that lesson. He had not.

His father's words took him back to the ancient grounds of Saikyo-ji on Hirado. To a moss-covered altar of piled stone honoring his great ancestor, Matsuura Shigenobu. The same aroma of burnt-citrus incense had floated in the heavy tropical air.

Remember, my sons. To fear death is to die.

Akira had expected his wartime experience to mark him—for greatness. In life and even in death. And in the afterlife, if there was such a thing. Not for perpetual humiliation. Not for grinding shame.

None of those feelings were new. But when he'd been half a planet away, distance had dulled the edge enough to make the pain bearable. Now it was a knife slitting his heart.

It's not too late to make it right. Hadn't fate and weather directed their route farther north than they'd expected? Perhaps there was a reason. He'd mouthed hundreds—no, thousands—of prayers to the deities, at his mother's elbow and his father's. Could this moment be their answer?

Whose answer? The deities? Where had that idea even come from? He gave his head a brisk shake, as if a toss of his skull could hurl the nonsense away. He sighed away the tendrils of the past. *Hai,* he'd once harbored superstitions about Japan's supposed eight million deities, but he'd banished them since the war.

Still...another chance like this wasn't likely to come along. One final opportunity to redeem himself.

The thought came through with sudden clarity. *You belong there. In the depths below, alongside Nagai.*

Why was he getting mystical again?

But setting aside the sudden way the thought had inserted itself in his brain, his gut firmed at the truth of it. This was a one-time chance to rejoin his crew. To erase the past six years as if they had never been. To douse his shame forever in the spot where it was meant to end.

He gave little credence now to the spirit world he'd learned of on his mother's lap. But the smoke of spent incense clung to his nostrils, and the pulleys on the winch outside his porthole rattled. He had an unearthly sense that *someone* was there, calling him out to the railing. It was a call he was meant to obey.

He slipped on his coat like some kind of automaton and made his way to the strip of deck outside his cabin. He hung over the railing in the darkness.

The black depths five decks below called to him. It was a magnetic sort of pull, and his legs responded. They moved him down the ladders in something of a daze, toward the main deck where he could lean out over the water.

His shoes rang on the steel steps in a way that sounded more decisive than he felt. A few more paces, and his torment could be over. He could complete the job at which he'd failed six years earlier.

Each footprint he planted on the deck's slick planking left a momentary dint on the moist surface. In just a minute or two, the drizzle would erase any evidence he'd passed. And if he slipped into the waves, the ripple would disappear even faster. His shame and emptiness erased as if he'd never existed.

Lifeboats dangled above his head. They clustered around the ship's stern, spawning plenty of hidden crannies. He could blend into the shadows, unconcerned about anyone thwarting his purposes. *No* gaijin *interference this time.*

He came up level with the first of the boats, and his steps slowed.

Crashing waves. Driving wind. Howling bombs. Pounding pulse. He was back to the night of the attack, with Nagai at his side and Onishi and the others in a steel crypt beneath his feet.

A blinding explosion. A roaring blast. All of it gone. Those good men and *Nitto Maru* lay at rest on the bottom miles below. And that night, he had an invitation to join them.

The ocean shone dark beyond the rails. It would be cold, the plunge into the water. But ultimately, quiet. He'd struggle on the way down, but the fight would be over soon enough.

He'd worked so hard to kill himself on *Nashville* and failed. This was going to be easy. He just needed to give himself a quick push over the railing.

The wind had picked up. It tugged at the lifeboat.

Winches whined and waves smashed against the hull. The quiet in the depths would be bliss. The persistent buzzing voice in his head that told him he had no right to rejoin his family, no right to live, would be forever silent.

What did he think he was doing with this return voyage? They were better off without him. He didn't belong in Japan—or anywhere else. Better to bury himself in the sea he loved.

The wind had torn a jagged gash in the clouds at the horizon. A misshapen white moon hung in the break. Its reflection glimmered in shifting shards across the tips of the waves. They formed vague shapes, then merged into two bright oval patches. Broken gleams of light danced in uneven patterns around them.

I know you. Those were the eyes and silver scales of the giant helmet of the Dragon King Under the Sea, weren't they?

He blinked, hard. The eyes still glimmered below the waves. A distant, hungry roar rose in his ears. A chill all but convulsed him.

I've always known you. How many times had he burned incense beneath the Dragon King's painted image? The one that captured the mighty king in all the majesty of the moment when he'd gifted Hachiman, the Matsuura family deity, with control of the tides.

He couldn't tear his eyes away. An unearthly dread flooded him, turning his knees soft as bean curd.

Dark coils writhed in the waters below the moonlit eyes. Awe swelled through Akira, and a new voice—a commanding voice—boomed through every corner of his mind.

Come.

He froze. Did the Dragon King deign to speak to *him?* This was an honor beyond anything he'd imagined. He would have no need of a human priest to enshrine his spirit. He only needed to answer this call.

He grasped the top railing with both hands. He pulled in a deeper breath, then huffed it out. Why fill his lungs? It would only prolong his struggle when he answered the undeniable call. He placed his left foot on the lower rung.

Chapter Eighteen

SONO HAD CONCEIVED AROUND THE NEW year, the child inside her forming with the plum blossoms. The baby would arrive in the tenth month, as the tea bushes started to bloom and the sweet persimmons first appeared on the table.

What did it mean when her labor pains started in the eighth month?

Iya made her lie down. She rolled on her side, fixed her gaze on *Iesu*'s figure on her crucifix, and whispered urgent prayers.

A skilled midwife came at once from Hirado town. Lady Matsuura, Iya, Rin, and the older concubine, Tatsuko, all gathered with worried faces in Sono's chamber.

The grandmotherly midwife laid her head on Sono's belly to listen to the baby and probed her belly with her hand. "The baby has not yet dropped. It may be nothing to worry about. Some women's wombs like to practice. But"— she peered at Lady Matsuura—"you should set up your daughter's birthing chamber. And I prescribe complete rest until the baby comes. I also recommend she take the oyster-shell tea with peony and licorice."

Lady Matsuura pursed her lips. "*Hai. Arigato.*" She shot a glare at Sono. "This is what comes of it."

Sono's spine turned rigid, her shoulders grinding into the futon. "Pardon me, Honored Mother, but this is what comes of what?"

"You know exactly what I mean." She glared pointedly at Sono's belly. "Your stubborn and selfish refusal of the purification rituals that protect us all. It is no surprise my grandchild is in danger." She turned to the midwife, her features narrowing into a scowl. "Maybe the eighth month is not too late to restore some propriety. Rin, you will see to the priest right away."

"*Hai*, my lady." Rin bowed and ushered the midwife out.

Sono pressed her lips together. Tensions in the women's wing had escalated through the summer. She had taken a strong stance against the fifth-month ritual Lady Matsuura tried to insist on. And she'd learned her lesson from the debacle of the cherry blossom festival. She declined to join the family for the mid-summer Festival of the Dead.

Papa-san strode into her thoughts, with a cross on his chest and a *katana* at his side. He had fought a decades-long battle to free them all from the Buddhist and Shinto priests—and their tyranny of empty rituals.

She closed her eyes and mustered all her strength. It wasn't much. "Honored Mother, I pledge to rest and drink the tea. I pray you to reconsider the priest and the *sutras*. My baby and I do not need them."

Lady Matsuura shook her head firmly. "This is my grandchild. We will have a priest here. And we will have the *sutras* at all hours."

"Honored Mother—"

"This impacts the entire House of Matsuura, silly girl. It's not your decision." Lady Matsuura swept out.

Tatsuko started to follow Lady Matsuura, but she lingered with one hand on the *shoji*. She turned back and knelt beside Sono's futon. An awkward moment passed while she sat silent, with wide, fearful eyes. Then she spoke in a rush. "You will not hear the *sutras*, Lady Sono. They will not let the priest in here. He will have to chant them from outside."

Sono veiled her surprise. Tatsuko seldom said anything, and she'd never heard her utter a word that might cross Lady Matsuura. "*Arigato*, Tatsuko-san. That is a mercy."

Tatsuko adjusted her sheets with a fleeting smile. "Let us keep your dear baby warm." She sent a furtive glance after Lady Matsuura and lowered her voice to a whisper. "You understand why this is vital for her, do you not?"

"She does take an active interest in everything that passes among us." That was artful understatement. And admirable self-restraint.

Tatsuko gave her a second rare smile, with a wry edge this time. "*Hai.* And she has one thing in her bosom—

ensuring her own grandson inherits. Not one of Akiko's boys."

Sono narrowed her eyes. "*Arigato*, Tatsuko-san. I appreciate your insight. Even if the faithful words of a true friend are not always pleasant to the ears."

So Lady Matsuura hoped for a grandson she could control. *As she controls her son.*

Sono followed her treatment regimen to the letter, and it seemed to have a good effect. The cramping eased, then disappeared. Lying on her futon all day was tedious, but Iya kept her company. And Akiko took pity on her, visiting her and helping keep her entertained. Akiko's boys brought her paintings and sang her songs.

Hisanobu proved sweetly solicitous. He dined with her most evenings, bringing bush clover branches thick with delicate purple blossoms for Iya to arrange in a vase, and playing endless rounds of the poem-card game. But her bow lay sad and unused on a shelf.

He sat with her one evening after dinner, hand on her belly as the baby kicked. She made a face, and he grinned. "That was a strong one, ah? Boys kick more. I'm convinced of it."

She laughed. "Perhaps you are right, my lord. Our child seems unstoppable, even floating in calming tea."

"As he should." He reached for the box of poem cards.

She had a different plan. "Not tonight, my lord. I would like to ask a favor. Iya-chan brought me a letter from the brothers at church with some words from the Holy Bible. Perhaps you could write them on a scroll for my alcove? Your characters are so bold and strong."

He ran his hand along her belly. "How can I refuse you anything? Let's see your text."

She handed him the letter Iya had brought her. *Lord Iesu, I pray these truths find their mark.* She was supposed to be on Hirado to plant the seed for a *Kirishitan* dynasty. Why bide her time for the next generation? Why should her *Kirishitan* heir not follow on the heels of a *Kirishitan* lord?

He called for his writing materials. "Which part of the letter?" She pointed it out and he read out loud. "We are children of God. And if children, then heirs; heirs of God and joint heirs with *Kirisuto*, if indeed we share in His sufferings..." He gave her a sharp look. "Are you suffering?"

"*Hai*, my lord. I do not wish to tire you with complaints, but think of it. I cannot even walk in the garden. I can only peer through the *shoji* and long for a glimpse of leaves on the hillsides."

He gazed through the open partition. "I suppose that would be hard. Even for a woman."

"A woman's feelings aren't so different from a man's. Only her opportunities are different."

He stroked her cheek. "Once our new son has passed his first month, I promise we will go outside more."

"You are gracious, but"—she laid her hand on top of his—"you are not always available."

"Then I know you will pine for me when I am away." He gave her hand back and moved to the low writing table a servant had brought in. He positioned her scroll at the top and weighted it down. "You want all of this? It is a lot to fit."

"Every word is precious to me. This scripture says even women can be joint heirs with *Kirisuto*." She paused, biting her lip. "Not every woman survives childbirth, as you know."

He studied her. "Are you afraid?"

"A little." She forced a smile. "You face worse in battle. Are you afraid?"

"A little, sometimes. But the way of the *samurai* is found in death, so I calm my mind. To fear death is to die." He examined his brush, then arched a brow at her. "Perhaps we should put that on your wall."

She squeezed her eyes shut and silently asked *Deusu* for grace. "Perhaps a woman has more reason to fear death than a man. How would you feel if they told you you were destined for torment in Blood Lake when your spirit departs this life, my lord? Because you were born a girl. But a *Kirishitan* woman has an invitation into paradise. Just like a *Kirishitan* man."

He squared his jaw. "The wheel of life eventually returns everyone here. A woman's spirit can achieve better karma for the next life."

"*Hai.* And I would be better off reborn as a man, ah? Even a peasant. As a man I would at least avoid the torture of Blood Lake."

"You're not going to Blood Lake, darling. I will not permit it."

She broke into an exasperated laugh. "My lord is powerful, but you do not command life and death."

"No. But you'll have the best physicians and the best priests. You will not perish bearing my son."

"I will perish in time." She locked eyes with him. "When you are fearful, how do you calm your mind?"

"I remind myself that fear isn't real. Fear is a state of mind, and my mind is not my master. I am master of my mind." He pulled out an ink stick and ground it against his inkstone. "Smooth, mindful brush strokes. The accurate flight of an arrow. A tea ceremony completed without a motion wasted. All are means to practice subduing the mind."

She propped herself on one elbow and searched his face. "What I wouldn't give to see you forsake the wheel of life, darling, and come to paradise with me."

He stared at her, the warmth gone from his eyes. "You wish to set me against my father and grandfather? And generations of our ancestors? Or my Lord Regent?" He set the ink stick down. "Can you imagine my mother? She would be livid."

"But is serving the true God not worth the price?" *Of making your mother livid...*

"You serve what you call truth, Sono-chan. I will serve mine. My father will formally name his successor soon. The House of Matsuura is a Buddhist house. And I will not give its Buddhist lord any cause to pass me over."

"Pray forgive me, my lord." She stifled the bitter edge that tried to creep into her voice. "But it seems to me that the advancement of your house *is* your truth."

Saturday 26 December 1948

The command echoed again through Akira's mind. *Come to me.* The black surface of the waves rippled. His father's face materialized before him, bearing an expression of sublime pride.

That glow of pride on Papa-san's features sent warm bliss radiating through Akira's breast. He planted his right foot on the second railing and hoisted himself up.

"Whoa!" Feet pounded on the deck behind him. "Stop right there!"

He glanced over his shoulder, startled. A *gaijin*, running at him. The shock of it froze him in place for an instant before his foot found the next rung. It was just long enough for the man to lunge and get a fist wrapped around his collar.

A determined arm tugged at him. "What are you doing?" The man wrenched at Akira's jacket, yanking him off balance. He twisted toward the railing, but the stranger had a solid grip. Akira's feet thudded onto the deck.

A swell shifted, and the monster writhed and vanished. The stranger jerked him back two paces. Glaring light from a bulkhead fixture blasted his eyes. Irritation seethed through every pore. *Again!*

He looked the *gaijin* over. Medium height, for an American. Wavy dark hair. Slight receding hairline above a tall forehead. "Reverend Delham?" Where did he come from?

"You know me?" The man gaped at him, seeming as startled as Akira felt.

The irony struck with such force that he almost broke into a tortured laugh. Of all the times and places to meet Rev. David Delham, Doolittle Raider.

He made a desperate move to wrench himself from the *gaijin's* grasp. Delham braced his knees and clung to him with the determination of a Tosa fighting dog.

Akira seethed. *Why do these gaijin always get in the way?*

Delham clawed the fabric of Akira's jacket firmly into both fists. "I'm not letting go." His voice was steady but insistent. "You're not getting over that railing. I don't know what's happening in your life, but please trust me. There is help."

Help? Akira didn't need help. All he needed was the freedom to answer the call from the deep.

His laugh came then, a sharp-toned bark. Here they were, steaming across the North Pacific, within ten miles of the point where their paths had crossed six and a half years earlier. That encounter had cost Akira everything. And now Delham thought he could help.

If he was determined enough, this man couldn't hold him back. But it was no good now. He wouldn't slip quietly under the waves—that possibility had been shattered. If he jumped, the man would raise an alarm, and someone would be compelled to fish him out. It would only layer fresh dishonor on his crushing shame.

Delham's penetrating eyes were fixed on his. "You need to know there's a God who loves you. So much He sent me out here."

Delham's talk of gods jolted him. Rippling eyes swam through his mind, sending an eerie chill down his bones. "A *god* sent you." It came out a scoff.

Delham gave a little shrug, mouth ajar with his own astonishment. "I bet that sounds strange to you, but it's true. The call was clear as daylight. I woke straight from a dream, and I knew I was supposed to come out here and pray. I came, and here you are."

Akira kept his silence. It was stranger than this *gaijin* realized.

Delham eyed him. "I've stopped believing in coincidences. I've seen God's hand at work too often. This meeting, this night. My showing up in time to stop you. None of it happened by chance. You are *not* supposed to kill yourself."

"No?" Arrogant American, knowing all about what was destined for Akira's life.

"No." Delham gave Akira a brash grin that set him further on edge. "You're Japanese, I take it? I don't think we've met."

"No." Although they had shared a patch of ocean once, and an experience that had marked them both forever. "I'm

Junior Third Mate Matsuura."

"All right, then, Matsuura-san. God has a plan and a purpose for you. You have to believe that."

If I humor him for a while, maybe he'll leave me in peace. And I can finish what I started.

He needed to ratchet down the tension and make some pretense at conversation. "Do you have any idea where we are, Reverend Delham?"

Confusion clouded Delham's face. "Somewhere on the North Pacific, nearing Japan."

"Do you know that right now, this night, is the closest we will get to the point where your B-25 took off from an aircraft carrier in April 1942?"

Delham's eyes widened in surprise. "I'll be darned." He scanned the featureless ocean. "How close are we?"

Akira tried to sound like this was a matter of casual interest. "I don't know exactly. A little south of the place, perhaps."

"No kidding. You seem to know a lot about it."

Akira thought of saying several things at once. What came out was, "I hear you spent most of the war in a cell, ah? Why would you go back there?"

"Because God reached out to me when I was half dead in that wretched cell. Gave me new life. I couldn't have gotten any lower, Matsuura-san. Lonely. Desperate. Hungry. I hated everyone—myself most of all. There wasn't a day I didn't think about taking my own life. There probably wasn't an hour. But God wasn't through with me. And He isn't through with you."

Delham relaxed his grip a little. "I'm speaking from personal experience. There's hope, even in the darkest places. Now, how about we go inside? Find some coffee or something."

The undulating waves beyond the railing beckoned. But it seemed Akira had little choice. He would need to spend an hour or so to mollify this American.

He let the man guide him toward the nearest door.

"That's it. Good man." Delham used a coaxing-a-reluctant-animal voice. He kept a grip on Akira's collar as he swung the hatch open.

Akira twisted for one more glimpse of the water before he passed inside.

Delham clanged the hatch shut behind them, then ushered him through a door into a carpeted corridor. The wind that had whipped the waves outside was a murmur now.

The American whooshed out a sigh. "Please, Matsuura-san. Tell me how I can help you."

Akira stiffened. *If you want to help, get out of my way.* "Can you turn back time?"

"If I could, what would change?" A moment passed while Delham regarded him, eyes soft with what looked like compassion. He went on, his voice muted. "I can't do that. But I can give you assurance that God has a purpose for your life." Delham pointed him toward the dining room. "Can we talk more in there?"

Akira shook his head. "I'm not supposed to be in this part of the ship."

Delham shot him a surprised glance. "Why not?"

"Deck officers aren't encouraged to mingle with passengers. I can't be seen here. I'll go back to my cabin." He pulled his arm from Delham's grip.

The American lunged for him and got a fresh hold on his forearm. "You try to take off, sir, and you'll be amazed at how much commotion I can raise. Let me make your options clear. You can give me a chance to help you. Or we'll head up to the wheelhouse and let the watch officer handle it. I'm guessing *Meigs*'s brass won't want to risk having to account for a man overboard. I'm sure the cost and delay for a vessel this size would be significant. I bet they'd be well motivated to prevent that."

Akira bristled. A moment passed as he stared into Delham's eyes, which had gone steely with determination. The American's fingers pressed grooves into his forearm.

Delham was a fool if he thought he could make Akira go anywhere he didn't choose to go. But he wouldn't be free to do what was required, in peace, until he got rid of the man. And the last thing he needed was for Healy to find out about this. He'd be confined to quarters for the rest of the voyage, with any chance of getting over the ship's railing gone.

He had a better chance of slipping away from the reverend. He let the tension in his muscles go. "The library? We should be alone there."

Chapter Nineteen

Fifteenth Day of the Ninth Month, Anno Domini 1588

LATER THAT NIGHT, A SHARP PAIN woke Sono. Hisanobu lay beside her. She jostled his shoulder. "Sweetheart, I am very sorry to trouble you. But I must summon Iya-chan to make my tea."

He grunted, rubbed the sleep from his eyes, and caressed her belly. "What's wrong? Are you not well?"

She breathed through another cramp. *Fear is a state of mind.* She forced calm into her voice. "I have a little pain now. It should pass. The tea always helps."

She reached for the bell at her elbow and jangled it loudly. A moment passed before sandals shuffled along the warrior's run and a tousle haired Iya hurried in. "What is it, my lady?"

"I am having a little pain."

"Pray do not worry. I will make your tea at once." But she bit her lip, her delicate features crinkling in concern.

Hisanobu stood and pulled on his trousers. "Women's affairs...I leave you to manage it."

Sleep eluded Sono that night. By morning it was clear something was wrong—something that neither tea nor Iya's soft strains on the *shamisen* could fix. The pains grew in strength until they were much worse than the cramps that came with her red days.

Iya hovered over her. "Perhaps it is time to tell Lady Matsuura, my lady?"

A whole month early. Lord, not yet. Not yet. Tears moistened Sono's lower lashes as the tightness started in her lower abdomen again. "*Hai.* It is time."

Iya left, and another wave of pain took Sono. It dissipated as Lady Matsuura rushed in, Rin and Iya in her wake. She knelt next to Sono's futon and peered into her face. "How fast are the pains coming?"

"She has had four since the dawn bells, my lady," Iya said.

"You are laboring!" Lady Matsuura stood, hauled back her arm, and struck Iya across the face. Sono's handmaiden reeled into the artfully arranged shelves, gasping, and lifted her hand to her cheek.

Rage exploded through Sono. She pushed herself to a sitting position. "Lady Matsuura! That is too far." Of course a noble lady wielded absolute authority over the women in her household. And this lady could certainly lash with her tongue. But Sono had never seen her strike someone.

Lady Matsuura made a dismissive gesture with one hand while she railed at Iya. "Stupid girl. You should have told me at once." She turned to her own handmaid. "Rin, have them fetch the midwife and the physician. And bid the guards alert the priest." Rin bowed and scurried out.

Sono twisted on her futon and closed her eyes as a fresh cycle of pain crumpled her abdomen.

Lady Matsuura's merciless voice grated on in full rant. "We need everyone in white garb. And Iya, if you are done sniveling, fetch Tatsuko and Akiko. They can help you bring Sono to the birthing chamber. She has polluted our women's wing enough." Her voice rose to a shriek as she stormed from the chamber. "This is a disaster. We need the priest!"

Iya knelt and blotted moisture from Sono's face with a cool, damp cloth. "Do not concern yourself with her, my lady. Or with me. No one matters now except you and your child. You are going to be fine. When this is over, you will have your lovely baby."

Fear wound a sash around Sono's chest and pulled it tight. *I hope so. Dear Lord Iesu, I hope so.*

Saturday 26 December 1948

Akira let Rev. Delham guide him into a small interior cabin lined with walls of books. Akira's guess proved correct. They had the library to themselves.

A pair of wingback chairs stood facing each other. The

reverend closed the door and took the nearest one. Akira settled grudgingly into the other. "Do you mind if I smoke?"

"Not at all."

He pulled out a cigarette and clenched it between his lips, then offered one to Delham.

The reverend shook his head. "I'm going to pray for you, if that's okay." He intoned a few sentences while Akira shifted in his chair.

Delham studied the bit of pine garland decorating the table for a moment, then raised his eyes to his face. "How much do you know about me?"

"I read a little in the papers, Reverend Delham." He'd *seen* a bit more than was in the papers. But he wasn't ready to admit that.

"Please, call me Dave. Then I guess you read how I sat in prison for forty months, starting in 'forty-two. Mostly in China." He paused, pain lacing his features, then plunged into his story. Torture, starvation, solitary confinement. Three buddies executed. In a choking voice, he told how he'd watched a fourth friend suffer an agonizing death from slow starvation. "And I was pretty darn close myself. Can you imagine how much bitterness was rooted in my soul?"

Akira nodded. Perhaps no one had tortured or starved him, but he knew that choking sense of powerlessness. It colored all his prison memories.

Dave rested a hand on the table. "God is real, and He has power over our circumstances. And once you get that truth into your head, no situation in this world can defeat you."

"No?" Akira had seen his share of 'situations.' "Your ship blown to bits?"

Dave shook his head. "If you die, you die for heaven. If you live, you live for Him, and you trust Him to carry you through."

"Your crew dead?" Akira shot the words like bullets.

"All the more reason to serve Him. He's given *you* the gift of a second chance. Now, I told you my story. Will you tell me yours?"

Akira took a long pull on his cigarette. "Your navy sent my ship to the bottom. Every man killed. Except me." *And what I owe them is to join them.*

"What a tragic shame." The reverend gave a heavy sigh. "They deserved a lot more years."

"You don't think they were Jap vermin who deserved to die?"

Dave winced. "Good Lord, no. They were people—someone's sons and brothers. The whole thing was a wrenching tragedy. I hope—oh, I hope—it's our last war. Surely the human race will learn something from this."

They lapsed into silence. Dave's lips moved slightly. Prayer, perhaps. He spoke again after a moment. "What happened after that?"

Akira's jaws clamped like they were riveted together. This was mortally hard to talk about. Why did he owe this man any explanation?

"Look, I'm no psychiatrist," Dave said. "I'm just trying to figure out how I can help. How I can get you to fix on God's truth rather than the enemy's lies."

The enemy's lies. Covell-san had said something like that. "What do you mean?"

"God wants to give you an abundant life, full of peace and purpose. But your soul has an enemy, and that enemy wants you full of misery and fear. If you throw yourself over that railing, who are you pleasing?"

Covell-san had said something like that too. Probably some kind of standard line—although her seeming sincerity had left a lingering impression at the time.

Akira jutted his jaw. Bitterness soured his mouth and gave his voice an edge. "All my life people have talked about gods. Gods will protect Japan. Gods will lead us to victory. But in the end? They failed us. They were just fairy-tale things."

Like his Dragon King delusion. What under the four heavens had come over him out there? He'd seen fragments of moonbeam, insubstantial as the water that reflected them. Yet he had somehow duped himself for a moment that the spiritual was real.

He tamped his ashes into the ashtray, flicking the last clinging tendrils of those eerie sensations away with them. "Two years ago, I heard the emperor himself say that none of those things were true. Today? I have no use for spiritual things. You know what real power is, Dave-san? Aircraft carriers. B-29s. Atomic bombs. That is the power that wins wars."

Dave shook his head. "True power is living like Jesus, through His strength. That's the kind of power that keeps you from hurling yourself in the ocean."

Akira took a long pull on his cigarette. This man thought he lived like Jesus, ah? He knew a way to put that to the test. Thanks to Covell-san, he was familiar with a few words of their precious Christ's.

Father, forgive them, for they know not what they do.

Akira crossed his arms. "There's a thing I haven't told you yet. Last night was not the first time our paths crossed."

"What?" That made Dave's eyebrows shoot up.

"Here's your story as I understand it. Please say if I get something wrong. The task force saw an enemy vessel, and your mission launched early. So you ran out of fuel. And you were captured. Right?"

Dave's lips pursed in puzzlement. "Yes."

"And you spent the rest of the war in prison. That's why four of your friends died. They might be here today, but that little Jap ship got in the way."

Dave leaned back in his chair. "You seem to know a lot about it."

Akira delivered the next words with cool purpose, like throwing stones into the center of a *koi* pond. "I was taken prisoner by *U.S.S. Nashville*. On April 18, 1942, in waters not far from here."

"You were here? That same day?" Dave gawked at him. "Yes."

Dave was still groping to grasp what Akira had revealed. "You were captured during our raid?"

He answered with a decisive nod. "*Nitto Maru* was my ship. I was in command. We sent the transmission that killed your friends."

Dave's face sagged into an expression of deep pain. He sat silent for a long moment. "You," he said at last, his lip curling slightly.

"Now what do you think of me?"

The American's focus dropped to the table. Seconds passed before he raised glistening eyes to Akira. He blinked a couple of times. "What do I think of you?" He gave a small, resigned smile. "I think you did your job and I did mine. A lot of bad things happened for me after that. But God used them for good, to open my eyes to Him. He'll do the same for you, if you let Him."

Akira searched Dave's expression. No hostility. Not even a trace. "So I'm not your enemy? I'm the reason your men are dead."

"After everything Jesus has forgiven me, how can I hold that against you? There were guards who beat the daylights out of me, day after day. And starved me like an unwanted animal. But the love of Christ compels me to forgive them too. They didn't know Him, or His ways. As for you, you did your wartime duty. Nothing more."

"It's that easy?"

That drew a dry chuckle. "Oh, it's not easy. Never think it was easy." He leaned forward. "What those guards did to us was unforgivable. Someone had to pay a blood price. But that's the point. The price has been paid, Matsuura-san. Much better blood than theirs was shed, so it's covered. Everything they did against me. Everything I've ever done against anyone else."

Dave's face glowed as he talked about Jesus. It took Akira back to that hospital room in Colorado, with Covell-san's brown eyes fixed on him. So much grief in describing her parents' deaths. But when she moved from that to how Jesus had helped her forgive, her face lit like a beacon.

He recoiled inside. How was that possible? It wasn't human.

He settled back in his chair, weariness flooding every cell. "I can't think any more now. Maybe we can talk tomorrow."

Dave tensed and eyed him. "You're not going back out there. You're not leaving my sight. We'll sit here all night if we have to."

Akira studied the set of Dave's chin. The man did seem determined enough to keep him in that stuffy little library all night. Or worse, report him to Healy.

The ship's vibration thrummed through the soles of his shoes. Every rotation of the giant steam turbines carried him farther from the bodies of Nagai and his crew. But what could he do? He saw only one way to get rid of this interfering American.

"It's all right, Dave." He dragged the next words through lips that didn't want to speak them. "I'll still be here tomorrow—I promise." The way Dave was angling his head told Akira he wasn't convinced. "In Japan, an appointment is a very strong thing. Japanese don't break appointments. Deep dishonor."

"You're sure?"

"I'll bet a finger on it if you want."

Dave's lips quirked. "You'll do what?"

"The *yakuza* use this for keeping promises. You know, the Japanese crime gangs. If you break your word…" He made a slashing motion across his little finger. "Cut off here. On your sword hand. Very serious."

Dave's eyebrows arched. "Really? You'd put your sword hand on the line?"

"Yes."

Dave's expression went serious. "Here's the promise I want, then. You'll give your word of honor you won't take your life until we meet again. You can wait that long."

One more day. He didn't know where *Nitto Maru*'s remains rested—not exactly. His bones wouldn't settle next to his men, anyway. But by tomorrow night, he'd be four hundred nautical miles away.

He hated it—at least, he meant to hate it. A hint of rebellious relief murmured from some back corner of his mind. A tiny piece of him grasped at the sliver of hope a few hours' reprieve might offer. He gave it a stern thrust back.

"Okay, Dave-san. I promise we'll meet once more." Beyond that, he would make no guarantees.

Chapter Twenty

AKIRA WALKED INTO THE CABIN HE hadn't expected to see again. His shame closed in on him like the lid of a coffin.

Once more, he'd lacked the courage to end his life.

The charred remnants of the incense stick he'd burned earlier pointed accusingly heavenward. The scent of burnt citrus hung in the air. His bottle and glasses stood where he'd left them, next to the bowl.

He slipped off his shoes while a dark weight of humiliation wrapped him like a heavy cloak. He staggered under the mass of it and half-collapsed onto his berth.

Hearing voices tonight. What was that? But his cabin was still thick with it. Strong. Undeniable. The sense there was a *presence* there, besides his own.

A pulley rattled outside his porthole.

Dragon King. Utter nonsense. No such entity had been out there speaking to him. No matter what he imagined he'd seen in the water.

But the voice in his head had been as clear as his own. And the eerie sense of a presence in his cabin remained.

He mopped beads of sweat off his forehead and drew in slow, steady breaths. What kind of infant was he, to let a few night noises rattle him like this? The drumbeat of his pulse slowed and faded.

The liquor. That was it. Some sort of hallucinogen in that strange Hawaiian booze. He would sleep this off and forget it all by morning. He curled up under his sheets.

But a stubborn image of dragon-eyes woven of shifting moonbeams writhed beyond his closed eyelids.

Of course, he'd believed it all as a kid. He'd burned incense to his ancestors. Helped his mother arrange offerings of rice and fruit and flowers at the family altar. Prayed for gifts from the Star King's daughter at the midsummer Sky Festival celebrating her union with her starry oxherd prince.

But it had been years since he'd put any stock in it, hadn't it? His belief in the spirit realm had been fading since his capture.

Hai, he'd bowed in a school gymnasium, packed with tight rows of his grade-school classmates, before a shrine lodging the emperor's holy portrait. But the idea that a man had descended from mythical Shinto gods had suffered an ugly death with the end of the war.

God's truth, rather than the enemy's lies. Delham's words echoed in his ears. According to the American, there was an enemy—a real spiritual force that wanted him to hurl himself into the sea. Much as he wanted to mock the idea, what had happened to him that night? Could this thing be true—was there some reality to the spirit realm after all?

Covell-san, serving the people who'd murdered her parents. Delham, forgiving the guards who'd done the unforgivable against him. Something beyond human nature was at work in both of them. Solid evidence that a power Akira lacked reigned in their lives.

Phrases niggled at his mind. *Dwelleth not in temples...not far from us...*

Where had those words come from? Ah, the booklet Covell-san had given him. He still had it at the bottom of a drawer. He hadn't opened it since he'd read it through out of curiosity on an earlier voyage.

He got to his feet, rifled through his desk drawer, and found it. Flipped the pages until he landed on the words that had jumped into his mind.

...Lord of heaven and earth, dwelleth not in temples made with hands; Neither is worshiped with men's hands, as though he needed any thing...

The last time he'd skimmed the page, nothing it said had resonated in him. But the words from the Christian's holy book jumped off it now. They hit him as if they were written to him.

Temples made with hands. Japan was filled with those. Tens of thousands of shrines sprinkled the landscape, dedicated to eight million deities, so they said. And maybe he hadn't shaken as free of all that as he'd thought.

And this One Creator God. Clearly, if He existed, He wasn't a puny thing dependent on priests and temples.

All nations of men...that they should seek the Lord...and find him...

The world was a vast place. If there was a Creator God, His perspective couldn't be limited chiefly to a single chain of islands, like the Shinto deities.

The Creator wasn't far from anyone. He invited *all* to "seek after Him and find Him."

What a simple invitation. And it all made simple sense. If the One Creator God existed, didn't He deserve that much? What could it hurt to seek after Him, and maybe find Him?

Find Him. It felt like coming home. Akira had roamed the oceans of the world, but perhaps he'd just found what he'd always been seeking.

He bowed his head and folded his hands, as he'd seen Dave do. *I'm here, Lord. Seeking after You. Please let me find You.*

Then, also like Dave, "*Amen.*"

Sixteenth Day of the Ninth Month, Anno Domini 1588

Iya hurried back into Sono's chamber with Akiko and Tatsuko in her wake. The ladies helped her don a white kimono and hobble to the birthing chamber, a large space she had not seen at the end of a corridor she didn't know existed. Only two pieces of furniture graced the chamber. She sank onto one of them, a white-draped stool.

The other was an altar, complete with a priest chanting *sutras*. Wisps of aromatic smoke rose from a line of incense sticks before him and a thicker column from a small bowl. The man hastened to bow his way out, leaving a small statue of a fierce four-armed deity wreathed in flames to glower at her.

Ghastly thing. But she lacked the will to fight them about the altar. She lacked the will to fight anything but the pain. She fixed her eyes on an embroidered design in the white drapes that covered the wall. A contraction convulsed her, and a moan tore from her throat.

Akiko stood behind her, supporting her back and massaging her shoulders. The shrill rise and fall of the priest's *sutras* filtered through the *shoji*, a nerve-jangling counterpoint to the undulating rhythm of her pains.

Lady Matsuura strode in with the midwife from town. They all carried on a murmured conversation about her, and whether the poppy-seed smoke from the incense bowl should be having some effect by now. Their voices faded as Sono drifted into a dark cave of misery.

Hisanobu's self-assured voice in her head carried her through. *To fear death is to die.* She found a place where she could drift above the pain and outside the fear. But it took concentration to stay there. She closed her eyes, whispered petitions to *Iesu*, and pushed through the agony.

Conversation floated around her, mixed with the wailing of *sutras* and the sound of breaking plates— someone was smashing them on the floor to ward off evil spirits.

Time passed, measured only by crashing crockery and the rhythmic ebb and flow of pain. Then a moment came when the feeling changed. There was stinging, then burning. More and more intense, until she was certain she could take it not one moment longer. Then, in an instant, it eased.

The midwife crowed. "Here is the head!"

Sono leaned back on Akiko's chest, tears collecting in her eyes. "Is the baby fine?"

Iya gave her wrist a reassuring squeeze. "Beautiful, my lady. Perfect little head."

A plate smashed.

"But so tiny." Someone else's voice, a disbelieving whisper.

Sono drifted back into her cave. Not pain this time, but a blissful absence of it. Someone produced a cushion, and she collapsed on it. A woman's voice conveyed the tidings. "So fortuitous! It is a boy!"

Male voices from somewhere outside the chamber erupted in a cheer, and the cave where Sono's mind now lived flooded with dazzling joy. *A son! Our heir!*

More time passed, a length of it, gliding like silk between fingers, before she knew any desire to come back.

See him. I need to see my son. That thought tugged at her and finally pulled her back to the birthing chamber.

She opened her eyes and gazed at her baby boy. He lay very still in the midwife's arms, as if he felt as weary as she did. Tiny eyes ringed with dark hollows squinted against the light. Ruddy skin hung in wrinkles as if there was not enough of him to fill it out. Wisps of dark hair lay matted against his scalp. Delicate fingers clenched.

She watched him in awed wonder. *Will you live?* He had come so early.

He stirred and let out a thin cry. A tidal wave of compassion swelled in her breast, like nothing she had felt before. The joy and the pain of it, all at once, stole her breath. "Ah! Look at you, my precious little firstborn son. My *taro.*" She held out her arms. "Let me hold you."

The midwife moved him out of reach. "You stay there and rest, Lady Sono. I will clean him up a bit before you take him."

He crinkled his little face and issued another weak wail that coiled itself around her heart. "Hasten back, my *taro.*" She did her best not to let him out of her sight as the midwife bore him off. "Wait until your father sees you!"

And live. I pray you will live. Grow big and laugh and play at wooden swords like Akiko's boys.

Something whispered to her heart that he would. She smiled, eyes following the midwife, letting herself drift on a current of relief.

Lady Matsuura intercepted the midwife at the back of the chamber. "Let me see the boy." She took hold of one of his wrists, lifted his arm and examined it, then made a disapproving noise. "I am not sure about this one."

Her tone punched a jagged hole in Sono's aura of serenity. She pushed herself up to a sitting position. "What do you mean?"

Lady Matsuura pivoted to face her. "You cannot be that inexperienced. Your infant is weak and tiny. Those spindly little arms—like a monkey! He will be a sickly child. Not suitable for Lord Hisanobu's *taro*."

"Not suitable!" Outrage exploded through Sono's chest and drove her, aching and unsteady, to her feet.

Lady Matsuura sniffed and gave her head a supercilious shake. "This is one your husband would want us to send back."

"Send back?" She flung the words in the woman's face. Pain and weariness gave way to adrenaline. She somehow managed to stumble to the midwife. She snatched the baby and cradled his soft little body against her own. "What are you talking about?"

The baby squirmed and let out another pitiful wail.

Lady Matsuura gave her an unctuous grin and adopted an even, reasoning-with-a-child tone. "You really do not know? The midwife can dispatch him back to the water realm, of course. Where he came from." She glanced at the baby, eyes narrowed, but her fixed smile did not change. "It is always best to do it right away."

Her honored mother's words smashed like a battering ram into her chest. She squeezed her *taro* tighter and turned from Lady Matsuura, shielding him with her body. "That would be murder, Honored Mother. And I will have no part of it."

"Pray calm yourself, Lady Sono." The midwife spoke up in a voice she no doubt meant to be soothing, but it struck Sono's ears like a magpie's croak. "I am very skilled at sending them back gently."

Sono edged away from them, clutching the baby and shaking her head violently. She stared wide-eyed at her honored mother. "Your grandson, Lady Matsuura!"

The scorn in Lady Matsuura's eyes sent red-hot daggers into Sono's heart. "I will have a grandson when you give me one who will properly represent the House of Matsuura."

Sono stood as tall as she could. She loaded each syllable she spoke with all her clarity of conviction. "This is *our* boy—mine and Hisanobu's. The boy *Deusu* gave us. He is a beautiful gift. And the only place he is going back to is my chamber, with me."

Akiko took her arm and attempted to steer her back to

the cushion. "Pray sit, Lady Sono. No need to get agitated. No one is going to do anything except bathe him—until you are ready."

She thrust the young woman aside and spat her retort at her honored mother. "I will never be ready. *Kirishitan* do not send babies back."

"*Kirishitan* are fools, then. If you do not thin the garden, you will soon find that the weak things sap the strong." The corners of Lady Matsuura's lips twitched. "I have every confidence Lord Hisanobu will make his wishes known. I will carry the tidings to him now."

Chapter Twenty-One

Wednesday 29 December 1948
Port of Yokohama, Japan

AKIRA STRODE ONTO THE GANGPLANK ON a dreary morning just before noon. *Meigs*'s smokestacks towered behind him. A broad pier stretched below. Two duffels containing everything he owned jostled against his back. He'd never had much chance to accumulate things.

A beloved smell greeted him as he descended—seawater, fuel oil, fresh fish. A Japanese port.

Home.

There'd been progress since he'd seen Yokohama last. Structures sprawled around the docks, even if the construction appeared flimsy. A forest of rough, hand-lettered signboards jumbled the sidewalks, advertising every manner of business in a mishmash of pidgin English and Japanese.

Down the pier, a trio of U.S. battleships clustered. They projected a looming presence over the stretch of waterfront where a pleasant park had stood before the war. The *gaijin* had commandeered it and turned it into blocks of bland military housing.

Beyond the dock area, rubble blotted the cityscape, rendering it a disordered patchwork of ruins. A few more substantial buildings—clearly firestorm survivors—towered above the mess, with grimy, smoke-blackened walls and boarded windows.

Akira pushed back a choking sensation. He couldn't fathom now how he'd turned his back two years ago and left the family he loved to fend for themselves in a world turned upside down. Had he just emerged from some kind of madness?

He'd been so afraid, but of what? *Please*, Iesu. *Let it not be too late.*

When they docked two hours earlier, he'd left his station in the radio room and headed up to the wheelhouse to check whether Healy needed anything else from him.

He'd found the chief mate out on the command wing, gazing at the city. The man's face had lacked the usual sarcasm.

"Well, Jap-man. There's Yokohama. How does it strike you?" There was something almost sympathetic in the eyes he turned on Akira.

"It's...bad."

Healy nodded. "I think you did the right thing, deciding to spend some time at home and all. I'm guessing your family needs you."

Perhaps. I'll find out whether they want me. Akira willed himself to continue down the gangplank into this new chapter of his life. The reluctance that had dogged him for years was still a headwind he had to fight. But at worst, they would turn their backs on him, and he'd be alone—the same condition he was in now.

No, he'd be better off. He'd at least know what had become of them. But he had to start by stepping onto the pier.

He moved off the gangplank into a realm of shabby structures, crudely constructed with unpainted wooden siding. The thirteen hundred passengers from their voyage had long since scattered into shops and restaurants, or headed down the pier to collect their luggage—even Delham and his little family. Akira had spotted them from the gunwale earlier, waylaid by flashbulb-popping reporters.

He allowed himself a small smile. He'd met with Dave and Eileen several times after that first conversation in the library. What a pleasant surprise to see the Japanese press show such a robust interest in a former prisoner's journey of redemption. It boded well for the reverend's mission. And it gave Akira a small ray of hope for his own.

American President Lines had granted him a two-month leave. He hoped that would be long enough. He'd made few friends during his tenure with the liner, but it had left him more certain than ever of his calling. He couldn't imagine a life that didn't center on the feel of a great ship breasting mighty waves and a view that swept from horizon to horizon.

But his mission now was to find his family. The address he had was in Osaka. Mama-san's sister had taken ill with tuberculosis, so Mama-san had moved there with his brother and sister after he and Papa-san shipped out. That was the last he knew. But Osaka was several hours' journey by train. Tokyo was an hour away. He'd try their old neighborhood in Tokyo first.

He spotted a taxi stand on the far side of an open-air market. He made his way through throngs of people eddying around open stalls. A man hawked an array of battered pots and spoons from a large knapsack, his dirt-encrusted hands hovering over his inventory. An elderly woman with bowed shoulders sold second-hand clothes and household items from a plank table. Others offered mending and small repairs. A platoon of ragged boys with smudged faces and dirty caps vied noisily for shoeshine business.

In spite of the noise and mayhem, it felt surprisingly freeing to be surrounded by the sound of his own language, and to navigate without sparing a thought for *gaijin* and their customs.

American men in uniform swaggered everywhere. A young Japanese woman done up like a cheap version of a *geisha* stood in a doorway behind the taxi stand. Paper lanterns that matched her bright-red lipstick dangled above her head. She smiled an invitation at a pair of American sailors and played her fingers along the collar of her kimono.

An image of cigarette burns on fair skin rose in Akira's mind. Revulsion writhed through his stomach. What did they do to keep *this* girl working?

Lovely, delicate Mama-san. Vivacious, innocent Mi-chan. What had the war done to them? How could he have left them on their own?

He took in the whole tawdry street scene, and his stomach contorted with a toxic mix of horror, guilt, and shame. He, personally, had failed them all. He had been the initial link in a long chain of failure. Two years earlier, the crushing weight of this had been enough to drive him to sea.

He walked briskly on. He threw a lingering glance at his ship before he climbed into the taxi at the head of the queue. "Yokohama Station, please."

Akira's train rolled him past district after district full of relentless devastation, with shabby structures and twisted lengths of steel girder punctuating piles of ashen rubbish. They emerged at last from Yokohama's ruined core. Another thirty minutes brought them to Tokyo.

The desolation there was just as jarring. Even Tokyo Station bore the bombing's marks. The splendid domes that had once lit the towering main concourse had vanished, and it was two stories tall now, not three.

He walked out the blockishly modern front entrance in a steady rain into yet another thriving open-air market. It was going full-bore under strings of glaring electric lights. This one must have occupied at least ten city blocks.

He hesitated at the edge of it, disheartened to the core. For years, the prospect of this moment had cast a pall over every thought. The truth about his family could be a few minutes' taxi ride away.

His emotions were torn to bits with all the destruction he'd seen that day. If by some wild chance he did find them—which would be more than he deserved—he could no more face them now than an ant could drag an anchor. Better to brave the delicate first interaction after resting and cleaning up. For tonight, discrete reconnaissance from a taxi would be best.

He threaded his way around yet another line of vendors. A pair of teenage girls knelt behind a tattered blanket that displayed their wares—fried vegetables.

Why aren't they in school?

The younger girl's bony ankles showed beneath her wide pants. He glimpsed the rags that wrapped her feet. He tried not to stare as the answer to his question slammed into him like a gale-force wind.

Without shoes, there was no school.

Guilt-ridden sorrow tore at his chest. He overpaid them for two packets of sweet-potato spears and moved on.

A queue of taxis waited along a broken stretch of sidewalk. He gave the first driver the address of the home where he'd grown up, in a genteel neighborhood near Soseki Park.

Their route took them along the edge of the Imperial Palace grounds. The moat reflected the sodden light of the dreary day, and the ancient castle walls soared fifty feet above the water's edge. Towering gatehouses gave off a false air of impregnability.

But that was at odds with the story told by the broad patches of rubble on the city side of the moat. And somewhere behind those mighty walls, Emperor Hirohito had recorded the surrender message Akira heard at Camp Carson. If the rumors were true, His August Majesty had done it from an underground bunker, his residence smoking above his head.

Twenty more minutes along a major boulevard, three turns into narrower streets, and the driver stopped the car. "Your address is halfway down that block, sir."

"*Arigato.*" He didn't recognize a thing.

He stepped from the taxi and peered around in a daze. The storefronts he remembered so well—the cafe, the newsstand, the pharmacy—all obliterated. Where there had once been a tidy row of neat homes shaded by stately trees, there was now a ragtag assortment of shanties. On the left side of the street, bits of brick wall still stood intact, incorporated into new structures. On the right side, nothing seemed familiar.

The driver spoke from behind him. "Perhaps you'd like me to wait, ah?"

"Please." He took one step, and then another, leaving the taxi idling behind him.

He stopped on the broken pavement about a third of the way down the block and stared at the spot where their house had once stood. Rain spattered the concrete in front of him. A battered bicycle leaned against a rough wooden wall. A woman's voice crooned a lullaby, drifting through a window covered by a tattered burlap bag.

An older man emerged from the shanty next door. "Excuse me." Akira's insides were so numb he hardly knew he was speaking. "I'm looking for my mother. She used to live—we used to..." He glanced up and down the street. Could he have made some mistake?

No, their old street had angled just like this one. This was the place. "Right here." His voice broke.

"I'm sorry, young man. No one who lives here was here before the war. You might try the grocer two blocks down in the morning."

"*Arigato*." He choked out the words and retreated to the taxi.

Sixteenth Day of the Ninth Month, Anno Domini 1588

Sono's handmaid slipped a comforting arm around her shoulder. "Your *taro* does need a bath before his father sees him, Lady Sono."

Sono had no mind to let him go. "Have them bring in my washtub, then."

Servants scurried in with her lacquered washtub and filled it. She knelt and slipped the squirming infant into the warm water. He erupted in terrified wails.

Taro was not the first newborn she'd seen. *Hai*, he was weak. Skin hung loose around fragile arms and legs too slender for his torso. His torso in turn was too small for his head. His face was thin and his chin unnaturally sharp, and he wore a pained expression when he was not crying.

But watching him struggle against the world's harsh realities filled her soul with iron. She would gouge anyone or anything that threatened his tenuous existence. Shelter him under her wings. Never relinquish control of him for a single instant.

Control. Was that not the true source of this? Lady Matsuura wanted a grandson who would yield to her. Sono had proved to be a loose thread in the carefully contrived pattern of her life—and Lady Matsuura would force that thread into place.

A shiver ran across her shoulders. She was beginning to understand how far the woman would go to do that.

She lifted the baby from the water, cocooned him in a

length of soft cotton, and cuddled him against her chest. His frightened wails trailed off to silence. She brushed her lips against his tiny head and murmured comforting words into his fragrant skin. He took a shuddering breath and gazed up at her with trusting eyes. It rent her heart in two.

Akiko hovered at her elbow. "Ah. Look at him, the poor little thing. So exhausted." She fixed her eyes on Sono. "It seems the baby has extreme bad karma, Lady Sono, coming so early. Perhaps 'twould be best—"

"Stop! This *taro*—this little boy—deserves a chance at the life *Deusu* gave him."

Iya reached for the baby. "Will you let me take him, my lady? You need a bath too, before our lords come."

"True." Sono had not given a thought to her own state since she'd heard the words "send him back." More buckets of steaming water appeared, and she had a sponge bath. There were fresh white kimonos for everyone, including a tiny one for the baby.

She ached for him every moment he was absent from her arms. When they were both cleaned and dressed, Iya gave him to her. The warmth of his little body against her chest filled her with a fierce sort of contentment.

Lady Matsuura marched in, her face as implacable as the castle walls. Sono's soul chilled, and she clutched her baby tighter. Her honored mother shot her a glance full of veiled venom that yielded to a feigned smile. "Are you ready to greet your lord and husband, Sono-chan?"

"*Hai*, Honored Mother." She lifted her chin and steeled herself.

Lady Matsuura slid a *shoji* open, letting in a golden shaft of late-afternoon sun. Lord Matsuura stood at the threshold, flanked by his father and his son.

It felt like an eternity had passed since she had seen Hisanobu, although it had been but a few long hours. He seemed handsome and unruffled, but the stony glare on his face drove the air from her lungs.

To esteem, honor, hold, protect. He'd taken that vow. She would soon learn which of two women he esteemed more—his mother or his bride.

She stood, wincing at the soreness where she'd given birth, and bowed. She walked at a ceremonious pace to the *shoji* and held the baby toward his father like an offering. "Our *taro*, my lord."

He gazed past the child at her. "Mother says you are well, darling?" His formal tone chilled her.

"*Hai*, my lord. Well enough. And the baby is well too."

His expression warmed just enough to give her hope. "Let us see this little package we have awaited so long."

"I wish with all my blood and tears we could have awaited him longer, but here he is. With the breath of life *Deusu* granted him." She started to hand him the baby, but the cursed Buddhist rules of birth impurity forbade it—as they forestalled him from walking in. So she stood on her side of the threshold and held out their boy for him to examine.

Taro whimpered. A fragile hand flapped free of his kimono and twisted in the air, then came to rest against his jaw.

The young prince studied his son, and perhaps his face softened.

If only he could feel Taro's warmth. Hear his breath.

Lady Matsuura leaned over Sono's shoulder. "You see how tiny he is. This loose skin. Bony little wrists. This one is hardly going to make a name for himself on the field of battle."

"Look at his perfect little fingernails." Sono caught his hand and angled it to display them. "And I wish you could feel his skin, my lord. The wonder of it—like silk. *Hai*, he is small. But everything is in place, just as *Deusu* designed it." She stared into her husband's eyes. "It is no fault of his that he had the misfortune to come early."

Guilt speared her as she spoke. *Perhaps it is mine.* If only she had not moved around so much those last days, when she was supposed to be resting. If only she'd taken more tea.

Lord Matsuura crossed his arms and grunted. "His misfortune reflects his *karma*. This infant's poor *karma* is also a thing to consider."

Lady Matsuura tipped her head and jutted her chin. "So it is decided, I think."

Sono shrank back, dismay pushing her voice shrill. "Nothing is decided!"

The midwife, who had been hovering behind Sono's elbow, cleared her throat and made a deep bow. "If you please, my lords. This thing is always the mother's decision."

Sono gave her a grateful look. "*Hai.* And his mother says no to sending him back."

Hisanobu's grandfather spoke with solemn resonance, his face grave. "You must consider this with care, young woman. The House of Matsuura is not some shopkeeper's family. Hisanobu's *taro* will be responsible for the welfare of our entire domain."

Lord Matsuura exchanged a glance with his father. "Can you imagine this tiny thing leading our men in battle?" He issued a lengthy sigh. "Do you wish to condemn the boy to live as a failure, Sono-chan? Perhaps...if this one were a girl..."

Primal panic filled her breast. After loving the baby with a mother's love before he was even a swelling in her womb. After waiting so many months to greet him. After the agony of birthing him. How could they talk about ripping him from her now?

He squirmed and let out a pitiful little cry.

Her head swam with surreal disbelief. She inhaled deeply, doing everything in her power to reign in her wild emotions, and gave them her lowest bow. "I do esteem your wisdom, Honored Father and Mother. But I must seek *Deusu*'s wisdom first."

Hisanobu stood silent, glancing between his father and grandfather and his son.

Sono turned to him. "Your thoughts, pray, my lord."

Me? Or your mother?

He shifted his weight and folded his arms across his chest, echoing his father's stance. He moistened his lips. "Sono-chan, you are too emotional."

She had her answer, as cutting as if a spear had pierced her from a concealed window. He looked every bit a man, standing tall with the sunlight glistening from his smooth forehead and his luxuriant topknot and the hilt of his sword. But he was not man enough to take a stand for her, or their son.

But she'd said a vow on their wedding day too. The revulsion that twisted her stomach as she studied his face did not change her duty toward him. Nor did anything he said change her duty to their son.

Taro began to whimper. He nuzzled into her chest.

She turned her appeal to Lord Matsuura. "My lord, you promised my father and brother I would have freedom of religion in your house. This thing is repugnant to my faith. How can I agree to it?"

Hisanobu tried a conciliatory tone. "You have just gone through a tremendous experience—for a woman, maybe life's biggest. Perhaps you are too wound up in it all to make a balanced decision." He turned to his mother. "We can afford a few days."

A few days.

Little Taro wailed in earnest. Lady Matsuura peered down her nose at him and sniffed. "It is not worth all this discussion. He is unlikely to live anyway."

Sono stared around at their faces, the sense of unreality swelling again.

They all think I'm the crazy one.

Rin spoke up from the back of the chamber. "Pray excuse me, Lady Sono, but I believe he wants to suckle. Do you wish to nurse him?"

"I do." This baby had something to prove. He needed to feed, and to thrive.

Chapter Twenty-Two

Sunday 2 January 1949
Osaka, Japan

A FRUSTRATING FOUR DAYS LATER, AKIRA walked along the broad sidewalk of a boulevard in downtown Osaka. The First Evangelical Lutheran Church building loomed across the street.

He'd spent two days in Tokyo and learned nothing. He'd interrogated shopkeepers. He'd lingered for hours in front of bulletin boards propped against storefronts, thick with placards scrawled by desperate people seeking loved ones. He'd wandered to "Brick Street," once the site of a row of imposing government buildings, hoping to find someone at the Ministry of the Navy to question about Papa-san.

The Ministry of the Navy building was no more. In fact, the once-indelible institution called "Brick Street" was no more. Only a single building, the massive Ministry of Justice, had survived the air raids. Worse, the Ministry of the Navy itself was gone, abolished by MacArthur's Supreme Command. Pensions were no longer paid. MacArthur had no interest in supporting Japanese war veterans.

Akira stood on the sidewalk and kicked at a chunk of rubble. Where did that leave Papa-san?

On Friday, he gave up on Tokyo and traveled six hours by train to Osaka. He took a taxi to the last address he had for his mother, in Miyakojima Ward. That yielded no better results than his visit to his old neighborhood in Tokyo.

He was walking toward his hotel on Saturday night, thoroughly dejected, when his path crossed that of a balding American in a big coat. The man handed him a flyer. He took it and blinked in surprise at the photo on the front.

His friend, Rev. Delham. A single Japanese word was emblazoned above Delham's picture.

Horyo. Prisoner.

Akira thanked the man, who seemed pleased he'd

managed to give one away. "This will be a very special presentation. I hope you'll come," he said.

Go to church. Meeting with the Delhams on the ship was one thing, but to walk into a church building? That was a public declaration. Until the night he'd met Dave, he would have viewed any Japanese who would enter a foreign church as a cheap traitor, if he'd even heard of such a thing.

His friend's eyes stared at him from the flyer. Dave had emphasized the value of spending time with other Christians. Akira had put a toe in the water. Was he really ready to jump in the pool? "What time and where?"

The man flipped the brochure over to display the details on the back. "First Evangelical Lutheran Church. Sunday evening."

"I may come," Akira had said, "assuming I'm still in town."

And now, twenty-two hours later, he stood across from the church. Still in town, with no excuse not to go inside. He hesitated a long moment, the enormity of it sinking in. This would mark him publicly as a Christian. It was a step he needed to take. He knew that. And it would be wonderful to see the Delhams again—it would be the first time in days he'd seen anyone he knew.

The building appeared more forbidding than inviting. Was he this serious about following Christ? Maybe the whole thing had been a bad idea born of too much Hawaiian booze.

He fingered the brochure in his pocket. Daves's jaunty grin flashed through his mind. For better or worse, his course was laid in. He crossed the street and walked through the double doors.

Dave leaned against the far wall of the foyer, talking with a distinguished-looking Japanese man. His eyes landed on Akira, and his face lit with surprise. He greeted him warmly, then introduced him to the church's pastor. "Reverend Kagawa is extra happy to see you. The fellow he hoped would translate tonight isn't going to make it. He was worried he might have to do it himself."

Rev. Kagawa grinned and dabbed perspiration from his

brow. "It's wonderful to meet you," he said in Japanese. "Can you help us tonight? We'd be very grateful."

Akira cringed inside. Nothing like walking straight into the spotlight. "Of course," was what came out of his mouth.

"Any luck locating your family?" Dave said.

He replied with a weary sigh. "I'm afraid not."

"People will start to arrive soon." Rev. Kagawa talked them through how and when they'd enter and exit. He glanced at his watch.

"Before they start to come in," Dave said, "I think Akira has a story to tell too. About how Jesus found him on an ocean liner. We talked about this, didn't we, Akira-san?'

They had, or rather Dave had, at their last meeting on *Meigs*. Dave had studied him with appraising eyes. "You're an articulate fellow, Akira-san. The Bible says we must confess with our mouths. It would be good for you to learn to briefly share your testimony—three minutes about how Christ has worked in your life. It's an important discipline for a Christian."

Akira stared through the glass doors at the size of the sanctuary and felt his mouth go dry. "We did talk about it."

Dave clapped him on the shoulder with a hint of an impish grin and turned to the Japanese pastor. "I took the liberty of suggesting Matsuura-san prepare a brief three-minute statement. What do you think?"

Rev. Kagawa looked in Akira's eyes. "If you're comfortable."

Akira opened his mouth to respectfully decline, but Dave spoke first. "I know you can do this. Don't be shy. It will bless the congregation to hear what the Lord's done for you. And you can share a prayer request about your search for your family. Who knows? Someone here might have some information."

He stared back and forth between them, feeling just a little trapped. But something beyond the glass doors to the sanctuary caught his eye. A soft glow filled a tall window at the back of the room. A stained-glass depiction of *Iesu*, reduced to flat shards of vibrant color, His arms spread on the cross.

This God-Man had died for Akira. Surely he could say a

few words for Him.

"You're still searching for your family?" the Japanese pastor said. "Yes, please share that."

You know Dave's right. You should do this. "All right. *Arigato*."

"Great. I look forward to it." Rev. Kagawa turned to the double doors that led to the street. "Matsuura-san, you can stay here to greet people if you'd like, or there's a ready room in back if that's more comfortable."

"I'll wait in back." He was going to need some mental preparation for this.

Sixteenth Day of the Ninth Month, Anno Domini 1588

Sono settled on the futon with Taro against her chest. His tiny jaw worked like a *koi*'s as he rooted around for the nipple, letting out soft moans.

They all left her, except Iya and Akiko. And Hisanobu, who lingered at the *shoji*, arms folded. His eyes glittered with fascination. "The puny thing is so helpless. Cannot even find the breast for himself, ah?"

Sono stiffened. "There was a day when you were a newborn. I assure you that you could not either." The baby lost the nipple and fussed. She guided him back to it with tender fingers.

He was more serious now. "I know your heart beats for this baby. Mothers' hearts have done so for all of time. But it is foolish and dangerous to put pity for a weak infant above the security of an ancient house."

She speared him with her eyes. "I will perish before your son and I are separated."

"No matter what I say?"

"I hope my lord will defend me."

"That is difficult when you're being unreasonable."

"I am being a mother." Bitterness gave her words a barb. She cuddled the baby, wrestling with the maelstrom of emotions swirling inside her. "And my lord?"

"*Hai?*"

"I beg you to keep *your* mother out of this."

She had no more to say to her husband. He drifted off.

Iya slid the *shoji* closed behind him. "I am so sorry, my lady."

The adrenaline that had driven fire through Sono's veins drained away, leaving nothing but empty misery. She glanced down at her infant, now asleep with that same look of pained perplexity on his little face. One tiny, perfect fist rested against her breast. Her heart filled with fresh wonder.

Sono's next words to Akiko dragged through her lips, pulled by some morbid compulsion. "Have they ever sent a baby back, as they call it? From this house?"

Akiko dropped her eyes. "Ah! That is not for me to say, Lady Sono."

Something in her chest hollowed. *So it has been done here.*

Akiko went on. "It is always a difficult decision. You would not be the first to hesitate."

She wasn't sure she wanted the answer, but she could not help asking. "How do they do it?"

A flicker of pain crossed the concubine's features. "It is not so hard when they are tiny. A little wet mulberry paper across the nose and mouth, and the baby just stops breathing. Good paper is quite strong when it is wet."

Or they just leave them outside. She had seen that herself.

Akiko seemed to be having difficulty swallowing. Had she witnessed such an act? Those bright little boys of hers. Had there been another child, once?

Or Tatsuko. Why did she not have children?

Sono shivered and buried her baby's head against her shoulder. A fox's shrieking cry reverberated through her mind. Her pulse mounted. She clutched him so firmly he woke and started a thin wail.

She moved his mouth back to her breast and watched him through a fresh film of tears. "If only I could be certain he is getting milk. How can I tell?" She stared up at Iya. "I am paralyzed with fear for him." *And for my whole venture here on Hirado.*

Akiko spoke up brightly. "They have summoned the wet

nurse. I can bring her in, ah?"

Sono kissed Taro's head and nodded. Akiko bowed and left.

Sono turned despairing eyes on Iya. "At least we can talk here more freely. I have to ask you something. The midwife said it should be my decision, yes?

"*Hai*, my lady."

"Did you hear any of them agree to that?"

Iya's eyes widened in slow realization.

"Did they? Did any of them say 'twould be my choice?"

Iya's lips parted too, but she gave no answer.

"That is what I thought. Lord Hisanobu said only that they will wait a few days. And even if they did *say* it, you heard Honored Mother's words. The baby will die no matter what we do, ah? There are so many ways something might come to pass and appear to be an accident. Was she setting a table for that? Even this wet nurse—this Hiroko-san. Such a great friend of my honored mother's. Why should I trust her?"

Iya found her voice. "Surely Hisanobu will come to himself and take his son's part."

"But would it matter, if Lady Matsuura can convince them it was an accident?" She heaved a troubled sigh. "In her mind, this baby should perish, if only to prove me wrong. As for my husband"—bitterness swelled again, turning her mouth sour and her voice hard—"he is so quick to fall into his mother's sway. I am convinced he loves his house—and his prospect of ruling it—better than he will ever love me."

Iya spoke into her ear. "You know they would take Taro gladly at the House of Mercy. They have physicians there. Men who have studied with the Portuguese surgeon in Buzen."

Sono's insides melted. "They would take him. But how could I give him up?"

She cradled Taro's head, his cheek a little silken pillow in her hand. "And there is something else, Iya-chan. Something even bigger. How can I be part of a house where they can even discuss such a thing as 'sending back' a baby?" She shuddered. "Remember those horrid foxes? How could anyone…"

"I do not know, my lady. But do not forget why you are here, ah? A *Kirishitan* ruler could change all that."

She squared her jaw as she peered into Iya's eyes. "Here is something else I've realized. Lady Matsuura will never let that come to pass. No heir I produce will be good enough until she knows she will be able to rule me—and him."

She put the baby against her shoulder and stroked his back. "I need you to fetch my writing box. My brother has to learn that the freedom of religion I was promised is as substantial as"—her eyes drifted to the altar—"incense smoke. Or clouds racing before the moon. Sadly, by the time he receives my letter, the grandson our father sent me to bear is likely to be gone."

The incense smoldered. The icon sent its hideous glare at her, its back to the white-draped wall.

White. The color of death and birth. And poor, foolish brides, who understand not that promises, like eggs, are easily broken. Not to mention foolish daughters, gullible enough to believe their fathers and brothers have their best interests in mind.

"Was there anything else, my lady?" Iya said.

She focused on her handmaid's anxious face. "*Hai.* Pray bear my letter to town yourself and find a courier. I dare not trust anyone here."

Chapter Twenty-Three

Sunday 2 January 1949

AKIRA FOLLOWED DAVE AND EILEEN ONTO the platform at the front of the sanctuary. Rev. Kagawa had just given them a glowing introduction, and the air vibrated with a rising hum of expectation.

The hall appeared much bigger from the front. Cavernous. Hundreds of eyes fixed on him. His pulse mounted and his head went a little light at the idea that he would soon confess to his new Christian identity.

A pair of U.S. Marines stood stationed at either end of the banister in front of the platform. Candlelight glinted from their holstered pistols. He hadn't noticed them earlier. Perhaps they'd taken their places as the service began.

Surely they weren't a usual feature. That had to be for Dave. Did the American authorities think he needed a protection unit?

"Please welcome another special guest," Kagawa said. "Matsuura-san has recently repatriated. He will translate for Reverend Delham tonight."

Akira throttled his choking anxiety and made a deep bow toward the congregation.

Rev. Kagawa stepped back and Delham came to the microphone. "*Konnichiwa.*" He tried his best to deliver a couple of sentences in Japanese. Akira had to work not to wince at the result, which was barely comprehensible.

The pastor gestured Akira up to the microphone. "Matsuura-san, if you please."

He took his place at Delham's side. "I am honored to assist my great friend, Reverend Delham, with the translation."

Delham told his story. Akira knew the outline, but he'd never heard the details.

The airman had spent two days running from the Japanese army, but they'd caught up with him about the time Akira woke in the sick bay on *Nashville*. Dave told how he'd spent the rest of the war—forty endless months—

undergoing the worst the *Kempeitai* secret police could devise. "They executed my buddies by firing squad. Two men from my own crew, and one other fine man who was my friend. Simply for participating in the raid. I watched a fourth man, Lieutenant Meder, die from slow starvation. That's a"—he groped for adequate words to convey the details—"a hard death to watch." He stepped back from the microphone, choking over his emotions. "And I was darn close myself."

Akira's translation trailed off, the flavor of dry toast rising in his mouth. Shame burned through him at what his army had put his friend through. Dave and his buddies had starved in solitary, while he'd complained about sauerkraut in an officer's mess.

In the middle of Dave's darkest days, someone had given the airmen a few books. Among them, a Bible. They'd shared it between the four of them. Dave spoke moving words about how much that gift came to mean to him.

Akira warmed with compassion. He'd had whole libraries at his disposal, and they'd been a lifeline to him as well.

Dave brought his story to its conclusion. "What I realized as I sat there, day after day, reading the Bible, is that I was rotten to the core. And I was a man about to die. I wanted to be confident God would usher me into heaven, but I was pretty sure that wasn't the direction I was headed.

"Jesus didn't have to die for me, but He chose His death on the cross. God's one-time sacrifice for me—for us all. I prayed to accept Jesus as my Lord, and I can tell you that decision changed everything. I am here speaking to you today because I want Japanese people to have a chance to know him too."

Rev. Kagawa returned to the platform. Delham took the cue to wrap up. He peered over the podium deep into the congregation, his voice quavering with emotion. "Do you know what I said when they released me? I said, 'No man set me free. Jesus Christ did that, over a year ago.'"

Akira delivered the translation. The men and women in front of him greeted it with beaming faces, glistening eyes, even a few dabbing handkerchiefs.

Satisfaction swelled inside him, tinged with a dollop of pride. *Dave stirred some hearts this evening.* And he had helped.

Rev. Kagawa bowed repeatedly to Delham as the American moved off the platform and took the seat next to his wife. Akira turned to follow him, but the pastor laid a hand on his shoulder. "You were going to share something, Matsuura-san?"

He glanced out at the congregation and nodded, his mouth going dry as the Colorado grassland in August.

"Thank you, Reverend."

Rev. Kagawa had to gesture to the crowd to settle down. "Before we close, Reverend Delham has asked our friend Matsuura-san to share a bit of his story and his very important prayer request. Matsuura-san?"

Akira stepped to the microphone and spoke in Japanese. "My name is Matsuura Akira. When we embarked on the war in the Pacific, I had recently graduated from Eta Jima. I was assigned to *Nitto Maru*—"

His voice caught as he spoke his vessel's name. He stared at the podium, banishing Nagai's face and the echo of his ensign's voice to the back of his brain.

He told the story as simply and directly as he could, up to the point he'd signed on for the journey home. "It will be very difficult to see my family again. But I wish it now with all my heart. I once believed a defeated life had no value. But I look now at *Iesu* and I begin to think that a defeated life can have value."

His eyes rested on the Delhams in the front row. The colossal irony of how this had unfolded still amazed him. That was the point he hadn't brought home.

He lifted his eyes to the rows of faces behind the Delhams. "God's intervention in my life was no accident. I was alone on deck, in soggy weather, in the middle of the night. I had my foot poised on the railing, ready to hurl myself into the water. What were the odds that anyone would interrupt?"

He planted a fist on the lectern. "Only God could orchestrate something like this. God brought this man, who flew in the very raid that destroyed me, to my side at the moment I needed him most. And thanks to Reverend Delham, I stand before you with a new mission. To reconcile with my family. I've searched everywhere, but so far, no news of them.

"Our old neighborhood in Tokyo is nothing but ash. I would appreciate your prayers that I'll be able to get in touch with my father, Matsuura Saburo, who was captain of the *Aoba*. My mother, Matsuura Ayako. My brother and sister, Hiroshi and Miyako." He paused. "And please, pray they'll accept me when I do."

He gazed into the congregation. Into rows of faces, eager for a final word. "No matter how deep your shame, how complete your failure, I believe God still has a use for you."

He stepped back. Rev. Kagawa gave him an appreciative bow as he made his way off the platform. He took the empty seat next to Rev. Delham, flushed with relief at getting through those torturous three minutes.

The Japanese pastor led the congregation in a heartfelt closing prayer. Akira's heart flushed with gratitude knowing prayers were rising from hundreds of hearts for his situation. He stood with the congregation for the final hymn.

"*Sleep in exceeding peace. Sleep in exceeding peace.*" His heart swelled with a profound sense that somehow, everything would be well.

The chords faded. Rev. Kagawa dismissed the congregation. A queue of well-wishers formed to greet Dave and Eileen as they joined the pastor on the platform.

Two men who'd been sitting in the second row walked up to Akira. "Welcome to our church, Matsuura-san," the older one said. "I'm sorry you've had so much trouble locating your family."

The second man nodded. "Sadly, people were driven about at the end of the war like leaves in the wind."

The older man told his own story of a daughter lost and then found. He'd paused to blot his eyes with a handkerchief when a deep male voice boomed from a few paces behind Akira.

"I have found the sister of Matsuura-san." He announced it in English.

What? Akira spun toward the voice. A burly policeman stood, grasping a cane with one hand and the arm of a young woman with the other.

A wall of cold water smashed into his chest at the way she appeared. Stylish perm, bright red lips, pink sweater emphasizing feminine curves. And several inches taller than the girl he remembered. Hardly the picture of girlish innocence that lingered in his mind.

Her wide eyes and round mouth reflected his own astonishment.

He started to shake his head. This couldn't possibly be Mi-chan. But didn't something of his mother's delicate beauty shine in her features? Maybe...but if this was his sister, what had seven years done to her?

Eileen called out from the podium. "Akira-san's sister? Here? How wonderful!"

Akira got to the young woman in three brisk strides. "Mi-chan?"

She was quick to drop into a low bow.

The policeman reverted to Japanese. "There is a slight complication Matsuura-san will want to hear about." He sniffed. "I assure you this is your sister. But there is a small matter of her profession, ah? She's a known prostitute." He dropped her arm with a visible tweak and stepped back, leaning on his cane.

A crater formed in Akira's chest. This felt like all his fears colliding. His sister, a prostitute? She looked the part.

Your little sister. You've come seeking her from halfway around the world. Tell her it doesn't matter.

But if she'd sold herself, that shamed them all. And that did matter. What came out of his mouth was, "Is this true?"

Her lower lip trembled. "*Onii-san.*" *Honorable brother.* His old honorific title came out of those brash rouged lips in a whisper.

None of this made any sense. It was incomprehensible that he would find his sister in a Christian church in

Osaka—especially if what the police officer said was true. Yet this woman seemed to be acknowledging she was Miyako.

He shook his head. "My baby sister, here?"

How had Papa-san let it happen? How had they made her do it? Something had gone terribly wrong.

A deep sadness descended on him. His hands moved to her shoulders. "I don't believe it. I never thought I'd find you here. But you're so..." The word was *brazen*, but he settled for, "different."

She spat out a retort. "You aren't exactly what I was expecting either. They gave us your ashes, *Onii-san*."

His turn to burn with incredulous shame. "My ashes, ah?" *Hai*, he'd chosen to hide behind an assumed name. But how had his family received—and buried, presumably—a box of ashes? Who would have dreamed up such a ghoulish trick? "I didn't know, Mi-chan. I did use a false name during those years in America. I assumed you'd rather believe me gloriously dead."

Her response was savage. "We'd rather not have spent six years believing a glorious lie."

"We? Where is everyone else?"

She answered in a softer tone. "Papa-san is in the hospital."

Hospital. The word hit him as a relief. After so many deadly naval battles, so many newsprint photos of smoking ships, he'd braced himself for even worse news. "The hospital? With what?"

She cocked her head toward a quieter side aisle. She led him there, then turned and faced him with a deep sigh. "Leukemia."

"Leukemia?" He stupidly repeated the word while his heart caved in on itself.

She dropped her eyes and nodded. "They sent him into Nagasaki."

He sucked his breath in hard. "Nagasaki? He's *hibakusha*?" An explosion-polluted person. It was all he could do not to stagger before he formed the next question. "And Mama-san?"

"*Gaijin* bombing raid." She shot a glance at Delham.

"You have no idea what those firestorms were like."

He studied his sister's face. Was she saying Mama-san was gone? The bitter glint in her eyes told him she was. Consumed in a firestorm. A horrific death. That stung more than Akira could take in.

"Hiro-chan?"

She threw a second glance at the missionary, then took a small step around Akira. He swiveled to face her, turning his back to his companions on the dais.

She tipped her chin up. "Another bombing raid." She gave a harsh little laugh. "The night you died." She went on tiptoes to whisper in his ear. "Your friend behind you, ah? Your Delham?"

"*Hai?*"

"He dropped the bomb that killed your brother."

"What?" She might as well have slugged him in the gut. He reeled back a half step and lowered his voice. "You know this?"

"*Hai.*" The vitriol in that word was thick enough to scorch skin.

He stared at her, images cycling through his mind. Hiro-chan's fresh little face as he'd seen him last, all chubby cheeks and glittering eyes. Mama-san, elegant as she presided over that last wonderful sukiyaki she'd prepared for them. Even the sweet little sister he remembered, flushing as she presented him with the *senninbari* he'd wrapped around his waist the day *Nitto Maru* sank.

A new set of images wiped out the first set. Newsprint photos of downtown Tokyo, leveled. The fire and cascading water that had consumed the *Nitto Maru*. A tight paragraph announcing his father's ship, the *Aoba*'s, demise, her bridge cratered by eight-inch shells.

He forced all the images away and riveted his attention on his sister—his *now* sister. She was watching him intently. He opened his mouth, but no words came. He gave her a long, slow shake of the head.

Eileen called to them. "Akira-san, won't you bring your sister over and introduce us?"

Miyako snapped her gaze away from him, looking past him at the *gaijin* couple on the platform. A calculating glint sparked in her eyes.

What is she doing here? She hadn't come to expand her spiritual horizons with Christian teaching. The mocking curves of her mouth told him that.

He leaned toward her, uncertainty growing. "Are you all right? Maybe I should see you home?"

"I'm fine." She flashed her teeth. "I'll meet your new friends." She pushed around him and stalked toward the railing that separated them from the altar.

So strange. He caught up with her and laid a hand on her arm. "Mi-chan, what exactly are you doing here?"

Sixteenth Day of the Ninth Month, Anno Domini 1588

Sono's baby continued his cycle of rooting, fussing, and sliding off her nipple until his little face turned red with frustration. She felt red with frustration herself by the time Akiko ushered in a handsome woman who had seen perhaps thirty-five springs.

Hiroko-san. The wife of one of Lord Matsuura's captains. Lady Matsuura's friend. She came in, bowing, and knelt next to Sono. "Ah! I heard he is tiny as a sparrow's tear." She folded her hands on her lap, which was sensibly swathed in sturdy blue silk, and watched Taro try to feed.

Sono studied her over the baby's head. Could she trust her? What choice did she have? Hiroko had experience. She had borne four children, three of them fine, strapping boys.

"Hiroko-san. I am desperate," Sono said.

The lady's forehead gathered in deepening furrows as she watched Taro. "It is going to be a battle for this one. I regret to say it, Lady Sono, but he does not find a steady rhythm. And he gives up too readily."

"Is that normal?"

She hesitated before she answered. "Feeding is a skill you will both need to learn."

What was she leaving unsaid—and why? "Is there

something else?"

Hiroko winced, then sighed. "This one seems to lack the motivation. Perhaps your baby is not ready for life."

Outrage pushed Sono's spine straighter. Was the woman prepared to give up on Taro already? That would make Lady Matsuura happy, no doubt.

"Perhaps. But it is our job to fight for it for him, ah?"

Hiroko's reply came with a hint of a wistful smile. "He must decide he has the will to fight. All we can do is help." She glanced at the altar. "I have learned a trick or two. But first, I would advise an offering to *Ususama*."

Sono glared at the monstrous little red-eyed icon. "I look only to *Deusu*, who has a plan and purpose for every trial." *Even trials that involve the suffering of innocents.*

Her gaze drifted to Taro, and her eyes misted. Her baby. Her marriage. Two of *Deusu*'s unfathomable mysteries.

Iya brought her crucifix from her chamber. But none of the prayers they fervently repeated, and no trick or technique Hiroko offered, goaded little Taro to a vigorous suck. The night passed in mounting cycles of frustration and heartache.

Iya left early the next morning with Sono's letter. Soon after the midmorning bells, a male voice—Hisanobu's—called in from the warrior's run.

Sono spun to face the *shoji*. She had been so intent on Taro that she had not heard him walk up. She greeted him and gave the baby to Hiroko.

Hisanobu followed Taro with his eyes, wearing an expression she could not read. "How are you?"

She knelt before him. "Taro does not seem to want to take milk, my lord. Either mine or Hiroko's."

"Mother told me things are not going well." The chill in his voice sent ice shards into her chest. How did his mother know? *Hiroko.*

"I understand this is very emotional for you, Sono-chan. But there is nothing I'd like to see more than my wife and my mother living in harmony. Not battling like dogs and monkeys. And as the daughter, that burden naturally falls on you."

"Does it, my lord?" She gaped at him, her world

crashing around her. "When your mother is determined to murder our son? It might be best if you leave us now." She stood, gave him a stiff bow, and turned into the chamber.

"Sono-chan—"

She shook her head and walked away.

It was nearing noon when Iya returned. One glimpse at her stricken face told Sono something was wrong. She dismissed the other ladies.

Iya waited until they had gone. "I gave your letter to Koteda-san, my lady..."

"What is it, Iya-chan? What did you learn?"

Iya peered at her, anguish in her eyes. "When I told her what is happening here, I heard things I was not ready for. Tatsuko-san..." Her chest heaved.

Sono finished her thought. "She was the one. Tatsuko sent her baby back."

"Babies." Iya's features were sharp with agony. "A girl and then a boy. At Lady Matsuura's insistence."

"Lady Matsuura! And after that she had no more?"

"Two miscarriages. And the rumor in town says she has never recovered from it."

"Poor Tatsuko-san." Sono stared at her own sleeping infant's tiny fringes of lashes, and her eyes narrowed to slits. "How abandoned she must have felt with no one to take her part against that horrid woman. But what about Akiko-chan? She was able to keep her boys, ah?"

"Akiko had her babies after Lady Matsuura had two boys. An heir, plus one more. That is the talk in the back rooms of Hirado town, anyway."

"So Lady Matsuura had no stomach for watching someone else's children inherit Hirado domain." Sono pressed her lips together. "One thing in her bosom, as Tatsuko-san said."

She fingered the silken ribbon that ran down the edge of a floor mat, where the House of Matsuura's mulberry-leaf crest shown in gold. "The more I learn about this splendid house, the less I like it. Think of my lord, riding out at the head of a column of hundreds of men. Bridles glinting. Banners waving. How grand he is! All these mighty *samurai*. All this pomp. But this great house lacks the capacity to protect one tiny infant."

She leaned over Taro on his cushion, her stomach roiling. His eyes flicked open, then his face relaxed as he eased back into sleep, his even breaths punctuated with adorable little sucking sounds. She reached out with trembling fingers to stroke his sleeve. "To think I was meant to hand poor little Taro over to Hiroko-san, Lady Matsuura's choice. Just a square of wet paper. How hard would that be?"

No help from her husband. No access to her brother. And Lady Matsuura's spy—or assassin?—at her elbow day and night. She ran a finger down her baby's soft cheek. Poor little Taro. What could she do for him?

The *Kirishitan* of Hirado expected a prince. Her family in Omura expected a lasting alliance. So many people expected so much of her. Yet she was powerless to keep this one tiny person, whom she loved with her entire being, from murder at the hands of his own family. He lay asleep with his little face pinched with pain. And she could not assure him of even one more day of life.

Sono's handmaid spoke softly in her ear. "Should I summon the others, my lady?"

She pursed her lips. "I wish we didn't need Hiroko-san. I do not trust her."

"You need not trust her. But you can trust *Deusu*, my lady. Taro's life is in no hands but His."

Sono murmured heartbroken prayers over his head until he woke and started his pitiful fussing.

Iya summoned Hiroko, who watched the baby, then sighed. "I have been hesitant to mention it, but I have heard of one more method. I do not know anyone who has had to try this. But there are tales of it working."

Did Sono dare hope? "What is it?"

"He does not seem to want to suck. But if we can get a little milk into his mouth, he might swallow."

Taro wailed in a thin voice.

"By all means, let us try," Sono said.

Hiroko leaned over a lacquerware cup and expressed an acorn's volume of milk. Sono nestled her baby in her arms. He quieted for a moment, eyes fixed on her face. Hiroko managed to pour a few drops into his mouth. He sputtered and coughed, his face balling up with displeasure. Less than half of it stayed in. But somehow, he swallowed the bit that did.

Iya nearly danced with glee. "He took some! He took some!"

He seemed a bit more content after he spluttered and swallowed some more. He lapsed into a peaceful sleep. Did Sono dare let a ray of hope bloom that they'd hit on something that might work?

That *Hiroko* had hit on something that might work, *graças a Deusu*. She thanked Lady Matsuura's friend many times over, her gratitude overwhelming her.

"You see, my lady?" Iya said. "*Deusu* is trustworthy."

Hai. And as long as He was trustworthy, even Lady Matsuura's hand-picked informant could serve His purposes.

Chapter Twenty-Four

Sunday 2 January 1949

AKIRA'S SISTER PULLED HER ARM FROM his grasp and walked toward the Delhams on the platform. Dave extended a hand toward her. "I'm so glad to meet you."

She maintained that unnerving grin. Her handbag dropped to the floor, and a lipstick spilled out. Something flashed in her hand.

On reflex, Akira lunged for her. "No, Mi-chan!" Her arm arced toward Dave's midsection. He threw himself between her fist and the American's belly. Something bit into his flesh where his neck met his shoulder.

Her blade clattered to the floor. He cried out and put a hand to the spot where she'd sliced him. It was instantly warm and wet. He slumped against the railing behind him, pressing on the spot where blood leaked from his neck.

His sister stood before him, mouth gaping, his blood spattering her blouse. "Akira-san! What have you done?"

Me? What have I done?

Pandemonium erupted. The barrel-chested police officer stumped over, surprisingly agile in spite of that cane. He dropped it and strong-armed Miyako into a chokehold. One of the Marine guards sprinted up, pistol leveled. Rev. Delham vaulted the railing beside Akira and circled a supportive arm behind his back.

"*Ishi!* Is there a doctor here?" Dave helped Akira over to the front pew and made him lie down. Eileen was there too, with a wool muffler. She made a horrified little gasp and pressed it against his wound. He flinched at the sting of it.

Voices buzzed above him. Someone called out, "Keep the pressure on it."

A crowd formed around him, but Akira wasn't concerned with them, or their words, or the stinging where she'd slashed him. He focused only on his sister.

The police officer had her in cuffs, but her eyes lingered on Akira, agony written across her face. "*Onii-san!* Forgive me."

He stared between a forest of thighs as the policeman bundled her toward a side door. Papa-san's voice whispered Confucius' ancient words in his ears. *You mustn't sleep under the same sky as your enemy.*

There'd been sheer hatred on her face when she told him Delham's bomb had killed their brother. Did she feel honor-bound to vengeance? Was that why she'd come to church?

The policeman gave her a savage shove.

All the tragedy she'd witnessed. His years in American camps had reshaped his perspective on this *gaijin* enemy. Blunted the edge of the ancient philosophies men like his father had inculcated into him. Miyako hadn't experienced any of that. The inner voice driving her was still their father's.

Desperation to speak with her filled him. To express how badly she needed to make room in her heart for new ways. But all he could manage was, "Mi-chan, not this way."

A young woman pushed through the crowd to his side. "Excuse me. I'm a nurse." Eileen made room for her.

Dave sank to one knee by Akira's shoulder. "I think she was aiming at me," he said, voice faint with wonder. "You stopped her."

Akira looked up at him. "Dave-san. Forgive her. She doesn't know. You must tell her."

Dave nodded, moisture brimming in his eyes. "Don't worry about a thing. You just rest until they get you some help."

The nurse moved the blood-stained fabric and peered at Akira's wound. She pressed the muffler back into place, a relieved sigh whooshing from pink lips. "Thank God, she didn't get the artery. Let's get you bandaged and stable for a trip to the hospital."

A motherly Japanese woman stood over them, wringing her hands. "I should call an ambulance, then?"

"*Hai. Arigato.*" The nurse bent her diamond-shaped face over Akira's gash again.

The policeman had Miyako almost at a side door. She pushed an elbow into his belly. "Let me talk to Akira-san!"

Her shrill voice carried through the sanctuary.

The officer set his jaw and gave her a shove.

She gaped over her shoulder into Akira's eyes. "Akira-san, please forgive me. It wasn't meant for you."

The nurse propped his head and shoulders on a pile of coats. His eyes didn't leave his sister. "Mi-chan," he said. "You must listen to Dave."

The officer conducted her roughly out the door. Akira laid his head back and closed his eyes, an acid taste in his mouth. *Too late.* His rage at himself was enough to make him burst.

What madness had driven him back to sea two years ago? This was his fault. He could have prevented it. He'd come too late.

Dave jogged up to the ambulance as they were lifting Akira's stretcher into it. He settled on the bench seat across from Akira. "I won't be much help since I don't speak Japanese. But it's not right for them to haul you away on your own."

Akira couldn't meet his eyes. How much misery were he and this airman destined to inflict on each other? "*Arigato.*" It came out sounding flat. "Eileen is okay?"

"She's in good hands this evening. But she's very worried about you."

The ambulance attendant slid in next to Dave, and the vehicle rolled off.

"I have to ask," Dave said. "She really is your sister?"

Akira bit his lip and nodded. He grimaced as they hit a pothole—and not just from physical pain. The ache in his heart was torment, and he would soon have to inflict it on the man facing him. The explanation he owed Dave would not be fun for either of them.

"What a way to find her." Dave studied his face. "Why would she attack me?"

"Dave-san, I am so sorry." Akira paused to summon the right words. "Let me—"

Dave gave his head an adamant shake. "First, let me say something. Thank *you*. What you just did for me was incredible."

Akira focused his eyes on the storefronts rolling past the window. "Our lives are locked together." *In some kind of death grip.*

Dave's shoulders slumped against the back of the seat. "Even more than I realized, it seems."

Akira glanced at the attendant next to Dave. No way to know how much English the man spoke—and whether the police might interview him. "I learned some things tonight. We should talk later."

Dave's eyes followed his. He gave a nod and a tight smile.

Seventeenth Day of the Ninth Month, Anno Domini 1588

Hisanobu made no appearance the rest of the day, but Sono got the dubious pleasure of Lady Matsuura's company. From the moment she entered the room, a swirling malevolence seemed to eddy around her.

They had succeeded at their delicate feeding operation three times by then. But under Lady Matsuura's hawk-like gaze, something startled Taro. He jerked and jostled the cup. Milk splashed onto his tiny cheeks. He shrieked, made faint gagging sounds, then went silent, thrashing about with reddened face in a way Sono hadn't seen before.

She grabbed him from Hiroko, disbelief fading into horror as his coughs grew weaker and his cheeks gave way to pallor.

"My lady! He is choking." Hiroko snatched him by the ankles so he hung upside down. "Give him a good smack on the bottom. Quickly!" He dangled from her hands, perfectly still.

Sono crooked one arm around his tummy and slapped his bottom with the other hand.

"Again!"

She struck him harder. He coughed, took a long gasping breath and wailed.

"*Graças a Deusu.*" Sono pulled him to her in a tender, rocking hug. "I am so sorry, Taro." She gazed up into her wet nurse's eyes and found her own fear and heartache mirrored there. Hiroko sagged onto a cushion and sank her head into shaking hands. "That was a near thing, my lady."

Lady Matsuura watched them with frigid eyes. "Your baby cannot nurse." The scorn in her voice jarred Sono's ears. "Yet he is meant to rule this domain one day. How long do you intend to live under this delusion?"

She spun on her heel and left. Hiroko watched her go, her expression unreadable.

Taro's brush with death marked a turning point. It wore Sono as thin with anxiety as a length of fine gold thread. She and the other ladies had less confidence feeding him, and he resisted it more. By late afternoon, the newborn she'd longed for was fading like a plucked flower.

Sono persuaded Hiroko to step out for a respite in the gardens. With the wet nurse beyond earshot, Iya bent toward her ear. "My lady, the baby needs to—"

"Go to the House of Mercy. That was exactly my thought."

Her desperation mounted as she studied him. "The way he looks scares me. He hardly moves or makes a sound, and those shadows around his eyes..." Was it too late already? She clutched him against her chest as if holding him could somehow send her life force throbbing through his veins. "Pray summon my lord."

I will give him one more chance to be a father.

Hisanobu came, but to Sono's chagrin, so did his mother. Her husband could not cross the threshold, but Lady Matsuura bustled in.

Sono bowed to them both. Hisanobu opened his mouth to speak. His mother broke in before he could. "Your handmaid made this sound urgent."

"It is urgent, Honored Mother." She fixed her eyes on Hisanobu. "I am sorry to report it, but our Taro weakens, my lord."

"That's hardly news," Lady Matsuura said.

Sono battled to keep her tone even. "Ever since that choking incident this morning, he has been getting sicker."

Who could know whether the chill Lady Matsuura brought into the room helped provoke the incident? She pressed her lips together so they wouldn't spit out that thought. "They have wonderful doctors at the *Kirishitan* House of Mercy, my lord. Men who have been trained by the foreign physician up in Buzen. We could summon one."

Lady Matsuura cut in. "They have powerful men of prayer at Saikyo-ji. No doubt my brother would be happy to send us one."

"I am not after *sutras*, Honored Mother. Someone who knows the new medical approaches from outside—"

"Would take all the credit should the baby improve," Lady Matsuura said.

"He would agree to do it discreetly, Honored Mother." Sono appealed again to Hisanobu. "They would minister to the baby, even if there was no glory in it. I know they would."

"My dear daughter." Lady Matsuura's voice clanged against Sono's ears, insistent as a temple bell. "We will have a priest or no one."

The truth hit Sono like a winter wind. Lady Matsuura hated *Kirishitan* more than she loved her grandson. Maybe she lacked the capacity to love anything as much as she hated the *Kirishitan*.

"Mother," Hisanobu said, "perhaps you could give me a minute with my wife?"

Lady Matsuura graced Sono with a smile that made the room even colder. "Certainly." She dropped in a rigid bow and left.

"I am sorry, Sono-chan." Hisanobu shifted on his feet. "But you see how much our mother objects. This is not a step I can agree to."

"So you will give up on this little life we made together, this little miracle *Deusu* gave us, to avoid making your mother unhappy." Her rage was thick enough to choke her.

He stared her down. "You tell me how powerful your *Deusu* is. Why should He need physicians?"

She snapped back. "Can you not see this is ripping out my heart? To watch our son slip from this life without ever leaving the chamber he was born in?"

So many other dreams would slip away with him. Her father and brother's dream of an alliance that would stand the test of time. Padre Lucena's dream of an heir for Hirado who would stand for the cause of *Iesu*.

And her own dream, that there was some purpose to her caged-up life on Hirado. "My lord, if you will let your mother steal this baby's chance at life, what will stop her from moving against our next child?"

"Be reasonable, darling. We can all see how weak this infant is. Our next boy will be more suitable. I'm confident of it."

Not if your precious mother has her say.

Chapter Twenty-Five

Sunday 2 January 1949

SOME HOURS CREPT BY BEFORE THEY had Akira mildly sedated, sutured, and settled in a hospital room. Dave hadn't left him.

Akira tipped his chin at the open door. "If you could close that, please, I can finally answer your questions."

"Thank you." The American did as Akira had asked, then settled in the chair next to him and gazed at him with eyebrows raised.

"I know this is going to hit you as hard as it hit me. My, ah...my sister believes a bomb your plane dropped"—he paused, moistened his lips, then forced the next words out—"killed our little brother."

Dave stiffened in astonishment. "Your brother?" His features went sharp with pain. "Please tell me that isn't true."

"She said he died in Osaka, on the day of your raid."

"From an explosion?"

He nodded, fresh misery swelling in his chest and souring his gut. "That's what she said."

A gurney clattered along the hallway. A long beat passed before Dave spoke. "One plane flew over Osaka. *Payback.*" His voice was as hollow as his eyes. "If your brother died in the raid that night, your sister is right. Our mission caused his death. I'm so sorry, Akira-san. I don't know what to say."

Akira knew he needed to speak some words of forgiveness, but he couldn't bring himself to form them. "Maybe she was with him when—" His voice broke. "She had that knife in her purse because she may feel her honor requires her to kill you."

Our honor. A fresh pain surged through his chest. How her memories of his death must have tormented her, feeling she should have prevented it somehow.

Dave pressed his lips into a line, clearly finding this concept hard to digest. "So your sister tried to knife me because she blames me for your brother's death."

"Maybe. I don't know that. But we have a very old tradition called *kataki-uchi*. If your close relative has been murdered and the authorities will not act, you must. We have many old stories about this. Some of the great heroes we tell our children about." He lapsed into silence and studied Dave's face, so foreign, with his pale skin and prominent *gaijin* nose. "You can see how, if this is what she believes...and maybe what my father asked her..."

Dave sat staring into his hands. He gave a slow nod, then looked up at Akira with a face sharp with pain. "How old was he? Your brother?"

"He'd just turned eight."

Dave rolled his head back so it thumped against the wall. He sat there, fists balling then releasing. When he turned his eyes to Akira again, they were moist. "I need you to know this, Akira-san. We only hit military targets. The Sumitomo Aircraft Factory. The Maruzen Oil Refinery. All direct hits. We never targeted civilians. I wasn't up there to kill kids." His voice rose. "All those years we were in prison, they called us war criminals. Accused us of indiscriminate bombing. It was a lie."

Akira nodded and pushed his words past the thick spot in his throat. "I believe that." He couldn't even start on the other news she'd given him. It was going to take a long time to work through it all.

A cane clacked along the hallway floor. Someone rapped on the door, rescuing Akira from having to talk more. The intruder swung it open without waiting for an invitation. It was the police officer who'd hauled Miyako out of the church building earlier.

Dave rested a hand on Akira's shoulder and stood. "Call us tomorrow when they release you."

"Thank you, Dave-san. We'll talk more then."

A sour note rose in his mouth as he watched Dave give the police officer a polite bow, then trudge out the door, face stricken.

"May I?" The policeman swiveled and lowered himself ponderously into the visitor's chair. He propped his cane against the wall. "Matsuura-san, welcome back to Japan."

"*Arigato.* I wish it felt more like home."

"Ah! This is our new Japan. We all wish it felt like the home we remember, ah?" He leaned forward and peered at Akira. "We're well acquainted, young man, although you may not recall it. My name is Oda. Your father is a dear friend, going back to our academy days at Eta Jima." He shot a resigned look at the leg extending in front of him. "Thanks to this leg, I'm a police captain now."

"Of course, Captain Oda. I should have recognized you right away." He had rehashed every detail he could remember of that last afternoon with his family. A few of Papa-san's close friends had come by to wish him well. A more agile Oda had been prominent among them.

Oda grunted. "Everything has changed. You hardly recognized your own sister. Of course, she has changed more dramatically than most, regrettably."

His tone bore a scornful edge Akira didn't miss. "*Hai.*"

"And you wouldn't be the first not to know me with this cane. Your sister said the same when they hauled her into my office about a week ago." Oda's lip curled with a hint of smirk. "That was after they caught her out at night, in a particularly unsavory district."

There was something about the man that made Akira's hackles rise, but he pressed the feeling down. *I need this fellow.* "Maybe you know more about my family, then? I have many unanswered questions. I've seen only two people I know since my return, and you're one of them."

Oda's eyes glinted from beneath thick brows. "And the other is in jail, ah?"

"Exactly. Mi-chan"—he made a deliberate choice to use her pet name—"didn't get a chance to tell me much before she...had to leave."

Oda delivered a deep sigh and a pensive nod. "Sordid incident. We'll come to your family shortly. But first, I have police work to do." He pulled a notepad from his breast pocket. "I must say, the circumstances of your return took me by surprise."

"I imagine I'll get that reaction a lot."

The policeman responded with a grim laugh. "We have

a term for men like you—men presumed dead, who somehow reappear. There was a rash of them a couple of years ago. We call them two-legged ghosts."

"Two-legged ghosts!" Akira had to chuckle in spite of his deepening dislike for the man. "My sister did look like she was seeing one. But please understand, it wasn't my choice to get rescued."

Oda eyed him. "That's the story all the two-legged ghosts seem to tell."

Akira's pulse throbbed in his wound. If the man was trying to make him angry, he was succeeding. He directed his eyes to the notepad. "You have some questions for me?"

"A few, for the record." Oda positioned his pencil. "When did you arrive in Japan?"

"Last Wednesday, aboard *S.S. General Meigs*."

"And what is your business here?"

"To find my family and recover my life. I hope you can help."

"I'll do what I can." He ran through a list of routine questions about what Akira had observed, then fixed him with keen eyes. "You weren't her target, ah?"

Careful. "I'm...not sure."

"It appeared to me she lunged at the American. Why would she do that?"

Warning bells went off. Was he giving away too much? *No need to tell him anything he doesn't already know.* "How would I know?"

Oda's brows lowered. "You must have some guesses, ah? You two spoke at length before the attack. Perhaps she said something?"

"She told me about Papa-san. And about our mother."

Oda leaned toward him. His eyes took on a fierce glint. "Nothing else? About your brother, perhaps?"

Weariness washed over him, and desolation welled up from inside. "*Hai*, little Hiroshi too. She mentioned he died in a bombing raid."

"And you have no idea why she would have attacked Reverend Delham, ah? It's strange, don't you think? She was quite friendly with a number of Americans." He placed a not-so-subtle emphasis on the *quite*.

Akira went rigid. "Have you asked her?"

"Please forgive me, Matsuura-san. My work makes me cynical." He slipped the notepad into his breast pocket. "That's all I have for now, in an official capacity. Let's talk about the rest of your family, ah?"

"Please. I'm eager to hear anything you can tell me."

Oda leaned back in his chair. "To my great regret, I was out of touch with your father for some years. I didn't know your mother landed here in Osaka until they brought your sister into the station a few nights ago. That was when I learned about your mother and brother." His eyes sank to the linoleum floor and his jaw jutted. "Tragic. What a hell those bombing raids were."

"I saw photos—"

"If you weren't here, you can't imagine it. The barbarity. Entire districts leveled. Death kept raining from the air until the toll ran into tens of thousands. Civilians, Akira-san. Tragically, we believe your mother was one of them."

Hope stabbed him. "We believe?"

"All we know is that she was never seen again after the firestorms in March of forty-five. We have to assume she was among the unidentified remains." He glanced up at Akira. "Thousands of remains, Matsuura-san. So now you know everything I do. I don't have the words to convey how deeply I feel your loss."

Akira closed his eyes while his sorrow rose like a tide, engulfing him. The woman who'd raised him, with all her warmth and charm and beauty, hadn't even left a grave to visit.

Oda waited a moment, then went on in a flat-sounding voice. "As to your father, when I interviewed your sister a week ago, she didn't mention him. She had her reasons. Her story didn't connect, so I decided to investigate. I was able to track him down." He let a moment pass. "He is a very sick man, Matsuura-san. She told you this?"

"*Hai*. Radiation poisoning. But I know little else. Where is he? When can I see him?"

"That will be...complicated."

Not what he wanted to hear. "Why?"

"I'm afraid his condition is fragile. You must

understand that your reappearance, under such"—Oda's eyes narrowed—"unexpected circumstances, will be a tremendous shock to him. It might be more than he could bear."

Something hardened in Akira's stomach. "He would have preferred me dead."

"He has believed you dead for a number of years. Unwinding that belief is something that will have to be done with care."

If at all. Oda didn't say it, but Akira heard it hanging in the air.

Oda penciled his home phone number onto his business card and handed it to Akira. The captain wished him goodnight and left.

Akira lay in the darkened room, the miserable truth soaking into his soul. How much time did Papa-san have? If Oda spoke for Papa-san's doctors, Akira might lose him without ever seeing him again. Like he'd lost Mama-san and Hiroshi.

He'd come to Japan on a mission to reconcile with his family, and only two of them were left. One was sleeping in a jail, hating him for protecting her enemy. The other slept in a hospital somewhere, ignorant of his existence.

He was at grave risk of losing them both—again. This could not happen.

Seventeenth Day of the Ninth Month, Anno Domini 1588

Sono's husband left, and she sagged to her knees before the crucifix. For a long while, she could not even muster a whispered prayer. Her heart held nothing but sobs.

Iya dismissed Hiroko, then knelt at Sono's side. *Graças a Deusu*, she voiced prayers for both of them.

The golden light of late afternoon had faded before Sono managed to drag a handful of words from a spirit heavy as lead. "I don't know why *Deusu* is against this baby. *Deusu* gives, and *Deusu* takes away. I know I must accept what comes from His hand—even that."

Iya gave her shoulders a squeeze. "Remember what

Koteda-san said the last time she came to us. Our God is not father to the sparrows. But He neglects not a single one of them. How much more will He care for us, His children? And for Taro? If *Deusu* has marked him to perish in your arms, my lady, it will be a better death than by foxes."

A chill ran down Sono's spine. She narrowed her eyes and shuddered. "Don't even mention the—"

Foxes. Wait.

Iya gazed at her with a stricken expression, then bowed all the way to the floor. "Pray forgive me, my lady. I did not mean—"

"No matter, Iya-chan." A sliver of possibility opened before her like a glowing gap between clouds. She spun to face Iya, grim laughter on her lips. "That woman thinks she can make me give up. But she's wrong."

"Of course she is."

She grasped her handmaid's wrist, a new hope quickening her heart. "What I mean is, I may know a way he can see a physician."

Iya's eyes widened with incredulous joy. "How?"

"I hate it. But it is insane enough it might work."

"Tell me, my lady."

"You could tell them I have decided I'm ready to expose him—"

"What? No!"

"Shh! *Tell them* that. But we would have someone from the House of Mercy in place, awaiting his chance to collect the baby."

Iya's mouth formed a little circle of surprise. She closed it, then opened it again. "It could work, but—"

Sono's surge of hope was already fading. "But can you imagine poor little Taro, in a basket under the pines like our foundling boy?" She twisted her hands together in her lap. "There are so many ways it could end badly. They could decide to kill him outright rather than leaving him."

Iya's features pinched. "'Twould be kinder. Or they could leave him at a different place than we expect."

"Or they could guess at our game. And place a guard."

"Or the foxes could get to him first."

They fell silent once more, the remembered howls of a

224 | THE MULBERRY LEAF WHISPERS

fox echoing through Sono's mind.

"My lady?" Iya's voice trembled. "Last Sunday when I went to service, it was *Mōse* the Lawgiver's Saint Day. You remember *Mōse's* story—how his mother had to save him?"

"She had to hide him from the wicked king. In a basket. And *Deusu* kept him from the river monsters."

Iya nodded. "Like He saved our foundling from the foxes."

"Ah, Iya. What a great example for us. We know how *Mōse's* story ended. But his mother did not, when the best she could do for him was to lay him in a basket among the reeds. Can you imagine the despair she felt?"

Iya bit her lip. "Your idea is perilous, my lady, but—"

"But so was hers." Sono mused. "I could yield to their wishes and agree to expose him, but only if it is done in a certain way. A way that ensures our friends can get to him. So...something like this, ah? I can accept leaving him in the woods, but not outright murder."

"No mulberry paper."

She shuddered. "No. That way *Deusu* has a chance to intervene and save him." Her eyes rested on Taro's sleeping form. Fear drilled through her chest. "Didn't *Mōse's* mother leave his sister to watch him? Who will watch our Taro?"

Taro let out a little sigh in the soft innocence of slumber. The urge to protect that innocence pressed like a weight on Sono's ribs. "Ah, Iya-chan! I cannot believe we must consider such a dangerous ploy." She blinked away a mist of tears. "And how can I convince Lady Matsuura I've had a sincere change of heart? I have been so adamant against this act."

"I am loath even to suggest it, but perhaps you can make the thing a triumph for your honored mother. Use your tears and tell her you have decided to stop fighting her. Make it your peace offering."

Sono snorted. "Quote a little Confucius, ah? Something about obedience leading to harmony."

"Maybe she will be eager to believe you have yielded to her superior wisdom. And she will not ask questions."

"Or"—tears fogged Sono's vision again—"eager enough to be rid of my baby."

Chapter Twenty-Six

IT WAS WEDNESDAY BEFORE AKIRA PENETRATED the police bureaucracy and arranged a meeting with Miyako. Dave begged for the opportunity to go with him. "I'm not sure when I'll be back in Osaka," he said, "and I'm desperate to ask her forgiveness. I'll stay on an extra day if I have to."

Akira's sister was sure to read it as a betrayal. He conceded reluctantly. "Can we meet for lunch first?"

They met at a noodle shop within easy walking distance of police headquarters. The place felt narrow and dark. But the air was full of the savory fragrance of onions and mushrooms mingled with the tang of salted mackerel. The kind of aromas Akira had longed for all the years he was gone.

The instant he saw Dave, the hollow in his chest pressed against his ribcage. His new *gaijin* friend had dropped the bomb that killed his little brother. The day that had passed since he'd seen Dave last hadn't made the ache any less profound.

The American stood and bowed with his usual breezy grin. "I'm so glad this worked out. I didn't want to miss the chance to see her." His expression softened with concern. "Again, Eileen and I are terribly sorry about...everything you've learned."

Akira pushed back the grief that threatened to strangle him. He'd had far too much time on his hands, with little to do but think about Mi-chan and what she'd revealed. "I just hope I didn't get back too late to make any of this right."

A woman bustled over, bowed, and wiped her hands on her apron. "You like fish or vegetables? Very sorry, but I have no other meat today."

Akira conferred with Dave and put in their orders for fish. Akira pulled a fifty yen note from his wallet and laid it on the table. The waitress brought a pot of steaming tea and slipped the cash into an apron pocket.

Dave took a hearty sip. "You have to coach me on how

to say this to your sister. I want to express how profoundly sorry I am for her"—he gazed directly into Akira's eyes—"for *your* tragic loss of a brother. And I want her to know I forgive her for Sunday night."

"Maybe we need to coach each other. None of this is what I hoped to come home to." Including the part where he shared a meal with the man who had killed his brother. Good thing Papa-san couldn't see this. He'd have another reason to scorn his son.

Dave focused earnest eyes on him. "Here's my coaching. Don't be afraid to show her you love her, no matter what she's done. You don't have to help her continue down a wrong path, but you do have to love her. And one more thing. Prayer is the root of any transformation."

Akira toyed with the tin ashtray in front of him. *Transformation.* Dave had talked about his own on Sunday night. From bitter hatred for his enemies to compassion. How did that work? Because whatever was supposed to empower it, Akira wasn't finding it in himself.

He pulled out a pack of cigarettes. "How about forgiveness? Is prayer the root of that too?"

Dave nodded. "That, and a bit of scriptural truth. Why dwell on something Jesus has already paid for? If He bought you, whatever that person did to you is no longer your concern. It's His. The cooks in the kitchen may have made the noodles we're about to eat, but you've paid for them now. Do they belong to the restaurant or to us?"

"To us, I guess."

"Yes. And I can do what I like with mine. I could choose to toss mine out, or to bless a stranger on the street with them. That's not the restaurant's concern, right? The noodles are mine."

Akira gave him a slow nod.

"I miss those men like crazy, my friends they killed in prison. But I have to trust God with it, like a child trusts his father. He saw every moment of what happened. Does He know what He's doing with the universe, or not?"

Every moment. When the *gaijin* bomb killed Hiro-chan in all his innocence, God was there. He was there when men died at Pearl Harbor and at Coral Sea and during Doolittle's raid, and on every other clod of blood-soaked dirt in every battle of the war. People would forget how bad it was in time, but God felt the agony of every dying gasp.

Dave pressed his mouth into a hard line before he spoke again. "I have to confess something to you."

"What's that?" *Do I want to know?*

"I had hatred in my heart the day we dropped those bombs. I wasn't out to murder children, but I wanted the Japanese nation to taste what we experienced over Pearl. I would never have targeted innocents like your brother and sister, but I can't say my conscience is clear of ugly motives." Dave rolled his head back and squeezed his eyes closed with an expression of abject pain. "I am so glad Jesus's blood is enough to wash away everything that happened that day."

Akira studied the tea in his cup. He hadn't taken a sip. "The day my mother didn't come home, there were four thousand dead in Osaka. A lot of men dropped a lot of bombs, Dave-san." He balled his hand into a fist beneath the table. "They had to know civilians would die."

"It had been a long war by then. Lots of room for hatred to thrive." Dave focused his blue eyes on Akira. "Hatred is very human. But it's a prison. It poisons everything around you. Overcoming it with forgiveness goes against everything that's natural. It's a clear sign God is at work."

Father, forgive them, for they know not what they do. Quite a contrast to the unending cycle of vengeance that had driven his sister's knife.

Their waitress hurried past with a pile of take-out cartons for a customer at the front door. Savory steam scented with soy sauce and roasted onions rose to Akira's nostrils.

Iesu had freed his soul, hadn't He? Maybe he could box up his unforgiveness and let his Savior unburden him of that too. Like a take-out order that *Iesu* had paid for.

Dave's voice broke into his thoughts. "Sometimes the hardest thing is to forgive yourself."

Forgive myself? His crime still confronted him whenever

he saw himself in the mirror. He'd failed to fight to the death to stop the bomb that had killed his brother. Maybe it was time to heap that in *Iesu's* carton, too.

Seventeenth Day of the Ninth Month, Anno Domini 1588

Taro sickened during the night. He made wheezy little grunts with every breath now, breaking Sono's heart and destroying any possibility of sleep.

She held him close and listened to his labored breathing. Deusu *gives, and* Deusu *takes away.* Sobs choked her, and she started to pray. *Our Father...*

The words stalled in her throat.

Thy will be done. In days past, the simple formula had heartened her. She had loved the straightforward reminder to cling to *Deusu's* will above all things. But with Taro balling up his little face and grunting in pain every time he inhaled, there was no comfort in it now. Could it really be His will for such innocence to endure so much agony?

If He was her Father, would He not want to hear from her heart? The way she had once addressed her Papa-san, even though he was a great *daimyo.*

A very different prayer rose from her lips. A presumptuous prayer. A ferocious flood of her own broken, tormented words. Who could know whether *Deusu* heard her better or worse? But she somehow *felt* more heard. And did He not know everything she thought and felt anyway?

Sleep overcame her at last.

Iya left to see Koteda very early the next morning. The shadows in the garden lay directly beneath the trees by the time she returned. But Sono had to wait until the baby had coughed and choked his way through another thimbleful of milk before she could speak to her handmaid alone.

She stood with the baby over her shoulder, swaying and attempting to burp him, while Iya whispered in her ear. "I have tidings that will interest you, my lady. It seems"—Iya made a dramatic pause—"Koteda-san's husband had a role in directing some covert work in the Shimazu campaign."

Sono let out a gasp. "Covert work? You speak of the *shinobi*—the assassin bands." She lay a hand on Iya's forearm and gave it a quick squeeze. "Koteda-san's husband is in contact with them?"

"Our friend is full of surprises. Snatching an abandoned infant from a forest will be nothing for *shinobi* mercenaries." She held Sono's eyes. "But their services are not free."

"No." Sono lowered the baby from her shoulder. He fussed for an instant before he quieted, taking in wheezing little breaths. She grimaced at the pinched, pained expression on his face, then shifted her gaze to Iya with a sigh. "So our smuggling venture is on once more. Ah, Iya-chan! I hate to ask you to risk the thing again."

"You know I will risk anything that might save our little Taro." Iya ran a gentle finger down the baby's wan cheek. "We need to get him there as quickly as we can."

"I would say you have earned my undying gratitude, but you did that long ago."

Iya waved her words away. "What is our excuse for me to go? A visit to the herbalist?"

"Suppose..." Sono settled on the futon, then bit her lip, thinking. "Suppose Koteda-san knows where to get some special holy oil we can anoint him with. But you need to go back to town to retrieve it."

"Good." Iya mused. "And when it has no effect, that gives you reason to start to question everything you believe."

"That might work. Iya-chan, you're clever as—" She stopped and thrust her fingers over her mouth.

"What is it, my lady?"

"I almost said 'clever as a fox.'"

Sono and Iya selected a kimono for Iya to smuggle out. Iya summoned Hiroko, then left on her errand.

Sono's afternoon crawled past. Her chest constricted every time she thought about her handmaid, taking yet another grave risk for Taro's sake. The early-afternoon bells sounded, and a little of the tension drained from her. Iya should be past the castle gate, at least, or she would have heard about it.

Hisanobu came by as the first streaks of pink stained the sky. Sono knelt near the *shoji*, baby in her arms, and repeated her story about the wondrous holy oil.

He gazed at his motionless son. "I wish I could share your optimism about your *Kirishitan* cure. And I do wish I could hold him..."

His unspoken *before he's gone* floated in the air between them. The melancholy written across his face seemed to go deeper than mere words. So he'd had at least some change of heart toward his son. Was this *Deusu*'s response to her prayers?

Iya returned a few moments after Hisanobu left. She produced a small glass flacon from her sleeve with a flourish and a triumphant grin. "I barely got through the gate before they closed it for the night. But here I am, and I have the oil."

Sono accepted the ornate bottle with her most hopeful smile. She removed the stopper. The scent of lavender and clove wafted through the air. "Its fragrance is like a touch of heaven, Iya-chan. Let us start right away!"

Iya beamed sincerity at her. "They said you must pray first, of course."

They knelt before the crucifix. After a moment, Hiroko joined them, a bemused expression on her face.

Sono recited a series of prayers, including several in Latin. She added a stream of her own words in her new style of prayer, pouring out her soul's deep longing for her son's life. Iya's eyebrows lifted, but she echoed her heartfelt "Amen." Even Hiroko repeated those two syllables.

The baby lay sleeping. Sono applied a few drops of thick, amber-colored liquid to his forehead and massaged it in gently. She opened his little kimono and rubbed some into his chest. His tiny ribs felt delicate as a bush warbler's. He flinched and his eyes flicked open.

She blinked away tears and met Iya's eyes, which also glistened. "We shall see, ah?"

Sono encouraged Hiroko to slip away to her family for a few hours. Once the lady had left, she eagerly sought her handmaid's report. All was arranged. The *shinobi* needed a day to get watchmen in place. When they saw Iya exit the gate with a group, they would follow.

"And," Iya concluded, "as soon as the baby is alone, they will rescue him."

Taro whimpered. Sono picked him up and held his little body close. "So failing the miracle we've prayed for"—she kissed his smooth head—"I will have to part with him tomorrow. Iya-chan, how will I do it?"

Iya stroked the infant's frail shoulder. "Remember *Mōse.* You must push your son out into the reeds. Then trust *Deusu.* Like with *Mōse,* He may have a bigger plan."

Sono and her handmaid repeated the oil treatment, with impassioned prayers, throughout the night. She dared to nourish a hope, however faint, that morning light would reveal some change for the better. With dawn seeping into the chamber, she woke and cuddled the baby as he slept. But as the light grew, the thin wisp of hope she'd nourished fled like a cloud driven across the moon, leaving a bitter void.

There was no change.

She stroked Taro's tiny hand, longing to see him curl his fingers around hers. But he did not stir. She laid him down. Hiroko watched her with her baby, the corners of her eyes creasing with something that appeared to be compassion. She uttered not a word about the failure of the *Kirishitan* cure.

Sono asked Iya to comb her hair, then to send for her husband. She awaited him, steeling herself, her chest constricting with dread. If her contrite guise failed to convince them, Taro's last faint glimmer of hope could come to naught.

The four bells sounded the hour of the snake before Hisanobu and his mother appeared. Lady Matsuura wasted no time on pleasantries. "Your *Kirishitan* remedy has done no good, ah?"

Not one glance at her grandson. Sono thrust back her anger. She dug deep for all the meekness she could find.

She stammered out a few sentences she and Iya had worked out about how she had meditated on the words of Confucius. "I wish to be more conscious, always, of the sort of conduct that will bring pleasure to Lord and Lady Matsuura and honor to our house."

Hisanobu shot his mother a glance with a good bit of triumph mixed in. He fairly glowed at Sono. "That is very mature of you, Sono-chan. 'When you have faults, do not fear to abandon them,' as Confucius also said."

Lady Matsuura's eyes glinted. "I know another adage worth heeding. 'I hear and I forget. I see and I remember.' I would prefer to *see* this new humility of Sono-chan's in her deeds. Shall we invite in a priest?"

Sono loosed a deep sigh. She'd prayed for days that *Deusu* would grant a miracle, but He had chosen not to. *Thy will be done.* She had to trust it, even when she did not understand it.

"*Hai.* Perhaps the *sutras* will help the baby after all." She squirmed inside at even suggesting such a thing. But *Deusu* knew why she had to make such a hideous pretense.

Lady Matsuura harped on. "I just hope this has not come too late."

"As do I, Honored Mother. And if the Buddhist cures do not help him..." The enormity of what was coming made her words jam in her throat. She forced them out. "I think I will have to concede you were right."

"How so, daughter?" There was no mistaking the triumph in Lady Matsuura's eyes. She wanted to hear Sono say it aloud.

"Perhaps it would be best to end little Taro's suffering." The words tore a hole in her heart.

The priest arrived well before noon, and *sutras* rose from outside the chamber. Lady Matsuura thrust Sono's crucifix aside and rekindled the incense on the altar herself.

But naturally these worked no better than the oil from Koteda-san's dresser. By late afternoon, Taro no longer woke to feed. When Sono jostled him, he squinted at her through drowsy eyes over colorless cheeks, as if to let her know that feeding was an unwanted nuisance he no longer cared to endure. He pulled air into his chest only with tiny grunts and a visible effort.

Hiroko stroked his forehead. "If I could give up my own breath so he could have it, I would."

Sono's heart flooded with humble gratitude for how hard Hiroko and Iya had worked—both of them. "I am deeply thankful for everything you have done, Hiroko-san. You have been a true friend." She felt ashamed, now, that she had been so suspicious. "And Iya-chan, I would sooner lose my right arm than you. But I think Honored Mother is right. This has continued long enough."

"Ah! Lady Sono." Hiroko's eyes filled with tears. "What are you going to do?"

She had to force the next words out. "I am going to do as Honored Mother has suggested."

Hiroko patted her hand. "This death will do a great deal to erase his bad *karma*. He will earn a better rebirth, I swear. That should be some comfort to you."

Iya stood, her face working with the force of her effort to contain her emotions. "Would you like me to summon Lord Hisanobu to…"

To take our son away. Sono could not speak. She only nodded.

Chapter Twenty-Seven

Wednesday 5 January 1949

AKIRA WAITED IN THE VISITATION ROOM at police headquarters for his sister to appear. Dave leaned against the dingy counter by his side, facing the glass partition that would separate her from them. A policeman occupied the chair behind them, arms folded over his chest in a way that said he wouldn't budge.

Dave's lips moved in silent prayer. Akira watched him, amazed at his dedication to this woman who had nothing but venom for him.

Goes against everything that's natural. Clear sign God is at work. Dave had said it himself a few minutes earlier.

A door on the jail side of the glass partition swung open. Miyako walked in. When she saw him, her eyes went wide with surprise, and her face lit. He couldn't hear her well, but her lips appeared to form his old honorific title. "*Onii-san.*"

Akira stood. He had to look pathetic with his neck wrapped in stained gauze. But she looked worse. Sunken eyes, disheveled hair, streaks of dirt across her clothing. His first encounter with her at church had delivered a shock, but this was a broadside. What had they done to her?

She took a step that was almost a skip toward the glass before her eyes landed on Delham—and she stopped.

The gaunt-faced policeman who'd walked in with her gave her some heavy-handed encouragement into her chair. It seemed he intended to stay too.

He directed a malevolent glare at each of them in turn. "I will remind you of the rules concerning this visit. You will confine your conversation to approved matters. You will not attempt to communicate with the *horyo* by gesture, in writing, or"—he glanced at Delham—"in any foreign tongue. The visit will last no longer than thirty minutes." He focused on Akira. "I am authorized to conclude it at any time I deem you've violated these rules. Understood?"

Akira affirmed it with a bow. "*Hai.* May I translate this to Reverend Delham?"

The policeman nodded and waited for Akira to finish. "Proceed," he said.

A narrow steel-mesh band ran across the thick glass partition, allowing sound to carry through. Miyako leaned toward it and began in a rush. "Please forgive me, brother. I am very happy to see you. I hope you know I never meant to hurt you."

Akira cringed inside at the subtle emphasis she put on the word "you." Not a word or a glance for Dave. Watching her work so hard to stay the indomitable warrior—it broke his heart. How to tell her she didn't need to? "I've been trying to visit for days. But it was nearly impossible to get clearance."

"It's wonderful you've come. I'm so relieved." She paused, then went on in rapid syllables. "But tell me the truth, ah? Why is *he* here?" Clearly, she expected that if she spoke fast, Delham couldn't follow her. She'd heard the reverend's halting attempt at Japanese at the church.

Dave's face was a blank. It seemed Miyako was right. Akira replied slowly, enunciating each syllable. "Reverend Delham asked to come. He has something he wants to say to you."

"To me?"

Akira gave Delham the nod to proceed. Delham started in English. "Please—"

The policeman beside her rose to his feet. "*Japanese!*"

"Sorry—uh, *sumimasen.*" Delham tried again. "*Wata...ah...Watashi ha anata...woyurusu.*" He made his best effort at the Japanese phrases Akira had taught him. *I forgive you.*

She flushed, clearly at a loss. Had she understood?

Delham turned to him. "Please help me out." He gestured in her direction.

Akira nodded. "Here's what Reverend Delham came to say. I can perhaps express it better in our language. It's true he piloted a plane that bombed the refinery and the aircraft factory. But he is brokenhearted about"—the reality of Hiro-chan's death slammed into his chest again—"little Hiro-chan. Sometimes bombs kill the innocents." He looked into her eyes through a mist that had formed in his own. "Reverend Delham wants you to know that's not anything he wanted."

She stared at him before she shot back, delivering every syllable as a barb. "Ten thousand dead, Akira-san. Ten thousand, here in Osaka. One hundred thousand in Tokyo. I walked and walked, day after day. Never found them. Not Mama-san. Not our grandparents." She trailed off into fuming silence.

Delham stood and gave her a gracious bow. "*Watashi o yurushite, kudasai.*" Please forgive me. "*Senso wa warui kotodesu.*" War is a bad thing. It wasn't eloquent but should have gotten his meaning across.

His sister sat in stony silence. A wave of sorrow rocked him. How old was she when the first bombers came? How old when she lost every adult who'd taken care of her?

"Mi-chan," he said in his gentlest voice, "I don't know what those firestorms were like. I've had my own experiences with American bombing." He flexed his scarred hand. "But I don't know how things were here. I forgive you for whatever you had to do. And"—here was the root of his own despair—"I hope you can forgive me for not coming home to you."

He waited for some kind word from her lips. She sat with a stony face. No word came.

"You know some of my story. I know so little of yours," he said.

"Really?" Her reply rang with bitterness. "I was sure Captain Oda would tell you all about it."

"I've gathered a few things, but here's the important one—you've been taking care of Papa-san since the war. Alone." His heart ballooned with tenderness for her.

She met his eyes, and he hoped she read the depth of his soul-searing regret in them. "Here's a lesson I'm doing my best to learn, Mi-chan." He was glad he had Dave's words to echo. "Hatred is a prison. Forgiveness is a gift of God that frees you from it."

The policeman beside her bristled like a watchdog. "Foreign religion. Not approved topic."

"I'm sorry, officer." He throttled his exasperation. "We've all been through so much, sister. Many wounds. Deep wounds. It's time for healing."

Her eyes went wide, as if she'd actually forgotten for a moment. "Your stab wound, *Onii-san*. Does it hurt much?"

He gave her a rueful smile. "It hurts a lot, little sister. But bodies mend."

She made a low bow. "Please forgive me, Akira-san."

"I forgive you." He could feel the sincerity of her contrition—toward him, at least. "I told you that."

"*Arigato*." She bowed again. "Did you see Papa-san? How is he?"

He went stiff with stinging misery. "Oda has informed me he believes seeing me would be too great a shock for Papa-san in his current state."

"I am sorry," she said in a soft voice. "I'm sure that was painful to hear. But he does know Papa-san well."

"I hope I can see our father soon. I hope he can find some forgiveness in his heart for me."

She snorted. "He found none for me."

He longed to speak to her from the heart, and it would be easier without Dave there. "*Kudasai?*" He glanced at his friend, then at the door.

"*Hai.*" Delham took the hint and gave her a low bow. "*Sayanara*, Matsuura-san."

Akira waited until the door had closed behind him. "You can't do it, ah?"

"Do what?"

"Grant him your forgiveness."

"Of course not." Her tone blistered with irony. "What would it even mean? But apparently you can."

"I couldn't have, even a month ago. But when—" He glanced at the policeman, weighing how far he could go. "Let's just say I see a lot of things differently now. In the hospital, and in the prison camp, I heard things and saw things that gave me a great deal to think about. There's strength and discipline in the Yamato ways. But there's also a very real power our way doesn't teach us. A real freedom."

"And you're learning this power? From your Delham?"

"*Hai.* You think you can honor Hiro-chan's death through another death?"

"Approved subjects," the police guard growled. "I won't warn you again."

He made a quick bow. "Forgive me." He gazed into his sister's eyes. "It doesn't work that way."

"How does it work, then?" She lifted her chin. "You and your new friend are wiser than Confucius, ah?"

"There's been a death already. It's paid for already. *Iesu's* death, Mi-chan." He was working to fully grasp the implications of this himself.

The police guard glowered. "Approved subjects only. The visit is done. *Horyo,* come."

Akira squeezed his hand into a fist and pushed it against the glass between them. "You know I loved Hiro-chan, too."

She rested her palm on the glass behind his fist. "I know."

The brute grabbed her wrist. "*Horyo.* Come." He yanked her off the chair and propelled her through the door.

Akira burned at the rough handling they were giving her. He called out after her. "I love you, sister. And I'll find you an attorney."

The police guard showed him out to the vestibule. Delham was pacing in front of the window. They walked in silence out the back entrance and down a smoke-blackened granite stairway

Delham spoke in a low voice. "This place looks grim."

Akira nodded. "Very. I know she broke the law, but what they're doing to her is not right."

The American gave a little shudder. "It brings back memories I wish I didn't have. How long can they keep her here?"

He wadded his fists deeper into his pockets and peered miserably at the pavement. "I don't know. But I did not come back from the far side of the world to stand still while they brutalize her."

Nineteenth Day of the Ninth Month, Anno Domini 1588

Sono asked the women to leave her. She was on her knees before the crucifix when sandals squelched on the path outside. She rose to greet her husband.

His eyes were soft with grief. A flicker of hope sparked in her heart. "My lord, I will ask you one more time." She hurried on, not daring to pause for breath. "If we send him to the House of Mercy, they might still be able to do something for him."

"Sono-chan, you must believe that sending the child back saddens me. But I will not defy my mother. And the truth of her position is becoming clearer by the hour."

The bitterness in her soul drove a tart edge through her voice. "Then there is nothing left for me but to follow my Honored Mother's desires in all respects. Perhaps my agreement to this will make up for some of my prior faults in her view."

He reached for her hand. She flinched back, but he seized it anyway. "I knew you would see wisdom. What is this baby, after all, compared with the value of harmony within our household?"

A long moment passed while she struggled to master herself enough to speak the words she had practiced. It was stepping off a high balcony again, like the evening she'd uttered her wedding vows. But that night, there had been a delicious sense of adventure. A dizzy excitement that there might be a rampart worth capturing on Hirado. Now there was only a dull desperation.

"He cannot be murdered by our hands, my lord. You must carry him into the woods, in case *Deusu* might take the opportunity to intervene. Perhaps near Saikyo-ji, where Hiroko-san tells me Jizo might also take care of him."

He squeezed her hand—in spite of the birth impurity. "You're sure this is what you want?"

Hot words sprang to her tongue. "What I want—" She dropped her eyes and swallowed the rest. *Calm your own mind.* She went on in her meek voice—she'd been using it a great deal in the past hours. "What I want is for Honored Mother to be pleased. But there is one more thing. Since I cannot leave the birthing chamber, I would like Iya-chan to accompany him until you leave him."

Hisanobu gave her a soft smile. "Certainly. And Mother is pleased. As am I. But we should leave soon."

Iya had said to give the *shinobi* until the hour of the sheep. The sheep's eight bells had sounded, but Sono was not ready to part with her baby. "Pray, my lord. I need some time alone with—" Her voice broke.

"We can leave as late as the seven bells." He squeezed her hand again and stood. "I shall return then."

Sono's remaining moments with her Taro passed all too hastily. She cradled him, resting her cheek against his warm little head. *This will not be the last time I hold him. This will not be the last time.*

Iya brought the basket. The weave was tight, and it was just the right shape to keep him snug. They had fitted it with soft red cushions. Sono nestled Taro into it. He lay very still.

She brushed her lips against her baby's smooth forehead. *I must push him out into the reeds.*

Men's leather sandals fell on the path outside the birthing chamber. Sono gave Taro one last kiss. "Goodbye, my little angel. We will meet again. Whether here or in heaven is up to our Heavenly Father. But I know He will guard every step of your journey."

She watched his face intently, longing to see some response to her voice. Some last token of his little personality she could carry with her.

Hisanobu's shadow fell across the closed *shoji*. A tiny furrow creased Taro's brow between two labored, grunting breaths. That little change of expression would have to do.

She handed the basket to Iya. "Take him now." The words ripped from her breaking heart.

Time passed. Sono could not have said how long. She'd watched their retreating backs until she could no longer see or hear them. Now she lay crumpled on the straw floormats, empty arms hugging her chest, aching for her son.

Hiroko padded into the chamber and knelt beside her.

"Come, Lady Sono. No need to lie on the floor. Please move over to the futon, and I will make some tea."

She shook her head and curled into a tighter ball. "When will Taro drink again?"

"You must let him go, lady. His destiny is out of your hands."

She sat up. "Let him go?" His tiny robes lay folded on a shelf, with a ceramic cup next to them. No doubt a few drops of milk coated the bottom yet. The whole room was still dressed in white—the white futon where he had slept tucked up against her chest. The white-draped dais and white-hung walls. The glaring icon stood brazenly in the center of the altar with his corona of fire to combat her "birth impurity."

What was the use of a birthing chamber with no baby?

No son for Hisanobu. No twenty-eighth lord for Hirado. No tiny warm body at her breast. The ache of her loss was a consuming void. And if Lady Matsuura had her way, what would keep her next pregnancy from ending the same way?

The afternoon had turned bitter cold, a chill wind whipping from the sea. The walls rattled. A loose tile clattered above their heads.

He will not do it. He will not leave our baby out there.

Hiroko layered more charcoal on the fire in the sunken hearth, then sat beside her, massaging her back. "I know this is difficult, Lady Sono."

"I see him everywhere, Hiroko-san. In every corner of this chamber, where I birthed him and where I held him—"

"This chamber, where he endured so much pain, my lady." Hiroko's voice was firm. "You did the right thing. He will shed that pain soon."

Being torn by foxes is better? She managed to choke back those words, but she was powerless against the bitter storm raging in her soul.

I pray, dear Iesu, that You do not let him suffer. Let the shinobi do what we hired them to do.

Hiroko went on. "And your husband is pleased with you. That is most important, ah?"

He should be pleased. This is his fault. She bit her lip until it hurt holding back her bitter words.

The sympathy in Hiroko's eyes seemed real. "Perhaps a change of scene would do you good." She leaned toward Sono confidentially. "There is a Buddhist custom you might find helpful."

She doubted that, but she felt compelled to ask. "What is it?"

"A birthing hut. They do it more in the villages. It is the same idea as this chamber, only not so grand. And farther away from everyone else. A simple space designed for relaxation. And meditation."

"Far away from everyone sounds perfect." *And I mean everyone.* All the people who had betrayed her son. And her.

"Would you like me to ask Lady Matsuura for you? It is one small way I can help."

"I cannot imagine Honored Mother has much interest in doing anything for me."

Hiroko gave her a knowing little smile. She glanced at the icon on the altar. "If she is convinced you are taking an interest in True Word Buddhism, she will be."

Torchlight filtered through Sono's *shoji*, heralding Iya's return. She slipped in and shed her hat and veil, revealing tear-stained cheeks under red-rimmed eyes.

It is done. My husband really left him. Everything solid in Sono's world dissolved. She collapsed onto her knees, buried her face in her hands, and broke into a wracking sob. "Ah, Iya! I kept hoping he would have a change of heart."

Iya gently drew Sono's head onto her shoulder. "I think it was not easy for him, my lady. He insisted we nestle Taro's basket among the pines you love, in a nice sheltered spot. He got on his knees to make the bed of leaves himself. He sought out a place"—her voice broke—"a place within view of Saikyo-ji's pagoda."

"And the foxes?"

"We did not hear them, *graças a Deusu.*"

Hiroko reached for Sono's hand and patted it. "You have done a hard thing, Lady Sono. Everyone understands that. Now that you have Iya-chan for company, I will seek out Her Ladyship and see if we can get you moved."

Sono thanked Hiroko, and she departed. Sono rose to her feet, her hands clasped in a tight knot. "Iya-chan, did you see anything of the *shinobi*?"

"I hope not, my lady. We did hire them for secrecy."

"We will know nothing until you go to town tomorrow, will we? I think I'll expire first."

"Koteda-san promised to send word in the morning. And in the meantime"—she glanced at Sono and bit her lip—"I imagine Hisanobu will come by."

Sono groaned. "So I shall have to act grateful."

"*Hai*. Heartbroken, but grateful."

Sono edged closer to the hearth, but its warmth could never fill the void her babe had left. "How can I go back to my old routine like nothing has passed? Like I never held poor Taro?"

She had been confident, when she came to Hirado, that *Deusu* sent her. Supremely confident, thanks to her father, and her brother, and even a special dispensation from Padre Lucena himself. But if *Deusu* was with her, how could this have ended in such disaster?

Deusu, *if you* are *listening, I want nothing to do with this life. How can I sleep under silk sheets with a man who would leave our infant out in the cold?*

Chapter Twenty-Eight

January 1949

AKIRA HAD NO IDEA HOW DIFFICULT finding an attorney for his sister would prove.

The first three men he interviewed claimed they were fully engaged. The fourth attorney fidgeted with the corner of a brief on his mahogany desk, then looked into Akira's eyes. "Your sister is the daughter of a former navy captain. She attacked a prominent American. Her recent history includes an arrest for prostitution."

"But not a conviction." Akira was quick to insert that.

"It doesn't matter. The arrest tarnishes her record enough." He shifted his wire-rimmed glasses up his nose, frowned, and gave his head a resigned shake. "I don't think I can help you, Matsuura-san. In the current climate, I don't think anyone can keep your sister out of prison."

What? Akira's frustration was a wall that slammed into his chest. "You're the fourth attorney I've met with." And the first who'd been forthright. "And you won't even try to defend her?"

"I'll be honest, Matsuura-san. I am sorry about your sister, but I can't tarnish my reputation with the judges. I have to think of future clients."

Akira sat back in his chair, squeezed his eyes shut, and willed himself not to explode. He formed fists, then released them before he could manage a reply. "I look in Miyako's eyes and I see my mother. She squares her jaw and I see a prettier version of my father." He glared at the man. "But every attorney in this city seems ready to throw her out like a pail of rotten fish."

That meeting made him desperate enough to seek out Oda's advice. They met two evenings later for a beer at a restaurant the captain suggested. The little place specialized in fried shrimp, and the delicious aroma that filled the room summoned saliva to Akira's mouth.

A waitress brought them two beers and a platter of shrimp balls thick with breaded crust. Oda brandished a skewer. "You were a very young man when you last saw Japan. No experience with legal matters, as far as I know." "That's true. So I'm grateful for your insight." "Which shows your customary wisdom." The captain's lips curved in something that bordered on a smirk. "Japan's system works rather differently than other nations'. Our prime concern is getting to the raw facts. A criminal like your sister"—he took a hearty bite of shrimp—"is best served by facilitating that process."

"I trust she's doing that. There were dozens of witnesses. What would she imagine she could hide?"

"That's what you would think, but I spoke a couple of days ago with the prosecuting attorney, Suzuki. He is convinced she's holding something back. And he will make her life miserable until she persuades him otherwise."

Akira's skewer sagged in his hand. He'd lost all interest in shrimp. "Any idea why he would think that?"

"Instinct, maybe. She hasn't named any accomplices, but Prosecutor Suzuki doesn't believe she worked alone." Oda pressed a napkin against his lips with incongruous delicacy. "I have tried to help your sister, believe me. I owe that to your father. But I can't help her until she's willing to help herself." He eyed Akira. "Think about it. You've been gone so long. What do you really know about her?"

Akira let loose a deep sigh, his mind swirling with uncertainty. "Not as much as I hoped."

"Exactly." Oda picked up another skewer and twirled it. "As an old friend, I can offer one more piece of advice."

"Please."

"I have observed that a significant contribution to the right political organization can sometimes force a door open, even when it seems firmly shut."

A bribe. Akira froze, his glass halfway to his lips.

Oda gave him a disingenuous smile. "You asked for my advice." The smile faded. "It's a sad thing, but that is the Japan we're living in. Men consume each other to stay alive."

"And my sister has become someone's dog meat." Rage made his shirt feel tight. "If I ever find out whose, I'll make sure his bill comes around. As for my father, that's another topic."

"Naturally, you want to see him."

"*Hai.*"

"This is a difficult matter." Oda pinned Akira with his eyes. "I heard your little speech at the Christian church the night of the attack. Am I to understand that you have renounced the religions of your ancestors?"

Here it comes. "I have become a Christian."

Oda leaned back in his chair, lips pressed into a grim line. "And you expect your noble father, who has devoted his life to defending our nation and our emperor, to welcome a Christian son with open arms."

"Not exactly, but—"

"You do understand that all this time he has remained confident"—he spoke the word forcefully, his eyes drilling into Akira's—"that you died showing the same devotion. I'm not sure you fully realize how impossible it will be for your father to reconcile himself to your return, first as a *horyo*, but even more as a Christian."

Shame coiled like a serpent through Akira's gut. He ejected it. "I wouldn't have to confront Papa-san with everything at once. But, Captain Oda, I've come back from the other side of the world to rejoin my family. I must see him. I must do my best to explain."

Oda set his glass down and regarded him, eyes cold. "A man as near death as he is wants to enjoy some certainty in what's left of his days. Certainty, for example, that his children will honor him when he departs this life. That they will venerate his spirit according to our ancient traditions."

The captain picked up a paper napkin and squeezed it in a weather-beaten fist. "It would be a bitter shock to him to learn that you live, but that he can't be sure of you." He dropped the crumpled napkin on the table. "Your father has taken you to Hirado, yes?"

"Of course. More than once."

"Then you've seen the memorial to your great ancestor Shigenobu, the hero of the Korean campaign."

"*Hai.* It's a vivid memory, how Papa-san took us to light incense there."

"That means you honored the tomb of the twenty-sixth *daimyo*. And maybe you also visited the twenty-eighth. But you never saw the tomb of Hisanobu, the twenty-seventh lord, did you?"

"No." He pushed back his irritation. Why was Oda drifting off topic? "I suppose every warlord can't go down in history."

"Indeed. I'd like to show you something." Oda pulled a battered hardcover book with yellow-edged pages from his satchel. He set it on the table.

Age of the Warring States: A Military History.

Akira gave him a quizzical look. "A textbook?"

Oda nodded. "Your father and I took this course together at the academy. We teamed up on our final project. A report on the strategy the sixteenth-century Lord Regent Toyotomi used to subdue the Island of Kyushu."

Akira nodded in recognition. "Ah, second-year military strategy. That was a tough one."

Oda opened to a page he'd bookmarked and pointed to the top of a paragraph.

Akira read: *One major challenge the Lord Regent confronted in his drive to unite Japan...*

The text explained how a number of warlords had allied themselves with the Portuguese by claiming the *Kirishitan* faith and thus gained the advantage of European firearms.

Akira peered at Oda. "What—"

"Keep reading," he said.

Notable among these was Omura Sumitada of Hizen Province, who went so far as to cede the fishing village of Nagasaki to a Kirishitan *religious order called the* Jesuits. *Prior to this duplicitous act, the House of Matsuura had established the island of Hirado as one of Japan's foremost centers for international trade. Sumitada succeeded in making Nagasaki the principal port of call for the Portuguese "black ship."*

The text went on to describe how handsomely the House of Omura profited by displacing the House of Matsuura as the conduit for European trade.

Akira reached the bottom of the page and handed the book back to the captain, puzzled. "This is mostly common knowledge."

"*Hai*. But since it concerns your own house, your father was struck by it. Such an injustice suffered due to foreign religion. It set him on a path that pushed well beyond the bounds of our project."

Oda's eyes went glassy as he reminisced. "He traveled to Hirado that winter break and met with a third cousin or something. He toured the family residence and they showed him some of the treasures of your house—very precious heirlooms. Shigenobu's armor. A banner with your family's mulberry crest that Shigenobu and his son, Hisanobu, may have carried on the Korean campaign. A set of handsome old palanquins. A copy of the Lord Regent's 1587 Edict Against Christianity, believe it or not."

"They have that on Hirado?"

"*Hai*. It's very rare. It bears the Lord Regent's own signature. Your father was also given a chance to delve into some of the chronicles of your house. And he was deeply shocked by what he learned. You know, of course, that the Tokugawa shoguns forcefully ejected this seditious foreign cult from Japan. What you don't know, I suspect, is that your own family had a brief deviance with it."

Akira jerked to attention, startled. "My father never said anything."

"Of course not. What he learned is this—Hisanobu, the twenty-seventh lord, ended his life in such disgrace that no one even knows where he's entombed. But his wife is buried on Hirado, among all those *torii* gates and spires. Her virgin name was Omura Sono. A daughter of Omura Sumitada."

Oda leaned forward, his eyes intense. "Do you see it yet, Akira-kun? The blood of the most infamous *Kirishitan* warlord in that entire infamous era runs in your own veins—a fact your family has done its best to bury for generations. A *Kirishitan* warlord who robbed your house of ascendancy and wealth. Your father learned this while we were students at Eta Jima, among all those noble—and loyal—officer candidates. Can you imagine the shame he felt?"

Akira groped for words. None were adequate.

"Shamed to the core, Akira-kun. I'm not surprised he never chose to divulge this to you."

Akira shook his head. "I didn't know."

Oda toyed with the last skewer. "So I think you'll see

how disconcerting it would be for your father to learn that, after all these generations, his own son has opened the door again to this outside religion."

Disbelief cottoned Akira's brain. "*Hai.* But I'm not sure I understand, Captain Oda. Because of something that happened centuries ago, you're saying the doctor will refuse to let me visit my own father?"

Oda drained his beer. "Given how things are, I think it's best to see what happens with your sister. If you can get her freed, that might help cushion the blow for your father. At least he'll have one child he can count on."

Akira all but gasped at the verbal punch. *That stung.* And had the captain just made seeing his father contingent on a bribe?

Oda stood and pulled his wallet from his pocket. "I hope you'll consider the advice I gave you concerning her case. It could dramatically shorten her path back to freedom."

Akira rose and choked out an *arigato.* He glared through a haze of angry disbelief at the captain's departing back.

Nineteenth Day of the Ninth Month, Anno Domini 1588

Sono's husband did not visit her that evening, and she was delighted to be spared the sight of him. She tossed on her futon, her mind rushing about in despairing circles. The nine bells sounded at midnight, and then the eight, and the seven, and on to the six bells at dawn. She heard them all.

The time crept by somehow until the hour Iya could hasten to the kitchen to retrieve their letter from Koteda-san. Sono paced, straining to hear the clatter of her wooden sandals on the paving stones. What tidings would she bring?

Her heart jolted at the sound of footsteps. But they were the slap of a man's leather soles, not Iya's wooden sandals.

Hisanobu? Her stomach lurched like it was falling off a precipice. She hurried to pat her hair smooth and knelt facing the *shoji*.

He looked haggard, with topknot askew and bleary eyes. He glared around the chamber. "You're here alone, ah?" He smelled of stale sake.

A warning blast blared through her mind. "*Hai.* Welcome, my lord. Are you well?"

His voice went from gruff to savage. "Perhaps you wondered where I was last night, ah?"

"*Hai,* my lord. I had hoped to see you after—"

"After I had to handle the matter of the baby."

Handle the matter. She froze. The silence prickled with tension. He cleared his throat and cast his eyes to the ground. "I did my best for him, Sono-chan."

Remember, heartbroken but grateful. "*Arigato.* Iya-chan told me."

"And afterwards, I went up to Saikyo-ji and prayed for him. I made an offering to Jizo and prayed all night, Sono-chan."

A form of prayer that involved imbibing *sake,* apparently. "And you saw our uncle, the abbot, there?"

"*Hai.*"

Irony blistered in her voice. "I suppose he said what passed concerning the baby is all my fault. And *Iesu's.*"

He glowered. "You have neglected the rituals we have always observed in this house. From ancient times, Sono."

"Twenty-seven generations. I have heard all about it. But when you married a *Kirishitan,* what did you expect, my lord?"

He loosed a string of curses. "I did not expect this. I did not expect to have to lay an infant on a bed of pine needles."

The slightest tremor shook his lower lip. This was the heart of it. Was all the drinking to mask the pain?

She wasn't feeling gracious. "You did not *have* to do that. You could have had the physician come, as I begged you to do. At least then, if our son perished, it would have been in my arms."

He thrust out his jaw and hurled words at her like throwing darts. "You know why I couldn't do that."

Yes. Your mother. She cringed at the odor of *sake* that

hit her face. "Why did you come here?"

"To command you to be reasonable. Give up this foreign heresy. Return to the religion of your ancestors and mine."

"Buddhist babies never perish, then? Never come early. Never have to be 'sent back.'"

"Of course they do. But mine will not."

It was all she could do not to burst into a scoffing laugh. "Why? Because the Matsuura make sacrifices to the deities and give alms to Saikyo-ji? Then what of Tatsuko's babies, ah? I imagine your father was in the habit of giving to Saikyo-ji then."

His eyes turned frigid. She had gone too far. She put her forehead on the floormat. "Forgive me." She raised her eyes to him. "I do not pretend to know why *Deusu* allowed this baby to suffer so. But maybe *Deusu* is trying to say something to you. Trying to get you to turn to Him. To face your own mortality in the person of your son."

"I am *samurai.*" His tone blistered the air between them. "I face my mortality daily. It is my duty. And it is time you do yours. When you conceive again—and you will—you shall adhere to the rituals. If in the end you bear a girl, you can do what you like. But when you bear another boy, you will do everything the priests recommend. And we will present him at Saikyo-ji."

"What about *Kirishitan* baptism? I was promised—"

"You want someone to sprinkle *Kirishitan* holy water on him? I do not object. But you will complete our rituals first." His red-rimmed eyes fixed on her chest and widened. "What is that?"

She put her fingers to the cross pendant dangling against her breastbone.

He stiffened, his muscles tensing under his silks. "Take that off."

"My pendant? You know I never take this off."

"Take it off, or I swear I will rip it off you."

"My lord." She clutched the pendant and scooted back, well out of his reach, using the impurity of the birthing chamber as a shield. "Leave me now. We can discuss these things when you have not been drinking."

He growled in frustration. The rage distorting his face

sent fear skittering through her, and not just for the delicate chain on her pendant. The sword thrust through his belt could sever her neck as easily as his fingers could rend the golden chain. She had seen it done.

He slammed the side of his hand into the wooden doorframe so hard that her heart jumped in her chest. She pressed her forehead to the floormat. A long moment passed while she knelt servant-style, praying he could bring his rage under control. He stood, and she listened as he stalked off.

She slid the *shoji* closed, then slumped against the doorframe. She sat a long moment without moving before she whispered into the empty room. "He never really saw you, Taro, did he? Until the moment came to leave you in the woods."

Chapter Twenty-Nine

Thursday 13 January 1949

AKIRA SETTLED INTO A CHAIR IN the dingy visitation room of Osaka police headquarters. The attorney he'd engaged, Namura, took his place beside him. Rev. Kagawa's suggestion had finally brought Akira to the man who seemed to be the only attorney prepared to take Miyako's case. Which raised cynical questions in his mind as to whether this man had any reputation to worry about.

"Last time it took them a few minutes to bring her in," he told the man.

Namura gave him a lethargic nod and pulled a magazine from his briefcase. Akira stifled his irritation and his growing concern that this stately older fellow didn't have the energy for a tough battle to save his sister.

The door opened on the jail side of the dividing wall. Miyako walked in, followed by a police guard. Akira managed to muffle a choking sound. He had thought she looked bad the last time he'd seen her. But today she looked worse. Her eyes moved listlessly across the floor. Dirt lodged under her nails and in the creases around her knuckles.

What were they doing to her? He could not let them keep her locked away in this place.

She raised her eyes to his, and her wan face lit with relief. "I am so glad to see you. You don't know how glad. I've been so worried about you." She dropped into a bow.

The guard on their side of the partition delivered the customary rules litany, then Akira introduced the attorney. "I am so sorry we couldn't come sooner. They say I can only come once a week. And Attorney Namura had to apply for clearance to interview you. I saved my visit until he could join me."

"I'm delighted to meet you, sir. Believe me."

Namura adjusted his glasses, registering no surprise at her roughed-over appearance. "I've heard a great deal about you."

She reacted with something that crossed a wince with an ironic smile. "I hope I live up to the expectations the newspapers created." She hesitated. "What do you think of my chances?"

The attorney cleared his throat. "Generally, as a first-time offender you would just need to convince the prosecutor you're serious about changing your ways. And that you have the family support to do it. Assuming we can give your prosecutor confidence you're a low risk for future offenses, he should be amenable to recommending that the case not move forward. And a judge will almost always accept that recommendation."

A flush of hope bloomed over her face.

"However"—Namura shifted his focus to Akira—"your sister's case has two unique elements. We have a high-profile American involved. And the case has become very visible. General MacArthur and the people at his Supreme Command in Tokyo are likely to take a stance on this. They operate like the puppeteers in black. Not off-stage, but we're all supposed to pretend we don't see them."

"And if her case goes to trial?"

"If it goes to trial, there's little chance of freeing her. Prosecutors don't move a case to trial unless they're confident they'll get a conviction. It's always best if a prisoner cooperates fully with the prosecution and avoids a trial."

"I have." Her voice sounded as bleak as the dingy wall behind her. "But they're trying to make me confess to something that didn't happen."

Akira's chest hollowed at the way every vestige of hope had fled her face. "Captain Oda also emphasized that, sister. Are you sure you're not holding anything back?"

"Oda!" She arched her neck and glared at the ceiling. "I don't expect any help from Oda."

"He said he's tried."

"I don't need his kind of help." The venom in her tone jarred him. But the man had been pretty rough when he arrested her. "Akira-san"—she glanced at the guard next to him, then fixed anguished eyes on Akira's face—"you have no idea what it's like in here. They keep pushing and pushing to get me to admit to...something. The only problem is, there's nothing to admit. It's like they want to make an example of me. Prove how zealous they can be."

He groped for a more optimistic angle. "We do have two things in our favor, ah? The high-profile American you mention is my friend, and he has no desire to see my sister prosecuted. He'd prefer to see her forgiven, freed, and whole."

Namura harrumphed. "Quite admirable—"

"And as the *actual* victim, so would I."

The attorney shifted in his seat. "Unfortunately, in an attempted murder case, that won't be your decision. But if the victim, or victims, indicate that the defendant has reached a satisfactory settlement of restitution, prosecutors often find that persuasive."

Akira persisted. "And surely it would mean something to have a famous war hero advocate for her."

"Delham?" she interjected. "Why would he do that?"

"He feels terrible about Hiro-chan. The army accused them of indiscriminate bombing, but he swears it wasn't true." He paused, searching for the right way to broach the topic that had weighed on his heart like an anchor. "Were you with our brother when he died, Mi-chan?"

She nodded, eyes fixed on the the grimy counter in front of her.

"So it was a bomb?" The deluge of grief he'd been holding back broke through once more. Poor lively, unlucky Hiro-chan. His bright little life snuffed out before it really started.

She nodded again, chin trembling.

"Dave-san will be devastated to hear that." He went on, speaking as gently as he could. "You'll have to tell me everything sometime. There's so much I don't know. About Mama-san, for example..." He faded to silence, his sense of loss swelling like the surf at high tide.

She blinked hard, then raised moist eyes to his. "There is a lot I haven't told you. And we won't be able to cover it all today." She gave an ironic little snort. "They can grill me for hours on end, but you get thirty minutes. You won't be able to come again for another week?"

"I'm afraid not."

She took a long look at the guards, weighing something, then turned back to him. "There's something I need to tell you before our time's up." Her grime-streaked face brightened. "I had a dream. I don't know what to think about it, but perhaps you can tell me."

"I'm no expert on that subject. But what was it?"

"I heard from *Him*, Akira. At least, I think I did."

He gawked at her. "Him? You mean *Iesu*? How do you know?"

"I can't tell you all of it. We won't have time. But He called me 'daughter.' And the way it made me feel..." She sighed. "If only I could live in that dream."

Akira gave her a wistful smile. "We all wish that. But what happened in your dream?"

"It's too long a story, but He invited me to ask for what I needed. And to believe." Her brows crunched together in puzzlement. "Believe what, ah?"

"That's amazing, Mi-chan, if *He* spoke to you." He glanced at the guard at her side. "Maybe I could bring you some Christian books."

The guard shook his head.

"Or you could come teach me, brother."

Akira turned to the attorney. "Could I?"

"Instruct her in religion?" Namura said. "We can put in a request. It's quite unlikely to get approved, but the fact that she asked can only help bolster the picture of a repentant criminal."

She leaned toward Akira. "It's not just a picture."

The jail-side guard made the announcement he'd been dreading. "Two more minutes."

Her face fell. "Ah! How can we be out of time? Quickly, then. Of course, no apology can make up for the thing I did. But please, *please* tell Reverend Delham I'm sorry. And have you seen Papa-san?"

He shook his head. She'd hit on his other great regret. "I spoke with his doctor. Papa-san is stable, they tell me. Not very lucid. The doctor is as adamant as Oda that confronting me might be harmful." He stood. "We have to get you out of here so you can see him."

"*Hai*. If he dies while I'm here...how horrible. I can't imagine not seeing him again."

Akira thrust his thoughts away from the anguish that loomed behind every thought of the family he'd grown up with. "I'm sure our father feels just as eager to see you."

She shook her head. "I wish I believed that."

Akira walked with the attorney through the detention center's tiled waiting room. Its battered wooden chairs were a depressingly familiar sight. Out the way they'd come in, through an unassuming back entrance onto a smoke-blackened granite stairway.

The instant they were beyond the range of any listening bureaucrats inside the looming red-brick edifice, Akira vented a surge of rage at Namura. "Did you see the state she's in? What are they doing to her? And what can we do about it?"

Namura let out a heavy sigh. "It is perfectly customary for them to put a high level of pressure on their suspects. They need to be sure they've obtained all the facts."

"The way they're treating her is *customary*, ah? Don't I have some recourse?"

"At this instant? I'm afraid not."

Akira glared at the sidewalk. "So you're saying my sister is at their mercy."

"Unless you have some well-placed friends you haven't mentioned to me."

"I don't have any friends." He cast an ironic look at Namura. "Except the man she tried to stab."

"If he's willing to provide a statement, as you suggested earlier, that would have some value."

The hopeless look on Miyako's face replayed through his mind. He picked up his pace toward the line of taxis at the building's front entrance, anger grinding his feet into the pavement. He wasn't going to let an idle moment pass before he got on the phone with Dave Delham.

Twentieth Day of the Ninth Month, Anno Domini 1588

Sono leaned against the doorframe and stared at the ceiling without focusing, her breath coming in short pants. *Take it off, or I swear I will rip it off you.* Her husband's vicious words howled like foxes in her mind.

Her fingers moved back to her pendant. Papa-san had given it to her at her confirmation. It had never left her neck since.

Iya hurried in and spoke in a whisper. "I brought tidings from Koteda-san." She pulled a small scroll from her sleeve.

Sono unrolled it with trembling fingers. She spread it on her futon so they both could read.

My dear Lady Sono,

The House of Mercy has a new occupant as of last night. They are tending to him as best they can. The brothers send you some encouragement from the Holy Scripture:

Trust in the Lord with all thine heart; and lean not unto thine own understanding. In all thy ways acknowledge him, and he shall direct thy paths.

Except a corn of wheat fall into the ground and perish, it abideth alone: but if it perish, it bringeth forth much fruit.

She looked up at Iya, tears of relief blurring her vision. "*Graças a Deusu.* Our men came through. Iya-chan, our mad plan actually worked."

Iya gave her a brilliant smile. "*Hai*, my lady. And now he is in *Deusu's* hands." She pulled a handkerchief from her sleeve and dabbed at Sono's teary face. "I saw Hisanobu on my way in. He looked terrible. Something passed while I was out, ah?"

Sono told her about Hisanobu's tirade. "I have never seen him like that. When the sake wears off, I hope he thinks better of what he said."

Iya made hasty arrangements for Sono's breakfast, then hurried to town for further news of Taro. But Sono could only pick at the whitefish a kitchen maid brought her. Taro's pathetic little cries haunted her. How could she fill her stomach when she knew not whether he was feeding?

She gave up the pretense and curled up on her futon. But sleeping came no more readily than eating. She cycled through her memories of her baby, her heart tipping between warmth and pain.

His tiny body snuggled against hers. Trusting little eyes gazing up at her. Three and sometimes four women exhausting themselves to fulfill the trust in those innocent eyes. With her eyes closed, the room still echoed with the noise of them buzzing around.

Trust in the Lord with all your heart. That was the verse the brothers had sent her. If a group of women would do all that for Taro, would his loving, eternal Father in heaven do less?

They had sent another scripture. What was it again? She sat up and groped for the scroll.

Except a corn of wheat fall into the ground and perish, it abideth alone: but if it perish, it bringeth forth much fruit.

The words punched an insight straight into her heart. *Iesu* had given himself on the cross, and *Deusu* had transformed that sacrifice of His own Son into something even greater than anyone had expected.

Mōse's mother had given up her son, floating him in a basket in the reeds. *Deusu* had transformed that mother's sacrifice into freedom for a whole people.

Sono had sent her son in a basket to lie beneath the pines. *Deusu* willing, that sacrifice could become something much greater than she could foresee or imagine. Couldn't it?

She had come to Hirado trusting in men. Her father, her brother, Padre Lucena. And they, in turn, had trusted promises from the Matsuura.

Nothing here had gone as she had hoped. Maybe it was time to stop trusting men and trust *Deusu* instead. Her little seed had been planted in a bed under the pines. *Deusu* willing, He could transform even this incredible hardship, this apparent death, into something wonderful.

At least she did not have to trust her baby to Pharaoh's court. In her version of the story, he would rest in loving *Kirishitan* arms. As for Pharaoh's palace, she was the one imprisoned there.

Sono's eyes flew open at the sound of the *shoji* sliding. Had she slept?

Iya stripped off her traveling coat, beaming. "Taro made it through the night. He is very weak, but they are tending to him."

The room was instantly brighter. "What do they say? Will he live?"

"It is too soon to tell. He has a long road to travel."

"Still!" She stood and threw her arms around Iya. "*Graças, graças, graças a Deusu!* And to you, Iya-chan."

Chapter Thirty

AKIRA STOPPED AT THE FIRST PAYPHONE he saw and placed a call to the Delhams at the house they'd taken in Tokyo. Dave answered, and Akira quickly brought him up to date.

"She looks awful, Dave-san. From what I hear, they'll do almost anything to get a confession in that place." His impotence was enough to choke him.

"What's your new lawyer say? What can you do about it?"

"He was not encouraging. And maybe not so good a lawyer." He caught his breath while fury mixed with guilt gave him another pummeling. He summarized Namura's pessimistic assessment, ending with, "If she goes to trial, he thinks there's little hope." He stopped and breathed a quick prayer before going on to his request. "But he said one more thing."

"What?"

"If the victim confirms that the defendant has made an acceptable offer of restitution, that would be a factor in her favor."

"Restitution? What would that mean here?"

Akira ground the sole of his shoe into the pavement. He should have explained things in a different order. "She told me something remarkable that I know will make you and Eileen very happy." He related what his sister had said about her dream. And her change of heart toward Rev. Delham.

"That's fantastic!" Dave's exuberance had Akira holding the phone away from his ear. "I'm delighted. And Eileen will be so pleased."

"I knew you'd feel that way. And about the question you asked a minute ago...I'm told they like to hear that the victims have seen evidence the defendant is truly sorry. And that there's an agreement on how she can make it up to them."

"And you feel you've seen that?"

"I hardly know her now, but she seems sincere. And this dream meant a great deal to her. She asked for someone to teach her about Christianity."

"Did she? Can we—"

"Her attorney plans to ask for that, but he says they'll say no."

"Dang!" The line went silent for a moment.

Akira cleared his throat. "They seem to view us both as victims. So, I know it's a lot to ask, but if you believe she deserves your time—"

"Thank God, Jesus didn't wait until I was deserving! I'm happy to do whatever I can. But what can I do?"

Praise God for Dave. "I am not sure. The attorney wasn't very helpful. He said something about the mysterious ways of Supreme Command. Said they're like a puppet master, manipulating things from the back of the stage."

Dave went silent for several seconds. Then: "I know a man in the administration. Colonel Cyril Hill. He met us at the dock when *Meigs* arrived. He's with the Judge Advocate Corps, and a wonderful Christian. Spends his weekends distributing care packages to villages. Perhaps he'll have some advice."

Akira's day had just brightened, in spite of the drizzle. "I don't know how to thank you, Reverend Delham." If the man had been in front of him, Akira might have done a very un-Japanese thing and hugged him.

During the next days Akira learned a new verb. *Robī.* "To lobby, or attempt to influence."

Dave spoke with Col. Hill, who agreed with the fear that somewhere in the halls of General Headquarters, someone might exert a little behind-the-scenes influence. Dave reported this to Akira by phone. "He says there's a very real risk they'll want to lock her up and toss out the key. He said we'd better get in front of it."

Toss out the key? "What do we do?"

"He offered to introduce me to some people at G.H.Q. He says it's MacArthur's goal to see Japan take on Western ways in many areas. Maybe most areas. Democracy, the vote for women, etc. Matters of faith are no exception. If we can approach the men at Supreme Command from the perspective of a budding, repentant Japanese Christian whose faith is in jeopardy, he felt the story might pluck all the right strings."

"The prosecutor could move her case to trial any day."

"I'll call the colonel again."

Akira woke every morning with a knot in his gut, anticipating disastrous news. His sister in detention awaiting trial. His father in the hospital awaiting eventual death. And he seemed powerless to do anything meaningful for either of them.

His campaign to save Miyako was moving too slowly. He'd had no trouble getting Rev. Kagawa to agree to visit a prisoner. But as Namura had forewarned, getting approval from the faceless authorities proved to be another matter.

It was Monday morning before he could get Dave on the phone again. "What did Colonel Hill have to say? What else can we do?"

"Things are moving forward. Colonel Hill and I are having lunch with a couple of people tomorrow."

"Would it help if I go up there? I can take a sleeper train and join you for lunch."

There was an awkward pause. "I asked Colonel Hill that exact question. He doesn't feel it's needed at this point."

Akira heard what Dave wasn't putting into words. MacArthur's people at General Headquarters weren't interested in what a Japanese had to say.

"I'm coming up," he said. "Where can I meet you?"

A beat passed. "We're having lunch at the Officer's Club at G.H.Q. I'm afraid you won't be welcome there, my friend."

"Dave-san, I can't just sit here."

"Okay." Dave drew out the two syllables. "What is it? Seven hours by train?"

"I think so."

"We're meeting at noon. If you want to wait in G.H.Q.'s lobby around one, we'll see what happens."

Tuesday 18 January 1949
Tokyo, Japan

Akira perched on a hard leather chair in the vaulted granite lobby of MacArthur's General Headquarters in Tokyo. He stifled a yawn.

The jostling night spent in a sleeping berth had not left him well rested. For nearly eight hours, the wheels had clacked out a rhythm that echoed Dave's grim words. *Lock her up, toss the key. Lock her up, toss the key.* He battled all night with a deepening sense of doom.

His train had disgorged him at Tokyo Station at seven in the morning, leaving him with six hours to while away. He was very glad his stint on *Meigs* had taught him to appreciate coffee.

A burnished brass elevator door slid open and several Americans walked out. Dave was among them. His eyes locked on Akira, and he said something to a balding man next to him wearing officer's insignia.

Col. Hill? Akira stood. Dave gestured toward him and the two men angled his direction.

The colonel's shoulders drooped with age, but he still made Dave appear small. He gave Akira a firm handshake and introduced himself in a decisive voice.

"Pleased to meet you, sir. I've heard so much about you."

"Likewise. I have about fifteen minutes before I'm needed upstairs. Shall we have a seat?"

They found three of the hard leather chairs grouped together and sat down.

Col. Hill put out his opening shot. "It sounds like your sister gave everyone a real show a couple of weeks ago."

Akira winced. "She's very sorry, sir."

"From what Reverend Delham tells me, I'm sure she is." His face darkened. "I don't care what she's done. We'd all like to see Japan shake free of the kind of police-state techniques they seem to be employing on her."

"Is there anything you can do?" With fifteen minutes, he had to drive the conversation to the point.

Hill quirked a grizzled eyebrow. "Democratizing Japan is a huge undertaking. We've had to attack things piecewise. And so far, we've chosen to meddle with your system of justice only in a very limited way."

He'd come to Tokyo to *robi*. It was time to do it with everything he had. "I hope that limited way might include exerting some influence to help my sister."

The colonel gave him a ghost of a smile. "This one's strictly a matter of Japanese civilian legal processes, and for the most part, we've been leaving those alone. If we were going to pick one to weigh in on, why this one? And why on your sister's behalf?"

"Sir—"

Hill lifted one hand. He wasn't finished. "A young woman gets arrested on suspicion of prostitution, then released. A week later, she attempts to assault an American war hero. Why wouldn't we want to see her prosecuted to the full extent of the law?" He glanced around and lowered his voice. "You may not have been back long enough to notice this, but for a free-speech advocate, MacArthur is quite intolerant of overt anti-American sentiment."

Akira sighed. "Maybe that's why they're working her over so hard. Maybe they think they'll make friends up here at G.H.Q. by making an example of her."

"My mission here is with the war crimes trials, and believe me, it keeps me fully occupied. But I'm in legal work because I love justice. I believe even hardened criminals deserve a fair shake and a chance to reform." The colonel jutted his jaw and his eyebrows lowered. "It doesn't sound like your sister is getting either."

"No, sir."

"I think I have a little good news for you, son. The reverend and I had lunch today with a couple of men. One of them might be able to help you."

"That's great," Akira said, relief flooding through him.

"It is. We were fortunate to get the ear of the man who's responsible for public relations in the Kansai region."

"Public relations?" What did that have to do with Miyako?

"Yes. And I think your eloquent and quick-thinking friend here was able to convince the fellow that he could wring some publicity value out of this. Illustrate for the Japanese how fair, yet merciful, our concept of justice is."

Dave beamed at Akira.

Akira packed all the intensity in his heart into his next words. "Sir, if you're able to get her a fresh chance, I promise she won't fail. She's not the kind of person you might think she is." At least, he hoped not. "She did what she did a couple of weeks ago because she was forced into a life she wouldn't have chosen. That won't happen again."

Col. Hill exchanged glances with Dave, then nodded at Akira. "That's what I was waiting to hear. If we are able to help in some way, I want to be sure it won't backfire on us. And I feel better hearing that straight from your lips. Your commitment to come up here speaks volumes."

A tinge of triumph ran through him, but it was too early to celebrate. He fixed determined eyes on the colonel. "Thank you, sir. You have no idea what this means to us. I promise she—we—won't disappoint you."

"I believe you," he said. "Now bear in mind, I can't vouch for the Japanese side of things. The most we can do for her is some indirect influence. You'll want to work the Japanese angle as well. But insofar as there's something I can do to help her get a fair shake, I'll do it."

Akira thanked the colonel profusely. It seemed at least one person at G.H.Q. cared what a Japanese had to say.

Twentieth Day of the Ninth Month, Anno Domini 1588

It was mid-afternoon when Sono's honored mother marched in and swept her hawk-like eyes around the birthing chamber. They lingered on the fierce little statue glowering from the altar, and a flicker of satisfaction crossed her face.

She directed a strained smile at Sono. "How are you, daughter?"

Heartbroken but grateful. "As well as can be expected, I suppose." She kept her voice properly subdued. "*Arigato,* Honored Mother."

"I imagine it was not an easy night for you." Her voice took on a syrupy quality. "Well, this heart-wrenching incident is behind us now. And I have some tidings I believe you'll appreciate."

The gist was that Lord Matsuura had graciously volunteered his own teahouse for Sono's use through the seventh day. It was a stunning offer. She loved that place, and she was grateful. Both to him, and to Hiroko for suggesting it.

But moving someone with "birth impurity" a third of the way across the castle grounds proved to be more involved than Sono had imagined. She stepped from her palanquin—draped in layers of white so it could safely contain her impurity—and into the teahouse in the last golden light of day.

As always, no detail inside the small, rustic space had escaped Rin's attention. For the most part, it was lovely. A set of white cushions on the floor. Luxuriant white drapes on every wall. Charcoal smoldering in the sunken hearth.

Soothing, except for the miniature altar in the alcove. Sono grimaced to see that Ususama, the fiery four-armed deity, had arrived at the teahouse before her. A row of incense sticks smoldered in front of him, scenting the air with sandalwood and pine. True to custom, her honored mother had prepared the space in her own way.

But the music of the small stream bouncing over rocks outside made up for all that. Sono closed her eyes and let the water's melody fill her soul in the same way it filled the compact space.

Rin and Iya came in behind her. Rin inquired whether there was anything else she needed, kindly passed on Lady Matsuura's good wishes, and left.

The instant Rin was gone, Sono strode to the alcove and turned Ususama's face toward the wall. "Let's drape something over him, Iya-chan. You will have to bring my crucifix from my chamber."

Iya's eyes went wide with dismay. "You know someone

will come in and see that. And your supposed fresh interest in their deities is why you are enjoying so much favor."

"I cannot have him staring at me all day, Iya-chan. And you know what else I cannot do?"

"What, my lady?"

"Keep up this Buddhist pretense forever. And how am I under any obligation, ah? Their cures worked no better than our pretend holy oil." She dropped to the cushion, suddenly weary. "But apart from our fiery little friend, it is better here. The sound of the brook is lovely. Maybe I can even venture outside to look at it."

"I hate your Buddhist pretense as much as you do, but you had better keep it up a little longer. Until we see how Taro fares. Until he is well enough to blend in with the foundlings at the House of Mercy, or—"

Or he's gone. Any pleasure she had gleaned from her new surroundings evaporated. "I suppose you are right, as always." She angled the statue so his empty eyes glared into a corner. She settled in the opposite corner, near the hearth. "If we sit over here, at least our stony friend isn't glowering at me."

"And about going outside—"

Sono pursed her lips, exasperated. "What else?"

"This teahouse is in full view of the fourth gatehouse, as well as the sentries on the keep. We may have privacy inside. And you can probably venture as far as that latticed patio. But Hisanobu's men will see every move you make if you step farther."

The last breeze sapped from Sono's sails. "Then I am no freer here than anywhere else."

A light rain started as dusk gathered. Iya piled charcoal into the firepit. Sono prodded the fire to life while her friend walked up to the kitchen to arrange for their dinner—the warming yang foods that a woman who had just delivered was expected to favor.

But once servants brought the meal, every bite of fowl in piquant sauce accused her. If she was a new mother, where was the babe in her arms? She put her chopsticks down after three bites, and no amount of encouragement from Iya could persuade her to pick them up again.

A long evening stretched ahead of them. They knelt side by side and cried out to *Deusu* for Taro's life. Sono squeezed her eyes shut and pressed her hands together and begged with all the yearning in her soul.

When they had exhausted themselves, they spread out their futons—the room was barely large enough to hold them both—and lay down. Firelight cast a warm glow over low eves and unfinished rafters and unadorned mats on the floor. An image of Mama-san, with all her fussing over the details of Sono's dowry, rose in her mind and sent a wistful pang through her chest. She preferred that rustic teahouse with Iya to all the splendid things in the Matsuura mansion.

She picked up the poker and prodded the embers so they sparked. "You know I love this place, but it feels all wrong to enjoy it now. Thrust aside, while someone else fights for my baby's life."

Iya's voice was thick with drowsiness. "Maybe it is not such a bad thing to end up in the place where there is nothing to do but trust. You *can* trust *Deusu*, Sono-chan."

Iya's voice trailed off. Her breathing slowed.

Sono watched the fire, her handmaid's words echoing through her mind. If she was going to start a new way of life, trusting *Iesu* rather than fathers and brothers and padres, what would she do differently?

The rain came down harder, drumming on the roof and all but drowning out the sound of the stream outside. She rolled over and the fiery four-armed icon glared into her eyes.

There was a time when she had refused compromise like this. Even when it had cost her the joy of an evening under the cherry blossoms. Was that just a few months earlier?

Her heart twisted. They had brought her to this. She was playing host to a Buddhist deity to win favors. She rose and upended the demon-faced thing onto its face.

If she wanted to trust *Deusu* rather than men, she would stand for no further compromise. She would perish before she let what had passed with Taro take place again.

And more than that. The vision of the *Kirishitan* heir was a mirage. At best, any son she raised in Lady Matsuura's women's wing would be a *Kirishitan* in name. He might wear a cross, but these people would squeeze any real faith out of him. As they were doing to her.

How much did Akiko-chan see of her boys? A couple of hours a day. How much influence did she have over them— their mother, versus their instructors?

Her husband would choose her sons' instructors. The man who had left his infant in the forest as a meal for foxes, then demanded she rip off her cross. If she trusted *Deusu*, she would never go back to that.

But what was she supposed to do? What leverage did she have? Her only recourse was to write her brother again and beg him to retrieve her. If he did it, the alliance would be broken. No *Kirishitan* heir for Hirado. No assured respite from Matsuura raids for Yoshiaki and his family. What if they snatched her nephew away as a hostage, the way they had carried off her brother?

And what of her own lost son? How would she ever see Taro again?

She curled up with a bitter groan. *Unless I'm prepared to desert my husband and baby, I am at their mercy.*

Chapter Thirty-One

Tuesday 18 January 1949

AKIRA SWITCHED ON THE LIGHT above his berth on the sleeper train back to Osaka. He pulled down the shade that would spare him more tragic views of the ruined city. Allowing himself a triumphant grin at their success in pleading his sister's case at G.H.Q., he slipped between crisp cotton sheets and picked up his brand-new issue of the weekly *Asahi Picture News*.

He leafed past the advertisements and paused at the table of contents. A woman's photo regarded him from the bottom of the facing page. A middle-aged lady wearing glasses. Her pleasant expression drew him in. What did she have to say?

Today marks the one-year anniversary of the arrest of the "Demon Midwife" of Kotobuki. Ishikawa Miyuki killed more than one hundred unwanted infants.

More than one hundred. His dinner of braised eel churned in his stomach, and the magazine sagged against his chest.

He didn't want the lurid details—and yet he did. He tried to flip the page, but his eyes found the next sentence faster than his fingers moved.

I am writing because I find it an imminent occasion to remind your readers of the urgency of the mixed-blood-baby crisis that afflicts our nation.

Of course, with Americans trolling every street and female flesh for sale on every corner.

His stomach lurched again. That trade had kept his own sister in groceries while he'd chosen to sail the seas. He turned the page and numbed his mind with some unrelated story. Tried to push his thoughts away from the hundred young mothers of those murdered infants and the despair they must have felt when they learned of their unwanted pregnancies.

And the babies' hundred *gaijin* fathers. Beaudoin's leer loomed in his memory, ogling the mulatto girls on the streets of Havana. If a man like him stooped to buy a few minutes of pleasure from a girl, would he care what misery might follow for her?

He thrust the magazine aside and switched off the light. He pushed his head into the pillow as the wheels clacked out a new phrase.

Must get her free. Must get her free. On every level. Free of prison and free of the shadow of the horrible choices she'd been forced into because he didn't come home.

What else could he do 'on the Japanese side,' as Col. Hill had put it?

There was Oda's suggestion—and Akira didn't have any better ideas. *A significant contribution.* How big was *significant?*

A queasy feeling swelled inside him. He'd debarked from *Meigs* thinking his savings account had plenty of cushion for a two-month leave. But it turned out having a sister with legal problems was expensive. He might have a big enough sum to bribe his way to the best table at a restaurant. But if Oda was right, and a bribe was what it would take to purchase Miyako's freedom, there wasn't enough for that.

Unless he was ready to go back to work.

American President Lines expected him in Yokohama on March 1, ready for a fresh voyage. Could he eke out his cash that long?

And with his father in the hospital, battling for his life. And his sister in jail, battling for her freedom. How could he turn his back on them and steam away—again?

A naval career was the life he'd always longed for. He was born for the wind and the waves and the cry of the gulls and the fresh tang of ocean spray. The thought of himself as a *salaryman*, with an office and a briefcase and a daily commute by train, made the mahogany walls of his sleeping berth close in.

But there were two newspapers in his briefcase, each with a few pages of classified ads.

Could he give up the sea for his father and sister? And if he did, what was he good for?

Attorneys, police, bureaucrats. Law offices, detention centers, headquarters buildings. That's all Akira's next days consisted of. That, and his weekly jail visits.

He hounded Namura until the attorney was clearly sick of him before they achieved the next bit of progress—a meeting with Prosecutor Suzuki.

Namura cautioned him not to be too optimistic. "He and I meet Tuesday morning. But it will be only the attorneys, I'm afraid. This isn't a conversation to which the victim is privileged."

The following Tuesday, Akira paced the Regional Public Prosecutors Office lobby, waiting for their meeting to conclude. The elevator door slid open and the attorney's dignified silver head appeared behind the smooth hairstyles of a pair of well-dressed women.

Was that a hint of a smile on Namura's face? Akira strode to him. "What did he say?"

"Well, it's unprecedented in my experience. Your friend at G.H.Q. seems to have engineered a turnaround. Prosecutor Suzuki will accept her original confession. He is preparing his recommendation of suspended prosecution to the judge."

"Which means?"

"Which means our hard work has paid off. She is likely to be discharged with a probation agreement. As long as she follows that document to the letter, she won't be tried."

He tipped his head, doubting his ears were working right. "Never?"

"Correct." Namura broke into a relieved grin. He pulled out a handkerchief and blotted his forehead. "You should be able to collect her in a few more days."

Akira left the building, his steps lighter than they'd been in weeks.

Akira spent the next couple of days rushing around in a buzz of happy anticipation, preparing his small walk-up apartment for Miyako to move in. He bought an extra futon and more dishes. Picked out a few items of clothing so she'd have something to wear until he could take her shopping.

But once he had everything ready...nothing. Day passed after quiet day. No further communication from Suzuki's office. No probation agreement. No release date. No response to phone calls.

Akira agonized over his bank statement. Half his two-month leave was gone. And much more of his savings than he'd anticipated.

A significant contribution. He ground the point of his pencil into the bank statement's margin, fear mounting that what Oda had suggested weeks ago might be his sister's only real path to freedom. How would he raise that kind of cash?

His weekly meetings with Miyako were heartbreaking. She wasn't getting any information either. And every week, she seemed thinner. "They don't even interrogate me now," she told him. "I just sit in my cell. It's like they've forgotten me."

"But they do remember to feed you, ah?"

She grimaced. "To a degree." She glanced at the policeman next to her. It was a different fellow this time—not the gaunt, snarling one. "I think all the time about that dream, Akira-san. I'm trying to believe, like the voice told me. But it's hard to hang on to hope when I sit in my cell day after miserable day, and I hear nothing."

He'd been feeling a bit like that himself. "My pastor says there are times when *Iesu* lets you walk in silence for a while. That's where faith comes in. You must cling to the truth He's given you, no matter how bad things look."

She gave him a petulant little scowl. "What truth? In my dream He called me daughter. He said believe. And He set me free. That's it."

"Daughter. Believe. Free. Those are key truths. If you've decided to follow *Iesu*, you can add eternally loved and completely forgiven."

She glanced again at the officer beside her. He sat impassively. "I'd like to learn more. I'm not sure what it all means."

The guard at Akira's elbow growled out the expected reminder that they'd strayed from approved topics.

Of course. Akira frowned in frustration. "I've been trying to find some way to get you more truth to hold on to. But they don't make it easy."

"No they do not," she said, every trace of light leaving her face.

Akira left the building, stopped at the first phone he saw, and got Miyako's attorney on the line. "What is Prosecutor Suzuki waiting for?"

"I wish I knew, Matsuura-san. Nothing about your sister's case has been ordinary."

He hung up and glared at the damp pavement. He couldn't sail out in a month. He would need to find something else. But who would hire an ex-*horyo*?

In the end, he had to call American President Lines' station manager in Yokohama, plead a family emergency, and ask for another month of leave.

Three more weeks passed. He fumed and worried and tried to figure out a way to raise cash. He borrowed a typewriter from a neighbor, pecked out a resume, and dropped it off at a growing list of businesses.

He'd just returned from one of these expeditions when he finally got good news. A date had been set for the judge's review of Miyako's case. She should go free within the week.

Twenty-First Day of the Ninth Month, Anno Domini 1588

Sono woke the next morning to the rustle of silk. Iya moved about the room, fully dressed.

She sat up and rubbed the sleep from her eyes. "You're off to town for tidings, ah?" She let out a wistful sigh. "I wish I could go with you. Or sail on a bird's wings above you." She stood and helped Iya tie on her veil.

Iya slid the *shoji* open—and stopped, her gaze fixed on the wooden slats at her toes. "My lady!"

Sono came up beside her and stared. Her bow lay alongside the threshold, in all its supple beauty. Her quiver with its full complement of arrows rested next to it. A red tie bound a small scroll to the bow's shaft.

Iya knelt to pick them up and handed them to her. She stroked the bow, relishing the smooth feel of its bamboo back. How her fingers had ached for it. The string felt newly waxed. Had her husband done this for her?

She laid it down with care and untied the scroll. When she uncoiled the fine paper, a spear-shaped mulberry leaf larger than her hand sprang out and drifted to the floor. Dark red characters—her husband's bold strokes—marched in precise columns down its bright-green length.

She picked it up. "It's a poem." She read out loud.

"This mulberry leaf
Whispers a lonesome warrior's
Words of deep longing.
Dearest, when will our arrows
Take flight side by side again?"

She glared at the leaf, then crushed it in her fist. "Can he truly believe we are going to take things up again where we left off, as if nothing has passed?"

"He is our lord. It is his right."

Anger thrust her spine straight. "Does he understand me so little? Does he even care to understand me?"

Iya gently pried her fist open and removed the crumpled leaf. "I wonder why he left it here in the middle of the night. 'Twould be more like Hisanobu to hand it to you with a flourish, yes?" She laid the leaf on the shelf in the alcove and smoothed it back into shape as best she could. "Your lord will expect your reply. I had best retrieve your writing box before I go."

"My lord. That's precisely the problem, ah? He is a lord to me, but not *the* Lord. Yet he thinks he has the right to tell me how to think and feel. And what to worship."

Iya shot her a quizzical look. "I will leave you with a thought, ah? Perhaps all of this has humbled him a little. Perhaps he left your bow with such a pretty poem by way of apology."

Sono snorted. "An apology. From Hisanobu. That would be a miracle."

But after Iya left, her anger waned. She read the poem again. If she trusted *Iesu*, did she not expect to see Him work? And when He did, might it look like this?

A miracle indeed. A husband's changed heart.

Unless I want to leave, I am at their mercy. She had

thought that, but it was not true. She was at *Iesu*'s mercy. As was Taro.

As were the *Kirishitan* of Hirado. When *Mōse's* mother floated her son in a basket in the reeds, it was no grand design she had. It was a last desperate ploy to save a baby. But *Deusu* had a bigger plan. Not just to save a baby from sword and from river monster, but to free a whole people.

She needed to step forward in faith, somehow, and trust *Deusu* with the outcome.

She gave in to her urge to get reacquainted with her bow. She slipped the string over its tip, went to the window, and tied back the heavy white drape. She nocked an arrow and drew it halfway back. The feel of the weapon straining against her arms set her pulse humming with familiar exhilaration.

Hisanobu did not realize what this meant. She was no longer helpless. Defenseless. Her bow gave her leverage.

How did *Deusu* mean her to use it? She knelt before the crucifix, rested the bow across her lap, and prayed.

Wooden sandals clacked across wooden planking. Iya walked in carrying a lacquered box. She halted and gave Sono a measuring look. "You strung your bow. What are you doing?"

"I am making sure it's in good working order. And then I am going into the garden."

"You will scandalize the Matsuura."

Sono examined the piercing iron tip of an arrow, then lifted her eyes to her handmaid. "I have reached a decision. I do not believe the Lord *Iesu* wants me to keep living a lie. A lie where we all say I am free to live as a *Kirishitan* when in a hundred ways, I am not. A lie where we all say I can raise my children as *Kirishitan* and then they're ripped from me. When they come to take me back to the women's wing, I do not intend to be easy to collect. From this moment on, I will live unashamedly as a *Kirishitan*. And if someone doesn't care for that, I will accept the consequences."

Iya watched Sono finger the arrow. "What became of turning the other cheek?"

"You know how long it's been since I last drew this bow." She let out an ironic little laugh. "I doubt I could shoot anything if I wanted to. But I can use it to make a statement my husband will not ignore. If he wants my surrender, he will hear my terms."

"Which are?"

"Only this—I will demand the freedom of religion I was promised. For myself, and for my children. My life here is meaningless without it. And then I will take your advice and trust *Deusu* for the outcome. And depending on how my husband responds..."

"*Hai?*"

"I long to have our Taro back. But I need to know whether we can trust Hisanobu with our little secret." Sono laid the bow down and slipped an arm around her friend. "Now, dear Iya, hasten to town and find out about Taro. I will have a message for you to carry to my husband when you return."

Iya did not return until after midday, which gave Sono plenty of time to consider and pray through her next moves.

Calm your own mind. That horrid day when Papa-san had passed into paradise, Suminobu had teased her over her dream of being a great general. And he was right. It was a flight of girlish fancy. What a child she had been.

But now she had to think like a general, or at least like a captain. What did she need to carry out her plan? A position that would give her cover from at least two sides. A place she could lurk with her bow, seeing without being seen, until her husband came to seek her.

She stepped onto the screened patio and surveyed the little garden. *Perfect.* One of the few spots in the castle designed more for privacy than defense. A wall enclosed it on the far side of the stream, tall enough to hide her. A row of mulberries screened that from behind. As long as she took care to stay in the very shadow of that wall, she would be out of view of the gatehouse sentries and invisible to anyone who approached. Until they rounded the corner and walked through the narrow gate—and into her bow's range.

Iya could take her message to Hisanobu. Sono and her bow would await him there.

Chapter Thirty-Two

Monday 21 February 1949
Osaka, Japan

AKIRA PACED THE TOO-FAMILIAR WAITING ROOM at police headquarters. His efforts, Dave's, Col. Hill's—the hard work of so many people was on the verge of paying off. Miyako was coming home.

Namura hadn't been able to clear his calendar to come. But Suzuki, the prosecuting attorney, had just arrived, introduced himself, and perched on one of the battered chairs.

The thick steel door that led to the detention cells swung open. His sister stood, blinking in the light. He took a step toward her. "Mi-chan!"

She squinted at him, strangely hesitant. "Brother?"

The guard beside her gestured her forward. The instant she crossed the threshold that made her a free woman, Akira strode to her, swept her up in his arms, and swung her in an exuberant circle. He put her down, and she braced herself against his chest. She laughed, a sound like tinkling crystal.

"Akira-san, are they releasing me?"

He gave her a big grin. "*Hai.* Let's get you out of this place. We can talk more in the taxi."

She clung to him for a long moment. A not-so-faint whiff of dirty clothing hit his nostrils. It didn't bother him. She was warm, and real, and family.

Prosecutor Suzuki stood. "Congratulations, Matsuura-san. The judge has agreed to release you into your brother's custody."

Her eyes landed on the prosecutor, and she went stiff before she bowed. "*Hai. Domo arigato.*"

Akira handed her a package. "I brought you new clothes." She beamed, and his heart warmed. This was a small sampling of so many good things he had in store for her. After waiting so long, what a joy this was going to be.

She hurried off to the ladies' room wearing a dreamy

smile and clutching the package to her chest.

The attorney watched her disappear, then turned to Akira. "I am sorry. In a normal case we might have released her sooner, but"—he dropped his voice—"it seems someone at G.H.Q. wanted to time this for publicity purposes."

"Publicity? Those reporters outside—they're here for my sister?"

The attorney nodded, wincing. "I'm afraid so. The Americans would be gratified if she'd say a few words about how she has benefited from their gracious brand of justice."

Akira tried to picture her talking into a bank of microphones. "You saw her. She looks awful. She can't talk to them now."

"It can't be helped."

Akira shook his head in stunned disbelief. "I don't think it would leave the impression G.H.Q. wants. Another time, ah? They have to understand she's not..."

She reappeared from the ladies' room, silencing them. The dress he'd bought her sagged around her skeletal limbs. How much weight had she lost?

"I'm ready, brother."

He forced a smile. She might be in wretched shape physically, but the new light in her eyes boded well. She could bounce back from this, and he was going to make sure she did. "That's much better. We can go shopping tomorrow, ah?"

Suzuki took a long look at her and sighed. "I need to be able to tell them we asked her, Matsuura-san."

Akira turned to her. "It seems someone leaked news of your release to the press, Mi-chan. Quite a few reporters are waiting for you."

"Reporters! Akira-san, no. What would I say?"

The guard spoke from the vestibule door. "If I might make a suggestion?"

"Please," Akira said.

"Prosecutor Suzuki could keep them occupied out front, ah? There's a fire escape at the rear. I can take you two through the back office."

Suzuki gave Miyako another appraising look, then

acknowledged defeat. "Fine."

Ten minutes later Akira smuggled her out the fire escape and into a taxi. And half an hour after that, miracle of miracles, they were home.

He showed her up two flights of stairs to his flat. It was a small, cheerless space in a battered brick building he'd furnished on the cheap. A place both of them would have squirmed at spending time in before the war. But the floor mats were clean and not too frayed, and he had a usable tea set on a table in the corner where he kept his kitchen things.

He draped her coat over the hook next to his own. She looked around, eyes wide with clear delight at the basics he'd put in place. How their perspectives had changed.

He had a few more things to give her. Enough to get her by until they went shopping. And he did have one special item for her. He bowed and made a formal presentation of a box covered in silver foil. "It's the most important thing I have for you."

"I'm overwhelmed, Akira-san." She slipped the box open to reveal a Bible bound in blue leather. She ran her fingers along its silver-etched title. "It's beautiful. But what is it?"

"You told me you don't know what it means to be a *Kirishitan*. This book will teach you."

She caught it to her chest. Tears filled her eyes. "You are so thoughtful."

He broke into a grin. Her reaction to it all—starting a new life at home with him—met all the hopes that had kept him going through the past weeks. "Ah, Mi-chan! I can't believe you're finally here. What would you like to do? Eat? Sleep?"

She sniffled and almost laughed. "*Hai* and *hai*. A little something to eat first, please."

"Do you want to go out for noodles?"

Her eyes widened, and she flinched away from him. She gave her head a vigorous shake. "If we could have something light here, that would be perfect."

So anxious. Like a cat who'd been driven away from too many doors. His heart folded for her. "I'll make tea and we can catch up, ah?"

She settled onto a cushion and followed him with her eyes as he moved around the room. "How under heaven did you get me out of that place?"

He carried a tray with snacks and the teacups to the table. "Our friend Reverend Delham did it. He pled your case persistently with many people. All the way up to General Headquarters in Tokyo."

She looked at him, astonished. "After what I tried to do to him?"

"*Hai.* He wouldn't give up. He used all his connections. He's a war hero, after all."

She blinked away tears. "That was so kind of him."

The teakettle whistled. He got up and returned with a steaming pot. He said a heartfelt thanks to the Lord over their first meal together, then she poured for them.

The worst is behind us. You'll see. Watching her across his table, it was easy to picture her as she would be. The sweet sister he'd left behind, restored. No more brash red lips. No more cheap perm, partly grown out now. Only a little older and more world-weary. As was he.

She set the pot down, the remaining light in her expression fading with some fresh concern. "*Onii-san,* there is something you need to know."

"I'm sure there are a lot of things I need to know." He managed to smile. "Everything that happened while I was gone."

Her gaze slid away from his. "No. This is serious."

"All right, Mi-chan. Tell me."

She took a lingering sip of tea, seeming not so eager to respond. "When you invite me to stay, you need to know it's not just me."

"What do you mean?"

She paused again, a long one, her face a picture of warring emotions. She was gathering her strength to say something. Sudden fear withered his stomach. Was he ready?

Dave's advice echoed in his ears. *Don't be afraid to show her you love her, no matter what.*

She looked up at him. "I'm pretty sure I'm pregnant."

His cup clattered on the table.

A few months, and there could be a baby. His sweet vision of her innocence restored shattered into a hundred shards of tawdry-colored stained glass. His sister, marked for life, as what she'd been when he met her. A worthless woman who'd sold herself. Who'd conceived a child who would have no father.

She fingered the rim of a bowl. "I guess I'm in my third month."

His pulse surged. Who was the despicable brute, and where was he? What man thought he could use his sister, then discard her like a filthy soda bottle? And leave her carrying his child. If he ever found that guy—

Those guys. His rage made the air feel thick.

She peered at her hands, clasped in front of her. "There are other places I can stay. I think my friend Kimi would—"

"No, Mi-chan."

Show her you love her, no matter what. He'd said the wrong thing at the church and regretted it for weeks.

He forced himself to lay his hand on hers. Breathed a quick prayer for grace and understanding words. "I've waited years to find you. You are not leaving now. No matter what."

"No matter what?"

He shook his head.

"No matter if I don't know who the father is?"

Another quick-breathed prayer. "No."

"No matter"—she gnawed on her lip, seeming to withdraw into her emotions for a second or two—"if the father might be American?"

"No matter. Whatever happens, we will deal with it together."

"Really, *Onii-san*? A mixed-blood child?"

Her words hit him like a giant sledgehammer. He couldn't look at her. He pushed to his feet, made his way to the window, and fixed his eyes outside.

A young family walked out the door of the building across the street. The mother wore a traditional wide-sleeved jacket. A tiny dark-haired head peeped over her shoulder, and a small girl in a bright kimono marched at her side. A slice of proper Japanese family life, the woman looking every inch the Confucian ideal of *good wife, wise mother*.

The full magnitude of Miyako's problem—*his* problem—unwound itself in his mind. A child who looked different. Round eyes, pale cheeks. Or dark skin and hair in kinks. Either way, there'd be no future for such a child in Japan. Born to lifelong shame. Scorned and ridiculed wherever he or she was seen.

A weight of despair pressed into his chest. They would make a lovely family, ah? A former prostitute. A former prisoner. And a child who was only half Japanese.

For years he'd imagined resuming life with his family—at one point with dread, and then with determination. But it had never looked like this. Proper families like the one on the street would cross it to avoid sharing the sidewalk with his. Not so many years earlier, he might have done the same.

The little girl in the kimono tripped over something and fell to her knees. Her mother was quick to kneel and gather her in her arms. She brushed off the tiny kimono and pulled a handkerchief from her sleeve to dab at the little face.

There was a lot he didn't know about being a Christian. But it was a call to selfless service—that much was clear. Dave and Covell-san had both shown him that.

No matter how deep your shame, how complete your failure, I believe God still has a use for you. Hadn't he said that himself? Was a mixed-blood child somehow less redeemable than he was?

He heard a choked-back sob behind him. His sister. He turned. She sat slumped, her eyes riveted to the table.

Hai, she'd stumbled. Badly. But God had answered his prayers and brought her to him. And she needed him. In a different way than the little girl below needed her mother, but just as much.

He spoke around a lump in his throat. "Your child. My nephew or niece. A person *Iesu* died for. That's all that matters, Mi-chan." He eyed her with a rueful grin. "I may be just a two-legged ghost, but I'm not going to vanish. This ghost is here for you. And your child."

And the ghost isn't going back to sea any time soon. The realization brought a sour taste to his mouth. He'd have to put out another round of resumes the next day.

He knelt beside her and gave her shoulders a squeeze. He pushed the bowl of pickled plums toward her. "Now. Please eat."

She leaned into his chest, dabbed at her cheeks, and shot a relieved grin up at him. "*Arigato.* For everything." She picked up her chopsticks. "You must tell me all about how the war went for you. I want every detail."

"Of course. But I'd rather start with you."

"With me, ah?" She set the chopsticks down, clenched one hand into a fist, and chewed at her lower lip. "Here's where we'd better start, Akira-san. It may not be too late for an abortion."

He studied her profile, and a ghastly specter rose behind it. A hundred tiny corpses in a line that faded into the distance, with grayish flesh and staring eyes. The Demon Midwife's victims. He moved back from the table, his stomach clamping as taut as her fist, and pushed down the bile that rose in his mouth. His own niece or nephew would not take a place in a line like that.

But sick as it made him, he couldn't blame her for considering this. She knew what lay ahead for a child like hers. And how easy this solution sounded. A quick operation versus a lifetime of poverty and shame.

He spoke as gently as he knew how. "I'm a Christian now. I make decisions in that light. They've talked a lot about this at church, with this new Eugenic Protection Law. How there's an age-old battle over the fruit of women's wombs. Life has only one source—Almighty God. If there's life in your womb, He put it there. It's not ours to take."

She raised her eyes to his, and they burned with pain. "An illegitimate, mixed-blood child. No one likes the idea of abortion. But surely, in this case, it would be kinder."

He wrapped his hand around her fist. "I don't think *Iesu* cares about labels like 'mixed-blood' or 'illegitimate.' Any more than 'prisoner' or 'prostitute.' And I promised I would follow Him, even if it isn't easy."

Even to a cross.

He stifled a sigh. *Even to a desk job.* "But what about you? You had some kind of encounter with *Iesu* in jail, didn't you?"

"Ah, how I've been clinging to that dream. But you know how dreams are. Details fade."

"Then tell me everything you remember. Please."

She related her dream in a depth the police hadn't permitted during their jail meetings. The folds across her forehead softened as she recounted the details. A powerful stallion, garbed in full *samurai* armor. Tantalizing fruit dangling from a distant tree. Forbidding bars that blocked her way to the fruit—steel prison bars that stretched to the clouds.

"And then..." She paused and lifted glowing eyes to Akira's. "His voice, Akira-san. That's when I heard Him speak."

"And He said...?"

"He called me daughter. He said that I should ask for what I needed. I asked, and it happened. The bars in the dream just melted away." She gave him a wistful smile. "If only it had been true in real life."

"He made it happen in real life." Didn't she see *Iesu*'s hand in the events that had set her free? "It just took longer."

She sat for a second, digesting this.

"He said something else, didn't He?" Akira said. "You told me when I visited you."

"He said 'Believe.' But believe what? I was heartbroken that I didn't know."

He laughed. "It's obvious now, isn't it? Believe that *Iesu* would free you. And He has, physically. He wants to free your spirit too."

She gave him a pensive nod. "I've heard that. Do you remember Kusumi-san, the guard who showed us out today? He's a Christian, and he was very kind to me. The only light in that dark place, besides you. He said I have to accept *Iesu* as my Lord, and He will save me if I trust Him."

"You'll never be sorry if you do, Mi-chan. *Iesu* will

always be there for you. But He will demand some changes in your life." A real commitment to Christ would make all the difference for her. *Iesu* alone could breathe hope into her dark circumstances. Nothing could be more important than helping her understand that.

She sat gazing into her tea for a moment. "I have so many questions." She looked up at him. "Why hasn't *Iesu* spoken to me since? If He's real, where has He been? All those weeks, they were on me. Screaming. Threatening. Pressuring me for hours at a time, trying to make me admit to something that never happened." She crumpled her napkin. "We've all been to the realm of the dead and back, Akira-san."

Her voice trembled with emotion, and her pain was another knife in his flesh.

"Bombing raids, Akira-san. Firestorms. Hunger. Radiation sickness. Oh, and crooked police. If He cares for us so much, why does He allow it, ah?"

Patience. Just love her. And trust the Lord to lead her along her own path. "I wish I had an answer for every question. I don't. But *Iesu* did have a plan to get you out of that place. Every day you spent there, Christians worked to free you. The man you meant to kill. An American officer you don't even know. Not to mention your two-legged ghost of a brother, who materialized just in time."

She looked at him, abashed. "I hadn't thought of it that way. I'll never be able to repay any of you for what you've done for me." She fingered her teacup. "It was more than what *happened* in the dream. It was the way it made me feel. Like *Iesu* knew everything about me and loved me in spite of it. With a fierce kind of love I've never known before."

"I experienced something like that." His eyes flinched shut and he was back aboard *Meigs*. Both hands gripping a cold steel railing, staring into colder waves. "That's why I'm alive today and not a pile of bones on the ocean floor."

Her intense eyes drilled into him. "Do you have it? That sense *Iesu* is with you?"

"I've never had a dream like yours. Or heard His audible voice. That's something special *Iesu* gave you, Mi-chan. But I feel His presence. You know what I am—the dishonor I bear. I attempted twice to end my life. *Iesu* returned what I was trying with all my strength to throw away." He gave her a steady look. "And now I know why it was so important, why He brought me back across two oceans."

"Why?"

"I need to be here for *you.*" *And you're going to outlast this.* He'd do anything in his power to make sure of it.

She tossed her head and huffed. "But you won't help me with an abortion."

"I could not support it. Please trust *Iesu.* He'll see us through this, together."

"Isn't there some other way? Some special offering we can make to appease the spirit?"

"Like an offering to Jizo *Bosatsu?* No. Christians only have one mediator. *Iesu.* And the offering we make Him is to believe Him enough to follow His ways."

"But lots of women have abortions. What about them? There must be some means of forgiveness."

"What about failures like me? The Lord always holds out forgiveness and grace. But we need to use all the strength we have to follow Him the best we know. Even when the path is steep."

Her shoulders heaved with the depth of her sigh.

"*Shinzeba,* Mi-chan. Believe."

A moment passed before she gave him an American-style philosophical shrug. "If *believe* means the baby must come, I will try to reconcile myself to that."

He did his best not to think about where she'd learned that little shrug. He rolled out a futon for her in what had been his bedroom. She knelt on the far side of the *shoji,* offered him a quivery smile, and wished him goodnight before she pulled it closed.

Three souls. There were three souls in his apartment now, where the night before there'd been just one. Since his return to Japan, his family had done nothing but shrink. Tonight, for the first time, it had grown. And he wished he could feel excited about it.

This family was *Iesu's* will for him. Not the picture-perfect one on the street earlier. *Lord* Iesu, *let me see my family as You see us. Let me be your loving arms for them. Both of them.*

Chapter Thirty-Three

Twenty-First Day of the Ninth Month, Anno Domini 1588

IT WAS NEARING THE HOUR FOR the noon bells when Sono's handmaid brought back her good report. "Taro keeps taking the milk bit by bit. He is a fighter, it seems. Like his mother."

"*Deusu* sent him to inspire me. How I wish I could see him." She knelt by the teakettle on the hearth and picked up her ladle. "The water is hot. Pray rest a minute and let me serve you tea. Then you can take my note to my husband."

"What does it say?"

She beamed her handmaid an innocent smile. "It is an invitation to tea. What else? As far as any other plans I might have, you know nothing of them."

Sono ladled the steaming water into a tea bowl and whipped it into a lovely green froth. She placed it before Iya, then bowed her head to the floor, servant style. "I am not sure how this day will end. So I want you to remember what I am about to say, in case—"

Iya shook her head, stricken. "Sono-chan—"

"Dear, dear Iya. Let me say this while I have the chance. *Domo arigato* for everything you have done for me, as long as I can remember. No matter what passes next, I am forever in your debt. True friendship is known first in hardship, they say. I have been completely undeserving of yours."

Iya's elegant hands trembled as she picked up the tea bowl. She studied Sono over its rim, tears blurring the line of dark paint below her lower lashes. "It has been my honor to serve you. And I will keep serving you, as long as we both have breath."

"Nonsense. You are going to marry a good *Kirishitan* man and have a family and a household of your own." *And Deusu willing, I will live to see it.*

Iya took a tiny sip and set the tea bowl down.

"Is it passable, at least?" Sono said.

"It is wonderful. *Arigato.*" Iya picked up the bowl again and cradled it in her slender fingers. But she did not drink.

Sono sat still for a moment, memorizing every detail of her beloved friend's appearance. Her long white fingers. The grace of her dancer's neck. Her expressive lips, quivering with emotion.

Hard as it was to part with such a friend, even bigger issues were at stake. She gave Iya a resolute smile. "Drink your tea, please, so you can deliver my message. But after you take it to him, you should stay away for the rest of the day. And I do have one more request."

"Anything, Lady Sono."

She pulled a handkerchief from her sleeve and dabbed at her eyes, then made another deep bow. "If I am no longer here to care about him, do not forget poor Taro."

"I could never forget him. I swear it."

Wednesday 23 February 1949

Akira woke the next morning and went down to the building's compact lobby to pick up his morning paper. He returned to find Miyako wrapped in a cotton kimono, leafing through the stash of old news magazines he hadn't bothered to throw away.

"Here's today's paper," he said.

She grinned at him. "It hardly matters, since I haven't seen a newspaper in weeks. It's nice you kept these old issues so I can catch up."

"They'll have this week's *Asahi Picture News* when we're out today."

Her expression froze. "Out?"

"You want to see Papa-san, don't you?"

"Of course." She laid a hand on the table in front of her, as if she were trying to steady herself.

She seemed overwhelmed at the idea of leaving their four walls, but after breakfast he managed to coax her into a taxi. She looked around in silence, eyes wide and mouth tight, while the driver navigated the city streets.

The cab slowed as they approached the hospital's main

entrance. "When did you see our father last?" he probed gently.

She studied her hands, clenched so hard in her lap her knuckles were white. "A few days before I got arrested. That was the night he disowned me."

"He what?" The broadside knocked the air from his lungs. She'd hinted at a distance between them, but he'd disowned her?

What an awful blow.

"I neglected to tell him exactly how I was paying our bills." She turned her head away.

He studied her, and a hollow carved in his chest. Mental gears clunked into place like tumblers inside a combination lock. *No wonder it meant so much when the voice in her dream called her "daughter."*

A moment passed before she spoke in a lifeless voice, eyes still fixed outside. "I wonder how long I have before he figures out I'm pregnant." She heaved a deep sigh. "If he makes it that long."

Akira's eyes drifted to her belly, still perfectly flat—for now. Papa-san would not take this news well. How tragic, for both of them.

Bitter regret burned through his chest. If he'd been here, he'd have kept her off the streets somehow. This was one more heartbreaking consequence of the madness that had kept him from home.

They got out and walked through the hospital's majestic double doors. He gawked at the condition of the lobby. The once-grand building had been the veteran's hospital the last time he saw it, and an object of national pride. But now? Smoke had blackened the tops of the columns. Plaster flaked off cracked walls. The chairs in the waiting area were mismatched and worn.

The venerable building was in as tragic a state as his family.

There was a short queue at the reception desk. They joined it. When they reached the front, Miyako inquired after Papa-san. "We'd like to see Matsuura Saburo. Is he still in the cancer ward?"

"What are your names?"

"I'm his daughter. Matsuura Miyako."

The receptionist flipped through a box of filing cards with manicured fingers. She pulled one out and adjusted her reading glasses. "I'm sorry. I don't see your name on my approved visitors list."

Miyako went stiff. "There's a list? I'm his daughter."

The receptionist looked vaguely sympathetic. "I'm very sorry, but visits to the cancer ward are restricted to approved guests."

Akira managed to stifle a not-so-Christian comment. "Who do we talk to so we can get added to that list?"

She peered at the top of the card. "It says 'Guarantor: Oda Jinzaburo.'"

They looked at each other. Akira's voice rose more than a notch. "Captain Oda. I didn't think—"

"*Onii-san.*" Miyako rested a hand on his sleeve. "*Arigato,*" she said to the receptionist. "Is Doctor Nakamura still Father's doctor? Could we speak with him?"

"Unfortunately, he's not on duty today. Do you know how to reach him at his office?"

She nodded. "*Hai. Arigato.*"

Not fifteen minutes after one taxi had left them at the hospital's entrance, they slid into another. Miyako turned to him. "We have to talk to Captain Oda. He'll need to update the list."

"You can be sure I'll talk to him." *I hope it's just a mistake.* He directed the driver to the Nishinara district police office.

She clawed at his arm, eyes wide. "No, Akira-san. I can't go there."

"Why not?"

She gave him a vehement shake of the head. "I won't go anywhere near that place. Not after..."

He cursed himself silently. Oda had mentioned questioning her in his office. How could he have forgotten? "I'm sorry. You don't have good memories of that district office, do you?"

Her voice carried the chill of a North Pacific winter. "No."

"I'll take you home." He studied her pallid face, a

protective instinct surging through him. This had really shaken her. "I can find him there tomorrow." Papa-san would have to wait another day.

He gave the driver his address and turned to her. "It's one thing for me, but he can't do this to you. He won't keep you from seeing Papa-san."

Her gaze slid to her knees. "I didn't quite know how to tell you, but this is not my first encounter with Captain Oda. He's a sick man." She darted a fiery glance at him. "Guess who put Papa-san up to disowning me?"

"Oda did?"

"*Hai*, after they arrested me. And there's more." She was gone again, lost in thought for a few seconds, before she tossed her head. "But please don't ask me. When he says he's operating in Papa-san's interests, let's just say I no longer believe him."

"He told me he tried to help you in jail."

A scornful laugh erupted from her. "Help me! Of all the ridiculous demands they made on me in that place, his was the most outrageous of all."

"What—"

She turned her head and focused outside the window. "Please, I can't talk about it."

Frustration throbbed through him. "All right. But I haven't seen our father in more than seven years, Mi-chan. And we might not have much time."

"I know. I want to see him too." She issued a dry laugh, her hand grazing her belly. "Soon."

"What do you think Oda's trying to achieve?"

"I've asked myself that a lot. He'd like us to believe he acts out of some kind of twisted loyalty to Papa-san. But he seems to expect us to live up to an imaginary standard of the perfect family he never had."

"He never married, ah? Odd. I wonder why."

She bit her lip for a second, as if deciding whether to speak. "Did you ever notice the way he watched Mama-san when our father wasn't in the room? She told me once that she knew them both, before she got married. Back when Papa-san was at Eta Jima with Oda. I've often wondered if something happened back then. Something we never heard about."

"You think she jilted him for our father?"

"Maybe."

Or had an affair with him. His muscles tensed beneath his shirt.

Incendiary bombs had blackened the once-grand halls of the hospital. A *gaijin* airman had destroyed his sister's future. And now, yet another event from a past he couldn't change. Oda and his decades-old wounded feelings were not going to keep him from his father.

Akira had hoped to take Miyako shopping when they got home. She needed so many things. He tried several times that afternoon to tempt her beyond the four sturdy walls of his apartment building. He proposed shops, movies, restaurants.

But she only repeated a soft "*Arigato,* but no," with a hunted look. Taut lips and wary eyes.

She might be free, but that didn't mean she was whole. Watching her, realization sank in. Getting her out of jail had been the first step on a long road. A long journey toward healing for her, and atonement for him.

The next morning, he lifted his coat off the rack by the door at eight-thirty. "You're sure you'll be all right here by yourself for a few hours, ah?" He was determined to track down Oda and get immediate access to Papa-san. For his sister, certainly. And for both of them, if he could.

"I'll manage." She shot him a timid smile and picked up a magazine from the stack.

He took the stairs to the ground floor, formulating what he would say to Oda. The man's smug face scored with hardened lines formed in his mind. His pulse picked up and his feet hit the steps harder. He flung the front door of the building open, marched through it—

And stared into the police captain's face a mere twenty steps away.

Oda crossed the street toward him. "Good morning, Matsuura-san."

He masked his astonishment with a quick "good morning" and a bow. Had the man come to discuss Papa-san's visitor list without any prodding? Maybe he'd judged him too harshly. Maybe.

"I'm here to see your sister." The captain's tone was formal.

That set an alarm off in his mind. "She's not in trouble, is she?"

"No." Oda's lip curled with vague amusement. "But I expected you'd be happier to see me. I'm one of the three people you know in Osaka, after all." The trace of amusement vanished from his face. "And I've come on business from your father."

"What business?"

"He wants to see her. And frankly, she'd best hurry. My car's around the corner."

Akira's chest caved in on itself. *She'd best hurry.* What did Oda mean? "We're very eager to visit him. I'll get her."

Oda put his bulk between Akira and his front door. "To be clear, the invitation is not for you."

Akira bristled. "We'll discuss that." He maneuvered around Oda and took the stairs two at a time.

When he burst into their apartment, he found Miyako kneeling at the table with one hand resting on the newspaper. Hollow despair painted her face.

"Mi-chan?"

She blinked, seeming to come out of a sort of trance.

"Captain Oda's outside. He says Papa-san wants to see you."

She pushed to her feet, eyes wide, still holding the newspaper. "I'll get dressed."

"He says we should come quickly. He offered to drive you there."

She made an abrupt stop with one hand on the *shoji* and pivoted to face him. "No. *No!* I'm not going anywhere with Captain Oda." There was a hint of desperation in the eyes she anchored on him. "Please. You and I can go together."

"Of course." That was how he wanted it anyway. "I'll tell the captain to go on without us. We'll follow in a few minutes."

Twenty-First Day of the Ninth Month, Anno Domini 1588

Sono watched her handmaid leave, then slung her bow over her shoulder and walked out to the latticed patio. She stole down the steps and edged along the garden wall.

The spot where the wall bent was as concealed as she had hoped. The teahouse hid her from *samurai* stationed at the gatehouse. The wall at her back hid her from all eyes downslope—even the guards at the castle's outer wall. As for the keep on the ridge above her, only the top floor was visible.

A lovely breeze caressed her face. Sunlight glinted from ripples on the pool's surface and from the smooth rocks beneath the shallow waterfall. A bush warbler sang from somewhere outside the garden. She drank it all in, squeezing every drop of joy from sight and smell and sound. It felt as if the world existed for a single purpose—to flaunt the beauty of *Deusu*'s creation. Give her a hundred reasons to want to live. Tempt her to set her bow aside.

Fear is not real. To fear death is to die. Her husband's words. Ironic that she would dwell on them as she strained to catch the first sound of his footsteps. The warrior's calm detachment he had described. The steady disregard for death. She would need all of that if she was going to force a change in her circumstances—or perish in the attempt.

The stream cut a path across the garden the way the River of Heaven angled across the bowl of the sky. Sunlight sparkled on the water's surface, turning it into a causeway of twinkling stars.

The River of Heaven. He had written her a poem about it once, while he awaited her passage up the long waters of Hirado Channel to his bed.

...a simple oxherd's words of deep longing...When will our eyes and arms meet?

It was his turn to cross the water. Her voyage up

Omura Bay had marked the beginning of their marriage. Would his leap across a narrow stream mark its end, with their eyes locked above weapons?

A man's footsteps echoed outside the gate. She squared her stance, drew her bow, and sighted down her arrow at the garden's entrance.

He passed through the gate and came to an abrupt stop. "What is this?"

"This is your wife, letting you know that I will not go back to the women's wing."

He laughed. "You will if I command it."

"No. Respectfully, my lord, I will not. You will have to kill me where I stand."

His mirth faded. He took a stride toward her. "Put down the bow, Sono. Otherwise, I'll deem it treason."

She adjusted her aim. "Stop where you are. Pray stop, my lord."

His foot lifted. She angled her bow up and let the arrow fly. It whooshed past his shoulder and plunged into a tree trunk behind him. She nocked another and focused down its length at his heart.

He froze at the far edge of the garden, his palm on his long sword's hilt and his face clouded with confusion. "What are you doing? You know, if I snap my fingers, there are ten *samurai* here. And traitors get no mercy."

She strengthened her stance. "The life I live in your castle is not worth keeping."

She had given away the advantage of surprise, a realization that made her heart sink. But she still had the advantage of distance. She stood a good four paces beyond his sword's range, with the stream between them. But one good lunge across that little stream, and he would have her.

Unless she was stalwart enough to shoot. She adjusted her aim.

A moment passed, filled with the water's music and the bush warbler's song. She studied his face. In spite of all his bluster, perhaps something raw shone behind his eyes. Was he more angry, or more hurt?

"Whatever you say, wife. Put down your bow and we will talk about it."

She dropped her aim by a hand's breadth. "I will not put down my bow until you hear my demands."

"You will not dictate terms to the next Lord of Hirado." He bared his teeth and lunged at her. She let her arrow fly as he slowed to splash across the stream. But did her skill fail her, or did she lack the heart to put it in his chest? Either way, it dinted the garden wall behind him and plunked to the ground.

His sword flashed from its scabbard and slashed at her on a diagonal. Her bow flew from her hands, severed in two. He stayed his weapon with the front edge a finger's breadth from her belly. "What was that about demands, ah?"

She dropped to her knees. He repositioned the blade against the side of her neck, frigid eyes fixed on her. If she had seen a glimmer of vulnerability a moment before, there was no hint of it now.

"My lord." She stopped to swallow. "You know there is no wheel of reincarnation for me. I have only one life to serve *Iesu*. I will not spend that life in a manner that achieves nothing for Him. Pray either grant me the freedom of religion you promised, or kill me now."

The point of his sword slid to her throat. "You live to serve me and this house."

She gazed up his silver blade and into his pupils. "I am honored to serve you, but I live to serve Lord *Iesu*. I am unable to do that in your house."

A dozen warring emotions played across his face. Her life depended on which of them won—and she shrank inside at that knowledge. She'd seen how quick he could be to order a head dispatched, with a blade just like the one at her throat.

Deusu, if this is my end, may it be a pleasing offering to you.

He lowered the blade just enough that she could breathe without feeling its edge. The world rotated, then righted.

"Very well, Sono." His expression was stony. "I grant you one chance to explain yourself."

Chapter Thirty-Four

Thursday 24 February 1949

AKIRA SLID INTO A TAXI'S BACK seat, next to Miyako, and it pulled away from the curb. She turned a pleading face to him. "Find a way to come up to us, please. I know how much you want to see him, and we may not have much time." She leaned toward him, her voice throbbing with intensity. "And I don't want to be alone with him and Captain Oda."

"I'll be there, Mi-chan." *If there's a way to do it.* Did the hospital have any real security to stop him?

Her face lit with relief. "*Arigato.* The cancer ward's not hard to find." She reeled off a list of directions.

Twenty minutes later, they walked into the lobby of Osaka Hospital for the second time in two days. This time, Oda waited for them, leaning on the reception desk.

"Matsuura-san," he looked pointedly at Miyako, "if you could please come up with me." The receptionist gave her a nod.

She lifted her chin. "What about Akira-san?"

"Your brother didn't tell you, ah?" Oda threw a glance full of veiled malevolence at him. "The doctors believe his visit would not be in your father's interest. The shock might be too much for him."

Akira's hackles rose. "As his children, don't we have some voice in that decision?"

Oda's response was cutting. "*Hai.* If your father acknowledged that relationship."

Please, God, let that change today. Why else would Papa-san have asked for Miyako?

She sent a pleading glance his way, then started up the stairs behind the captain.

Akira settled in a chair with a raw feeling in his gut. Slipping upstairs to materialize at Papa-san's bedside had seemed like a good idea in the taxi. But what if Oda and the doctors were right? The shock of seeing his son alive might prove more than Papa-san's overburdened system could handle.

His poor decisions had cost his father and sister enough already. This one could join that list.

He pulled a magazine from his briefcase, then whispered a prayer for guidance. The receptionist was watching him over her reading glasses. He stared at a page without focusing.

His father had so little time left, and his sister's pleading eyes refused to leave his thoughts. Conviction pressed a weight into his chest. He couldn't sit gathering dust in that decrepit lobby. He'd have to find his way to the fourth floor. By some more roundabout path than the sweeping staircase that rose before the woman's desk.

An elderly gentleman with a cane shuffled through the entrance and crossed the chipped tile toward the receptionist's desk. He moved at a glacial pace, putting each foot only a few inches in front of the other.

Lord willing, the fellow would keep her occupied for a minute or two. Akira meandered toward the bathrooms. They were tucked around a corner, out of view of the reception desk. A hallway extended beyond them.

There had to be a back staircase—probably several.

Look purposeful. Akira pushed through a set of swinging doors. A storage closet stood open to his left. Closed doors lined the hall beyond. Trying them all would certainly appear suspicious.

Thankfully, one of them popped open and a nurse rushed through, eyes glued to her notepad. He spotted a bit of steel banister behind her.

A staircase. He walked briskly through that door. If he could make it to the fourth floor without getting stopped, he should be able to pass himself off as a visitor who was supposed to be there but might have lost his way.

As he mounted the dingy stairs his feet took on ballast. For seven years, Papa-san had loomed in his thoughts. Was he ready to see him now?

He'd be a withered husk of the determined commander who'd once loomed so large as Akira's hero. And how would it feel to see abject scorn for what Akira had become written all over his face? Because that would happen when he walked into Papa-san's hospital room.

Ascending the last set of stairs felt like battling a headwind. He willed himself to move one foot forward, then the next.

He left the stairs on the fourth level, turned down the hall, and the headwind took on gale force. But if he couldn't find the courage now, when would he?

A pair of heavy wooden doors loomed ahead of him. They fit Miyako's description of the cancer ward. But as he passed a row of smaller rooms, the buzz of voices carried through a thin wall.

A woman. "Papa-san, I tried to do something terrible." It was Miyako—her words. He halted.

Her voice again. "I went to jail for it."

Miyako, speaking to their father. They'd moved Papa-san, then. Realization stabbed into Akira's chest, pushing a hard mass into his throat. The move was needed because they didn't keep dying men in the ward. It had to be hard on the others.

The conversation continued in softer tones. He extended a hand toward the door handle but couldn't make himself grasp it. Couldn't bring himself to walk in and confront his father with the truth that he existed.

Maybe it was best to let Oda keep running his charade, if it led Papa-san to a good death, his face composed in peace.

Miyako's voice bled through the wall, more animated than before. "It was Akira-san. He's—"

Oda cut in smoothly—the first time Akira had heard him speak. "*Hai.* You honored your brother's spirit as well. I'm sure he's smiling now with pride."

Brother's spirit. Oda's little charade was making him a ghost and his sister a liar. Of all the poisonous—

He pushed through the door and looked straight at the hospital bed. What he saw wrenched the air from his lungs.

Pain laced his father's face. A bruise stretched from one sharp cheekbone to where his frail shoulder disappeared into his hospital gown. His ribs etched clear stripes through the gown's thin fabric. Purple splotches covered his hands.

He'd read about leukemia and its terrible advanced stages. But reading it hadn't prepared him. Akira wouldn't have recognized his father if he hadn't known he'd find him on that bed.

Papa-san's eyes focused on Akira and went wide. "Akira-kun? My son?" It was little more than a wheeze, but it carried a pitiful depth of emotion.

Miyako had the chair on the far side of the bed. She lifted her eyes to Akira's and her face brightened.

Oda leaned against a wall, the power of his presence filling the small room. He pushed away from the wall and cursed. "You! I warned you—"

Akira gave his father a deep bow and slipped into the other chair, facing his sister across the hospital bed. "I'm here, Papa-san." He shot a glare at Oda. "Your friend asked me not to come, out of concern it would be too much for you."

Papa-san coughed and made an effort to sit, his translucent skin going ruddy.

Miyako laid a hand on his shoulder. "Shh. Please don't get excited." She squeezed the hand she was holding.

Papa-san gave her hand a tiny squeeze back. Akira's heart swelled to see how tender she was with him and how he accepted her touch.

"I'm so sorry, Papa-san," he said. "I've been away for too many years. It is a long story, and it's my deep regret I did not come to tell it sooner."

His father lay very still now, watching him with luminous eyes.

Oda also eyed him, cold but calm. "It's not a long story, young Matsuura. I can tell it quickly. Your father hasn't heard from you because you spent most of the war"—he turned his eyes to Papa-san and spewed out the next words—"in camps in America. For *horyo*. That's the shame I hoped to spare your father. But you disregard me and come anyway."

Papa-san's face froze in stunned disbelief.

Akira gaped at the captain. This was the man's idea of sparing his father pain? It seemed his real concern was keeping Papa-san isolated and in his own orbit. "I would never choose to shame you, Papa-san."

Oda gave Akira back an even stare. "Tell your story, then. Where have you been? And what have I said that isn't true, ah?"

Papa-san's features twisted with tragic pain.

Akira appealed to him. "Please. I haven't seen you in seven years. Let me explain it in my own words."

All Papa-san's gestures were compact, as if to conserve every last iota of precious energy. He gave a slight nod, his eyes lingering above Akira's collar.

Akira pulled his collar away from his throat. "Part of what Captain Oda says is true. You see my scars, Papa-san. You remember when they assigned me to *Nitto Maru*. The enemy blew her up under me." He took a deep breath to calm himself. "I commanded her in the end, Papa-san. All the men did their duties bravely. You would have been proud of us."

Papa-san nodded again, a slight smile softening his features. He fixed hungry eyes on Akira as if he were memorizing every detail of his son's appearance.

"They were all rewarded with good deaths in our nation's service. But that wasn't my destiny. I alone had the misfortune to survive—at least, that's how I saw it. The *gaijin* fished me out of the water, unconscious. I woke in a sick bay, on an enemy ship."

Papa-san's face darkened. He opened his mouth as if to speak but managed only a rasping cough.

Akira hurried on with his explanation. "You can imagine my shame. I knew I needed to end my life. It was the only honorable path, and I tried very hard. But always, the *gaijin* prevented me."

Oda cut in. "And in the end you made your peace with your useless life. How did you accomplish that?"

"Papa-san," Miyako said. "Make him stop. Akira and I are your dutiful children. That's why we're here. Let's end this visit in peace, ah?"

Oda sneered. "I think your father deserves the truth."

Papa-san's jaw worked for a second before he eked enough air for a few precious words from his pneumonia-scarred lungs. "Want only...truth. Dying, Akira-kun. They don't say it, but I know. No time."

Akira met his eyes. "Then you'll have the truth. All of it. I have become a Christian. It's my new faith that has given me the strength to return to you, in spite of my grave dishonor. I desperately want to be reconciled to you. So does Mi-chan."

Miyako spoke up. "And Akira-san is helping me so much, Papa-san. He and his friends kept me out of prison. I'm determined to lead a better life, and with his support I will."

Papa-san's eyes lingered on her. She went on. "I did my best to care for you. I'll do it again. I'll come and read to you." She broke into a winsome smile. "I'll fix Doctor Furata's tea you always hated."

He started to return her smile, but his eyes jerked back to Akira. "Matsuura...do not tolerate...Christians." He gasped it out with what seemed to be the last breath in his lungs. His focus moved to Oda.

"Papa-san, don't be so stubborn," Miyako said.

The captain's voice was unctuous. "I've explained it all to your son. I reminded him that the House of Matsuura has always been a staunch Buddhist house. But there was a brief era when this Western religion tainted the House of Matsuura. And the cost was extreme."

Miyako's brows creased in puzzlement. "What are you talking about?"

"You don't know? This stain took the form of a woman, Omura Sono, daughter of that infamous Christian warlord. She married your most illustrious ancestor Shigenobu's son, the twenty-seventh lord of your line."

Miyako still looked confused. "But...so long ago. Why—"

"Think about it. When you pray to your ancestors, you pray to the *Kirishitan* Omura Sumitada as well. Consider what his spirit must make of that! In any case, he was a fool, sending his daughter off to Hirado to found a Christian dynasty. But it meant nothing. Hers was the last Christian generation on Hirado."

Miyako frowned and shifted in her seat to put her back toward Oda. "This is crazy, Papa-san. It's ancient history.

How could this possibly matter to you and your children today?"

Papa-san's hand made a small flick in Oda's direction.

"Suspicion attached to your house, thanks to this treacherous Omura daughter. Your eminent ancestor Matsuura Shigenobu had to burn down his own castle to prove his loyalty to the new shogun. An entire castle. Why such an extreme gesture? I wonder. Perhaps this Omura woman infected her husband as well."

Oda folded his arms across his broad chest. His face went red, his voice low and menacing. "The sixteenth century, Akira-kun. That was the last Christian generation on Hirado. Your noble forebear saw to that. And you!" Oda the lecturer visibly swelled, completing his transformation to Oda the bully.

Miyako cowered, as if she'd seen it before. *Why?*

Papa-san had his eyes riveted on Oda. But where Akira thought he might read disagreement or anger, or perhaps at least confusion on his father's face, he saw only gratitude.

Gratitude.

Oda bellowed at Akira. "And you dare come to your father professing this foreign religion. Who will do your duty to honor your father's spirit once he's gone? This is weakness. Profane weakness. But what can one expect of a *horyo*?"

Papa-san's eyes turned to Akira. "You...give up this...Christ?"

Akira shook his head. "You said you want only truth. *Iesu* has saved me from grinding shame and a pointless death, and I'm convinced now that"—he slowed for emphasis—"He is the truth."

Papa-san stared at him. "Dishonor." His nostrils spread. "Leave me."

Miyako released his hand and stood. Tears shone in her eyes. "I must go too, then." She said it softly, then glared at Oda. "I don't know why it pleases you to see Papa-san suffer without his children, but you're about to get your wish."

Papa-san's eyes followed Miyako, his expression

stricken. "Mi-chan? Why?"

She fell to her knees at his bedside. "Because I believe in *Iesu*, like Akira-san. Please reconsider this, Papa-san. If you can't accept Christians, you can't accept me."

Akira gaped at her in astonishment. *When did that happen?*

Oda sputtered. "A Christian? That's worse than abandoning your father in this life. You'll abandon him in the next."

Papa-san clamped his jaw shut and glared at his daughter. A tense moment passed before he closed his eyes, pressed his head into the pillow, and rasped out three more words. "Make them leave."

Akira ushered his sister from the hospital room. They walked in silence until they reached the top of the main staircase. He shot her a sidelong glance. "You've decided to trust Christ, ah?" He hoped with all his heart it was true.

Her features were taut with pain, but there was a stubborn set to her jaw. "It's not the first time Papa-san has disowned me, you know. And all I did was try to care for him." She squeezed her lips together and marched on two paces. "I couldn't watch him treat you like that. After everything you've done for me."

He stopped and turned to her, pushing back his disappointment so it wouldn't color his words. "So you only said it to support me?"

She met his eyes. "No. It wasn't just that. I'm learning there's a different kind of Father. One who never casts His children out, no matter what they've done."

"Then...you're ready to follow *Iesu*, wherever that takes you?"

She managed a crooked smile. "Where else is a girl like me supposed to go?"

His heart exploded with joy. "The path may not always be easy, but you won't regret this decision, Mi-chan."

She looked solemn now. "I know."

They descended half a flight of stairs. Happiness for his sister and a tragic sense of loss over his father buffeted him by turns, leaving him drained.

Miyako spoke again. "Imagine what it was like for poor

Sono. They married so young back then. And she was alone against all those brutal *samurai.*" She let out a dreamy sigh. "Doesn't it make you want to go back to Hirado? We could look for her grave. Oda even hinted that her faith may have *infected* her husband, the lord of the land. That's not a small impact."

This was the first time she'd mentioned wanting to go anywhere. And that was heartening. "We can take a trip there when your probation is over. But we won't burn incense this time." A shiver ran through him at a vivid memory. *Monroe's* railing, and a pair of glimmering moonlit eyes reflected on the shifting black waves of the Pacific.

A little laugh burst from her. "No."

"Not everything Oda said was true, by the way. That was not the last Christian generation. You know where Shimabara is, yes?"

"Just north of Mount Unzen. Not far from Hirado."

"Exactly. Three decades after the Lord Regent triumphed on Kyushu, there were still enough Christians to raise the Shimabara rebellion. And enough seasoned Christian warriors to lead them. Who knows what part Matsuura Sono or her children might have played in that?"

An idea hit him. "They should have something on all this history at the library." Could he lure her out of the apartment for the library's quiet halls? That would be a small victory. "We'll go later today, if you'd like."

She shot him a wry look. "I can't say I've read many books lately." The vitality drained from her face. "But why not, ah? Rather than sitting around thinking about Papa-san."

Their father. His first meeting with Papa-san after seven years had left his emotions as beat-up as Yoshigumi's gang had left his body. He could only pray this wouldn't be their last meeting.

He met his sister's eyes. "Matsuura Sono. Alone against her Buddhist house. This is what it can mean to follow *Iesu.* Are you sure you're ready?"

She looked pensive. "I'm feeling some kinship with her now." She shot him a sidelong glance. "I guess I just chose my side."

Chapter Thirty-Five

Twenty-First Day of the Ninth Month, Anno Domini 1588

SONO HAD DELIBERATED LONG ON HER next words. It was no surprise that she would deliver them with Hisanobu's sword at her throat and her knees in the mud.

He glowered down his blade at her. "How is your life so worthless here, and what are these demands?"

"My lord, I pray you have seen something of it in the way I live. Faithfulness to *Iesu* is my life and breath. I must have the freedom not to do things that grieve Him. I must know that our future children are protected. I must have your oath that you'll never again ask me to send a child back."

He exhaled in an exasperated huff. "I did what you said you wanted."

"What you pressed me to accept. And poor Taro! I miss him every moment of the day. I fear we will both regret what we have done until the instant we leave this world."

A grimace crossed his face, and his sword arm sagged. He raised its point back to her collarbone. "Is that all?"

"I took the liberty of writing out a few things. If you will permit me, I have it in my sleeve."

"An edict?" A hint of the old amused light danced around his eyes.

"*Hai*, my lord, if you choose to name it so." She reached in her sleeve and pulled out the scroll she'd written earlier that day. She bobbed the best bow she could with his blade at her throat and presented it to him.

His *katana* made a *schlick* sound as he sheathed it. Her rebellious muscles sagged with relief like a fistful of noodles. She forced her chin up and her back straight.

He unfurled the crisp paper and read out loud. "You request living quarters outside the women's wing and away from my mother." He looked at her and angled an eyebrow. "But I am permitted to keep you under guard there if it suits me."

"*Hai*, my lord. I am suffocating in that women's wing."

A breeze ruffled the corner of the paper. A half-dozen mulberry leaves drifted down. One settled on the water behind him, where it bobbed along until it caught in an eddy.

He read on. "You request to give alms to *Kirishitan* charities as our mother does to Saikyo-ji."

"Your domain needs the work they do at the House of Mercy, my lord."

Mulberries were not planted for show or beauty. The humble mulberry tree lived to serve, giving up its leaves to be chewed into silk and beaten into paper. The ancient Matsuura clan might have forgotten the meaning of their crest. If she survived this day, 'twould be to remind them.

"You request to entertain *Kirishitan* ladies at will."

"*Hai*. Teaching and fellowship are central to our faith."

"You request my agreement that you can teach our children about *Iesu* yourself. And send our boys to town for *Kirishitan* education."

"*Hai*, my lord. You promised me freedom of religion. The list you hold is what that would mean to me."

He peered at her, forehead creasing with incredulity. "You thought you could wrest these concessions from me at the point of an arrow, ah?"

"I hoped to make you see that for me, this is life and death. If you cannot honor my requests so I can live for *Deusu*—as you did promise—then I beg you." She moved her hair aside to better expose her neck and bowed her head to the earth. "Kill me now. I have given you cause."

"You have." He said it in a matter-of-fact tone. He pulled a fan from his sleeve and strode onto the patio. He sat on the bench and fanned himself. "Come."

She fingered her neck with an enormous sigh of relief that her head was still on it. She followed him up the step and knelt at his feet.

He rested her scroll on his thigh. It curled around his fingers. "I am prepared to make allowances for your behavior today, Sono-chan. These past days have been a grueling experience for you. For both of us." He moistened his lower lip, reached out, and stroked her hair. "I have missed you. By all the deities, I have missed you."

Her spine went rigid. "And about my requests?"

He gave a tolerant little laugh. "This edict of yours. I want you to be happy here, Sono-chan. I told you that from the beginning. You know I cannot commit to most of these points without agreement from Papa-san. And he will bring our mother into it, and things will get"—he swallowed visibly and looked into her eyes—"difficult."

His mother, still. "So nothing will change, my lord?"

He slid her scroll into his sleeve, took her hands between his, and gazed into her eyes. "I pledge this. You and I will never send an infant back again. I know many argue how essential it is to prune a garden, but I found no joy in leaving the pitiful little thing in the woods. We can manage in the future without that." He stroked the back of her hand, his eyes fixed on hers. "I will not hurt you again that way."

"*Arigato*, my lord." She gave him a grateful smile. It was a heartening move—and it was tempting to let it be enough. The inviting breeze, the play of sunlight on the stream, the way her pulse still throbbed at his touch—they all conspired to persuade her to let it be enough.

But the mulberry leaf bobbed, making its brave stand against the current, as if to remind her—she had to stay strong. "And the rest?"

"Is that not the heart of it? 'Twould be best if you could accept this offer. Then I have no need to bring your requests before my father. You will go back to the women's wing tomorrow, as our mother expects, and we will keep what happened here between us. For myself, I care not where you live. But we must honor my parents' wishes." He cleared his throat. "I do want my father to name me his successor."

She stared at him for a long moment. Her Taro needed a father who would stand up to his grandmother. And Hirado domain needed a true *Kirishitan* heir, not one in name. She parted her lips and gave her head a slow shake.

A pained expression lodged on his face. "Must you make this difficult, Sono-chan?"

"I cannot help it, my lord. I will not go back there. I will not raise our children"—*my Taro*— "where their faith will be attacked every day."

He released her hands. "You stand by your terms, then."

"I do."

He planted his feet and stood. "The Lord Regent has taught me much about dealing with enemies. You start by softening them with a siege. Even hardened soldiers get more accommodating when they go without food and water for a time." He peered down at her, his expression fixed as stone. "Do not make me treat you as an enemy. Or worse, as a traitor."

There was a moment when she could have reversed course. Could have taken his offer and the safe path that led to the women's wing. The breeze whispered its soft invitation. The stream murmured. And his eyes pleaded.

She let the moment pass. "I am truly sorry, my lord."

He pressed his lips into a line and angled his jaw toward the teahouse. "Back inside, then. And stay inside, on point of death. You will remain here under tight guard until Lord Matsuura and I decide what to do with you."

Thurday 24 February 1949

That evening, Akira was taking a fresh look at the classified ads, pen in hand. Miyako had finished with the most recent *Asahi Picture News* and buried herself in a back issue. Three library books sat piled beside her magazines. His plan to get her out to the library might have backfired. She had more reason to stay insulated in the apartment than ever.

She set the magazine down, her face creasing with revulsion.

"What is it?" he said.

She slid it across the table at him and stabbed a fingernail at the top of a column. She rose with her hand over her mouth and walked to the window.

The editorial about the Demon Midwife. She'd found it.

Idiot. Why didn't you throw that one away? He picked it

up and digested the portion he'd skipped on the train.

Ishikawa's lurid story is a powerful symbol of the desperate choices that confront the loving mothers of these babies, which so often serve as unwanted reminders of relationships that never should have been.

He looked up at her. "Did you know about this Ishikawa woman?"

She nodded.

"How did the babies die?"

"They strangled some. Others they just abandoned outside."

The magazine sagged in his hands. "A hundred. That must be the worst series of murders in decades."

"And they only gave her eight years." Miyako turned from the window, dabbing tears from her cheeks. "Eight years, Akira-san. For over a hundred babies. Mixed-blood babies don't have much value, ah?"

"Not to the men who judged her trial, it seems."

"Or to their fathers," she said in a choking voice. She crumpled her hands into fists. "I understand why it happens. Women can't take the shame of it."

He stood, trying to load his words with all the compassion in his soul. "Or they feel they can't support the baby after the father leaves them. But I'm here for you, Mi-chan."

"I know. And I'm very grateful."

He probed, proceeding cautiously. "Do you know who the father is?"

Her eyes sank to the floor. "I was a prostitute. No."

"But he might be American."

She looked at him, blinking away tears. "I've been thinking and thinking. Trying to get clear on the dates. The weeks in jail blend together. One long stretch of seamless misery." She seemed to deflate. "Unfortunately, there are a number of possibilities."

"I'm ready to hear them." *I think.*

"I had...American clients. One of them was my regular. George-san." She stopped.

"Or?"

"Or the baby could be full Japanese. But if it is..." She

turned from him, sank her head in her hands, and stood that way for a long moment, taking shuddering breaths.

"What is it, Mi-chan? You can tell me."

"I was raped," she said through her fingers. "Three of them."

He took a half-step back, rage pumping through his blood and putting a film over his vision. "Who were they?"

She walked to the window and stared out. "George-san asked me the same question. He thought he was going to get them arrested or beaten or something. I wouldn't tell him." She spun back to him. "And I won't tell you. I can't go through it, Akira-san. You know the likelihood of obtaining a conviction? Next to zero. And maybe you don't know what they'd put me through in the process." She shook her head violently. "No. That chapter's closed."

"But it's not closed, if there's a baby. What about this American? Was he"—Akira pushed down a noxious wave of spiraling fury—"good to you?"

"He was the best man I knew. He invited me to move in with him. If he didn't treat me well in the end"—she collapsed to her knees by the table—"I gave him good reason." She buried her face in her hands. "It's just as well that's over. He wouldn't want a mixed-blood baby. He would have left me. They all do."

A long moment passed before she raised her eyes to his. "You haven't been here, so you don't know. No one wants these children." She screwed her eyes closed, tears wetting her cheeks. "When the baby comes, it should be obvious if it's George-san's. But if the baby's full Japanese..." She clearly couldn't speak again about her rape. "I don't know which is worse."

Agony creased her face. "Are you sure we can't—"

He pushed his words past a wall of anguish that mirrored hers. "I couldn't be part of it."

She went on as if he hadn't said it. "Imai-san, the woman who runs the Oasis where I...where I used to work. She would know a doctor. I bet she'd even finance it."

"For what? For a renewed work contract?"

She nodded, her eyes on the floor.

"You don't want that life, do you?"

"Any life I want is out of my reach. So what do I do?"

"You cling to *Iesu*. And you believe." Akira picked up the magazine. "Did you read down to the author's biography?"

Miyako rose and paced the length of the small room like a caged lion. "I didn't."

"She has an orphanage in Oiso. All mixed-blood children are welcome. This says she's raising dozens of children there."

"Is that so?" Miyako took the magazine from him. She settled beside him, her eyes locked on the paragraph at the column's base. "Takanura Miki. The Tabitha Mills Home," she murmured, as if trying to engrave it on her memory.

"Oiso's a lovely place. It's on the coast, between here and Tokyo. We can probably tour the home if you'd like."

She studied the woman's photo for a long moment before she answered. "*Hai*. I would like that."

"I'll call."

Akira turned from stowing some dishes on his shelves the next evening to see Miyako at the coat rack, fingering her coat's lapel. "Remember how you said you'd take me out for something to eat?"

"Of course. Anything."

She fidgeted with a button. "I think I'm ready."

He grinned and reached for his coat. "Now? Great. What would you like?"

The answer turned out to be sweet bean soup. But not just any soup. Very specific soup, at a specific cafe, on the famous Shinsaibashi shopping street. There were probably a hundred restaurants closer to his apartment. But he wasn't about to argue with a pregnant woman about food. Anything that motivated her to brave the evening throngs on the subway was a milestone.

Forty-five minutes later, they stepped off the train at Shinsaibashi station and walked a long block. The warm, spicy aroma of sweetened beans flavored the air for a hundred feet before they turned into the shop, evoking powerful memories of Mama-san's kitchen.

It was a small place. Nothing remarkable to him. Maybe the selection of pastries in the glass display case was better than average. But the highlight, of course, was the sweetly spiced soup. A woman stood behind the counter spooning the thick, red-brown liquid into bowl after bowl, assembly-line style.

He fell in line to buy the soup. The place was crowded. Miyako stood almost against his side, gazing around, the anxiety he'd seen in the apartment haunting her eyes.

"Maybe you'd better go find us a place to sit." He suggested it gently, wanting to push her a little but not too much.

She bit at her lip, but she nodded. She wove her way through the crowd until she found two empty chairs at a bistro-style table. She sat gazing out the window with a wistful look, eying the shoppers on the brightly lit street.

Replaying some memory?

A couple walked in. A tall, blond American in a leather aviator jacket. A slim Japanese girl, fawning on him. The sight of them made his stomach churn.

He snapped his eyes away. Why did Miyako like this place?

A flash of movement from her direction startled him. She'd pushed her chair back, turned toward the wall, hunched her shoulders and dropped her head. A curtain of hair hid her face.

The American took a place in line while his girl went to find them a table. Akira paid for two bowls of steaming soup and a pot of tea and carried the tray to Miyako. "What's wrong?"

"We need to go, Akira-san." She said it in a whisper, then rose to her feet, keeping her face toward the wall. She started toward the door, hunching in an awkward way to hide her face. Of course that only drew attention. Curious eyes followed her from the tables around them.

The American turned from the counter, looked at her, and froze. "Hey." He took a small step toward her then stopped. His eyes flicked to the girl he'd come in with.

Miyako slipped through the front door. Akira left their soup on the table and followed her. He caught up with her outside. "What was that about? That American acted like he knew you."

She stared at him. Her lips parted but nothing came out.

"Is that him? The American who—"

She gave him a nod, wide-eyed with horror, then dissolved in tears.

So that was why she'd wanted to come to this specific place. And why the wistful looks. She'd been there with him.

Akira pivoted and stomped into the shop. The American had left his tray with his new sweetheart and returned to the counter for spoons.

Akira strode to him, stopped in his path, and glared into the eyes of the despicable louse who'd taken advantage of his sister's—and his father's—destitution. "Do you know my sister, Miyako?"

The scoundrel shook his head. "Doesn't ring a bell. Do I know you?"

I'm your sin, hunting you down. "The woman who just left. The one you were watching."

"I thought maybe I knew her. But I was wrong."

Akira stiffened, his pulse pounding in his ears. "Her name is Matsuura Miyako."

He passed it off with a shrug. "Sorry, fellow. I don't know anyone by that name." His eyes drifted above Akira's shoulder, to the corner where his latest girl was sitting.

Akira barely managed to restrain himself from slugging the *gaijin*. He took a good look at the American's face and at the squadron patch on his chest. A furious-looking dark bird rode a disembodied propeller, the number eighty-nine floating in a puff of clouds above its head. There was a leather name band too. *Sanders.*

He jutted his chin and took a half-step closer to the big American. He spoke in a low voice, only for the *gaijin*'s ear. "My sister is pregnant."

The airman tensed and his upper lip curled. "Congratulations. You must be excited."

"Weren't you the man who asked her to move in with you?"

His face darkened. "I don't know you. I don't know your sister. And I don't know what you're talking about." His hands made fists at his hips.

A fresh thought struck him. "You might know her as Miyako. And isn't your name George?"

That seemed to hit him. He stood for a moment, jaw ajar. But he shook his head. "Look, fellow, I am sorry about your sister. But you've got the wrong guy."

Bitterness pushed acid through his veins. Of course the man wouldn't admit to anything. What had he expected?

He packed all the scorn scorching his heart into his next words. "She tried to tell me you aren't worth my time. And you obviously weren't worth hers." He spun away and stalked out the door.

Miyako stood waiting for him just out of view of the cafe's windows, white hands clutched together at the base of her ribs. "Akira-san, he was with someone! What did you say to him?"

"I asked him if he knew you."

She focused enormous, anguished eyes on him. "What did he say?"

He paused, smiled through gritted teeth, and lied. "He said to tell you he wishes you well."

"He did, ah?" Moisture stained her cheeks. She brightened a bit, and his heart broke for her.

"Do you want to try another place? I know a spot—"

She gave him a decisive shake of the head. "No, thank you." She dabbed at her eyes as they started back toward the station. "I can't believe that happened. He's never on leave on a Friday."

They walked a few more paces. She spoke in a half moan. "He's found someone new. Of course he has." She turned tormented eyes on Akira. "Did he say anything else?"

"Not really." He wasn't about to admit that he'd confronted George with the fact she was pregnant. What a disaster that evening had been, thanks to the lousy American. He would never lure her from their apartment again.

The Lord promised to bind up the brokenhearted. Dave-san had assured him of that. But how long would it take *Iesu* to heal poor, broken Mi-chan?

Chapter Thirty-Six

AKIRA'S SISTER DISAPPEARED BEHIND HER *SHOJI* as soon as they got home, and by mid-morning the next day he had barely seen her. Her Bible and a pile of books had disappeared into her bedroom with her. The back issues of the *Asahi Picture News* had not, as he had quietly thrown those away.

Details from the night before circled through his mind. Especially the fact that he now had the *gaijin*'s name and squadron number—enough information to find him and confront him again. Should he?

Is the baby even his? It would be months before they'd know. But from what Miyako had told him, the likelihood was strong. And it was clear she still had feelings for the man.

The *gaijin*'s sneer rang in Akira's ears—and that wasn't the only thing. The scorn in his tone had been matched by everything else about him. The curled lip. The subtle but quick move to fists. If the American had been in love with Miyako a few weeks earlier, there'd been no trace of it the night before.

Still, George had gone back to that cafe. A place he and Miyako had visited together, it seemed. Was it possible he felt a little nostalgia, too? And if Miyako was pregnant with his child, didn't he deserve a chance to know it?

The louse knows. I told him. But Akira had come at him out of the blue. If he'd approached him better, maybe the man would have responded better.

Doubtful.

He needed to get some fresh air. Clear his mind. "Mi-chan?"

She murmured something from behind the closed *shoji.*

"I'm going out for a cigarette. I could stop at the grocery store if you want anything."

"No, thank you."

"Are you sure? You should eat something."

"I'm not hungry."

He went out, puffed through his cigarette while his thoughts spun in worried circles, then dug the mail from his mailbox on his way upstairs. Three items. One bore his sister's name, which sent a jolt of surprise through him. The creamy rice paper exuded a faint scent of jasmine. Their address was inscribed in a delicate hand.

He rapped on the *shoji*. "This came for you."

The *shoji* cracked and she took the envelope, eyebrows lifting in surprise. Her face went blank as she peered at the handwriting. She ripped it open, scanned the note inside, then crumpled it.

"What is it?" he said.

She stared at the envelope like it was infested. "How did she know?"

"Who?" Akira gently extracted the wadded-up note from her hand. He guided her to a cushion, then read the note.

My dear Midori,

Or is it Miyako now? How did your beloved father react to the news that you're expecting? Or those Christians they tell me you now call friends? I can only imagine how excited they will be to welcome your illegitimate child.

Or perhaps they don't know yet.

I can help you with your dilemma. But not if you wait any longer. Come see me.

Your devoted friend,

Imai

He dropped the crumpled note on the table. "Imai? She manages the brothel, ah?" Had the paper left a layer of slime on his fingers?

Miyako nodded, her forehead furrowed with distress. "How did she get this address? And how does she know anything about my friends?"

"I don't know." He gestured at the note with his chin. "What do you want me to do with that?" Was she considering the offer?

She stood rigid for a moment, then went to her futon, picked up one of the history books from the library, and thrust it at him. "Read this, please."

To cement this new alliance, the ailing Omura Sumitada married his fifth child, a daughter, to Hisanobu, the son of Matsuura Shigenobu. Her new family was adversarial toward her faith. The Jesuits' annual letters mention her by name on two different occasions, praising her perseverance and piety. She was allowed to baptize her children as Kirishitan.

Her firstborn son was small and sickly. One of many areas of contention between Sono and her Matsuura family was their desire to end this child's life, in accordance with the common practice of that time. She refused on the grounds that this would violate her faith.

He looked up to find her studying him. He snorted. "I guess it wasn't just the practice of *that* time."

"When I first told you I was pregnant, you said something. An age-old battle."

"I guess I did."

"Interesting, ah? This is all I could find about Matsuura Sono. All we know about her. Our *Kirishitan* lady ancestor fought for her baby when everyone around her said he shouldn't live."

"If she hadn't, you and I wouldn't be here."

"*Hai.* And I see what you were saying now." A fire lit behind her eyes. "They thought they could dispense with a baby that didn't suit them. But a teenage girl stood up to them. She knew that no one but God has the power to place that spark of life in her womb."

The light in her eyes. The determined set of her chin. He looked at the wadded-up note on the table between them. "You've decided about Imai's offer, then?"

She nodded, breaking into a slow grin. "Do you have a match?"

He reached for his pocket.

She pinned him with a level gaze. "I don't want what Imai has to offer. I'll walk the path *Iesu* has laid out for me."

He reduced Imai's note to ashes and made Mi-chan a cup of green tea. The question stirred again and rolled around in his brain. *If* he wanted to contact George—

He didn't. The thought of the man brought only withering distaste.

Miyako made a face and caressed her belly.

"You're sick, Mi-chan?"

She gave him a miserable nod.

What he felt wasn't so important. Like it or not, there

were good odds the little person growing inside her bound both of them to the airman in a manner that wasn't going away.

The question did another lap around his mind. Assuming he decided to contact George, how would he do it? How would he get in touch with an American airman at a base two hours away—a man who wanted the conversation even less than he did?

She dragged around the apartment all day, and his distaste turned to conviction. He had to try.

At church on Sunday morning, someone pointed him to a man named Kito-san, whose chain of bakeries had a contract with the base. Kito-san advised him that access to the base was only on official business. "So don't bother going out there. You'd waste a trip. And you won't be able to phone in to an airman. Ask the switchboard operator for his squadron command and leave a message for him. That's all you can do."

Akira thanked the gentleman. George's image rose in his brain, complete with arrogant stance. Upper lip curled in disdain.

Disgust made his teeth grind. Leave a message. What good was that going to do? Unless the *gaijin* was a very different fellow than he'd taken him for, he would never hear anything back.

He didn't linger after church but made a quick exit to the broad avenue leading to the station. Three Japanese men stood deep in conversation in the doorway of a storefront. Their laughter jarred him, so at odds with his own black mood.

A big placard hung in the storefront's window. *Jesus Saves*, in bold red characters. Both in English and Japanese. And underneath, in English only, *Servicemen Welcome*.

Servicemen. The base would have a chaplain's office, yes? A Christian chaplain should be interested in helping George do the right thing by a girl he'd made pregnant. He might get further there than via George's chain of command.

He'd make both calls on Monday. Nothing would come

of it. The *gaijin* had no interest—that was all too clear at the cafe. But at least he would have tried.

Monday morning came. Akira forced himself out on a couple of errands. He told Miyako about one of them—he needed to rummage the black-market stalls for a second-hand interview suit. There was no need to mention the phone calls.

The gray drizzle outside matched his mood. His forays with his resume had been getting a decent response. He was more employable than he'd guessed. Every business that sold to Americans needed people who spoke their language and knew their ways.

Which put a weight at the base of his gut. The desk job he feared was a real prospect.

He rolled it around in his mind as he walked toward the market. During Miyako's long weeks in prison, he'd made a daytrip to Kobe in search of Nagai's parents. He'd had little to go on. So he was disappointed, but not surprised, when he failed to glean any information about them.

He'd spent an hour or so walking the causeway where the bombed-out old port city met the bay. He put his face to the wind and filled his nostrils with the hearty tang of the spray.

It had been weeks since he'd scented the sea. It tugged at him.

But so did his sister. And for her sake, he would have to entomb himself in a desk job. Put the sea behind him for the time being.

Possibly forever.

He'd almost reached the edge of the black-market district when a payphone confronted him, thrusting George's face back into his thoughts. The wretched louse who'd made his sister a toy—a broken toy he had to stay in port to help mend.

He glanced at his watch. Nine fifteen. Not too early to get the calls to Itami Air Base over with. If anything came of the thing, that would be up to *Iesu*.

He dug in his pocket for two coins, dialed the main switchboard, and asked for the chaplain.

"Which one? Father Lawrence or Pastor Gould?"

Pastor. That was what they called Rev. Kagawa. "Pastor Gould, please."

The operator put the call through, and a male voice picked up. "Pastor Gould."

He'd actually gotten to someone. That was more than he'd expected. He cleared his throat. "Hello, pastor. I'm hoping to get your help in reaching an airman."

There was a brief hesitation. "My help? Did you try the switchboard?"

"It's nothing I want to describe to a switchboard operator."

"What can I do for you?" The voice wasn't as warm as Akira had hoped.

"I'd like to make sure this airman gets a chance to do the right thing. He may have made my sister pregnant. Could you help me let him know?"

A heavy sigh came over the line. "The girl can't tell him herself?"

"She, ah...hasn't heard from him for a while."

"Look, son. I'm no Ann Landers."

Who? "Sir?"

The chaplain let out another sigh. "You can leave me your details, and I will locate the fellow and pass this information along."

"Thank you, sir. That's all I—"

"But"—the man sounded weary—"I will also be obligated to advise him that the War Bride Act has expired. And that *if* he's interested in marriage, and *if* his marriage is approved, he will have to sign a pile of documents. He'll have to acknowledge that U.S. immigration laws give him no right to bring a Japanese wife to the U.S. Meaning that, at some point, he'll have to choose between this new wife and everything he left at home."

Akira stood frozen, the chaplain's words battering his ear.

And the man hadn't finished. "Most of them find that too hard a pill to get down. And...I feel compelled to add this. Between you and me, if the airman does have some interest in matrimony, I'm required to check with the police. It grieves me to say it, but with the rash of prostitution around our bases, many marriages get disallowed. Too often, we find the girl has a record." He cleared his throat. "I'm sure that doesn't apply to your sister."

Akira cringed inside. "She has become a Christian, if that matters to you."

"It matters a good deal to me. I'm delighted to hear it. But sadly, it matters not one whit to the Air Force." The line went quiet for a second or two. He went on in a softer tone. "I am sorry. And I do wish I could paint a rosier picture. I'll take your information. Who knows? Maybe some good will come of it. Maybe the young man will learn to keep his pants zipped in the future."

Akira's blood burned through his veins. How did *in the future* help his sister—or her baby? But he muzzled his indignation and gave the chaplain the information.

Not that it was going to do any good. Poor Mi-chan. She'd cried so hard after seeing her airman. There was no reason to tell her that her love affair with George had never had a chance. And every reason to hope she'd be pleased with the Tabitha Mills Home when they toured it the next day.

He didn't waste a coin on the second call.

Twenty-First Day of the Ninth Month, Anno Domini 1588

The teahouse was an empty place without Iya. Sono huddled inside, listening, while Hisanobu summoned a guard detail and issued instructions to the captain. "Lady Sono is not to leave the building. And no one is to enter."

A gruff voice responded. "Will they be bringing her meals?"

"No."

"*Hai*, Master Hisanobu. I will see to it."

She collapsed onto her futon. *Not just an enemy—a traitor.* From his perspective, that was true. And traitors deserved death.

She wanted to be brave, but her stomach ached with fear. He and his father were going to have quite a conversation. Would he be her advocate? She might have wounded his pride enough to make him her accuser.

The lengths of white fabric around her spoke both of birth and of death. And summoned an image of Taro. The ache to hold him once more stole her breath. And grief jabbed a spear into her chest at the thought of perishing without seeing her family in Omura again. What account would they receive of how and why she died?

But she could leave that in Iya's hands. And in the Almighty's.

Since she was under siege, she inventoried her provisions. It was a quick exercise. She had the water in the kettle and no more. A few lumps of coal to pile on the embers. And not a morsel of food. Not that she was likely to want to eat.

She had to hope Lord Matsuura wouldn't deliberate long.

The afternoon light was fading, and she had no means to light the lamp. If she was going to compose a death poem, she would have to do it now. She brought out paper and brush and ground her ink.

She closed her eyes. *Lord* Iesu, *will You speak through my brush?* The poem she had recited the day she met the Matsuura men echoed through her mind. *People gone... Grass withered, lifeless. Wistful thoughts.*

That poem made a lovely point, but it missed one eternal truth.

Not all things fade.

That was four syllables. She needed five for her first line. *Do all things fade? No.*

With that on the page, the next three lines needed for a poem in *tanka* form flowed out of her.

The grass withers, and the flower.
But Deusu *dwells*
In unapproachable light.

She still had the fifth line—seven more syllables to bring her message home. She twirled her brush in the ink.

I seek our little son there.

Tears welled up at the thought of him. *Ah! Taro. We may be together soon.*

It had grown too dark to write well. The poem wasn't everything she wanted. It captured the immortality of the Lord and of the soul. And it would continue to promote the idea that Taro was dead, which was crucial. But this was not just about poor Taro. If it had been, 'twould have been better for her to stay silent, at least for a season.

No. She was staring death in the face for her future babies—for all the babies. All the babies in her Lord's domain should have their chance at the life *Deusu* gave them—whether born in the Matsuura mansion or in Hirado town or in a remote village on Furue Bay. She needed the freedom to raise a *Kirishitan* lord who would put himself between *all* the babies and the foxes.

Chapter Thirty-Seven

Tuesday 1 March 1949

AKIRA STOOD WITH HIS SISTER AT the edge of a broad, rolling lawn. Roses bloomed around a fountain. The air echoed with the joyful sounds of children playing, somewhere out of sight, and carried a faint whiff of the sea.

He watched Miyako take it in. Before the air raids, the Tabitha Mills Home had been a baron's summer estate. Now, thanks to the baron's granddaughter, it housed dozens of children no one else wanted.

He touched her elbow. "We took a five-hour train ride so you could talk to them. And they are expecting us. You've done harder things than this."

She bit her lip and nodded. They crossed the stately grounds to a big, Western-style building with generous windows. A gray-haired woman in a severe dress met them at the door. She weighed Miyako with a single cool glance. "You're here to inquire about placing an infant."

"*Hai.*"

The woman turned to Akira. "And you are?"

"Matsuura Akira. Her brother."

"My name is Ito. Please come in, young lady." She peered at Akira. "You can come in if you wish, since you're not the father. We don't allow them here."

Miyako looked at her, eyes wide with surprise.

Ito-san led them through a towering foyer, spacious but bare, and down a long hall. A door stood open, revealing a large, bright ward with cribs. Row upon row of cribs.

And babies. Crying, chortling, crowing. Round heads covered with curly dark hair, smooth light-brown hair, and every variation in between. Skin of every shade. A pair of white-capped nurses presided over the scene.

She showed them to an office. "I'll let Takanura-san know you're here."

They settled into wooden chairs across from an empty desk. A collage of framed photos filled the wall behind it. The central decoration was a brass plate mounted on a handsome wooden plaque, engraved with these words:

As You Have Done Unto the Least of These
Matthew 25:40

Outside the window, a dozen small children wearing identical rompers clamored in a well-equipped playground. Two slides at different heights, swings, teeter-totter. All shiny and new looking. A matronly lady watched over them. Takanura Miki walked in—swept in might have been a better term. Akira knew her from her photo in the *Asahi Picture News*. She carried herself with unmistakable presence, every inch the baron's granddaughter. She also wore a prominent gold cross around her neck.

"You are Matsuura Miyako?" Takanura's cheerful smile seemed a bit at odds with her commanding manner.

Miyako gave her a demure nod. "*Hai.*"

"And you're her brother?"

"*Hai,*" Akira said.

"And you, young lady, are pregnant. The baby will be mixed-blood?"

Miyako dropped her eyes under the lady's sharp look. "I think so."

Takanura-san shifted her owlish glasses up her nose. "You *think* so?" She let that hang in the air while she jotted something on a notepad. She turned piercing eyes back to Miyako. "We take only mixed-blood children. You don't know if your baby will be eligible?"

"I...don't."

"I see. Let me familiarize you with a few of our ground rules. We teach the children English as well as Japanese. We raise them in a Christian environment and baptize them into the Anglican church. In short, Matsuura-san, we raise them with a future as citizens of the West in view. That is the society to which they are most suited. It's sadly clear these children have no place in Japan."

All of them? Without exception? Why would she take such a rigid stance?

Miyako nodded. "*Hai*, Takanura-san."

"Also, once you put the baby in our care, it will be best if you don't plan to visit. We find the children are most content with all connections to their birth family severed. We aim to raise these unique children in a protected environment, where we can shield them, and you, from heartache and shame."

Miyako nodded, but this time there was a minuscule quiver to her chin.

Takanura seemed satisfied that she'd attained agreement. "That's good, then. On the presumption that your child will be mixed blood, would you like to take a look around?"

"*Hai*. Very much."

Takanura ushered them through playgrounds, craft rooms, a library, a small chapel. She passed out advice as they went. "If your baby is mixed-blood, young lady, you mustn't contemplate keeping it. I've seen lovely young women like you rejected by their families, evicted from their apartments, and fired from their jobs once they've given birth to such a child. And after the mother suffers so, the child has nothing to look forward to."

She ushered them back through the foyer where they'd entered and delivered a parting admonition. "You're a bright young woman. You'll weigh for yourself what is better for your child. But please don't live in the fantasy that your G.I. lover will come back to rescue you. It never happens."

"Never?" Miyako said.

"I haven't seen it once. It pains me, but I must tell you the sad truth. Japan doesn't want your baby. And America doesn't want you."

Their tour hadn't taken long—forty-five minutes perhaps. They walked the winding path toward the gate. "Well?" Akira said.

"Takanura-san is very sure of herself."

"She has to be. I imagine there's plenty of opposition." He studied his sister's face. "Is this what you want?"

She looked around the gracious landscape. "It's lovely. But...sever all ties, Akira-san? No birthdays. No kites on Boys' Day or dolls on Girls' Day. I'll never know what became of my son or daughter."

"It would be a clean start. For both of you."

"An amputation." Her voice took on a bitter tone. "If I

bring the baby here, I'm no longer a mother. I'm an obstacle. Something to be kept out of the way."

It had sounded that way. He had to admit that.

"And we don't know about the baby. If my child is full Japanese..." She trailed off. The possibility that the baby was conceived through her rape seemed too difficult for her to contemplate.

Akira swung the gate open. She walked past him and down the steps, waiting until he joined her at the bottom. "Without a doubt, Takanura Miki is saving lives. But"—she tipped her chin at the sign that read Tabitha Mills Home—"I don't feel the name tells the truth. I'm sure they're doing their best, but an orphanage isn't a home." She ran a palm down her flat belly and sighed. "At least we don't have to decide for a while."

"We aren't deciding. You're deciding. I'm supporting what you decide."

She looked up at him and blinked moisture from her lower lashes. "*Domo arigato.* That means everything to me."

The next morning, Akira was skimming the front page of the newspaper when Miyako put down the section she was reading with a little gasp. She lifted a hand to cover her mouth.

"What is it?" he said.

"Look." Her fingers shook as she pointed out a headline.

Infant Corpse Found in Johoku River

"Last night. The bridge where they found her is six blocks from here." She pushed the paper at him accusingly. "A mixed-blood baby, dead in the river. And she didn't drown."

He dropped his eyes, his stomach roiling. "That's horrible. I'm so sorry, Mi-chan."

"I told you, Akira-san. No one wants these babies." She sank onto a cushion and wrapped her arms around her belly. "My poor, poor child."

"*Iesu* wants them. He said to let the children come to Him. And why do you think Takanura Miki does what she does?"

Her eyes sank to the floor. She sniffled and nodded. "Miki's children did seem happy. Wanted. Perhaps that is what I should do."

His poor sister. It weighed on her with every breath, how she could create a future for her child.

Twenty-First Day of the Ninth Month, Anno Domini 1588

The four bells sounded the hour of the boar. Long past dinner hour. Sono's stomach growled, but her thoughts lingered elsewhere. She heard a commotion outside—male voices at the teahouse's west wall.

"A box, ah?" The captain's voice. "I have no direction from Master Hisanobu on that."

A voice she did not know. "Lady Matsuura told me to bring it, no less. She says it is from her son, and Lady Sono must have it right away."

A box from Hisanobu. Her thoughts spun. This could mean everything—a decision handed down from his father. Or it could be as simple as he'd taken pity on her and sent something to eat.

"I will handle it." Sandals squelched on the patio. "Lady Sono? You have a package from your husband. I leave it here."

"*Arigato*, captain." She listened while his footsteps receded, then slid the door open a crack. The moonlight revealed a simple rectangular wooden box. She lifted it inside, settled next to the embers where the light was best, and pulled off the lid.

A *tanto* knife. The type Papa-san had taught her to plunge into her throat, should she ever need to end her life through the rite of *jigai*.

Every detail of the dagger captured the glow from the embers and emblazoned itself on her mind. Brass fittings glinted, and polished wood shone. The scabbard arced in a vicious curve, about the length of her forearm.

Perhaps she had seen this knife in Hisanobu's chamber—the precise pattern of green cord that wrapped its ivory hilt looked familiar. But it hadn't rested on a square of white silk. That silk was specific to a suicide ritual.

He had delivered her an invitation to end her own life.

Traitors get no mercy. He'd spoken to Lord Matsuura, then. And her death had been determined.

She closed the box as if she could cage what was inside it, then set it aside with shaking hands. She bowed her head and bid her pulse to stop racing.

Does my husband expect me to take my own life?

Except a corn of wheat fall into the ground and perish, it abideth alone: but if it perish, it bringeth forth much fruit. Even an ugly death for *Iesu* would be a thing of beauty.

She lingered with her head bowed for a moment, something niggling at her thoughts.

He knows better.

As a *Kirishitan,* she could not commit *jigai.* It was a mortal sin. Hisanobu knew that. So what did he mean by sending her a knife set up for the ritual?

She took a gasping breath, and then another, grasping with all her strength at this thin shred of hope. He'd sent her his *tanto* knife for some reason, but he could not expect her to use it. *Deusu* willing, the knife did not represent their final sentence.

She would know the next morning.

Chapter Thirty-Eight

Wednesday 2 March 1949

THE NEXT AFTERNOON, THE BUZZER SOUNDED in Akira's apartment.

Miyako pushed her sewing needle into a gray wool sleeve. She was finishing some alterations to the second-hand suit he'd picked up. "Someone at the door downstairs, ah?"

Was he really going to trade his crisp braided uniform for that nondescript thing?

He shrugged. He wasn't expecting anyone. "I'll go down."

He jogged downstairs to the lobby and peered through the glass door that led to the street. Oda stood on the sidewalk, mouth swept down in a heavy expression. He clutched a large envelope with both hands.

A court summons? But the envelope looked personal, not official.

He opened the door and stepped out. Oda extended the envelope toward him with both hands and dropped into a formal bow. "From your father."

"*Domo arigato*, Captain Oda." Equally formal. He took the envelope—mulberry paper, of the best quality, tidily secured with a black silk ribbon. His hands shook. "Is it..."

Oda gave him a terse nod. "Your father's death poem. He's wrapping up his affairs. You and your sister will want to read it sitting down."

"How is he?"

"His battle could end at any hour."

"Will he see either of us?"

"When you're ready to renounce your foreign cult."

Akira hadn't expected Oda to bring any other answer. He gave the man a cold thank you for his trouble and trudged upstairs to his sister.

She took one look at the envelope and went pale. "Is he...?"

"He's still with us. But he's written his death poem. His parting thoughts." He dropped on the cushion next to her and placed the envelope on the table.

"You should open it, *Onii-san.*"

He nodded, his throat suddenly dry. He fingered it for a long moment before he broke the seal and unfolded the single sheet of mulberry paper.

He cleared his throat and read, doing his best to banish the tremor from his voice and give his father's words every dignity.

"Bare branches once held
Myriads of blossoms. Gone,
Scattered. Fruit all ruined.
One mulberry leaf in snow.
Every wind blows to the West."

Miyako touched the paper, as tenderly as if she were stroking Papa-san's own arm. "He sounds desolate." Her eyes filled with tears.

"A lone mulberry leaf in snow. It's a haunting image." He read the lines again. "What do you think he means here? *Every wind blows to the West.*"

Miyako dabbed at her eyes. "West, where the Pure Land of Amida Buddha lies. He imagines his spirit drifting there." She sighed and looked up at him. "But, I'm sure it has a double meaning. About us. About Japan."

"The West has invaded. Even infecting his own children." His words came out with a wry barb. "It's a final reproach."

"A bitter one."

Seven years earlier, in the captain's cabin of *Nitto Maru*, he'd held another piece of fine mulberry paper. A ruined captain's death poem. How smug he'd been. He'd never imagined his own father would end his life in such bitter disappointment.

Miyako peered at the characters with despairing eyes. "We can't let him pass like this."

"I know. I asked Oda. You can guess how he answered. But let's write Papa-san a letter together. He might have a change of heart."

"*Hai.*" She gave him a slow nod, but no hope sparked in her eyes.

Twenty-First Day of the Ninth Month, Anno Domini 1588

Sono prayed until the teahouse waxed dim and cold. When she could resist her drowsiness no longer, she layered the last of the charcoal on the fire and curled up around the hearth to soak in every bit of heat from the dying embers.

"Sono-chan. Sono."

She snapped to instant alertness. "What is it?" *Who is it?*

"It's Hisanobu." Her husband's voice, filtering in from the patio.

What? "My lord?"

"I sent the men away. I decided to guard you through the night watch myself."

"You did?" Her jaw slackened. It took a conscious effort to close it. She settled next to the guests' entrance and slid the *shoji* open. He knelt on the patio, moonlight through the lattice casting a patchwork of shadows across his face.

She gave him a stiff bow from the waist. "Did you come hoping to watch me commit *jigai*, then?"

He recoiled with surprise. "What? No. I, ah..." He cleared his throat, then looked into her eyes. There was a softness there, and a vulnerable curve to his lips. "That is the last thing I want."

Relief slammed into her so hard her head spun. She braced a hand on the wall until the world stopped swiveling.

He went on. "I do not know what my father's decision will be. But I thought you should not spend this night alone. And"—he pressed the palms of his hands into his thighs—"I determined I have passed enough nights without you. So I will be out here, standing guard."

She searched his face. He'd had some change of heart. How far had it gone? "You have forgiven me for this afternoon, ah?" she said, testing him. "I hope you know I had no intention of hurting you."

"I see that now. I did not see it earlier." He said it without rancor.

"I am glad, my lord. Did you speak with your father?

What did he say?"

He shook his head. "I wanted to give some thought to how I put this before him." He clenched his hands into fists. "I don't suppose you have reconsidered any of your demands?"

"No. I'll join *Iesu* in His paradise before I give up even one of them."

He glared at her. "This could well end that way. You realize that, ah?"

"The box you sent made that clear."

"What box?"

"The *tanto* you had your mother's courier bring me."

He looked genuinely mystified. "What do you mean?"

"A courier brought me a knife. Yours, if I am not much mistaken." She retrieved the box and handed it to him across the threshold.

He lifted the lid and examined the knife. "That is my *tanto*. But I do not recognize the silk. A courier brought it?"

"*Hai.* According to him, Lady Matsuura said you wanted it given to me."

"My mother sent this?"

"So I was told."

He fixed his eyes on the knife as if he thought it might slither away. He made a disbelieving grimace and shook his head. "She sent you a knife prepared for *jigai*, and it seems she wanted you to believe it came from me."

"Your mother did this on her own, then?" *This thing was not even known to him.*

He lifted his gaze to Sono's face. A mirthless laugh burbled out of him. "*Hai.* And this was a bit much, even for her. I hope she did not expect you to use it. Maybe she meant it as a cruel joke. But in any case, stealing my knife for her ruse was conniving."

She watched through the lattice as the moonlight wove its magic across the surface of the stream. Then she speared him with a stare. "When you came here two days ago, you made some demands of me. Have you reconsidered any of those?"

He flinched and looked ashamed. "I am sorry. I blamed you for everything. That was not the man I want to be. And you are right. I agreed to accept your religion when I agreed to take *you*." He pushed out a huff of air and squared his shoulders. "'When you have faults, do not fear to abandon them.' I quoted that to you, did I not?"

"You did, my lord."

He gave her a taut smile. "I intend to rule this domain, Sono. But I see now that ambition has made me too concerned about Mother's opinion—and her influence over Father. I have not practiced the eight virtues toward you. For that, I am truly sorry."

"In *Iesu*'s name, I will always forgive you. But what now?"

"A wise hawk had best conceal its talons." The smile turned to a grin. "My mother may not realize it, but she has played into your hands. I will show this to Lord Matsuura, along with your requests. He cannot expect you to live with her now. And if he fails to see that, I will tell him I refuse to permit it."

"And my other requests? Will you demand that your father grant them?"

"I will do my best. And I am sincerely sorry you have not been able to rely on me for that. Can you forgive me? Can we start this thing over?"

She nodded, her heart so full she dared not speak.

He leaned toward her, the smallest hint of a smile in his eyes. "It occurs to me that I can guard you best from inside. With your permission, of course."

She managed to maintain her grave face, much as her lips itched to return his smile. "The birth impurity, my lord?"

"I'm already infected."

Sono's husband rested at her side until the guards reported for the next watch. His eyes clung to her as he left, his expression grim. "You will hear from me when Lord Matsuura and I have spoken."

She bit her lip, nervous now. "*Arigato*, my lord. Until then."

"Remember, my darling, to fear death is to die."

Sono's handmaid appeared shortly after the five morning bells, her best blue kimono and a basket draped over her arm. "Make haste, my lady. Lord Matsuura summons you."

In an instant, Sono found it difficult to breathe. "What do you think it means? Favorable tidings, or ill?"

"I wish for all the world I knew, Sono-chan. I wish I knew."

She shed her clothes down to the skin. Iya helped her into fresh garments and went to work on her hair. With each layer of fine silk and each stroke of the comb, one question droned through her mind. Was all of this bringing her closer to freedom—or closer to hearing her death pronounced?

Her eyes lingered on her crucifix. It meant freedom either way.

Sono's palanquin issued soft creaks as her bearers set it down in the teahouse garden. Iya gave her powder a final dab. "You will do."

She flung her arms around her handmaid. "Iya-chan, I gave up long ago on the idea that I could ever thank you enough."

"Do not be ridiculous. We will speak again soon." But Iya's eyes glistened. "And Sono-chan, I know your heart."

Walking out the teahouse's back entrance was like stepping away from a dear friend's embrace. It was a brooding morning, and with each lurch of the palanquin up the rise toward the mansion, the air grew more oppressive, almost a physical weight on her shoulders.

Iya helped her out of the palanquin under the ever-watchful eye of the glowering statue of Hachiman. She walked, weak-kneed, up the mansion's steps. She paused outside Lord Matsuura's grand audience chamber, her blood throbbing in her ears, and waited for the guard to slide the *shoji* aside.

To fear death is to die. She steeled herself and moved her feet across the threshold.

Hisanobu knelt alone on the dais at the head of the grand chamber. Surprise shot through her. Apart from the two of them, the chamber was empty.

She halted and bowed. "Do we await Honored Father?"

He shook his head with a severe face. "You may approach."

He was at his most imposing, in tall black court cap and crisp silks in the Matsuura colors. She willed her legs to carry her the length of the chamber and knelt before him. Once she got close enough to see it, the amused light had resumed its dance around his eyes.

"What is our father's decision, my lord?"

"The conversation was a bit...fiery. But in the end, Father said the decision was mine." He drew his back straight, looking stern and formal. "Accordingly, I hereby declare your edict approved and your requests fully granted."

"All of them?"

He broke into a grin. "All of them, darling."

The tension drained out her pores, replaced with a soaring sense of elation. Those were words she had longed to hear. They were not merely a reprieve from a traitor's death. They were a heavy stone rolled away from a tomb, revealing a glimpse of glorious dawn. The start of a whole new life on this island, sheltered from Lady Matsuura and her constant opposition.

I might even thrive here, where Deusu *has planted me.*

Hisanobu stood. "They are preparing a chamber for you in the west wing. Would it please you to have a look?"

"'Twould please me very much. But first, concerning this fiery conversation. Did Lord Matsuura bring up the succession?"

He stepped down from the dais. "He did not." He extended a hand to her. "But as you lay in my arms last night, I realized something."

She placed her hand in his and rose. "What, my lord?"

He took her other hand and pressed them both between his. "Lying there thinking I might lose you—through my own fault—" He squeezed his eyes closed, then opened them and gazed into hers. "It was the worst thing I have ever felt. I will brave any destiny rather than that, Sono-chan." He pulled her to him and held her tight against his powerful chest. "As long as I have you, I can accept any path the deities grant me. Whether or not I ever rule a domain."

Graças a Deusu. She loved that he'd so fully opened his heart to her. Perhaps over time he would open his heart to *Deusu* as well.

Chapter Thirty-Nine

Tuesday 8 March 1949

AKIRA'S SISTER HADN'T FELT WELL ALL day. She didn't protest when he made her sit down, and she let him prepare them a simple dinner with *soba* noodles. He'd just placed their bowls on the table when someone knocked on their door.

He gave her a quizzical look. "You weren't expecting anyone, ah?"

She widened her eyes. "Who would visit me?"

"A salesman, perhaps. I wish our neighbors wouldn't let these fellows in." He opened the door.

An American. Tall, with a cleft chin and a strong, straight nose and hair the color of corn silk.

Porcelain clattered behind him. He glanced back to see Miyako rise to her feet. "George-san?"

"*Konnichiwa.*" The American did a proper bow from the waist.

George? He looked very different from the cocky airman Akira had confronted at the cafe. His leather jacket hung loose around his middle. Ruddy skin sagged on his jowls. He fixed sunken eyes on Miyako, and his haggard face lit with a grin.

Seems he remembers her now. Akira pressed his jaw closed. He'd never told her that her lover had denied knowing her.

He stepped in front of the American, barring his path into the room. He puffed out his chest and squared his shoulders and loomed as big and threatening as he could— but still had to raise his eyes to look into George's. "What are you doing here?"

"Please pardon the interruption. I'm afraid I was rude to you the last time we met. I'm sorry." George said this while looking past him. "I'd like to talk to your sister, please."

Miyako joined them. "George-san, I'm very glad to see you." She spoke in English. "But you look not good. What happen?"

His eyes traveled up and down her form, and his grin faded. "I came here to ask you one question."

"Ask me anything. Please."

"Before God, you'll give me the truth?"

She nodded, with big earnest eyes.

"Your brother told me you haven't been with anyone since I saw you last."

"No. No one. Really, George-san, you...it wasn't just for money."

She was as eager to please this louse as a hungry puppy. Akira's stomach curdled with disgust.

"You said that, but after everything that happened—I didn't know what to believe." His voice went hard. "And you could be just saying it now."

"No." She bit her lip and studied the floor, then looked into his face. "Truth?"

"Truth, please."

"It's a dream you come here. Every day I think of you."

Akira cleared his throat. He thought of George too. Every time his eyes brushed past the swelling in her midsection. Thoughts that involved rearranging the *gaijin*'s arrogant face.

Thoughts he should repent of. But he hadn't tried very hard.

George's eyes flicked to him. "I'm sorry. I'm being rude again. I'm Captain George Sanders. It's a pleasure to see you."

"Matsuura Akira. And I'm not going to say it's a pleasure to see you."

Miyako directed a little pout at him. "Akira-san, please. Can George-san come in?"

"Actually," George said, "I was hoping I could convince you to take a walk with me."

Akira bristled. "My sister is not leaving with you." He didn't want George's breath to soil the air in his apartment, but this alternative was worse.

"Akira-san, please," she said again. "I can take care of myself."

He pinned her with a glare. *Can you?*

George lifted his hands in surrender. "Okay. I guess

what I have to say to her, I can say in your hearing. May I?"

Akira moved aside, doing his best to appear mastiff surly. George came in, bent and removed his shoes.

"Here, George-san. Please." Miyako scurried around to whisk their dinner off the table, set the teakettle on the burner, and plump a cushion for him.

They had no western-style furniture, so George settled on the cushion cross-legged. He looked very awkward doing it. She knelt opposite him, all demure and domestic. Akira stifled a gag and took a place beside her.

There was a pause while the two of them gawked at each other. George flexed his big red hand. Akira envisioned that hand on his sister's flesh, and sparks exploded in his brain.

Miyako dropped her eyes first. "I'll start. I'm a Christian now, and I feel so bad about how we were with each other. It was very wrong."

Red crept up George's neck and onto his face. "Funny you should say that. The chaplain mentioned that, in a note." His eyes flicked to Akira.

Her brows shot up. "The chaplain? What note?"

"You don't know? Your brother here got in touch with Chaplain Gould on base. Anyway, I've been a Christian as long as I can remember, although I sort of...forgot for a while. Will you forgive me for treating you like you were something I could buy?"

Her eyes drooped with sadness. "I *was* something you could buy. But not now. Not ever again."

"You don't know how glad I am to hear that." A grin made a timid appearance. His hand made a small twitch toward hers, but Akira shot him a glower and his arm froze.

Akira had restrained himself as long as he cared to. "Excuse me, Captain Sanders. This is my sister, and she's all I have left. I crossed an ocean to find her, and it nearly cost me my life. She isn't a toy you pick up when you want and drop when you're through. If you're going to stay any longer, I need to know what you intend."

George turned those startling blue eyes on him. "That's fair. But can I answer with a story?"

It was a simple question. "Is that what it takes?"

Miyako rose and brought the man a cup of tea. He took a big swig as if fortifying himself for a lengthy tale. "Some things have gotten knocked into my thick head. I need to tell you how that happened. And how I've come to realize the way I was living last winter was half crazy."

She looked at him with wistful eyes. "Not the half that liked me, I hope."

He flashed her a reassuring smile. "No. That was the sane half." Another swig, and his gaze drifted off somewhere beyond the window. "Ten days ago, my crew and I got assigned a training mission. Easy trip. Fly to Okinawa, refuel, come back. But the weather didn't cooperate, and soon we're fighting a pretty fierce headwind. About two hours in, we're over open ocean and there's a big bang from the right wing. My right engine throws a prop. I see it literally fly off the wing."

She gave a dainty gasp. "No."

He went on, absorbed in his tale. "Now the wings aren't balanced, and the plane is bucking me like a bronco. And to make things worse, that prop took the number one generator out. Something flickers and everything goes dark. Second generator is gone—overloaded, maybe.

"So there we are. Flying by flashlight. No radio, which means no beacon. We hope like h— like anything we can make Okinawa, but it's hard to keep the plane on course, and we're fighting that headwind. And we can't even put out a Mayday."

His gaze sank to the table and he paused, swallowing hard. "It's tough to talk about what happened next." A moment passed. "We didn't make Okinawa." He seemed to squeeze out the words.

"You...crashed?" Her voice carried a soft quaver.

He responded with a pained look and a minuscule nod.

"Your crew? What happened?"

He looked up at her, his eyes tortured. He pressed his lips together and shook his head.

They're gone? Akira's cup rattled into his saucer. Thankfully, he managed not to drop it. "Three men? Four?" Killed in a training mission. That was a bitter shame.

"George-san, I am so sorry," his sister said.

Nagai's face loomed in Akira's mind. With smashing columns of churning water and the pitching deck of *Nitto Maru*. A fresh gash opened in his pain—and a thin dribble of sympathy for the American pilot seeped through it. The first hint of warmth he'd felt for the man.

A moment passed before the *gaijin* spoke again. "Do you have any idea how big the ocean is? And how tiny an emergency raft is? I floated out there two days, alone, nothing to look at but sea and sky. The hour I gave up hope was the hour God started to talk to me. And do you know what He said?"

She shook her head.

"He said what you and your brother probably want to. He told me I'm a jerk, and there are a lot of things in my life I need to make right. And guess what one of those things is?"

She shook her head again, but a hint of a smile crept over her lips.

"You, Midori. He convicted me that the kind of relationship I had with you was the kind I should have with only one woman. My wife. So...I was hoping to get reacquainted."

She gave him an awkward little laugh. "I'm sorry, George-san. But maybe we start now with right names. Midori was only name for the street. My real name is Matsuura Miyako."

He looked at her as if she'd just said the most bewitching thing a woman ever uttered. "Miyako?"

His pronunciation was close. She nodded, dimpling up at him.

"A new name—at least new to me. That's perfect. It's better that way."

Akira thrust down a renewed urge to gag and shifted his weight. Noisily. "What's better?" The man still hadn't answered his first question.

George turned to Akira. "Are you sure I can't talk to the lady alone?" He stood and extended his hand. "You have my word of honor. I intend nothing but good for your sister."

His honor. Daring to bring that up was not his best tactic. But the glow on Miyako's face was something Akira hadn't seen since he'd returned to Japan.

He stood. "Fine. I'll go outside for a cigarette." He fixed him with his surliest glare. "But I smoke fast."

He brushed past the coatrack where their raincoats hung next to her pink parasol with its painted flowers. He wandered down to the street, mind abuzz. A light drizzle had started, so he lit his cigarette under the overhang.

What did the *gaijin* mean by "reacquainted"? He wasn't sure how to read these things with an American. George now claimed he was a Christian, but Akira had seen plenty of Americans whose Christianity seemed to be largely a Sunday pretense. And George's past behavior didn't line up with that claim.

Akira wasn't sure how to read these things with his sister, either. Clearly, she wanted this man in her life. What would she be willing to do to get him?

A soft light issued from his third-floor window. And it struck him that all its warmth emanated from his sister. He tried to picture his apartment without her. No flower-painted parasol keeping his dark coats company. No home-cooked meals. No laughter at his jokes.

No one to share his pain when he mourned his—their—many losses.

After everything the war had stripped from him, an American wanted his sister? The tiny place was going to feel cavernous without her.

If this American lover of hers wanted her after all, it would come at the price of a wedding. And Pastor Gould had made it clear how difficult that was going to be. So what was the man up to? Did he fully understand what he was getting into?

No matter. Akira would insist on marriage, and surely Miyako would want his blessing. But his gut went sour. There was something rather important that George-san didn't know yet. What kind of man would marry a woman carrying a baby that might not be his?

His cigarette was two-thirds gone. Good enough. He started back upstairs. When he reached his own door, he called in a greeting, then entered without waiting for a response.

George quickly stood, a little flustered, and bowed. Miyako shifted her weight as if she were about to do the same. A small velvet box, the right size for a ring, rested unopened on the table between them.

"No need to stand, sister." Akira stared George in the eye. "You have something to tell me?"

"I have something to ask you." He took a lingering look at Miyako. "After two days on a raft, I'm a lot clearer about many things. It became clear to me I love your sister. I count myself blessed that she seems to love me, too. We'd like to be married. But she tells me this is Japan, and I need your permission. So I'm asking you formally. May I marry your sister? I haven't done right by Miyako in the past"—he tripped a little over her name—"but I will make it my life's mission to love, honor, and care for her now."

Mi-chan beamed up at the American. In the glare of her smile, the weight of hard duty crushed Akira like five leagues of water over his head. So cruel, to see her hopes raised to such a lofty height, only to be dashed to the ground.

But it was better to be clear from the start. "Before I answer, Captain Sanders, I have to bring up a point that might be...difficult." He paused, groping for how best to approach such a delicate issue. "The timing—"

"I guess you're going to tell me it's possible the baby isn't mine. I've worked that out. The child still needs a father. And I know what happened wasn't by her choice." George rested a hand on her shoulder. "I'm committing myself to this woman. For better or for worse."

Akira studied the man, stunned. "If the baby isn't yours, have you thought about how hard it will be for you to watch the child grow up?"

"If she can live with it, by God's grace I can." George settled on his cushion again. "The chance that the baby might not be mine is a pill I get to swallow. But I have one you'll have to take. I don't know what's in our future or how we'll live. The Air Force isn't keen on us marrying Japanese girls. It turns out there are a lot of rules—well, we can get into all of that later. But with her pregnant, I want—no. I *need* to make things right between us. And I believe with all my heart that God will find a way for us."

George fell silent, and Miyako barely breathed. Both their eyes anchored on Akira with a pressure he could feel. He turned and took a pace or two. *He was the best man I knew.* She'd said that about George some weeks ago.

For his own part, he had no reason to trust this George and every reason not to. But if he believed in *Iesu*, he also had to believe in hope and second chances.

He looked at them together and his heart lurched. His sister and only surviving relative would go to an American husband. And maybe, someday, to America. He was as helpless to stand in the way of this union as he'd been to stop the bombers lined up on that carrier.

This marriage would be his deep loss—and time would tell whether it would be her gain. He hoped she'd judged George right. That he *was* a good man. But in the light of cold, hard reality, what were his sister's options? Didn't her baby deserve at least a chance to have a father?

"Miyako, you're willing to accept this"—he threw a glance at George— "pill, ah?"

"*Hai.*" The luster in her eyes said that and more.

George took Miyako's hand. "Akira-san, you talked about crossing an ocean to be with this woman. I've faced my ocean too. The Lord had to almost kill me to make me see this is the right thing. And my C.O. authorized the marriage." He cracked a grin. "He had what you'd call a soft moment. That's a miracle right there. I'm convinced this is what the Lord wants for me." He squeezed her hand. "For us. Will you give us your permission?"

Akira smiled for the first time since the *gaijin* had shown up. "Who am I to get in the way of God?"

George's grin went wider. He pulled Miyako to him and planted a lingering kiss on her lips. "We need to marry while I'm on leave. Another week. Can we do it?"

"I'll talk to Reverend Kagawa," Akira said.

Chapter Forty

SONO'S PALANQUIN SWAYED, BUT HER STOMACH lurched much harder than that could account for. She twined her fingers around her cross pendant and murmured urgent prayers. She hadn't ceased those prayers all night.

Gracious Lord, preserve my son.

Sixteen months, she'd bided her time. Cherished every tiding Iya brought her from the House of Mercy. Treasured every instant of her weekly service visits there—one of the concessions she'd won with the arrow aimed at her husband. Hisanobu didn't know those visits permitted her to steal a few priceless moments with their son.

What a little beam of light he was! How she had ached to share those moments with her husband. *Deusu's* grace on Taro was apparent. The infant Hisanobu had called "puny" and tried to "send back" was a bright-eyed bundle of happy energy now.

Can I trust my husband with the truth? For sixteen months, she'd observed him. Not a day had passed—no, not an hour—when that question had been absent from her mind.

As long as Taro was one more foundling at the *Kirishitan* House of Mercy, he was safe. Safe from Lady Matsuura and her murderous designs. And safe from any sudden flare of Hisanobu's temper.

He never spoke of Taro—nor did she. But abandoning his tiny son to die seemed to have changed him. He had shown himself a different man. He'd stood with her against his mother on many occasions. And she'd not seen rage distort his face the way it had when he came to her drunk at the teahouse. Or when he executed Sato before her.

When their second child proved to be a girl, her heart had quailed in her chest. She knew their abiding lack of an heir disappointed him, but he said nothing. And he held their tiny daughter so tenderly. As if doting on their newborn child could win him atonement for his terrible wrong against their first.

But a man's heart could be changeable as the autumn sky. She had seen how hurt could bleed over into wounded pride for him. If he learned she had kept *this* from him—if he felt betrayed—a *katana* could strike again like lightning. How could she be sure she wouldn't be its victim? Or Taro. Or anyone else her warlord husband concluded had deceived him.

She squeezed her fingers around her cross, the shopkeeper's dead eyes staring at her again from the floor of her palanquin. *Gracious Lord, preserve us all. How we need the* Kirishitan *heir.*

Her darling son might stay safe as one more foundling. But he would never rule. Never bring *Deusu's* peace and justice to their blighted land. The dilemma ripped her in two.

Her bearers' shoes pattered on packed earth. The muddy streets and green terraces of Hirado town jolted past her viewing lattices. Hisanobu's fine stallion high-stepped down the street before her, whinnying. He bore her husband as nobly as his people expected.

As for his people, prostrate backs and the crowns of heads were all she saw. Her honored father had stepped down from his throne a few months earlier. Now, in his nineteenth winter, Sono's pirate prince was absolute lord of Hirado domain. And so far, he had proven a good one.

As it happened, this had forced her to weigh a move. The Lord Regent had mustered their house. The next day, the new Lord Matsuura—her Hisanobu—would ride out at the head of a thousand men.

The battle would rage many weeks' journey away. Farther north than Osaka, or even Heian-kyo. The Lord Regent had declared war on the Hojo of Sagami Province, halfway up the big island of Honshu. Months would pass before the vast army the Lord Regent was mustering would take the field. And it could be months more before the siege engines ceased lobbing boulders and the acrid smoke of the cannon no longer clung to men's nostrils.

And the cries of the dying faded to silence.

Signs of preparation were everywhere. Cannonballs piled in the castle courtyard. Vessels of all sizes crowded the docks. It gave her the same sick feeling it always had. Every male face she looked into—would he, or would he not, be among those *Deusu* willed to return? And every lady—would she be counted among the widows?

A chill ran through her, and she hugged her winter coat to her chest. It could be autumn or even winter again before she knew whether her husband would return to her. The emptiness of long weeks of waiting and wondering. The quiet courtyards where few male voices echoed. It was a somber scene she knew too well.

And if he fell—either to battle or disease—without an heir? Her whole mission to Hirado would be in vain. All the fanfare of that voyage up the sparkling water two and a half years ago. All the hopes the beloved souls she'd left behind in Omura had packed on that vessel with her. All the painful battles she and Iya had fought since they'd arrived. All would come to naught.

Can I trust him with the truth? In a few minutes, she would be forced to decide. Staking her son's safety versus his destiny was a gut-wrenching choice. But if their little one was meant to rule, he could stay a secret no longer.

Hisanobu's stallion whinnied. Her husband rode proud, his shoulders square and his silks lustrous and his spine arrow straight.

Her pulse throbbed in her temples. It wasn't too late. She could still opt for the path that would keep them all safe. A single word to Iya, walking beside her palanquin, and the moment could be put off.

They mounted a set of flagstone steps. Her bearers eased her conveyance into the courtyard of Koteda's gracious mansion. They settled her on the gravel, and Iya helped her step out.

Hisanobu handed his stallion's reins to a groom. He shot her a teasing grin. "You have been very mysterious about this meeting."

I wish for all the world I could keep it a mystery. Until I can be certain of you.

That very morning, he had asked to see their three-month-old daughter. Lifted her from Sono's arms with a tender touch. Softly whispered in her delicate little ear how very much he would miss her.

Akiko's boys swarmed him as he held his baby girl. He had laughed, but no mirth had touched his eyes. There was often something a little haunted in his expression—unless she merely imagined it.

Ah, how he ached for a son. That much was clear. Could she send him off to battle without the pleasure of knowing he had one?

He chose this. He abandoned Taro to the foxes.

But her heart whispered he regretted it.

Gracious Lord, preserve my son. As long as *Deusu* was trustworthy, she could trust her husband too, yes?

That thought decided it for her. She anchored her eyes on him. "It is my dearest hope you will be pleased, my lord."

Koteda and her husband, one of Hisanobu's foremost advisers, stood elbow-to-elbow at the mansion's front entrance. The couple bowed low to greet their young lord, then showed Sono and her husband into a handsome reception chamber that overlooked a garden filled with winter-bare trees.

Iya hovered at the side of the room. Her smile looked as jittery as Sono's voice sounded.

The older couple made an effort at small talk. It faltered. Servants hurried in with finger food and bowls of tea, but Sono's throat was too tight to swallow and her stomach too knotted to digest.

Her friend Koteda caught her eye with an unspoken question. Her gut tightened as if a strong man were sitting on it. She breathed one more incoherent prayer, then shot her husband a thin smile rife with nerves. "Before I reveal my mystery, may I start with a little story?"

He nodded assent, a bemused quirk to his lips.

"My lord asked me a few days ago about my happiest day in Omura, before I came to your house. I had no ready answer then, but I have one now. And if you care to, you can renew that joy for me today."

He laughed, but it came with a questioning look around the chamber. "And you gathered witnesses to see whether I would be willing, ah?"

She forced her lips to form another smile. "You will see how our friends are implicated in a moment."

He arched an eyebrow. "I will endeavor to be patient, then."

She paused, inviting the years-old feelings—which had faded little with time—to sweep over her. "You know my brother Suminobu spent his childhood as a hostage of the Ryuzoji. He was a toddler when a *samurai* caught him up on an enormous warhorse and took him away. I did not see him again until his eleventh summer.

"I cried and cried for him. We said *novenas* for nine years that *Deusu* would bless him and bring him home." It was the best way she had known to pray then.

"And your *Deusu* did that for you, ah?"

"*Hai*, and I think it was the first time I really believed He heard me. Ah, that was a glorious day, when my baby brother rode back through our castle gates. The horns blaring, the white banners with gold crosses flying. He was quite the young warrior by then. Strong and tall on his own stallion. I told Iya-chan once, it was as if he came back from the dead."

Hisanobu tipped his tea bowl to her. "I would leave you with a pleasant remembrance if I can. What would it take to make you happy like that again?"

She bit her lip and gave her friend Koteda a slight nod. Koteda clapped twice. Sandals clattered on the wooden planks outside and a servant girl appeared with a toddler in her arms.

Their Taro.

He squirmed against the girl's chest, gave Sono a gummy grin, and reached his babyish arms out for her. Clever Koteda had him dressed in a tiny kimono in the Matsuura colors. Sono's breast swelled with tenderness and pride.

"What is this?" Hisanobu demanded.

Koteda gestured the girl from the chamber. Sono gathered her little son into her arms.

The mystified furrow between her husband's eyes deepened. "I see you made a friend. You met him doing service at the *Kirishitan* House of Mercy, ah?"

Sono beamed him a bright smile over the toddler's head, hoping to disguise the riotous churning inside her. "Not just any friend, my lord. You do not know him?" "No," he said. But realization began to dawn in his eyes. "This is our Taro, my lord."

He froze, his face an utter blank.

What was Hisanobu thinking behind that inscrutable mask of an expression? Sono's pulse drummed in her ears. She pushed back her fear and gave her husband a level gaze. "Will you welcome our Taro back from the dead?"

He sat very still, wide eyes fixed on the lad. "That is...my son."

"*Hai*, my lord." *Graças a Deusu*. No explosion—yet.

Hisanobu's cheeks showed a little pale. "He *is* back from the dead."

"Not exactly. They have been keeping him for us at the House of Mercy."

He peered around between the four of them. "You plotted this on the sly, wife? And you three knew about it, ah?"

Her heart flapped like a bird flushed from the brush. Had she judged him wrong? She squeezed Taro to her breast. "Please, my lord—"

Their host—a man Hisanobu trusted more than anyone who was not of his own house—cut in. "My lord, we were confident that, given time, you would think better of the decision you made when your son was an infant. And look at him now."

Sono turned him to face his father and set his little feet on the floor. He grinned and cooed and took a tottering step or two, his fingers twined around her hand, before he landed on his rear. He cackled happily, looking around with bright, intelligent eyes.

She chewed her lip, her eyes on her husband's face and her mouth dry as rice paper. Was Taro winning him over? His own father could not resist such charm, could he?

A pirate preys on the weak. A prince defends them. This moment would reveal which her husband was in truth.

She wrapped the toddler in her arms. "Suminobu was a little older than this when they ripped him from us, my lord." She blinked away a mist of tears. "In a way, I have a chance now to gain those years back."

They lapsed into anxious silence while Taro settled into his mother's lap. He wrapped stubby fingers around her gold cross.

Hisanobu studied his son, a tendon in his neck working. He held out his arms and spoke in a choking voice. "Can I hold him?"

Sono nodded, not daring to speak, and placed her child in his father's arms. Hisanobu bent his face to the little head, took a gasping breath and...sobbed. "I am sorry, Taro. You are so precious. How could I have done anything to hurt you, my son?"

He lifted red-rimmed eyes to Sono. "Not a day has passed that I have not wrestled with what I did. What I compelled you to do. And look at the lad. It is clear as the morning sun that you were in the right. And we—my parents and I—were utterly wrong." He clasped his son to his chest. "I have never in my life been so glad to be wrong."

He gave the boy another squeeze. "You all took a great risk to preserve the heir to the House of Matsuura. And I owe you an enormous debt of gratitude." He firmed his jaw. "But how best to address this with my father? Koteda-san, you and I must discuss this." He fingered the small mulberry-leaf crest on the boy's chest. "I promise, Sono-chan. We will bring our Taro home."

"Soon?" Could she really have Taro with her every day? Was it possible? Everything in her longed for it, but it had not the solid feel of reality yet.

Hisanobu tore his eyes from his son and looked to his key retainer. "My father needs to know at once, ah? We cannot sail tomorrow with this unsettled."

"I agree."

Sono's husband spoke in a decisive voice. "I will acknowledge our Taro before Father today, Sono-chan."

She swallowed down a parched throat. "And...your mother?"

"I am master of our house now, am I not?"

She bowed to the floor, her heart singing with gratitude—to her husband. To her friends. To her God. "*Domo arigato*, my lord."

Deusu had heard her. Her prince had relented. Both the missing piece in her young family and the aching gap in her heart would soon be filled.

Her mission to Hirado was set back on course. Her father's gamble in placing her here was poised to pay off after all.

And even in the face of armies and edicts and opposition, the *Kirishitan* from Hirado to Omura could rest a little easier. The struggling infant Sono had entrusted to a basket would come home in triumph, fulfilling his destiny as Hirado's heir.

Monday 19 September 1949

Akira's chair outside the maternity ward was hard, and he'd spent way too much time in it. Nearly six hours, so far, since they'd wheeled his sister, moaning, through those double doors.

That was after she'd labored several hours at home. Her midwife had directed him to bring her here. She'd tried to sound reassuring. "Don't worry too much. It's not unusual in a first delivery." But the concern that furrowed the lines around the corners of her eyes said something different.

George was wearing the shine off the waiting room's linoleum floor with his pacing. A perfect picture of an anxious new father. Akira had been relieved, and pleasantly surprised, when his brother-in-law walked in the room ninety minutes earlier. He'd left a couple of messages for him at Itami Air Base, of course, but since the airman was never allowed to tell Miyako when he was flying, there'd been no way to know whether he would make it in time.

Akira couldn't focus on his magazine. He stood to stretch his legs. He walked past two other nervous new fathers and a placid grandmother-to-be and studied the view through the window for about the hundredth time.

A nurse came through the swinging doors that led from the maternity ward. He swiveled, and her eyes met his. "Matsuura-san? I have good news for you—at last. Everything's going well."

Akira and George were quick to converge on her. "She's all right?" Akira said.

The nurse gave him a cheerful nod. "She's fine. Things are exactly as they should be. We'll be able to tell you more shortly."

Akira thanked her with a deep sigh of relief. It was the first time he'd seen this nurse. She was pretty, with a distinctive pointed chin that gave her face a diamond shape.

Her dimples flashed before she lowered her eyes and swished back through the swinging doors.

"What'd she say?" George's anxiety was painted across his features.

He translated the news for his brother-in-law.

"Thank God. That's great." George dropped into a chair and rubbed a hand across eyes that drooped with exhaustion. But after a moment he resumed his anxious pacing.

Akira couldn't bear to meet his eyes. *Every new father is nervous.* But perhaps this new father had a bit more than the usual justification. Was his brother-in-law really ready for anything this day might reveal?

As far as he knew, George hadn't raised the issue of the baby's parentage since the day he proposed marriage. And to this moment, he'd seemed every bit the doting papa-to-be. A baby with the wrong skin color wouldn't change that, would it?

Akira turned to the window. Between the roofs of the buildings across the street, a small stretch of the Yodo River sparkled on its way to the bay. The bay opened to broad ocean. And perhaps that ocean would see him again someday. But for now, his sister needed him. He had sacrificed the sea for her, and he was content with his reward for that. He would get to see his niece or nephew grow up, at least until George got reassigned.

A raw place in Akira's heart still ached over the fact that Papa-san's leukemia had taken him before Sono's baby came. If Papa-san had lived to see this day, would a grandchild have helped him make peace with the way things had turned out? After all, sooner or later there might be a grandson who could take up the ancestral profession of plying the waves.

Twenty-five more anxious minutes passed before the nurse reappeared at the swinging doors. She beamed. "Good news! You have a sweet little girl. Congratulations! Mother and daughter are both fine."

George raised an eyebrow at Akira.

"It's a girl, and everyone's fine." Akira clapped George on the shoulder and turned to the nurse. "When can we see her?"

"We'll have the baby ready shortly. We're going to give the new mother a few more minutes." She flashed Akira a smile that struck him as a bit...deliberate, then disappeared again through the swinging doors.

Something niggled at his mind. A sense that she looked familiar. And had her eyes lingered on his a little?

No matter. A pretty woman might give him an inviting look—or even several. But once she caught a glimpse at what hid beneath his shirt, her interest would evaporate. Nothing awaited him but a bachelor's life. He'd known that for years. He'd have to content himself with Miyako's happiness. And he hoped to God that wouldn't prove short-lived.

He conveyed the news about the baby to George.

His brother-in-law looked him directly in the eyes and cleared his throat. "Before we see the baby, I want to say something. And I want you to remember I said it. I am so excited to meet our baby girl. No matter what she looks like, she is my child as well as Miyako's. And I adore her."

Whoa. It took a big man to accept something like this. Akira broke into a grateful grin. "*Arigato.* My sister is fortunate to have you." He understood now what she'd seen in the fellow.

George shook his head. "No. I'm blessed to have her."

For Akira's part, it had taken a few weeks to move beyond revulsion at the sleazy transactions that had brought them together. And maybe, if he was honest, there'd been a hint of selfishness too. A bit of reluctance to so quickly lose the sister he'd just found. But this marriage—this man—was a wonderful thing for her.

And on the topic of wonderful things... What about that pretty nurse? Had he met her? When?

She reappeared a few minutes later. Again, a direct gaze into his eyes that made his pulse throb and a soft curve to her lips that looked like an invitation. "The baby's in the nursery." She announced it in a warbling singsong. "If you're ready, I'll show you."

"Please forgive me," he said, "but I feel like I've seen you before." Did he imagine her cheeks went a deeper shade?

"You have. I tended to your injury the night you translated Reverend Delham's message."

Ah. A sketchy memory came to him. A sweet-faced woman bent over him, pressing clean gauze against his shoulder. What focus he could muster had been elsewhere at the time, but how had he missed noticing her at church since?

In any case, that night she'd gotten an intimate view of his maimed chest. Was she flirting with him now? He wasn't sure. But if she was, maybe she had some idea what she was getting into.

He held her eyes and blasted her a return smile. *"Hai."*

Her cheeks flushed a lovely pink. She turned and led them down a narrow corridor. A bank of long windows gave a view into a nursery with ten cribs in rows.

"There," she said. "The one with the pink blanket on the end."

Akira and George moved as close to the little bundled-up form as they could. The half-dozen little dark heads on mattresses looked virtually identical. George held his breath and peered through the window, his eyes glued to the baby the nurse had pointed out.

The nurse was a fountain of effervescent cheer. "Isn't she adorable? We all love her cute little chin."

Akira craned to get a better view. There was a tiny indentation beneath the baby's pacifier.

He studied George's jawline. No question about it. The baby had a miniature version of George's cleft. Precisely the same little dimple. "Your chin, George-san."

The American nodded, his features relaxing. It was a small move, but visible. "I'm so glad." He said it in a low voice, not much above a murmur. "For Miyako's sake." He turned to Akira. "You know this wouldn't have happened without you."

"You don't think so?"

"Absolutely not. Without you, I wouldn't have found her. And she wouldn't have found herself."

The three of them stood enraptured, staring in breathless wonder at the tiny new human. The infant girl's chest heaved with a miniature hiccup. George and the pretty nurse murmured admiring "Ahs" in unison.

Papa-san. Mama-san. Hiro-chan. Their faces rose before him. He wished with all his heart they could witness this.

One mulberry leaf in snow. No, Papa-san would not have made his peace with George. Or the baby. But Akira had. His whole being glowed with contentment.

As for the implacable old mulberry leaf, it didn't need to end its days cold and alone. They would always live with the grief of their losses. So much excellent fruit had been ruined, as Papa-san's poem had said. But he stood elbow-to-elbow with his new brother, witnessing a living miracle in the crib behind the glass.

Better harvests lay ahead.

Author Note

When I finish a historical novel, I'm always consumed with curiosity as to how much of what I've read is fiction versus fact. I feel it's especially important to answer that for a novel based on the lives of actual people. Akira's story is entirely fictional, but it was suggested by a real man, Sub-lieutenant Kanegasaki Kazuo. Rescued from a life raft after the battle of Midway, Kanegasaki spent the rest of the war in prison camps in the U.S. Sometime during the final months of his imprisonment, he met Peggy Covell at a camp in Colorado. The specific circumstances of that meeting are shrouded in mystery, but we know she was employed as a social worker at the Granada Interment Camp for Japanese Americans ("Camp Amache"). And we know the essentials of the story she told him about her parents and the "Hopevale Martyrs"—a true event. Her example of stunning forgiveness in the face of searing loss made such an impression on Kanegasaki that he carried it back to Japan.

Sadly, Kanegasaki did not find hope and meaning in Jesus as my fictional Akira does. His story ended in tragedy. Like Akira, he chose to assume a false identity during his prison years. As a result, his wife, who pined for him for years after believing him lost at Midway, ultimately decided to remarry. Kanegasaki discovered this on his return home. Theirs had been a love match, a rare thing at that time in Japan. Heartbroken, Kanegasaki committed suicide.

But before he learned the sad news that drove him to end his life, he told a fellow veteran about Peggy—former captain Fuchida Mitsuo.

Fuchida was a prominent figure, the captain who directed the 350 planes that attacked Pearl Harbor. It was Fuchida who issued the infamously triumphant "Tora-tora-tora" ("Tiger, tiger, tiger") radio signal that communicated that the Japanese had achieved complete surprise—the signal that launched the deadly attack.

Heralded as a national hero during the war, Japan's defeat left him reeling in a deep quest for meaning. Peggy's story pierced his soul and he became obsessed with digging into the truth of it. Her shining example of a Christian faith lived out proved a key milestone on his road to finding Christ.

Fuchida soon took his place as a noted evangelist. A few months after he put his trust in Christ, a Japanese and an American veteran began traveling Japan and preaching to crowds together—Mitsuo Fuchida, the lead pilot at Pearl Harbor and Jacob DeShazer, the Doolittle Raider who inspired my fictional David Delham. They brought to thousands the message of God's sacrificial love for all people and the power of Jesus Christ to offer forgiveness from sin.

It was through Fuchida's testimony that Peggy's story and that of the Hopevale Martyrs reached the history books. And Fuchida always believed that, if only he had known Christ in time, he could have prevented Kanegasaki from taking his life.

Col. Cyril D. Hill is also a historic person, a man of deep faith and charity. Takanura Miki and her bold, life-saving work at The Tabitha Mills Home are loosely based on Sawada Miki, a Mitsubishi heiress noted for founding the Elizabeth Saunders Home for mixed-race children. Sawada is known as the "mother of two thousand children." The tale of how the baron's granddaughter heard and responded to the good news of Jesus Christ, and how she eventually devoted everything she had to providing a home for "the least of these" who were so tragically at risk, is another really beautiful one. I wish I could have lingered on it.

Lady Sono comes straight from history, as do most of the people who fill her story. The daughter of one of the most prominent *Kirishitan* of the era, she was married as a teenager into the House of Matsuura, just as you read in *The Mulberry Leaf Whispers.*

Jesuit chronicler Luís Fróis held her up as a model of resilient faith under adversity. But the details of the trials the historical Sono experienced on Hirado are sketchy. I find it interesting that when I began writing her story, I made many guesses as to what her life might have looked like. Some of those guesses were confirmed through determined research.

For example, it is a fact that she was deeply demoralized at being denied access to the formal church and to the padres. The role gifted Japanese laywomen, such as Koteda-san, rose to play in ministering to believers the formal church couldn't reach is a fascinating study of its own.

Other conflicts the fictional Sono experiences may or may not have occurred to her historical counterpart, but they are drawn from prominent mixed-faith households of the period. The best-known *Kirishitan* lady of the era is Lady Hosokawa Gracia, who loosely inspired the character of Mariko in *Shogun*. Some of the trials Sono suffers in *The Mulberry Leaf Whispers* came from Lady Gracia's life. The battle over the fate of an "unsuitable" son is one instance. Lady Gracia was also forced to witness a summary beheading, which her husband enacted to spite her.

I imagine you're wondering about the conclusion of Sono's story! She faced much adversity and tragedy, but she finished as she started—as a resolute *Kirishitan*. Her first son, who as an adult took the name Takanobu, enjoyed decades of rule as Lord of Hirado. Her husband Hisanobu's end is a fascinating mystery which just might be fodder for a third novel.

Discussion Questions

Discussion questions and other book club resources are available at my website! Come visit me at: www.lthompsonbooks.com/BookClubs.

I'd Love to Hear from You

As an author, I place tremendous value on your feedback! Reviews weigh heavily with readers when shopping for books, so if you enjoyed this novel, please consider leaving one! You could help another reader experience the power of this story. If you're willing, you can leave a review on Amazon Kindle version by simply swiping left from the last page of an Amazon Kindle book. My reader bonus page at www.lthompsonbooks.com/reader-bonuses provides easy links to leave reviews in other venues.

More Ways to Connect with Linda

Peggy Covell had a brother, David. For a free work of fiction exploring his response to their wartime loss, check out my reader's bonus page. *A Matter of Mind and Heart* is an exclusive offer for members of my Red Carpet Reader's Club. This and other bonuses that will deepen your experience with this *Brands from the Burning* series are available at www.lthompsonbooks.com/reader-bonuses

Other ways to connect with me:
Find my blog at: www.lthompsonbooks.com/blog
Like my author page on FB: @lthompsonbooks
Follow me on Instagram: @lthompsonbooks
Follow me on Pinterest: @lthompsonbooks
Follow me on Goodreads:
www.goodreads.com/author/show/18168157.Linda_Thompson